THE WICKED

L. A. BANKS

ST. MARTIN'S GRIFFIN ☙ NEW YORK

www.stmartins.com

Library of Congress Cataloging-in-Publication Data

Banks, L. A.
    The wicked / L. A. Banks.—1st ed.
      p. cm.
    ISBN-13: 978-0-312-35236-3
    ISBN-10: 0-312-35236-0
      1. Richards, Damali (Fictitious character)—Fiction. 2. Vampires—Fiction. 3. African American women—Fiction. 4. Women martial artists—Fiction. 5. Women in the performing arts—Fiction. I. Title.

PS3602.A64W53 2007
813'.6—dc22

                2006048681

First Edition: February 2007

10 9 8 7 6 5 4 3 2 1

This eighth book in the series is dedicated to all those who hold on to, and hold up, the Light. . . . No matter what demons attempt to drag you down, no matter what obstacles challenge your path, no matter what naysayers negatively spew, you valiantly keep trudging forward. Therefore, for anyone and everyone who has ever had to draw a line in the sand over a principle of righteousness and then quickly turn around to be their own army of one just to hold that line in order to protect what they believe in . . . yeah, we got your back. Ashe! Keep the faith and don't surrender. This is for you!

ACKNOWLEDGMENTS

Special acknowledgment goes to the winners of the 2006 "Name That Queen" contest, who did fantastic research to give more depth and dimension to the previously unnamed queens on Damali's Neteru Queens Council: Angela Tate, for her submission of the Native American queen, as well as for her submission of the Aztec queen; Valerie Johnson, for the Amazon queen; Katherine Gordon, for the Asian queen, and Candace Link, for her runner-up submission of the Aztec queen. (Thank you, Zulma Gonzalez, for always developing, managing, and judging the *best* contests!) Plus, as always, a Big Philly Hug goes to my Street Team; my agent, Manie Barron; my editor, Monique Patterson; the A-Team at St. Martin's Press (Michael, Harriet, Emily-squared, Colleen, and company); Eric-the-mad-scientist-artist; and Chris for being there. Special thanks to Liddy Midnight, Thomas Quinn, and Walt Stone, "cyber Marines" who helped me so much. Bless you!

PROLOGUE

In the Land of Nod . . . seven days later

Racked with agony, Cain sat naked at the edge of the sensation pool in his bedchamber, his legs dangling in the ether as he clutched silk sheets to his chest. Anything that would bring her to him, even if just her scent. He began slowly rocking back and forth, his hands trembling as he lowered his face to the fabric again with his eyes tightly shut, and then inhaled Damali's ripening essence. Her scent was set ablaze in his mind, fevered by the oil of Hathor she'd trailed. He winced and shuddered, the denial unbearable, the incarceration a suffering he'd never known.

Bitter tears rolled down his cheeks while decimating memories turned his saliva thick in his mouth. *She was his universe, the potential bearer of his empire!* Every breath he took felt as though his Neteru blade was piercing his heart. He could almost taste blood from the phantom wound she'd left.

Cain licked his chaffed, dry lips, remembering Damali's mouth upon his. A shiver almost arched his back. The desire to hold her had become a need, then an obsession, until it produced an incomparable ache. Just the memory of her touch, her sun-fired skin, her ecstasy-producing bite, her deep moans of pleasure, her incredible voice set to song . . . all of it was like a knife that carved at his groin and filled his sac with mind-numbing, unspent seed that could not be spilled in this sensationless realm.

But tasting her blood had made him feel it down to his marrow.

The peristaltic drive to release inside her without a way to ejaculate now tortured his mind to near madness.

"Devastation . . ." he murmured into the soft fabric that had been filled with her sweat. "How could you allow him to manipulate you this way?"

Feminine wetness that had overflowed from her valley entered his nose and clung to his palate, a razor of memory whittling his regal pride to sawdust. His apexing would last a month. Cain struggled to breathe as the reality wore on.

Days ago he'd abandoned the frenzied attempt to make love to her telepathically, to find relief in his desperate mounting against the bedding, his hands, the sheets, *anything* she'd touched, but to no avail. Her vibrations had ceased; his thrusts against inanimate objects futile, a teasing reminder that Damali was truly gone. All he had left to cling to was her delirium-producing scent and what remained of their last encounter in his mind. Even that was slowly vaporizing, as though she was being erased from his realm and his tortured psyche one memory cell at a time . . . leaving only the burn for her in its wake.

He couldn't conjure her in visions or connect to her astrally. The orgasm would crest and then die away, leaving him unfulfilled in a heat of raw desire. Everything in his chamber had soaked up the sound of his suffering—every lusty groan, every hot gasp, each time he'd wailed her name—and it now reverberated to taunt him with the knowledge that there would be endless days and nights until his solo apex finally ebbed.

"Damali . . ." A sob choked off his words as he nuzzled the sheets, remembering her voice, her caress, the way she'd reached for him and had arched under his hold, a plea in her eyes to love her hard. "I would have given you the world, and so much more. . . ."

Seven brutal days of suffering had lacerated his soul. Her blood had been a sweet tonic that still burned inside his veins. "Do not banish me!" he bellowed, throwing his head back as his fangs ripped his gums. Seven long, hard days and endless nights . . .

It was to be twelve days of mourning peace with Damali in his arms during a war hiatus that had also been reserved for his oldest friend. Everything had been so perfectly orchestrated, the strategy sound. The cease-fire had been established to quell civil unrest in his empire, and yet he was more bereft over the loss of Damali than the death of Zehiradangra.

His pool now remained eerily silent; Damali's vibrations blocked to his communion. Her voice was as unreachable as a distant star, dead to him, the flicker of its light only a resonance from the past.

"I loved you so," he whispered against the tear-dampened linens. "Come back to me . . . I beg you with all that is within me. Do not forsake me, angel . . . queen of all that I know."

The sensation tank remained still as Cain's agonized wails echoed off the white marble lair walls. The gold-and-silver mortar and every conductive metal object radiated pain so acutely that he reached his hand out and touched the glasslike blue surface of the ether with his fingertips. His pride in ruins, broken, he would settle for knowing her whereabouts even through the vibrations of another man.

Carlos had befouled his lair, his pool. Cain closed his eyes. Just to know where Damali was, he would link to his Neteru brother who also shared his vampire lineage. He had to know. Seven days was more than he could bear. Her absence had become a viral infection that fevered his mind, drove him to obsession, and had made his body ache with a craving worse than blood hunger.

But the moment he honed his focus to Carlos, Cain drew his hand back as though he'd been burned. The sheets fell away from him as he backed away from the pool shaking his head, going temporarily insane from the knowledge.

"No," he whispered, disbelief robbing his lungs of air. He went to his hands and knees, splaying both palms against the pool's surface, tilting his head, watching, listening—he had to understand. She *couldn't have* done this.

On his feet in an instant, Cain's body transformed into a ripping battle bulk. A war cry filled his chest and he released it like sudden thunder. Lightning arched from each digit on his hands. His eyes went silver, gold, and then black.

"Transgressor! Betrayer! Befouler! Be damned!" he roared, immediately materializing armor to cover his nakedness and with his blade of Ausar in his fist.

Capillaries burst in his temples; blood was in his eyes. "Married? You blotted her from my world by a treacherous act of matrimony? In a church? In the Light? *You*—on hallowed ground? I will behead you and make her a widow!"

With one long lightning bolt that cracked and singed the air as it ejected from the tip of his blade, every marble bench along the edge of the Olympic-sized pool overturned and exploded into rubble. The four-poster, solid gold, king-sized bed flipped over and melted, starting a blaze behind him. Eight-foot marble vases hurled against the wall, shattering into shards of marble as though made of glass with a wave of Cain's massive arm. Pillars began to crumble. His guard sphinxes came alive at the front entrance and rushed in to assist him, only to be summarily beheaded, leaving confused, stricken expressions that their master had harmed them in their glassy eyes.

The high, vaulted ceiling began to give way, but Cain stood in the midst of the destruction, so enraged he would not even shield himself from falling marble, boulders, and debris as he decimated his cliffside lair.

"You manipulated her to murder my father, Dante! You took my father's throne in Hell, stole his empire, and then threw it back in his face! You robbed me of my oldest friend after seducing her. You beset the Neteru Council of Kings against me to seal me in Nod with their shields of Heru! You come to my lair and desecrate my home. You steal my music, my nightingale, after you kept her from composing for one year—my Damali, the detriment of my soul! You break my mother's heart by causing me to cross into your world to seek the voice that I'd longed for."

Cain's eyes narrowed to enraged slits. "Because of you, my world is gone and my kingdom is under civil unrest! Then you betray my beloved's heart, take her body, and marry her away from me? Are you insane? Do you believe there will be no redress? I will have justice, Rivera!"

Pure fury roiled through Cain like a dark tornado, spiking adrenaline to rage in blackout proportions. In a sharp pivot with both hands on his broad sword, Cain sliced at a standing column, and then froze as the blade of Ausar shattered in his grip.

"Noooo . . . Imposter . . ." he whispered in utter disbelief, looking at the blade handle in his hand and then down at the broken steel at his feet. "For *millennia* you have deceived me? My mother's people . . . those of the Light?" Cain threw his head back and roared. "What game is this, Adam? Did you also deceive Ausar? What conspiracy is afoot amid the archons—I demand an answer! It is my due!"

Immediately Cain's eyes sought the horizon through the yawning hole in the destroyed lair roof, and his gaze tore around the multiple golden shields of Heru that still covered and sealed the thinning barrier between the Land of Nod and Earth.

"I believed . . ." Cain's voice quieted as he raked his fingers through his locks, incredulous. He stared at the blade on the floor that should have cut through stone, tears rising and then burning away with renewed anger.

The Neteru Council of Kings had betrayed him? Had given him a replica of the actual blade and had given the real mark of royalty to Carlos Rivera over him? Rivera—a man not made a Neteru by birthright through Eve, but rather through a late elevation? A man bitten and made a vampire, not sired from the original royal lineage of Dante and Lucifer? A common drug peddler made king over him? A man, who had also slain his sibling, lied, stolen, and God knew what else, was allowed to bed the millennium female Neteru, marry her in the Light, and sire? This transgressor, this interloper of dubious heritage, had been incarcerated for only a few short years, yet with full conjugal access to Damali, while he'd been locked away in the Land of Nod, devoid of carnal sensation *for eons*—when his only offense had been to execute his wearisome brother? *This* was the justice delivered from On High?

"Never!" He spat on the floor in disgust. "Then my father's people shall have me where my rule will be revered."

Cain was pure motion, his footfalls gaining in velocity until he reached the edge of the ravine. Headlong, he tumbled, burning through the energy atmosphere like a flaming arrow to land in the central kingdom square. His furious landing was greeted by the stunned amazement of his subjects, but constituents from the side of Light and the Dark drew away from their monarch. Blue-black flames flickered at the edges of Cain's nostrils as he whirred around to gain his bearings. Battle-length fangs had filled his mouth, and the lack of a blade hadn't left him unarmed. More dangerous now than ever before, he strode to the shadow wall zone. Patrons of the illicit sensations there scattered at his presence the moment he entered the dank alley.

Trembling with rage, Cain said nothing as he approached the rubbery surface of the wall of seekers. His footfalls thudded with lethal echoes as he stretched out his hands and dug into the flexible divide, plunging his fists into it up to the elbows. His massive hands grasped several faces, twisting and contorting them, causing the entire wall to wail.

"Warlocks, bring me Lilith," he said in a low, thundering tone. "Bring her to this wall that she might seduce modern men of science to run another barrier-shattering experiment. Tell her to open a hole and prepare my father's throne for me in Hell!"

Harpies genuflected. Level-Six vampire messengers cowered against stalagmites and stalactites and then fell to the floor, prostrate before Cain's passage. The Sea of Perpetual Agony ceased its cries and went silent. The molten, bubbling lava in the pit calmed as a slow glacier sealed over it and Cain stormed across the bridge toward the Vampire Council Chambers. Ice slicked the cavern floor behind him; the halting breaths of the bats and messengers came out in strangled puffs of frigid air.

The huge black marble doors leading to the throne room creaked open on frozen hinges. Ice weighed the golden, fanged knockers as the doors struggled to respond to Cain's royal entry, but seemed incapable of doing so fast enough to avoid being kicked off their hinges, each door exploding at the assault. With every footfall that Cain landed on the black marble floor, the blood veins in it oozed to a halt beneath his furious steps, icy fingers choking off the flow of life within it and spreading out in a frosted glaze behind him.

Lilith stood up from the pentagram-shaped ruling table that had been running with fresh blood. In her peripheral vision she watched it ice over into a shining, ruby, still resin. Her fingers and palm stuck to the golden goblet she clutched in her hand as she watched Cain stand in the center of the floor breathing fire and ice, his golden armor turning black at the edges until the hue of pure darkness overtook it all.

"Your throne awaits, Your Eminence," she said as chilly air made her words come out in visible white puffs. Going to one knee with her head lowered and respectfully motioning Cain toward his father's old throne, her tone was reverent. "Hell has frozen over, sire . . . it is your time to rule. Destiny."

Cain did not speak as he approached the old Chairman's throne, but he stopped to look at the last vampire's name that had been etched into the high, black marble back of it. "Imposter!" he bellowed, punching the top section of the throne away to rid it of Carlos Rivera's name before abruptly turning to claim his legacy. Then he saw Damali's name etched into the throne of every councilman she'd slain. A shudder of desire ran through him.

He sat quickly, his back straight, his jaw set hard, and closed his eyes. Tears of familiarity wet his lashes as satisfaction and knowing wafted through his cells. Dante's virile image was the first impression that careened through his mind, and just as quickly he saw his mother as a young, ripening virgin in Eden, and then watched his father uncoil in muscular fluidity to shape-shift from an enormous black serpent to take the first Neteru ever made.

"I will avenge you, Father," Cain murmured thickly as eons of vampiric information poured into his consciousness.

Profound pleasure began to burn away his skin as his vertebrae knotted and became welded to the throne. Huge bat wings with a twenty-foot span ripped through his shoulders, and his spine elongated, tearing flesh away from his back and permitting a razor-sharp, scaled, spaded tail to exit.

Cain simply steeled his jaw and gripped the armrests harder against the excruciating transition. *This* was power. He drew in a wincing breath and kept his eyes tightly shut. *This* was of his line. His father's people. He would not cry out as the metal armor he wore fused to his skin, becoming one with it and leaving him naked.

The transformation hurt so good it caused him to throw his head back as talons and twelve-inch fangs ripped through his nail beds and gums. He could feel his pupils dilate beneath his lids, and his inner vision showed him the gold bar that they'd become, now set in black orbs. Perfection . . . he had his grandfather's eyes . . . his father's fangs . . . his mother's tolerance to daylight . . . and power within the dark realms unlimited. He was a fucking king! He would slay the pure Light male Neteru!

Every deviant carnal act that had ever been committed on the planet imploded within Cain's groin simultaneously with the power of every evil that existed. His body convulsed and shuddered. But still he would not cry out, even panting, sweat leaking from his pores like black rain. No. Years . . . millennia of abstinence, pain profound for his kind, had been endured. He was a birthright monarch and would not cry out at his dark coronation or dishonor his father by a show of weakness. Not in the throne that his father had ruled since the dawn of time! Not in the throne that had broken Rivera's spirit into two entities! He would crush that bastard's memory from the throne of royal vampire lineage!

The moment the top of the throne reconstructed and the smell of sulfuric scorch emblazoned Cain's name within it, Lilith mounted him, adding to the exquisite torture of it all.

He savagely bit into her shoulder, still refusing to cry out until his transformation was complete. Her pleasure shriek made him tear his mouth away from her flesh to gasp as her spaded tail twined with his, slashing at the newly scaled flesh. The sensation of wet, hot, writhing female sheathing him, combined with the heart-seizing ecstasy emanating from the throne, finally caused him to arch while she rode him hard. Lilith's siphon as she dug her nails into the thick ropes of muscles in his shoulders dredged a slow, rumbling groan up from his diaphragm.

His wingspan instantly eclipsed hers as the leathery appendages beat in unison to each lunging thrust. Lifting her high into the vaulted ceiling in hovering flight above the throne, his talons tore at her ass, his mouth devouring her forked tongue until it bled black blood. Messenger bats swarmed around them, squealing in frenzied, airborne mating. Cain reached down, gripping Lilith's waist with one arm, his fingers craning as he pulled knowledge since the dawn of time up and out of the throne to him.

Torches blew out as he amassed power in a high-pitched, turbine whine of suction toward him. He lit the cavern with lunar eclipses from the first-world skies to better witness it all. Thunder and lightning sent black prisms to rain rocks down to the marble floor fifty feet below. Sound, sent in shock waves from Babylon, reverberated off the stone walls and he caught each note in his fist while still pumping against Lilith's nearly limp body, forcing the vibrations into her vertebrae one note at a time before allowing them to explode her disks in falling dominoes of pleasure.

Her shrieks of ecstasy drew him to her throat; his black laser sight on her jugular summoned the dead vein to the surface of her skin as he wound her raven hair around his clawed fist, yanked her head back, snapped her neck, and fed amid her orgasmic wails. Descending in a vanishing-point spiral of pure black vapor, he crash-landed with her splayed in the center of the pentagram-shaped table.

He was convulsing so hard against her that he couldn't control his thrusts. It had been so long, vanishing point a fantasy denied so completely that he was barely conscious when his body spewed every drop of agony his tortured scrotum held. Cumming in painful jags, he hollered until he was breathless. He grabbed the base of his shaft to try to slow the ejaculation, but was forced to yank his hand away when the throb along his entire length felt like it would split him.

Lilith's voice hit radar-destroying decibels that sent the bats in the crags in all directions, their disoriented flight patterns crashing them into the walls. Teeming vermin spilled over the ledges in search of a haven to avoid the sonar she'd released. Her damaged womb filled with thick, wriggling, maggoty life as Cain threw his head back and climaxed hard against her again.

"I'm not sterile like Dante," Cain said in a ragged whisper into her ear through his fangs, sending his Neteru apex scent into her nose and mouth with a punishing kiss. He broke away from her mouth, gulping air. "Sire the day heir that it might walk at my side as my son!"

"I can't," Lilith wailed, another orgasm ripping a gasp from her throat.

Cain looked down at her, snarled, and slapped her backhanded, bloodying her nose. "I said sire for me! Treacherous liar! You used to give birth to one hundred original demons a day—"

"The female Neteru gored my womb with an Isis blade," Lilith wailed, her black, Bedouin eyes ablaze with both fear and raw lust. She licked Cain's Adam's apple and wrapped her legs tighter around his waist. "Neteru, second to none ever created, my dark sovereign . . . I will find you a vessel just as I wrested you from Nod," Lilith moaned, closing her eyes as her head dropped back. "Just V-point fuck me as you apex and we can discuss it later. Hit me again— harder."

Winded from the feed and frustrated by Lilith's dead womb, Cain stood with her spent body still clinging to his torso, her legs and tail wrapped around his waist. Lodged deep within her, he slammed her against the council table, splattering blood everywhere. Her strike was a blinding bolt of black current that made him cum again so hard that initially no sound exited his throat. The seizure Lilith's bite produced was like none he'd ever known, and yet he needed more.

Her body was almost a rag of fatigued limbs, but driven by impulse, he extracted himself from her wickedly delicious pelvic hold and flipped her over onto her stomach.

"Your womb is dead, therefore the orifice leading to it is no longer of use to me," Cain snarled close to her ear. He entered her hard, sodomizing her with rage, dripping black sweat against her bruised spine as she moaned and writhed beneath him.

"Tell me your every wish," she cried out between gasps of pleasure. "Your grandfather will be so proud—just ask it and I will deliver it!"

"Raise the master vampire I request from the Sea of Perpetual Agony," Cain yelled, his voice echoing when a seizure of pleasure overtook him.

His head dropped back, his long, dark locks sweeping his ass as his deep lunges against Lilith increased in force. He cried out, unable to conceal the years of unfed desire with her blood polluting his system. It felt so good he didn't even care that he might bleed her out and fuck her to death. But he needed her direct access to the Ultimate Dark Power of their realms in order to raise the exterminated. She was already midway between black mist and pure vapor. Her voluptuous body was beginning to make him see double. The deal had to be finalized, but his cells had begun to deconstruct with hers again to the tonal frequency of the vibrating Babylonian chants in the cavern. Unable to scale back the velocity or stop moving, he sent hot-flash images of Sodom and Gomorrah into her skull, nearly fracturing it with a brutal mind thrust.

"Cain! Name your terms," she cried out, reaching backward and trying to hold on to his hips with her talons. Black tears streamed down her face and her breathing staggered as she tried to turn to score his jugular.

The need to release had also put tears in his eyes, and he held her heavy, pendulous breasts, vaporizing millisecond by millisecond as he spoke through his teeth. "The one not beheaded but felled by an Isis," Cain panted in Dananu, flattening Lilith against the table harder and pulling back from the edge of a V-point spiral. "My armies will slaughter Guardian teams worldwide with every setting sun. My hybrids will terrorize their days with bloodshed and chaos that knows no bounds! *I* will create the darkest night!"

"Yes! Anything—your scent, your voice . . . oh, great Darkness . . . your body—*I am damned for you, lover!*" Lilith shrieked near hysterics, sputtering black blood from her injuries, her talons digging deep grooves into the marble surface as her tail slashed at him wildly. "*Anything,* when you have surpassed even Dante's carnal abilities like this!" She dropped her head back and offered her jugular, craning her neck. "Do it, now!"

He abruptly withdrew from her with a groan that was sliced by her sharp gasp. Frustration caused her to hiss at him when he spun her to face him, and the sound sent a shiver down his spine that closed his eyes to half-mast.

"Just because I've been in Nod for a very long time, did you think you could take advantage of my celibacy, Lilith?" Cain's hand went to her throat as her eyes widened. "Do you know how many entities there are from here to the surface that I could fuck before worrying about you, bitch?" He leaned into her with a dangerous warning in his low, rumbling tone. "After all the centuries devoid of sensation, do you think I would give a damn if it is a she-wolf on Level Five, or an Amanthra serpent from above that? A succubus, a poltergeist—I do not care as long as it brings pleasure! Do you not yet realize that I am Cain, son of Dante, grandson of Lucifer?"

His black gaze locked with hers as he slowly anchored his tail to her waist.

"*I* run this council, Lilith, unlike Dante, who had to succumb to your rank as his father's Level-Seven wife—but you have been stripped of that military privilege," Cain whispered in a slow, even warning. "As a being impervious to the sun, not a dead, made-from-the-bite vampire—I was made all that I am *from seed*. *I* already have a waiting army and an empire and do not need to go through the laborious task of making vampires one by one, as in Dante's time. But be very sure that you understand that you do not even have a seat on this council yet. You are a familiar to do council bidding, just like you are for my grandfather. . . . Attempt a coup, and even he will not be able to save you."

"You saw the betrayal in Dante's throne . . ." she whispered, mesmerized, her hand reverently tracing Cain's cheek. "In the *first sitting* you received something buried so deeply within Dante's shame that it should have taken *years* to acquire?" Lilith's voice dropped to a low, quaking decibel. Her whisper was so gentle that the chamber went dead silent. "Fuck me again now, before I faint. I beg you."

Cain simply stared at her for a moment. There was no fraud in her eyes or her voice. Lilith's arousal spiked so radically beneath him in earnest that it was becoming increasingly difficult to negotiate with her. She was so twisted that the fear of his reprisal had sent a new slickness of desire between her thighs, making him tremble. Easing her backward against the ruling table, he kept a dark current protecting his throat to frustrate her strike.

"Do we have a deal on multiple levels?" His eyes slid shut as he brutally entered her and nipped her bottom lip.

"Yes," she whispered on a thick swallow and raked her nails down his stone-cut chest. "Take off the collar . . . please. I *must* strike you."

"Do you want to spiral up through the levels or take your chances with a knock on your husband's chamber door?" Cain whispered in her ear, nipping it and holding her tighter with his tail.

"Please, spiral up," she said, looking frantic. "Lately—"

"He's been stomping your traitorous ass into a black puddle," Cain said, chuckling, and then placed both hands on the table at either side of her hips.

Instantly the Vampire Council table developed a fissure and split in two. Cain's wings opened; Lilith screamed and slapped his face hard enough to draw blood. He smiled, reared back, and severed the vein in her throat as he opened the Harpies' chasm in the floor, then dragged her over the precipice dissolving into a V-point mist spiral headed for Lucifer's door.

It was an act so brazen that even Harpies whirled past shuddering and tried to hide, knowing they'd be collateral damage in a rampage. The caverns cleared. Roaring flames from the bottomless pit hissed and spit at the molecular violation. Damned souls retreated in cowering waves, cringing at the speeding intrusion. The scorching heat forced him to move against her faster, each cell bonding and breaking into hers at the atomic pleasure level, becoming one with the dense plumes of sulfur. What a way to die!

Lilith's orgasmic wails and deep talon gouges in his back added to the increased velocity toward the bottom of the pit. He couldn't slow down. Adrenaline and insanity had him in its grip. Pleasure had made him both blind and deaf, but he was anything but mute. Her sex felt so good that his moan rent the scorching air. The low sonic boom resonance of his voice began to implode the cavern in crumbling splinters that fell inward behind them. Two seconds short of an extinction wish, he pulled up, reversed polarity, and sent them both crashing through the backside of the council table to disturb the orgy of bats again.

He came hard in a black torrent of ecstasy so perverse he could only close his eyes as the images roiled through his mind with hers. Panting, his movements against her abated slowly and he kept both hands at either side of her skull while in the air, daring her to move by telepathy until he'd normalized. If she had just been Damali, it would have been perfect. Cain opened his eyes, temporarily sated but disgusted. Just the thought of Rivera having his Neteru through an apex made him want blood.

"Bring me the one vampire, the one master of masters that will carve out Rivera's soul to see risen again," Cain said between thundering breaths singed with flames.

"Just tell me, Your Eminence. I shall immediately take up your petition with my husband and convince him of your needs . . . just come to me like this again. Please. I beg you," she said, a sob catching the words spoken in Dananu in her throat.

"We have a truce. Avenge me, and what you did to Dante will be dismissed. I will see you often until my apex wanes. That is a promise . . . perhaps more like a vow." Cain righted the table and lowered them to rest on it, his giant, leathery wings thudding against the now-still chamber air.

The sound of slow, strolling hooves made Cain jerk his attention toward the battered chamber doors. The echo of calm, steady applause entered the Vampire Council throne room.

"Well done, grandson," a deep, melodic, baritone voice whispered in a murderous tone from the shadows beyond. "With a throne ascension like that, there is no need to go through my wife as an intermediary, although you can at your leisure, since she seems to amuse you."

Lilith cringed and buried her face against Cain's chest, her terrified grip tightening on his arms. "Don't provoke him," she whispered through her teeth when Cain lifted his chin. "I begged you to spiral us upward!"

"She'll do while I apex," Cain said, shrugging out of Lilith's hold and nonchalantly pulling out of her body. "Of greater importance, Your Majesty . . . let us decide how we might best rule the world."

Lilith gasped and closed her eyes, making her body very small behind Cain's hulking form.

A long sigh filled with amusement echoed in response. Each eclipse that had lit the chamber with thin rims of blue moonlight went out, creating pure darkness.

"Tell me the name and I shall consider your request to raise him. We are royal family. Heirs of the world, so to speak. If you can handle the job, you can rule it."

A low, mellow chuckle filled with heat began to melt the ice-crusted floor. "But do not *ever* freeze over Hell again without my permission. . . . I will allow this one transgression, given your Neteru arrogance from your mother's side and the insanity induced by your apexing condition. We don't see that much down here. It does intrigue me to witness it bloom on one of my thrones—even Dante never had that in him . . . and I must admit that I've never seen it turn so thoroughly, boldly dark as quickly as you have taken it. My compliments on the way you sire, as well." The sound of hooves began to retreat. "Well done. Yes . . . done outrageously enough to entertain me this evening. Therefore, tell me the name you seek from my prisons and we shall bargain."

Cain smiled, knowing the melodic, sinister voice had relented. He nodded and reinserted himself into Lilith's body with a shuddering wince. She covered her mouth to silence the pleasure gasp that threatened to bring her husband back into chambers less amused.

"Fallon Nuit," Cain called out in a tone of authority, moving against Lilith as he stared down into her stricken eyes.

"Nice move . . . very, very nice," a sinister voice thundered in the distance with another round of slow applause. "Done. You *do* take after our side of the family, after all. Vengeance served—*ice* cold. Great voice, too, kid. Excellent set of pipes and fantastic projection." Rumbling laughter with a hint of implied danger in it made the bats seek shelter again. "Think about what you want to give me later."

Both male entities chuckled.

Cain closed his eyes, threw his head back, and groaned softly, intensifying his thrusts as Lilith arched with a shiver. "Done."

CHAPTER ONE

La Paz, Mexico

Total contentment wafted through Carlos as he sat on a kitchen stool in their honeymoon villa, watching Damali bop around the kitchen. He leaned on his elbows on the wide butcher-block island and smiled. She looked so thoroughly happy and so in her element, buzzing around trying to fix their last private supper, he could only shake his head.

The last of the sun was bringing gold and rose-orange light in with the beach breeze from the decks and open windows, dappling the white rooms and Damali's beautiful brown skin. *This* was sanctuary; the Light had provided a few hallowed days of drama cease-fire and obligation so he could enjoy his new wife. It was a time that he thought would only happen when Hell froze over. *Jesus.*

He silently wondered what their life together would be like with children. After the way they'd been at it for four glorious days and nights, the result was imminent. He smiled and briefly closed his eyes just thinking about it.

Oh, yeah, this was a very personal gift from On High. He'd be reverent forever. The way Damali flitted from the counter to the refrigerator to the stove almost choked him up—the sight of it filled him up so. One day her belly would be heavy and loaded with a life they'd created. One day there would be a tiny little face with big brown eyes watching them tease each other and laugh. . . . He just wondered if what they'd make would have fangs or wings or both. He didn't care, as long as he'd made it with her. God apparently did answer prayers.

Pineapple and papaya that he was supposed to be peeling sat waiting for him, but try as he might, he couldn't focus on the fruit while he gazed at her. He was just glad that they were on the same wavelength about not wanting to go out for this last honeymoon meal together. Going back to their waiting Guardian team that was family had definitely lost its appeal, too. Although kidnapping her or stopping time to keep life at bay wasn't an option, there was something so private and so profoundly peaceful about this time that he'd tuck it away to savor it beyond the grave. He loved her. Period. End of story.

"You don't have to do this, you know," he finally said in a pleasant, mellow tone, just loving the way her white tank top fit her and the way her sheer white sarong hung low on her hips. He watched her unfettered breasts bounce as she moved. He wondered if she had on underwear. There was no visible line of a barrier, and the mystery of it all added to the excitement of watching her work. Did life get any better than this?

"I know," she said in a cheerful voice, seeming oblivious to his thoughts; then she stopped to kiss the bridge of his nose across the counter dividing them and went back to her disorganized puttering.

"But you're a vegetarian—you don't even eat steak." He laughed and poured them both another glass of merlot as a diversion, to give his hands something to do, rather than grabbing her.

"So? I know how to cook one, though."

Carlos raised an eyebrow. "Uh . . . you don't really have to cook it all that much for me . . . just a flash on both sides, and—"

"Yeah, yeah, I know . . . leave it running blood." Damali sucked her teeth. "I still don't see how you can go there with beef, but I'm not gonna start."

They both laughed.

"What can I say?" Carlos ran his tongue over the slight hint of fangs that had begun to crest just from the sound of her voice. "Baby, I don't want anything green on my plate, and you don't have to put a bunch of mushrooms and onions and stuff on the steak," he added in protest when she began making him a side salad. "You do the tabouli and hummus, and pita, and rice and beans and all that . . . just—"

"Carlos," she fussed. "You're still mostly human and need to eat a balanced meal. Vegetables are good for you."

He sighed. "Then go light on the garlic, okay?" His smile widened when she waved her hand at him. "I know all the blood-cleansing properties and what the health food digests say, but truth be told, it still gives me wicked heartburn," he said, laughing hard as she frowned. "Not everything came out of the sunlight straight, and if you smother that steak with that marinade you're concocting, you might as well drag me back to the family house on a livery tonight." He arched an eyebrow again and gave her a sly smile as he began peeling the fruit she'd shoved toward him. "I had other plans . . . but, uh, whatever you fix, I'll eat."

She set the small bowl of marinade down hard and chuckled. "Flash it, two seconds on each side—no salt, no pepper, no nothing?"

"Au naturel works best for me . . . you know that." He glimpsed her from the corner of his eye, and was rewarded by her brilliant smile.

"Fine." She moved to the counter and sipped her wine, keeping the butcher block between them, and then turned back to the stove.

As she moved about, all he could envision was the way her white wings would slowly unfold from her shoulders at the height of making love. Her satiny smooth legs peeked out from the sarong each time she pivoted to get something out of the cabinets or the fridge, and her bare feet sounded like a soft sigh. *Thank you, God. . . .* She was *his wife.* He could get used to the institution, for sure.

He burst out laughing as she pulled the steak out of the broiler, lifted it with a fork and a droll expression, then eased it onto a plate— her eyes saying yuck.

"Now do I act like that when I hand you a piece of fruit?" he asked, cutting off a juicy hunk of pineapple and feeding it to her over the counter.

"Fruit doesn't run blood, Carlos."

"Oh, no? Then what's this?" he said, leaning in toward her and kissing the juice off her chin, totally ignoring the steak between them. "The fruit is bleeding . . . just 'cause it's sweet and almost clear doesn't mean it's not—"

"Oh, man! You are ruining pineapple for me forever!" she squealed, wiping her chin with the back of her hand.

"Then come over here and sit down and let me make it up to you. Gimme that terrible image . . . and let me work with it," he said, his laughter becoming a low rumble in his chest. "Sun's going down, too . . . sheeit. I'll make pineapple your passion again before the night's over."

"Eat your dinner," she argued, playfully escaping his grasp but coming to sit beside him on a blond oak stool. "I went to all this trouble, the least you could do is taste it."

"All right, all right," he said resignedly, pulling her into his lap. He kissed her slowly and then looked at her. "I do appreciate everything you've done for me, baby." Closing his eyes, he leaned his forehead against hers. "Bless this food and the one who prepared it. Thank you, God."

They sat that way for a moment, her fingers stroking his hair, bare legs and bare feet touching, arms about each other in a loose embrace.

"I still can't believe we're married," she whispered as her mouth swept his temple. "You're my husband."

"Say it again," he murmured against her ear with his eyes still closed. "I love to hear you say that."

"You're my husband," she whispered and nipped his ear. "You're my sexy . . . wonderful, forever husband," she said against his throat, making his embrace tighter as she dotted each word with a kiss. "My . . . husband," she said over his lips, and then pulled back. "So eat."

He smiled and opened his eyes, then took her mouth hard.

"The steak!" she squealed, laughing as he stood up, toppled the stool, and started walking away from the kitchen with her in his arms.

"Oh . . . the steak?" he said, teasing her. "Oh, yes, the bloody steak." He looked at her, making her shake her head and laugh harder. "Decisions, decisions. My wife, or the steak—the steak, or my wife?

Her now and microwaved beef later, or the steak now and her re-heated later? I don't know, D . . . what should I do?"

"In four days and nights, you've practically starved me," she groaned, still giggling. "Just let me get a little bite of something," she said, laughing harder as he tilted his head to offer her his throat. "I mean something that I can *digest,* Carlos. Remember food? I'm *hungry.*"

"Ah . . . the lady says she needs human nourishment for stamina. Okay." He paced back to the kitchen, plopped her down on the counter, and stood in front of their plates, one hand on her thigh.

She swallowed a smile, the possessive move to keep her where he'd set her down not lost on her at all. With a mischievous grin, he began feeding her sections of pita dipped in hummus and seemed to revel in the way she slowly cut his steak and offered him a bite of it on his fork. *This* was heaven. She *loved* when he got that devastated expression in his eyes. But he shook his head.

"Why not?" She pouted, disappointed that he wouldn't try the steak, and she looked at him hard then at the cut meat, wondering what was wrong with it.

He smiled wider. "Take it off the silver and feed it to me au naturel . . . use your fingers."

"Oh," she said with a grin.

"Now *that's* good," he said in a sensual rumble, pulling the juicy meat from her fingers and sucking her index finger and thumb. "Way better. I think I'm developing an allergy to silver."

"Stop lying, man," she said, cutting him another hunk of steak. "Your eyes are glowing silver."

He knew they had to be; his tattoos were burning up.

"Do tell? I wonder why." He took another bite of steak from her graceful fingers and chewed it slowly as he brought her plate over to feed her more of her vegetarian selections. But he almost dropped the plate as she captured his thumb and drew it into her mouth in a pulsing suckle.

"You're starting to sweat silver, too," she said with an impish grin.

"Might go solid gold on you tonight if you keep that up," he said as he kissed between her breasts. "So you better bust a good grub now, 'cause there's no telling how long I'ma keep you hostage in the other room."

"Is that a threat, Mr. Rivera? 'Cause you know I brought my blade."

"It's a promise, Mrs. Rivera," he murmured against her warm shoulder. "Keep messing with me, hear."

"Well since you're talking possible all-out war . . ." she murmured, giving him another piece of steak and allowing a bit of the juice to drip on her thigh.

He looked at the red splatter on her leg, bent slowly to lick it while still looking up at her. "All-out battle—hard down, no negotiating . . . taking no prisoners tonight."

"Do tell?" she said, chuckling low and sensually as he came up to claim her mouth, cresting a hint of fang. "But I have to eat my salad first." She glimpsed him with a teasing smile, grabbed her salad bowl, and ate very slowly, munching the greens casually. "You're not allergic to balsamic vinaigrette dressing, are you?"

"Right about through here, you could take a bath in it, and it wouldn't bother me none." He winked at her as she ate a little faster.

"What just got into you?" she said, smiling through bites. "Like, a minute ago, you were all cool, and then all of a sudden—dang."

"I was watching you from behind," he sheepishly admitted, "and then . . . hey, spontaneous combustion. What can I say?"

She shook her head and kissed him quickly, getting salad dressing on his mouth. "There, at least I feel better knowing you got close to a salad. What am I gonna do with you?"

He pulled back a bit and sipped his wine, smiling, but no longer even interested in the steak. "I have several suggestions about what you can do with me, but the real question is, how are we gonna do this in the family house?" he asked with a smirk, then took another generous sip of wine.

"Very, very quietly . . . sneaky . . . vamp stealth."

He laughed and gave her a sip of wine from his glass. But it was the strangest thing . . . the later it got and the more he stared at her, the more the sudden testosterone rush slammed him. Yes he loved her, always wanted her, but damn, he was feeling something way past desire. And whatever was suddenly blasting through his system had an after-kick to it that was no joke. While Damali hummed and made a funny face at him, he could feel something summoning pure molten silver to his surface, and at the same time, his old days on a throne were calling out his libido at knock-his-head-back levels. Maybe she'd spiked his steak with some Queen's Council aphrodisiac, because he hadn't felt like this since she'd ripened the first time while he was all vamp.

"Don't ignore me by eating steak. You know I'm telling the truth, and we can't be going back to the house hooting and hollering, Carlos—so stop looking at me like that. And it's gonna be tight while we move the team around from place to place, so you'd better get all that out of your system *tonight*," she said, laughing at his slight scowl.

"Quiet."

"Yep, quiet," she said, briefly pressing her fingers to her lips and giggling. "Silent scream."

"Silent scream?"

"You wouldn't."

"Hmmm . . ." For a moment he just stared at her, wondering if he could take her to the point where a climax hit her so hard and fast that no sound would exit her throat. Maybe he'd been going about this all wrong, dragging it out? Carlos tilted his head and pressed one finger to his lips, studying her windpipe, then shook it off, making her laugh harder.

Yeah, it was their last honeymoon night and all, but he had to chill. This didn't make no kinda sense and was quickly about to border on insane, if he tried what was currently running through his head. Midflight she'd freak, and where *the hell* did that come from anyway? No. He took a deep breath, willed his hands not to tremble or quick-snatch her, and forced a smile. *Shit.*

Carlos kept his expression neutral and his tone light, but he was two seconds from battle bulking on Damali and wasn't even sure if he could pleasure-infuse the bite, he needed her so badly. If he made love to her in this condition, he knew he might actually hurt her, all fun and games aside. No.

"Vamp stealth only, then, huh? Girl, you know I can roll up on you like pure mist," he said, playing off his discomfort, "but uh, I don't think after I materialize, you're gonna be quiet, regardless."

He'd made her giggle so hard she set down her salad, losing interest in it. "You talk so much trash, Carlos Rivera."

"Husband, Carlos Rivera," he said, correcting her with a brief kiss. "And you love it, 'cause you know I can back it up."

"That ain't no lie," she said, her smile fading as her gaze went down his body with her hands. His skin was starting to swirl with energy colors beneath the coppery, golden tan the sun had kissed on it. She allowed her fingertips to trace down his stone-cut chest over his permanent brand of her fist clutching an Isis blade, and then slowly down his torso, almost willing his nylon black-and-white Oakland Raiders basketball shorts to disappear. When he obliged the thought and dropped his shorts away in one lithe move, she laughed and shook her head. "You need to stop."

"I'm supposed to give my wife what she wants, right?" he said, laughing in pain as he took her mouth.

She came out of the kiss serious and breathless. "You've always given me what I wanted, Carlos—you." Her arms wrapped around his neck as her legs wrapped around his waist. Whatever had set him off like this turned her on to no end. "That's all I ever wanted from you . . . was you."

This time there was no playfulness in her tone, or his kiss. As he stalked through the villa with her in his arms, she could feel his body changing and bulking to near battle proportions. The transformation was slightly unnerving, but she rationalized the fleeting nervousness away as a last-night-alone-throw-down-jones. However, the way he dropped her in the center of the bed and looked down at her like she was dinner, fangs fully crested, she briefly hesitated. Even his tattoo was different. It had gone silver, then gold, and was now white-hot, light, and smoking. She wouldn't even look down at the other one. Did she say silent scream? Probably.

He didn't need to tell her; it was brace herself now or never. Shame on her if she wasn't ready. Seeing that message blazing in his eyes oddly got her there in a heartbeat, though. For the first time since they'd been together, it was obvious that he was in no frame of mind to take his time with slow torture. Her man had immediate plunder in his sights and had started breathing hard without her touching him. Devastating.

"Baby, you all right?" she asked quietly, staring up at solid silver in his eyes that had began to turn gold at the edges of his irises.

He shook his head and then immediately blanketed her, not even waiting for her to pull off her clothes.

The full Neteru Council of Queens stood as Eve burst into Aset's violet-glowing meeting chambers in full Egyptian battle armor. Tears streamed down Eve's ashen cheeks, her once dewy, exquisite complexion in a ruin. With a stern look, Aset bade the other queens not to move or intervene as Eve rushed toward Aset and grasped her by the upper arms.

"You must grant me the ability to retrieve the Isis blade and the Caduceus!" Eve shouted, her hysteria increasing with every word. "Why have you blocked my ability to summon the blade of justice? I demand that you immediately release it to me and allow me to leave the Neteru Council realms! You cannot leave me unarmed or make me a prisoner at a time like this! Release me."

"I cannot, dear queen sister, and we both know why," Aset said in calm, loving tone. Pain rose from Aset's burnished skin in heat waves as she stared at Eve with unshed tears.

"He's my son!" Eve shrieked, pushing away from Aset and going into a battle stance. "Have you no mercy in your heart, and you call yourself my sister?"

Aset waved her throne lions and the other queens back. "I know he's your son, and it breaks my heart. We are all shattered by Cain's choice. No matter what you think of me in this dark hour, you will always be my sister and a queen to me."

Eve stood still for a moment, her eyes shimmering so much pain even Nzinga looked away. "Aset, he is my son. . . . If this were Heru . . ."

"My soul would die a thousand deaths, and I would need my queen sisters to hold me away from myself." Aset went toward Eve, but Eve slowly dropped to the floor within Aset's embrace, clutching her gown at her legs.

"My son," Eve sobbed into the gold woven silk. "He went to *his father's* throne after all these years. My queen sister, a Neteru, sent him there! Oh Heavens above, hear my lament!"

"They have heard you and the angels weep with us." Aset went to her knees and grabbed Eve to her breasts hard. "Our young Neteru sister did not send him to Hell. Lilith did that. She is the deceiver. She made human men open a new veil between worlds through their twisted science in ignorance. *She* was the one who originally brought Damali's voice to Cain on the channel of winds and vibrations. Do not blame Damali for that; we cannot have dissension among our queens. *Lilith* lured him to this fate with the assistance of her husband—but, yet, and still, the decision was Cain's." Aset began to rock Eve as her sobs escalated to inconsolable wails.

"My son, oh, Aset . . . he is still my boy," Eve cried, her face pressed against her queen sister's shoulder as she clung to the ruling matriarch. "I shall die and wither away from this. He bedded that shrew, Lilith . . . is in apex and could be attempting to sire in the unholy realms. . . . My grandchildren will be from the spawn of whatever is down there! Aset, hear me . . . the silver of my line is going to corruption. Adam is dressing for war to behead my son as we speak! I cannot let him do that— please just let me reason with my boy before Adam goes to war . . . I know Dananu," Eve said, her voice dropping to a piteous whisper and growing more desperate as Aset held her tighter. "Dante taught me; I can go to Cain and convince him! He would not deny his own mother's counsel or plea."

Nefertiti rounded the table, tears streaming down her flawless cheeks, weeping as she joined the huddle. "Heal her, Aset. Bring the Caduceus before Eve's spirit withers and dies and the light of feminine energy on the planet suffocates from the loss. All conception will stop; all gentleness of spirit and nurturing will be replaced with hatred and vile rage . . . war, anarchy, no respect for nature; Eve is the foundation!" She covered her mouth with her hand to stifle a sob. "No mother should know this pain—take it from Eve, I beg you."

Aset nodded, and Nzinga instantly produced the staff. "Please, dear sister Eve. Let me touch your heart and spirit. Let me draw this poisonous heartbreak from your soul so that you may rest peacefully to accept what must be."

"No!" Eve shrieked, trying to stand. "I will not forsake my son under any conditions! Give me the rod of Imhotep that *I* might heal *him*. I am of no consequence; it is my son who needs this now. For him I would give my life *and* my light."

"Don't say that," Aset whispered, aghast. "Never your light, Queen . . . not even for a wayward child. This is his path that he must walk; your prayers are his only salv—"

"You ask too much of me—to ask the first mother of all that is human not to be mother to her firstborn, not be humane to him, not be his light?" Eve whispered in a dangerously quiet voice as she pushed herself to her knees and opened her arms. "Are you mad, Aset?" Eve waved her arms and closed her eyes as more tears fell. Her next words came out in a thunderous shout. "Are you *deranged*? Has this Council of Neteru Queens gone insane in my presence?"

Gale-force winds blew the chamber doors open as hail and rain pelted around the council, inches from each queen in a serious threat.

"I will turn away from you and smite you if you do this to me, Aset," Eve screamed, making the floor rumble as the earthquake began building pressure under them. "That is *my child,* he is my heart chakra, every element within that makes me whole. Sister, hear me!"

The other queens rounded the alabaster seeing table, wiping their cheeks against tears that would not stop streaming.

"Form the pyramid of green light around her," Aset whispered while on her knees, outstretching her hands toward Eve. "My prayers are that it is swift. That the two mortal Neterus who are united in the Light make Cain's beheading a quick—"

"No!" Eve screamed again, scrambling to her feet. "Heal him,

Aset. Let me go to my son and let me touch his heart as his mother. Just that is all that I ask, all that I beg of this council. After all these years you owe me that one final request!"

Eve's panic-laden gaze tore around the group of agonized queens for support and came away lacking. "I ask for the Isis blade only, that I may battle my way to his throne room, not harm Damali," Eve said as she knelt before Aset again quickly and grabbed her hands. She closed her eyes, silver tears spilling in unstoppable rivulets, her words becoming thick. "I will grovel at your feet, Aset. Great Queen, have mercy in your heart."

"It is because of the unlimited mercy in my heart for you that I cannot abide your request. Just hear me out." Aset gathered Eve into a firm embrace as she spoke with halting words punctuated by repressed sobs. "Eve, my most revered . . . the entire pit would descend upon you—"

"I don't care," Eve whispered, pulling away so that her silver gaze could lock with Aset's. "I care not for my own survival. It is my son's that is paramount. My child's."

"And messenger demons would rip you into shreds on the way down," Aset said, undaunted as she pressed on, gathering Eve to her once more. "Succubae and incubi would adhere to your spirit like dark lesions so that you could not even communicate with any Light being."

Aset's voice began to rise, escalating as she tried to get her queen sister to understand the wrenching decision. "Light of Motherhood, the Amanthras would ensnare you and violate all that is clean within your wondrous heart. They would rape away the concept of all that is maternal in their mating ball swarms to devour it and regurgitate it as twisted energy. *Mothers would be no more.* Then, Level Seven would spew up the essence of Dante's father, who always held a grudge against you for never ceding to his son after the Garden. What would they do to Adam's mind, what serpent-inspired visions would they torture him with, my sister?" Aset urgently whispered into Eve's ear as Eve began to sob even harder.

"Adam, your husband, would lose his light, too . . . and Lilith would stand watch and screech with cruel laughter as this atrocity occurred. The One Who Remains Nameless could make you, the holder of world female fertility, the ultimate vessel for the Antichrist! Eve, you know that I speak the truth. This quest to stop the Unholy is the destiny of the paired, living Neterus—not yours. As much as my heart has been torn asunder, I cannot allow you to do this to yourself, nor could I bear witness as your shrieks for mercy went unaided. How could you ask me to watch you blotted from all existence?"

"Without my son in the Light," Eve said, her gaze unblinking as she leaned back from the embrace and stared at Aset, "I am already lost to existence. In Nod, he had a fighting chance. Hope has eclipsed in my heart if you will not allow me to try to retrieve him. I am, therefore, losing faith in my sisterhood . . . queens with sons who will not hear my pain . . . and with that, my love of you all is now in question."

Nzinga quickly went down on her knees beside Eve as Aset almost broke down into sobs.

"Dear, dear Eve . . . were we within our right to change the Master Plan, I would valiantly go to Hell to fight by your side. You *know* that! Any battle, any day, my sister of my heart, but do not lose faith, or love for us." Nzinga touched then cradled Eve's face. "Please," she whispered. "For the love of the Light, hope can always be restored . . . but faith and love are the cornerstones, the very *base* of the pyramid, hope its trinity apex. Do not lose the foundation in our midst. I will stand watch day and night without rest to be your energy beacon, my queen. You were the first female of our kind. If you are lost in spirit, we all die."

The Aztec queen, Chalchihuitlcue, who had previously hung back, moved closer to touch Eve's hair, her voice a gentle, harmonic murmur. "Work with us to send our youngest queen sister, Damali, every advantage of our collective skills in battle that she may do what must be done."

"I will give her my medicines of the world to heal her armies," the Asian queen, Lady Fu Hao, said, coming to Eve's side. "Our Damali did not cruelly lure your son to his demise; she was the one who sent him back and sealed him away with purpose for his own good. Give her reign over the elements of nature that she may use them wisely and with swift and sudden force as only pure elemental nature can render."

"I will give her the shaman earth harmonies I own and the fauna of North America," the fern-bearing, Native American queen, Est-santlehi, whispered. "We must work as one."

"I cannot commit to giving her my elements to behead my son. . . . Do not ask this of me right now."

Holding Eve away from her with a firm grip, Aset allowed her tears to wash her face. "Eve, how could you ask me to leave you to that fate in Hell you've requested? I would rather face your wrath of me for a thousand millennia than to watch you destroy yourself. I love you and could not bear it, nor could any queen sister who is witness to your suffering."

Eve shook her head slowly. "My son would not allow it. He would let me come to him to discuss it, to reason with him, once he saw how his decision has torn my heart out. I would go to him not as a huntress but as his mother."

Nefertiti dropped to her knees beside Eve and her voice became a pained murmur. "Your son is no longer your son. He would be faced with a choice. Either to go with a spirit queen that he has not seen in eons, his mother—one from the Light, who in his mind abandoned him—and again be cloistered in Nod without an empire or sensation. After tasting the forbidden fruit of excess, he'd side with the ultimate dark power conferred to him by his father's line. And with that side he'd have a chance to sire to start an empire through the living Neteru queen, Damali."

Nefertiti closed her eyes as Eve's body slumped. "He has just seen Damali, who is a much more recent image in his mind, and he will go after her, a female in season rather than you, dearest above all queen sisters. It is the nature of that line, and we all know this. Even if your hope is damaged, heed Nzinga and keep your faith in us, as well as your love for us. We say these things to you out of love and compassion, not cruelty. I also have children and know the terror of a mother's heart . . . never to want to face such a decision." Nefertiti kissed Eve's cheeks. "Give us each a little of your pain that we may all bear this burden with you. Allow Aset to heal you as much as she can, dear, dear sister of Light. I beg you that. Your son is gone. Do not look upon what he has become or you will go blind from the horror of it."

"I will keep constant prayer vigil," Joan said quietly. "I was never blessed with children before my demise, but I know that the Most High lost a beloved son and wept until the angels could weep no more. The Light will not abandon you. Do not leave us, or we shall never be the same without you."

"I will stand by Damali as an Amazon warrior who knows battle and loss of this kind, and I will guide her blade to be swift," the newest of the spirit queens, Penthesileia, said. "As your sister, this is my solemn promise. Your son will not suffer."

"He has family on both sides, and perhaps . . . his grandfather's people will show mercy, if his soul is not remanded into the Light?" Aset said with her eyes closed.

"Or maybe he will remember to die with a prayer in his heart," Joan murmured. "Carlos did . . . he listened to the living queen Neteru and was spared. I will start petitions immediately. Do not lose hope, even though corporeally, they may take his body below."

Bitter sobs consumed Eve as the other queens gathered nearer, each going to her knees to surround Eve with comforting arms.

"They cannot be allowed to desecrate my son's body or his spirit. We can take an army," Eve said, sputtering her futile complaint as she wept. "Both councils, every Guardian on the planet, to free my son!"

"If we do so—we—not Heaven, will begin the Armageddon . . . and the moment any of us saw Cain, we would do mortal combat," Aset murmured, petting Eve's hair. "And how many worthy warriors would we lose down in the bowels of Hell, thus making our side vulnerable to a war that will rage on for years?" Aset paused, allowing the reality to permeate Eve's mind. "Carlos and Damali must do this, as you are not capable because of your love, and we are bound to follow orders from On High."

Eve leaned her forehead against Aset's shoulder. "Then why didn't the warrior angels stop him? Why didn't they keep my Cain beyond the reach of Hell? Why didn't they intervene and abduct him the moment he left Nod?" Her voice was hoarse and weary as her arms slid around Aset's body in defeat. "Please, before you attempt to heal my wounds that will last forever . . . Great Queen Sister, tell me, before I lose my mind."

Aset motioned for the golden healing staff as Eve's frantic eyes sought hers. Aset touched Eve's face with trembling fingers and pushed her disheveled Kemetian braids away from her cheek. "Because," Aset murmured, swallowing another sob, "as much as it pains me to say this from one mother to another—it was simply *his choice.*"

"War is the only way! Give me the blade!" Adam growled, squaring off with Ausar. "Together we ride or die, side by side as a matter of honor, or you stand down and allow me to pass through to the Gray Zone alone!"

Ausar shook his head and kept his tone even and firm. "I will not grant you access to the Gray Zone, nor will I give you my blade. It has been conferred to Carlos Rivera this millennium, and Cain, as well you know, has been your Achilles' heel since the beginning. I will not see you sully your soul over this."

"Then we ride with Rivera now! How many battalions will stand with me?"

Two old warriors glared at each other, deadlocked at the Archon's Table, their towering six-foot-seven heights and sinewy girth evenly matched. Adam's long, silvery locks crackled with blue-static charge as his dark, Ethiopian face remained stone rigid. Ausar lifted his chin, sending a spill of jet-hued Kemetian braids over his shoulders. Hannibal slowly rose with Akhenaton, both kings prepared to separate potential immortal combatants.

"I, who will would ride with you, my brother," Hannibal said, his eyes shimmering pure silver in his near onyx face. Perpetual light in the realm of Neteru kings gleamed off his bald head as his aura gradually began to flicker with battle-prep silver. "But have you thought of the consequences to your wife's spirit should her husband slay her son?"

"That he is your stepson," Akhenaton said evenly, his tall, lean carriage slowly walking toward Adam, "will only make matters worse." He made a tent before his full mouth as he approached his outraged king brother calmly, his golden robes billowing behind him with unspent energy. "Before the other kings enter this chamber, my suggestion is that you think of what you are prepared to lose. Eve will never forgive you—and if you weigh what is in your heart upon the scales of Ma'at, you will find that murdering Cain has been there since Abel was slain. True?"

Akhenaton did not wait for Adam's response as he stroked his goatee. Solid silver glittered in his eyes, and his toffee-hued complexion held a tinge of angry crimson that made his cheeks become more ruddy as he spoke. "Ask Solomon to judge this before we mount up. If our wise counselor deems it so, then I will ride at your side with a winged steed of pure Light and place demon heads on pikes. We are always ready to go with you, this you know."

"This you know," Ausar said, repeating Akhenaton's words in a low rumble. "That you have doubted my brotherhood for you carves at my soul, Adam. You and I have ruled this council since the beginning. . . . Our wives are one. Blood sisters, beyond spirit. We are also brothers joined at the heart. Eve is thus and will always be my sister. My wife grieves at the sorrow of her closest queen sister. You and I, as men, *brothers* in spirit, have kept each other's deepest regrets at our core. Your loss is mine, Adam; your rage is my very own. I, more than you know, want Cain's head on a silver platter for doing this to Eve."

Ausar drew a steadying breath and walked away. "This turn of events tears at the fabric of the realms of Light Councils. However, I also want my brother whole—you. And if you are the one who assassinates Eve's now evil son, you will experience true eternity incarcerated in regret. I owe you more . . . enough to temporarily abide your fury. So what shall I do? My hands are tied by wisdom. The blade stays with Rivera."

"Then guide him!" Adam bellowed, snatching off his golden helmet and casting it to the white marble floor. "Teach him! Give him Hannibal's best strategies—a man brazen enough to take a thousand elephants over the Alps to crush Sicily, with the strength of a thousand kings—to make my queen's suffering end swiftly! He must be cut off from her energy and must stop dredging her heart! Even then her healing will take years!"

"Done," Hannibal said, going to Adam and clutching his forearm in a warrior's handshake. "Everything from every king of Light on this council I will collect and send to Rivera—my word as my bond, brother. From Nubia to Timbuktu, from Kemet to Songhai, from Athens to Persia, from Rome to the edges of Asia and beyond, the young king will be empowered and schooled by our old empires! It is done, tonight." Hannibal pointed toward the archon's table with his free hand, sending an arc of searing white light toward it. "He will feel the surge of power like he has never known. Here, we *are* our brother's keepers. Never doubt that alliance." Hannibal spat pure silver on the floor. "Cain be damned! I call a remote war advisory council, Ausar."

Adam let go of Hannibal's crushing hold, seeming somewhat mollified as he paced between Hannibal's hulking seven-foot frame and the massive, solid gold archon Roundtable that absorbed the silver blast and swallowed it into every Adinkra symbol and hieroglyph that surrounded it.

"I want that bastard Cain exterminated," Adam said through his teeth. "He has ripped out Eve's heart from its tissue anchors in her chest!"

Adam's voice hitched and broke as he paced away from the table again, giving the few assembled inner circle kings his back. "I don't want the other archons to see me this way when our war council convenes," he said, dropping his voice as the truth spilled from his lips. "Imhotep's Caduceus could not fully heal her. Eve is tied to Cain's energy by the eternal umbilical cord that binds mother to child forever—which has now become a black noose around her spirit. This is why I must have not only his head, but his heart gored before it is too late! The new Neterus must know how to sever all ties so that

Eve can eventually recover. This goes beyond business as usual or the normal reach of Heaven; it is *personal*. Eve was never to be destroyed at the onset of the Armageddon . . . or during it. My wife has paid her dues."

"We will not fail your quest—it is ours as well," Akhenaton said in a low rumble, throttling his rage at the indignity Adam faced. "We understand."

"Do you?" Adam asked with hot tears in his eyes as he spun to face his brethren. "*My wife* lies prone on her chamber bed staring at nothing, murmuring prayers, her gorgeous light diminishing daily. . . . How many years did it take her to come back after Abel's murder? I wanted to slay that bastard, Cain, the moment he reached manhood, but did not follow my first mind as I watched him manipulate his mother in ways that still slaughter me with outrage. Only the birth of Seth brought her around, and his conception is still a mystery to me because my wife was so aggrieved at Abel's death and Cain's subsequent banishment that . . ."

Adam's voice trailed off in a thick swallow as he walked away from the other kings and stood facing the towering white marble pillars that opened out to the perpetually lush Valley of the Kings. He stared at the monolith that bore the effigy of all the great leaders of old and willed strength. "Now, this heartbreak she must suffer as well?" Adam said as though talking to himself. He closed his eyes. "My ex-wife did this to her and used Eve's greatest blind spot, Cain, to drive a stake into my incomparable wife's heart. I will not allow it!"

"Nor will I," Ausar said in an authoritative tone, the fury-laden rumble coming from way down deep in his core. "Oh, my dear brother from the dawn of days . . . rest assured, nor will I. This is war."

CHAPTER TWO

Whew," Damali whistled, stopping Carlos's awkward apology with one finger before it could even begin. "I'm okay . . . but, whew."

"I know," he said, still gasping air. He gently turned her head to the side and tried to stop the jugular flow with trembling fingers. "Does it hurt?"

"Hell, yeah," she said, chuckling with her eyes closed. "You didn't even pleasure taint the nick, just—"

"Aw, baby . . . damn . . . I don't know where that came from. But, I'm serious, it won't happen again."

She opened her eyes and chuckled. "It was good, though."

"No. That was almost a damned battle bite." He slowly extracted himself from her and rolled off her to go get a towel to blot away the excess blood. "You might be a Neteru, and everything else underneath all that, but you're my wife, and I ain't *never* supposed to handle you like this."

Carlos's mind raced with panic as he walked to the bathroom. Something was seriously wrong, and any time something foul went down, the darkside was in it playing games. Damn!

"Relax," she murmured, trying to sit up, and then thinking better of it. She was dizzy from the sudden blood loss and exertion, and being with him had never done that to her before. "I'm okay."

He paced back from the bathroom and came to her side. "Lift your head and tell me how many fingers I have up."

She laughed and glimpsed them. "Three."

"One," he shouted and began softly dabbing her neck and shoulder with a towel. "Shit, D. Never again."

"Definitely not in the house. That was *not* a silent scream episode," she said, wincing as he touched near the area that was beginning to puff and bruise.

Carlos closed his eyes, not sure if he should blow on the bite, kiss away the offense, or if he could touch away the pain. There was nothing in his old DNA that told him how to heal a battle bite, since those were supposed to be what they were, fatal. And if one was delivered from his old throne knowledge on a female adversary that suddenly became a sexual negotiation during a death match, chances were she'd be a regenerative species, and sealing it up wasn't necessary on his part. The Neteru side of him wasn't much help, either, since he was the only one that had fangs . . . at least the only one he knew about this side of Nod.

"You're a hundred percent Neteru, baby . . . you can heal a battle bite, right, if you concentrate?" Carlos stared at her for a moment as her eyelids briefly slid shut.

"Yeah, I should be able to do that," Damali said, but there was no confidence in her tone. After a tense minute she opened her eyes. "I don't know what's wrong. It's like something is blocking my healing." Her gaze nervously searched his as her voice dropped to a pained murmur. "This hurts like hell and I can't stop the bleeding."

He almost couldn't speak as he stared at her, his heart thudding against his breastbone. If anything happened to her . . . "Baby, without the Caduceus—"

"Oooohhh . . . noooo. I am not going to the Queen's Council to ask for that for *this*. No way. Ice. Food. Water. Rest. The basics and I'm good. This one feels so bad that I don't even want Mar to see it when we go home. This sucker might need stitches—now how would that seem?"

Carlos dropped his head into his hands and sat back on the bed. "I don't know how to fix this or make the bruises go away. I've healed seduction bites, regular mortal-type wounds, and even helped do a vamp purge with Berkfield, but I don't know. This is different in the way it's delivered. It was a combo bite, I think. Has regular injury mixed with a battle bite, and those are different than turn bites or a seduction bite . . . I know what I'm saying probably doesn't make sense to you, but I can try a general healing if you let me touch it."

"Naw, that's all right," she said, laughing and edging away from him, then rolled over onto her stomach and smiled when he seemed hurt. "You made the other end feel *real* good, though. What were you cumming, white lightning? Dang." She peered up at him bleary-eyed, laughed, and sprawled out flat in a flop. "It's just the throat that's tender. Go easy on the jugular for a few days. Damn, I feel like a virgin all over again behind this mess."

He gently lowered his hands to her bruised shoulders, splaying his palms above the tender surface of her skin. "You've never been nicked in a battle by a vamp, but let me warn you, the battle bites are ugly and are designed for optimum pain. It's gonna hurt like hell in a few minutes, D . . . ask me how I know. You're still high off the endorphin rush. But the minute the battle bite sets in . . . you're gonna feel it."

Carlos wanted to kick his own ass. He'd held her so tightly and loved her so hard and recklessly that her wings didn't even get a chance to unfold. Had they done so, she might be lying there now with a broken wing that couldn't retract. He leaned down and kissed her shoulder blades. "Even when you were a virgin, I didn't manhandle you like this and leave you this sore—anywhere."

"True," she said, trying to make light of the subject. "See what happens to a girl when she gets married? All the romance is gone— poof—once the honeymoon is over."

"Don't say that, D," he said quietly. "Please, I'm sorry."

"Hey . . ." she said, turning over with effort. "You're really upset, aren't you? I was just playing, baby. Now I'm the one who's sorry. Don't worry. This will heal."

"I'ma take you into the bathroom and show you in the mirror. All right? Then you'll see why I'm so upset."

"Okay," she said, weaving as she tried to right herself.

"Let me carry you, D," he said quietly, shame singeing his voice. "You lost a lot of blood, too. I could barely seal the bite when I pulled out of it."

"No shit?" she asked, now trying to focus on his face as he gingerly lifted her and began walking. "Ow, that does sorta hurt . . . like everywhere and then some. Dang."

"No shit, D, and you know I've *never* come at you like that. Had you been on top, I mighta broken a wing if they presented. I grabbed you too hard."

"Baby, it's all right. . . . You just got caught up in the moment."

He shook his head and nodded toward the mirror. "Tell me *that's* all right, Damali."

The gasp escaped before she could cover her mouth with her hand. Horrified, she couldn't turn away from their reflection. Silver tears were in her husband's eyes, and her throat had been mauled. She leaned forward to get closer to the mirror, turning slightly to better examine the side of her neck, when she noticed the shoulder bruises from his grip.

"Honey, put me down," she whispered, "so I can see how bad it is. Baby, this wasn't your fault. It was . . . it was . . ."

Damali held on to the sink, at a loss for words as Carlos let her down slowly to stand, and she looked at the loose flap of skin that bunched around crimson, angry flesh within a black-and-blue knot. Instant pain shot through her, just seeing it.

"Don't," he whispered, as she leaned closer to the mirror and moved the flap with her finger.

"Holy shit," she said, swallowing hard, and holding on to his arm. "I think I'm gonna be sick. Ohmigod, I saw a vein. Oh, shit, I'm going into shock; that's why I can't feel anything. Ohmigod, ohmigod, I've never been battle nicked in the throat in my fucking life, ohmigod—this ain't a neat love-bite puncture. Move."

She went to the toilet in a wobbly path and hurled, clutching cold porcelain and breathing deeply as he held her up, rubbing her back. Hot coursing silver was running down her thighs. She was freaked out; he was freaked out, but she tried to play it off to help him deal after she finished vomiting, her words coming out in a shaky rasp. "I'm bleeding silver, so I guess I'll be okay."

Panic had put a sheen on his brow, and he held her more closely as he inspected her throat again. "No. Just red—"

"Look down," she said, pointing at her legs with her eyes squeezed shut.

"I gotta get you to a hospital, you're hem—"

"No!" she said, breathing hard and holding up her hand while leaning against him. "That's painkiller." She tried to smile before her husband flatlined with a very human coronary. "I asked you were you cumming white lightning, but shit. If you hadn't, I'd be in ICU."

"Damali, I swear I'm either taking you outta here to Marlene or to an ER buck naked if I have to and—"

"Stop," she said, leaning her cheek against his chest. "It was bound to happen sooner or later. A girl's gotta learn how to take a battle bite, sooner or later."

"What? Bound to happen sooner or later! This ain't nothing to joke around about, Damali. I'm your husband and I fucking bit you like—"

"Baby, just get me about a quart of water and let me sit down before I fall down."

"All right, all right," he said, picking her up very carefully but rushing to the side of the bed and then handling her like fragile glass as he deposited her on it. "Water. Right. Anything else? Talk to me."

"A banana, potassium. Garlic, an antiseptic in case any unwanted vamp buggies came with the bite. And bring me my purse. Mar taught me well. I always roll with a little somethin' something in there—a small vial of holy water, purified Red Sea salt, white sage, and anointing oil." She curled into a ball on her good side and panted through her mouth. "You were right. This shit hurts like hell."

"You're gonna try to do this purge *yourself*?" He stood in the bedroom door, incredulous, torn between going to the kitchen or her, unable to leave her immediately to go get what she'd requested.

"No," she murmured, suddenly becoming very sluggish. "We are one flesh now, so I'm gonna talk you through some serious female shaman healing arts, and you're gonna be my hands and strength."

She didn't have to tell him twice. He ran through the villa filling his arms with her antidotes and then found her purse and dashed back. On his knees beside the bed he dumped the full payload on the sheets and stared down at the gaping wound in her neck.

"Oh, God, Damali . . ." he whispered as he roused her. "It tore right over the first bite I gave you . . . that first time." He swallowed hard. "That was your sweet spot, baby."

"If we work fast, it might still be there," she said quietly. "If it doesn't keloid."

Carlos closed his eyes. "Tell me what I've gotta do."

"Clean it out."

He just stared at her.

"Old-school, honey," she said, reaching for his hand. "Don't worry. I'm in no danger of turning at my age, and you aren't all vamp. It's just gonna hurt like a mutha, but you know how to do this."

"I don't know if I can do this—I don't wanna hurt you any more than I already did."

Damali braced herself. "I'll be okay. Go ahead. Pour the holy water into the wound until it sizzles. Pack it down with salt; then make the sign of your faith—which in our case is the crucifix—over it, covering the length and width of the wound with anointing oil—using your right hand as you say a passage from the Good Book. . . . Then I want you to put my silver collar on to keep the burn going. The garlic and potassium is for me, and some mouthwash wouldn't hurt . . . neither would a trash can if I barf again. Light the white sage and ask for healing as you circle my body three times. Simple. Then, with anointed hands and a whole lotta love in your spirit, touch me wherever it looks real ugly and try to draw the bruised blood under my skin up and out. All right?"

He nodded, but was anything but all right, especially when she cried out. His whole body was shaking from sympathy pains by the time he was done. She lay there limp in a hot sweat, the wound leaking pinkish, sizzling ooze from beneath the silver collar, and he was practically rocking in a cold sweat from hurting her so badly. She took the mouthwash from the bedside table and swished her mouth out and spit in the wastebasket. He grabbed the trash can and lost his dinner into it.

"Jesus Christ, I don't know what came over me, D. . . . If you want a divorce, I can dig it. No contest. We don't even have to discuss it." He was talking quickly into the trash, fighting off dry heaves. When he looked up, he expected her face to be twisted into a hurt frown of disgust, but instead her eyes were serene and steady.

"You are so crazy, Carlos," she said, touching his leg and then letting her hand fall away for more comfort. "I love you." Her smile came out with a wince. "You're gonna be one of those dads that has to stay in the waiting room, aren't you?"

"What are you talking about, D? This was major. A battle bite? Having a baby is different. That's the culmination of—"

"Sheeit," she murmured, chuckling as she dozed. "I guess sitting in an all-male throne from a sterile vamp might not've had this info, but lemme tell you, brother. The way Inez, Mar, and Marjorie told me, this ain't nothin'. Try eighteen hours or more of hard-down work, your body convulsing in agony every three minutes without relent, a masked doctor standing over your stuff—your legs spread-eagle and all you hear is metal and all you see is lights, and dude is leaning way too close with a scalpel ready to put a stem-to-stern incision in a place you *definitely* don't want any loss of sensation or keloid scars, or maybe he'll just go through your stomach, move your intestines and whatnot out of the way—lay 'em on your chest to get the baby out, then will stitch you up later—just put a zipper right in your—"

"Oh shit!" Carlos stood up and began to pace. "They do a fucking Vamp Council wall on women in broad daylight like that, in this day and age?"

"Those are the better hospitals, not always found everywhere on the globe . . . and in those countries where women are having babies faster than you can spit it's in the bush with no clean water or meds, okay."

"How did we get on this subject in the first place, Damali? Can't they numb it up before—"

"Only if they get to you fast enough; otherwise, no drugs. You gotta suck it up like a woman or the baby is at risk, so you bite the bullet and holler. Then, after it's all said and done, you walk like you're tippin' on eggshells for a few weeks, they say." She looked at him hard. "That's why you guys have to wait six to eight weeks— who in their right mind would feel like all that after dropping an eight-pound baby and getting cut?" Damali sucked her teeth and then cringed as the mere action made her head throb. "Y'all are lucky to ever get any more in life, after that."

"Baby, I knew, but I didn't, you know what I'm saying . . . I—"

"Oh, please. The girls told me that your stuff hurts so damn bad as the painkiller wears off you can barely breathe, much less take a pee, with a hundred and fifty stitches in your ass . . . and there's sometimes this numb spot right in the most inconvenient place. But, you still gotta get up and take care of that little baby and nurse it, too, on real sore nipples." Damali sighed as she peeped open one eye to glimpse Carlos's stricken expression. All the blood had drained from his face, and she stifled a chuckle. "Life goes on."

"In this day and age? Oh hell to the no. A numb spot? For real, D, you ain't lying about that? Not my baby girl. That sounds like—"

"Medieval science. I know," she said, laughing softly to herself as she closed her eyes again, becoming peevish that her body hurt so badly from his drama. "Women go through some wicked shit in the name of love and life, brother . . . going into it, it's great," she added on a heavy exhalation. "Mind-blowing, life-altering, climb-the-walls fantastic. It's the aftermath that's the bitch. So a little roughhouse battle bite ain't nothin'. I can hang. Just don't do that shit again, or I'll cut you. I'm serious."

The man was so undone from the night before that he simply helped her into the Hummer, pecked her cheek, got in on his side, and drove. She couldn't keep the sly smile off her face. Dang, all she'd meant to do was use the truth to temporarily cool his ardor so he wouldn't get all rammy again and try her while she was healing. But in the morning, she was fine, and hadn't been able to coax him near her for one last round before heading home. Her bad. Damali sighed out loud. Carlos didn't even respond.

"Okay, listen, before we get back to the house and everybody swarms us, can I at least have a kiss?"

He leaned over and kissed her on her cheek and traced his finger over her silver wedding collar. "I love you, baby. Until I figure out what got into me, that's it. I'm done. I'm not putting my hands on you. Something like that is nothing I ever want to revisit."

"Carlos, your skin is still practically leaking silver—so it's not some dark influence. You're just a strong-ass male Neteru, and if you didn't have fangs, that would have simply been a love hickey . . . but, given the circumstances and the little issue of you having fangs, it got crazy. Baby, you just came out of an apex not that long ago and your body is probably still—"

"Damali," he said, swerving the vehicle to the side of the road and bringing it to a hard stop. "No. My original mark is still swollen on you . . . the place that I *revered* on your throat. My baby's sweet spot, and I dawged it like that? Me? I *never* made you cry out in pain, *always* pleasure—no matter what was running through me. Something happened, and I'm going to Ausar about this, because the last time we kept things all secretive, mad-crazy bullshit went down. This time you got hurt bad, and no. Uh-uh."

She opened her mouth and then closed it, and pressed her hand to her chest, staring at him. "Please tell me you are not taking our personal business up to no Ausar on the Neteru King's Council." Her voice had come out in a panicked whisper. "Oh, Carlos, you will embarrass me down to the toes of my shoes, if you—"

"Then what the hell happened?" He folded his arms over his chest with a look in his eyes that told her he would not be moved. "Sloppy, like that? Uh-uh. Nearly battering my brand-new wife's skull into a headboard 'til it split? Me? You crazy?"

Damali rubbed the top of her head, trying to make him laugh. "Did a sistah complain about that part?"

"Stop," he said, pointing at her. "A seduction fang entry is supposed to be dripping sensuality and feel so good on skin break that you bust a nut before the enamel is in your jugular full hilt, and—"

"Okay, okay," she said, hiding a wide smile behind pursed lips for a moment. "That part was a little rugged . . . but maybe it's your system converting back to not using that as a part of—"

"Shit . . . you think so, baby? You think I'm losing my bite?" He looked in the rearview mirror so fast and had pulled it so hard to turn it to him that it came off in his hands.

"Oh, Lord have mercy . . . no . . . but—"

There was no talking to this man.

"The other part was real good," she said, resting her hand on his arm.

"No, it wasn't," he said, his voice still laden with panic. "I had you in a caveman grip. Didn't do nothing to—"

"I was ready," she said, kissing his cheek. "Don't take no mess like that to Ausar. I'm healed, it's over, and . . . it's husband-and-wife stuff."

He let his breath out hard and rubbed his palms down his face. "I wasn't gonna go into that level of detail, but I need to know what that power surge I felt was all about. It was seriously go-to-war, pure adrenaline anger vibe all in it. But at the same time—the other side we try not to discuss—I was horny as shit, like I'd just done thirty years in the joint, or something."

Now it was her turn to just stare at him.

"You didn't tell me about that part," she said carefully.

"I didn't get a chance to last night. I was bugging so hard trying to get you healed up."

"How strong was it, Carlos?" she asked quietly, no judgment in her tone.

He closed his eyes and allowed his head to drop back against the headrest. "Damali, I felt something close to it on throne ascensions, all right. It was pulling my ass under in waves, sending fever up my spine 'til it felt like it would claw its way out the top of my skull if I didn't get laid. By the time I carried you into the bedroom, I couldn't even speak. Then the sensation flipped into war fury with you in my arms, and it took me to a place where I felt naked without a blade in my hand. Then it zapped back again, and the next thing I knew, I was hollering and cumming and slobbering on my damned self." He opened his eyes and looked at her hard. "That ain't hardly me by a long shot, now is it?"

"No," she said quietly, kissing him gently. "You always cared about making sure I was half outta my mind, *first,* and then whatever you did, under any circumstances, it never hurt. Even in the desert on the ground—on gravel and rock, I never got a scratch."

"That's what I'm talking about," he whispered, his eyes searching hers. "Never. I worship your skin. Leave a scar that might keloid over my original marriage to you . . . oh hell no. Make you scratch my back to get me off you during a lovemaking feed? What? Have so much fang in your throat that you're practically choking on blood, not pleasure. Me? You were calling my name, gasping, but not the way I ever wanna hear it coming from your mouth again. Then I don't listen, just put my tongue down your throat to shut you up—are you crazy, Damali? On our honeymoon?"

He was so outdone that he flung open the car door, walked ten feet down the deserted road, and then walked back to the vehicle. He leaned on the door, heaving air for a moment, and then got into the Hummer and slammed the door.

She kissed him again more slowly, wiped her finger over his damp mouth with the pad of her thumb, and smoothed her palm over his hair. "Let's go back to base camp, go in the house, make the greeting rounds, and then go get a private divination with our councils, because—"

"Do me this one favor," he said, stroking her hair. "Not that I have the right to even ask you for anything right now. But I'm asking you this as your husband, all right?"

"All right," she said, studying the deep pain in his eyes.

"This time, let me have a man-to-man conversation with Ausar first. Just a one-on-one. I do not want the queens in this, or Marlene, or anybody else. But if there's a problem beyond some transitional flux, then we come clean at the house. Together."

She nodded. "This is between man and wife."

The way Damali had said that she'd keep his concerns within their sacred union until he got answers made him even sadder. Just knowing that she unquestioningly had his back and always would made him need to dig harder for answers. It was all he could do to play the role when they walked in the door of the hacienda a few miles down the road.

Rider was on him like a pit bull, teasing him so hard he made the women in the house shake their heads as they spirited Damali away after she got quick hugs and love from the fellas.

"Well at least this time when you dragged your tired carcass over the threshold, you're legal, Rivera. How's it feel?" Rider slapped Carlos on the back and hugged him hard. "Four days wasn't long enough, I take it, because you seem a little reserved for a man who just tied the knot—like the gravity of it all is finally hittin' ya, or is it that your ass is so bone weary that ya need to lay down before you fall down?"

Carlos laughed as the house erupted in male mayhem and ribald humor. "A little of both, man," he said, dropping his grip on the floor with a thud and hugging Rider hard. "You're a sight for sore eyes."

"You're putting the pressure on, my brother," Big Mike said, laughing and hugging Carlos off his feet once Rider turned him loose. "I'ma hafta get a danged ring myself now," he whispered and then dropped Carlos down, still laughing.

Carlos shrugged, "Hey, man, what can I say? A man's gotta do what a man's gotta do."

Shabazz shook Carlos's hand then pulled him into a lightning fast chest-to-chest hug. Carlos wasn't even sure the hug had happened.

"Glad y'all made it back without incident. Nights get a little tense around here and we was worried about you two all alone. Figured you both had your radar down, and that's a good way for a man to get smoked. But you da man. Aw'ight." Shabazz looked in the direction of the family room, where Damali and the other female Guardians had gathered. He beamed as he looked at her. "You actually married my baby . . . in a church." Shabazz just shook his head, swinging his long, shoulder-length locks as though the whole thing had just occurred to him.

"Like somebody was gonna get in between them," Dan said, shaking his head at Shabazz's comment. "Be serious."

Shabazz just laughed. "The newbies will be next, watch."

"Hold it, hold it," Berkfield chuckled, slapping a hand down on Carlos's shoulder. "They've got a ways to go, but you, my man, I don't know what to say. How's it feel?"

"Fantastic, man," Carlos said, jettisoning the pain from his voice.

Bobby nodded and pounded Carlos's fist. "Good to have you back in the house."

Carlos raised an eyebrow and motioned with his chin toward Jasmine and Heather, and then glanced at Dan and Bobby again. "How's life treating *you,* is the question."

Bobby beamed and looked away. "Aw'ight."

Carlos cocked his head to the side as Dan's face lit up with a megawatt smile. "Cool."

"Everything's peace," Dan said with a bashful shrug.

Carlos shook his head with a huge grin. "Very cool. I'm impressed."

J.L. laughed and refused to look at Berkfield or Carlos. "Good to have you home, brother. Whew!"

Carlos laughed hard and slapped Berkfield on the back. "He'll do the right thing, man, relax. If I did, then shit."

Even Berkfield had to chuckle. "That does make me feel better by comparison, trust me."

Carlos looked around, mentally doing roll call and missing Jose and Juanita. Quiet worry filled him. The one person who might not be cool with all of this would be Jose. Truthfully, Juanita might not, either. Come to think of it, she might have more of a problem than Jose with everything. But that was squashed, he thought. Then again, as he glanced at the women who were grouped by a table of gifts . . .

"Where's Jose?" Carlos asked as casually as possible.

"Burnt to a cider," Mike said, laughing, "but you didn't hear that from me."

Carlos chuckled. "Then it's all good." He couldn't ask about Juanita and remain politically correct, so he held his peace.

"Oh, yeah," Mike said in a deep baritone designed to make them all laugh. "It's *all* good, *oh, baby.*"

"See, Mike," Shabazz said, laughing harder, pointing at him. "You ain't right. You ain't supposed to be using your special powers to get in our boy's business like that."

"Dude is a-okay, *hombre,*" Rider said, walking away from the group. "I'm just a nose, what do I know? But I didn't need freaking supersonic hearing. Shit!"

"I guess brotherman is aw'ight, then," Carlos said, laughing hard, following Rider into the family room to hug Marlene good.

"Jose is right *as rain,* man. Dude is chill," Shabazz said, slinging an arm over Carlos's shoulder. "Hey, Mar, guess what the wind blew in."

"C'mere, boy, and give me a for-real hug," Marlene said, grabbing Carlos to her chest so quickly that she almost knocked the wind out of him.

The women had Damali hemmed in by a sofa with her arm outstretched from her body, several hands on her forearm, turning her diamond in the sunlight like her arm just happened to be attached to the rest of her.

"Girl, how was the honeymoon?" Inez said, bubbling with excitement. "The rock is off da meter, and I know I saw it fast before, but, girl . . . how many carats is that blue-white sucker set in platinum? I know, after *all that,* the honeymoon was da bomb. *How was it?*"

Damali winked at Carlos. "Good. Real good."

Inez giggled and squeezed her hard, and Damali silently winced.

"It's too bad you kids couldn't have stayed away longer, but . . ."

Marjorie trailed off and sighed. "But at least you got away for a little bit, right?"

"I would hardly call being two or three miles down the road 'away,'" Marlene laughed, cupping Damali's cheek as she passed her. "But not here works, I'm sure."

"I cooked, y'all, 'cause I knew you was coming home today." Inez raced to the kitchen behind Marlene.

"I just think it's so romantic," Krissy said, practically swooning as Jasmine and Heather joined in her sigh.

"Okay, tell ya what," Damali said, "I'm gonna go drop this luggage in our room and—"

"*Our room,* did you hear that?" Krissy said, closing her eyes.

"Why don't you let the girl go lay down for an hour, 'cause I know she's tired," Inez shouted from the kitchen.

Damali shook her head as everyone in the room fell out laughing. Leave it to Inez to just flat blast her in front of the team. Marlene was laughing so hard that she had to turn her back and wipe her eyes. But the fact that Juanita and Jose were nowhere to be found made her nervous. Either it was a good sign that those two were in deep cohabitation and not to be disturbed, or it meant that they were somewhere nursing very old wounds. Still too taxed to summon a scan, Damali just made small talk and enjoyed being home.

"Let them get settled, guys. Lawdy-B!" Marlene fussed, trying to force authority into her voice, and then just broke down against the sink, laughing.

Krissy squeezed Damali into another too-tight hug, and this time Damali felt the tender spot beneath her shoulder blades give way, almost making her gasp as a damaged wing shifted.

"You're making me have to pee," Damali said with a tense smile, struggling out of Krissy's well-intentioned hold. "Oh, chile. I'll be back in a flash."

"See, Carlos," Inez teased. "You done sent her back here with a weak bladder—ya need to give her a break for twenty-four hours," Inez hollered, gaining more laughs as Damali slipped out of Krissy's love-fest embrace.

Almost numb from pain, Damali ran down the hall, leaving her bags, just needing not to be touched for a moment. Her whole body hurt, and yet pride kept her on her feet, smiling in front of the family. It was one of her best performances ever. But once in the still bathroom on the other side of the huge hacienda, she almost cried from the body aches that consumed her.

As carefully as she could, Damali opened the back of her silver collar to see if the redness and swelling from Carlos's bite had gone down. She placed the jewelry that was embedded with her seven collected stones on the sink with care and studied her throat. It was fiery red but sealed over, thank Heaven. However, the inside of the collar looked like an old Band-Aid, crusted with dried blood and wound ooze. Damali shook her head with disgust and glanced down at the necklace. The huge diamond Aset had given her covered her throat chakra, the same one that had screamed bloody murder, not passion, the night before. Even the pearl had splatter on it from the backside of the open settings. Carlos was right; this didn't make sense.

Damali rolled her shoulders and closed her eyes, stretching her back. A weeklong soak in one of the hacienda's old claw-foot tubs would be a luxury cure, but who had that kind of time? The team had been fortunate to get seven days of battle hiatus and, in a day or so, it would be time to move out to places unknown. Tonight, they'd party. Tomorrow, they'd sit in the makeshift war room, otherwise known as the family room, and figure out where the next safest place would be. In the interim, she and Carlos had to find clues as to what was going on while holding their shit together in front of the team. No emotion came. She was too tired to dwell on it right now. Tonight, after the welcome-home festivities, she'd slip into bed in her husband's arms and respect his personal space.

Damali plugged the sink with her eyes closed. The headache from the probable concussion was making her eyes sensitive to the glaring, bright light of Mexico's sun. She filled the bowl with cool water to splash her face, wondering how long she could endure the family hugs and slaps on the back before breaking down and begging them not to touch her. If Big Mike came at her—and he would because she'd slipped by him intentionally—one mighty crush from those huge arms . . . a two-hundred-and-seventy-five-pound-and-climbing weight category from Inez's loving pots, combined with an off-the-floor hug by the six-foot-eight team giant, would make her see stars and call on Jesus.

A light tap on the door jerked Damali's attention around, and she slowly said, "ouch," in a silent, openmouthed wince as she clutched the sink. Her necklace got bumped into the sink and was now submerged under cool water, but her arms hurt so badly at the moment she couldn't immediately move them to get it. If Carlos was sweating her to help fend off family, she couldn't.

"Come in," Damali said, breathing hard. "I can't come out; you'll have to come in."

When Juanita walked into the bathroom slowly, latched the door behind her, and kept her back to Damali, she tried not to bristle. Of all days . . . if girlfriend was gonna start some meeting-in-the-ladies'-room mess, today would not have been the day she would have picked.

"Hey, lady," Damali said, trying to be cool, and forcing herself to remember all the good things Marlene had told her Juanita had done from before.

"Hey, D. Welcome home."

The fact that Juanita kept her back to Damali wasn't helping matters, but there was something in the sound of her voice that gave Damali enough energy to push off the sink and meet Juanita midfloor.

"Girl, you okay?" Now Damali was concerned. Something wasn't right; even Juanita's voice was off. She held her body strangely, too.

Juanita turned around. She had on dark sunglasses, her hair was disheveled, and she was wearing a man's white cotton shirt with the collar flipped up and long sweatpants—in La Paz, in eighty-five degrees? When, of all the women in the house, 'Nita always showed the most skin?

"Are you all right?" Damali asked again, her voice steady as she approached Juanita.

"I have to ask you a question," Juanita said in a quiet, serious tone, unafraid. "This is nothing about your business. I'm just asking you this because I have a reason." She carefully lowered her collar and removed her sunglasses.

Damali didn't know where to look first. Juanita's eyes had dark rings under them as though she hadn't slept in days. Her neck was pocked by a series of purplish-red bruises, fresh ones that descended into scattered, older mulberry-hued tones that presented significant risks for blood clots. As Juanita did a slow striptease, removing her shirt to reveal a tank top and show skin, Damali slowly brought her hand up to her mouth.

"Father Mother God . . ."

"Did he ever do this to you?" Juanita asked, her voice just above a murmur.

Damali rushed to Juanita as fast as her sore body would allow, but stopped several feet away in the huge hacienda bathroom as the woman closed her eyes as though begging Damali not to touch her. Scanning Juanita's arms with a horrified gaze, Damali saw every easy vein point bruised. The insides of her elbows, her wrists, her throat.

"Girl, what happened?" Damali whispered through her teeth.

"When Carlos was half-vampire or part-vampire, did he ever do this to you?" Juanita repeated, her eyes opening slowly to stare at Damali without blinking.

"Let me see your throat," Damali said as softly as she could. "I'm a healer and won't hurt you."

"I'm a seer and never saw it coming," Juanita said sadly. "I only see very recent past events. I'm not like Mar or Inez, who see the future events in varying degrees of clarity. Marj can see a little, but is better at conjuring. If I was better, I would have seen it."

"Shushhhh," Damali whispered, allowing her hand to cover the left side of Juanita's throat without actually touching the tender bruise. "It's okay. When was the last time he bit you?"

"Jose bit me until dawn, then collapsed. You understand?"

The wild look in Juanita's eyes made Damali want to hug her. But for the sake of both their bodies, she dared not. The heat emanating from Juanita's skin was the closest human attempt at a vamp mate strike she'd ever seen. Raw passion almost arced a current in her palm as she tried to draw the blunt-edged strike off Juanita's skin.

"Where else?" Damali said quietly, going down Juanita's arms and lessening the pain. But Damali had to back up and breathe after a moment. Taking this on and coping with her own body aches made tears almost fall.

"I'm sorry. I know it hurts, but I couldn't go to Marlene with this . . . or Berkfield," Juanita said quickly, her voice quiet and panic-stricken. "He's never done anything like this before. . . . It would get intense, and I knew he had vamp way back in his family tree . . . but I swear to God—"

Damali held up her hand. "I know, I know, and baby, please don't swear to God about something like this." She sighed hard. "Look, I pretty much know where else a male vampire would bite you . . . and you can show me or not, but if it's bad, a femoral bite that gets a blood clot can be a for-real heart-stopping experience. I know we've had our shit between us, but—"

"It hurts so fucking bad I can't walk, girl," Juanita whispered through her teeth. When she shut her eyes two huge tears streamed down her cheeks. "Jose is the most passionate, caring, careful lover that . . . this isn't him, and you cannot say *anything* to anybody, *promise* me."

"I know—I mean, I suspect, given his personality," Damali said, quickly correcting herself before anything crazy jumped off in Juanita's mind. For a moment, she wasn't sure what to do and couldn't commit to keeping a secret this huge. The team needed to know about this; Carlos definitely had to know, but she also wanted to preserve some of her teammate's privacy. She just prayed that Juanita had enough sense not to tell her something she didn't wanna hear about Carlos, who *did* sleep with Juanita for years.

"Can you sit down on the edge of the tub?" Damali finally said. "And tell me you have on underwear because I'm not gonna be able to hang, unless you do."

"Yeah," Juanita said through a painful chuckle. "I was standing in the room by the door, trying to get dressed while he passed out. I knew you'd be coming home and was just trying to figure out how to get to you alone. . . . God is good."

Juanita inched her sweatpants down in agonized degrees, moving slowly not because of modesty, but from the bite welts on her hips, belly, and inner thighs. Damali fought to keep her expression neutral, but Jose and Carlos were definitely from the same old vamp line. Moving with calm authority, Damali sucked in a deep breath and placed her hands gently over each wound, grimacing as the pain shot into her skin and lessened on Juanita's. After a moment, Damali dropped forward on her hands and knees again, panting.

"That's all I can do today, just enough to take away the danger of clotting and make it bearable. I'm too drained right now and really need some other stuff to work with. But if you can keep him off you tonight, by tomorrow I can try another draw with my mini-Marlene version of purifiers."

"Thank you," Juanita whispered. "Bless you." She wept quietly and looked toward the door. "What's wrong with me, D? I'm like a fucking junkie. This shit hurts, and yet . . ."

"Oh, girl," Damali said, too tired to front as she pushed herself up. "Been there. At least the brother doesn't have fangs."

Juanita stared at her with wide eyes, and Damali could have kicked herself for the admission.

"All I'm saying is, you have to tell him—too rough. Your body won't heal like a Neteru's, and you could get put in the hospital, or worse, behind this craziness."

"I know," Juanita whispered, pulling on her sweatpants with effort. "Last night was the first time he went off on me like that . . . got this crazy look on his face, and then the outside of his eyes, the brown part, flicked a little silver, then gold, and the next thing I knew—"

"What?" Damali whispered, coming close to Juanita. "Jose's eyes changed?"

"Yeah," Juanita said, standing up with a wince.

"What time?" Damali was so close to her she could have grabbed her, but didn't.

"Like about an hour or so after sundown—Damali, he isn't a vampire, is he?" Juanita swung around and went to the mirror. "Please, God, tell me I'm not gonna change into the undead!"

"Keep your voice down. No. I'm trying to get a bead on what mighta happened—that's all." Damali raked her locks with her fingers. The coincidence was too eerie and completely unnerving. Both her Guardian brother and her man were linked by very old ties; that they went through some sort of simultaneous flip out was bizarre.

"Okay, can you re-create the episode for me? Spare me the intimate details," she added quickly, "but, like, what led up to it?"

Juanita nodded. "We was all eating dinner, and he didn't want anything but beef or lamb, something that you could cook rare and leave bloody, and told Inez not to season it. So you know that started some shit in the kitchen, right?"

"Oh, my God . . ."

"Yeah, you know it." Juanita flipped her long brown hair over her shoulders. "Okay, so finally all that was settled, and we ate. After he got halfway through the meal, we was all joking around, like always, and he looked at me and said, 'Baby, can I talk to you for a minute?' I was *so* embarrassed, girl, because it was plain as day that he wasn't trying to *talk* about *nothing.* So, me, I tried to play it off and said, 'Oh, sure, in a minute. Lemme help Inez get the dishes.' But he stood up from the table and said, '*Now,* Juanita. I'm not playing.' I was like, 'O-*kay.* I heard you, but don't boss me.' He walked away from the table and called me again. Like shouting, and the other brothers stood up and asked me if I was cool, because if I wasn't, they was gonna step to Jose about acting like that with me up in the house—no matter what we mighta been arguing about. But that's the thing," she said, her eyes holding hurt and confusion, "we hadn't been arguing at all."

Damali began to walk in a tight circle. "Were any of the other Guardian brothers, especially the newbies, acting weird like this?"

Juanita shook her head. "Uh-uh. I told the older brothers I was fine, Jose was just tripping. That's when it got ridiculous. I went down the hall to his room, and he snatched me in the door. I was like, 'Hey, hold up,' and before I could say another word, he kissed me so hard my head banged on the door. I was about to fight his ass . . .

but . . ." Juanita looked away. "He bit me. I ain't ashamed to say it, but—"

"I know, I know," Damali muttered. "Girl . . . look . . . get some rest in a safe room where there's another body other than his, and give me twenty-four hours to figure out what—"

"D, don't get mad at me, but for a lot of reasons I *don't* wanna go into, *please* don't go telling Carlos, okay?"

Damali closed her eyes. "That's my husband, 'Nita—my partner, the other half of this Neteru squad, and if anybody would know what's going on in a vamp line, even in a full human with traces, it's him."

Juanita walked away and lifted her hair off her neck. "I know . . . I just don't . . . Whateva."

"He won't step to Jose, if that's what you're worried about."

Juanita nodded. "I don't want that to happen. I shouldn't have even told you. Jose woke up this morning and was sick to death about what happened and made me promise I wouldn't tell a soul, but the wounds hurt so badly I had to get it numbed a little."

"Take some Motrin 'til I can go over you again, and—"

"You think I could be pregnant?"

"Oh, shit."

"I'm taking the pill, even though Marlene is dead set against any system-altering medications, but under these conditions . . ." Juanita looked at the floor. "I wanted to be sure that if some entity or something got to me again, I couldn't get knocked up and drop Rosemary's baby, is all I'm saying."

Damali bit her lip and went to the sink to begin picking blood out of her submerged necklace. It didn't matter that it was all gone by now; she needed something to do with her hands. "That's wise. I can't take anything that messes with my chemistry. So, if you're on the pill, why are you worried?"

When Juanita didn't immediately answer, Damali looked up into the mirror to see Juanita hug herself.

"Girl, what he shot was real different, is all I can say."

"What color was it?" Damali said in as calm a tone as possible, scrubbing her necklace harder.

"Like, hot silver and sorta glowing. What does that mean?"

"I don't know," Damali said quietly, picking at the intricate silver etchings around each stone even harder. "Just try to get some rest. When I learn more, I'll hip you."

"Thanks, D," Juanita whispered, and slipped out the door.

"Ouch!" the pearl in Damali's necklace complained. "I thought she'd never leave and it's about time you put me in some water. I'd have more clarity if you jogged down to the sea and—"

Damali scooped up her necklace as the she-dragon's voice began to fade within the now-glowing pearl the moment air hit it. She rushed through the house making lame excuses about having to commune with the sea to coax out a new song that was wearing a hole in her head. She blew Carlos a quick kiss but her eyes said, *Later, ask me then.*

"Zehiradangra! Ohmigoodness, where have you been?" Damali exclaimed in a tight whisper as she made it down the steps and headed for the beach.

"Sitting on your nightstand with *way* too much information," the pearl said in a huff, losing power out of water. "Waiting, waiting, *waiting* for you guys to get *done* honeymooning."

CHAPTER THREE

"Okay, Zehiradangra, talk to me," Damali said, stooping down with effort to lower her necklace into a shallow wash of sea by the rocks.

Her entire body hurt, and after getting nearly hugged into a stupor by her family and healing Juanita, the last thing she wanted was a lecture from a dead she-dragon. But Zehiradangra was an old friend and now an oracle that rivaled the one at Delphi, so Damali summoned patience. Although it seemed like it was taking forever for the pearl to glow again and come to life in her hands.

Damali steadied her voice and tried again with a gentler tone. "Z . . . all right, I'm sorry I snapped at you. *Please* talk to me."

"I didn't know what to say or if you wanted me around, you sounded so . . . upset."

Damali sighed with relief. "I was upset, but not at you," Damali admitted. "A lot of crazy things seem to be happening again. What's your take on it?"

The pearl glowed pink and then went white hot. "I did not want to intrude during a very private time, but are you all right now?"

Complete humiliation shot heat to Damali's face, and she made a mental note to be sure to shove her necklace in the bedroom drawer from now on when she wasn't wearing it. "I'm cool," she lied.

"You must be very, very careful during this time, Damali," the pearl warned. "I have never seen him this way."

"Yeah, well, me neither. But I really don't wanna focus on Carlos right now. Overall, I need to—"

"I am not speaking of Carlos," Zehiradangra said calmly. "I am speaking of his brother."

Damali leaned closer to the pearl. "Jose just went through—"

"No, no, no," she murmured impatiently, sending a small stream of bubbles to the surface of the shallow pool. "His older brother, my friend, Cain."

"Oh, him . . ." Damali turned and plopped down to sit on the rocks, no longer caring that her jeans would get wet and sandy. "I can't deal with whatever's going on in his twisted brain right now in Nod. As long as he stays there, then fine."

"There are several flaws to your statement, Damali," Zehiradangra said in a snippy tone that Damali had never heard her use before. "Cain loves you. He is a being that loves hard and deep, and you are very fortunate that he does."

Damali rolled her eyes and blew a stray lock up off her forehead. She had to remember that Zehiradangra used to be Cain's lover, so this was indeed going to be a delicate dance. "I'm married now," was all she could offer her.

"Yes. I know. I was at the ceremony, as you may recall."

Great. Just what she needed. An oracle with an attitude.

"Zehiradangra, listen . . . Cain seemed like a really nice entity going in. He is fine as all get out. Has a voice like . . ." Damali searched for an adequate description that would mollify the offended pearl. "Like a . . . aw, heck, the man can sing his ass off and is awesome. Comes from good people on his mother's side. Yada, yada, yada," Damali said, losing patience. "But I had to leave him in Nod for several reasons—reasons that you agreed with when he helped set you up to get your neck snapped. Or am I not remembering how this all went down correctly?"

"It is true," the pearl said, its glow dimming, its voice sad. "I just wished better for him. I am still connected to his light energy . . . what's left of it, that is. You should have seen how he suffered when you left him." The pearl sniffed. "I know you had to, but during his apex—the timing was horrible."

"Pearl," Damali said, her voice coming out as a plea as she used one of Zehiradangra's nicknames. "You know I had no choice about the timing of all of this!"

"Damali, he held his sheets to his face and breathed you in for seven days—unspent. He wept from the pain in his spirit and the agony riddling his body for you. He shunned regeneration and nourishment to the point of near energy collapse. . . ." The pearl stopped speaking and swallowed hard. "I am annoyed with you because his voice echoes and suffering clouded my vision. Cain needed to sire so badly, having come so close to you in the flesh that—I cannot even speak of it."

"Shit." Damali closed her eyes. "I wasn't trying to play with his mind, but there was no way I was allowing him to bring out his dark soul hybrids to take over the world."

The pearl again glowed a more mellow pink, and its tone became more philosophical and less judgmental. "This, I know. But as long as he could come to you telepathically, even in a one-way transmission getting your vibrations, he could . . . well—"

"Don't tell me," Damali muttered. "I get the picture."

"No, you do not have the full understanding of how deeply wounded he was—albeit much of this was his fault for his insistence on taking over the world. However, once you formally married in the Light, there was a sacred disconnection up in the realms from past lovers. Your energy receded from him, as did his ability to gain sensory impressions from you here on Earth. It became so maddening for my old friend that he even tried to relieve himself with inanimate objects and—"

"Stop," Damali said, removing the necklace from the water. "Waaaay too much info, Pearl."

"Well, it is true," Zehiradangra said in an amused tone once Damali had submerged it into the water again. "I have known Cain a long time, and I must admit that I was a bit jealous of his . . . duress brought on by his brief contact with you. However, I also am truthful enough to admit that I had heard of the legendary capacity of Neterus to drive an *amour* insane. Seeing it firsthand was a learning—"

"Pearl, you are dangerously on the edge of going back into the sea. The only thing keeping me from pitching you there at this moment is the fact that six other very precious stones sent by my queens are housed in this necklace. Are we clear?"

A melodic murmur of laughter filtered up to the water's surface, bursting in tingly bubbles against Damali's palm. "Oh, Damali, you tickle me. So modest. Why? You should be very, very flattered."

Damali closed her eyes and groaned. Her oracle was a flower child, if ever she saw one. "Pearl, can we get on to the more important matters, like what's going on in the cosmos?"

"This is all a part of it. Love and war are often combined, at least passion is at the center of both, one is light, one is dark, but this is the extreme of the balance of these energies."

"Please," Damali said, and dropped her head into one hand. She began rocking out of fatigue and frustration. "My head hurts. Be direct. What does this have to do with a decision I made about two men?"

"Everything," the pearl said in an upbeat tone. "Cain went mad, simply put. He was already teetering on the brink of insanity with his genius, but seven days in mourning for us both, combined with the unrequited physical hunger of a solo apex in Nod, just pushed him over the edge." The pearl sighed. "He is even more brilliant now, and has learned much. But I don't like his new mentor at all."

"And who might that be?" Damali said in a voice that wasn't her own.

"Why, Lilith," the pearl said, not the least bit fazed by Damali's tone. "She is his new lover, now. I don't think the three of us can be friends, as you and I are."

Damali leaned down very, very slowly. "Who?"

"It was awful. Their union wasn't lovely at all, it was more like a mating, beasts with two backs rutting, if you ask me, and I—"

"Where did this happen and when?" Damali crouched down over the pool, now holding the pearl with both hands.

"I knew you would be upset," the pearl said coolly. "You do still have feelings for him, as do I. Oh, Damali, maybe we can get him away from her, I don't know. But it would be just wonderful if upon occasion you made love to him with me there. . . . Don't you think we could share him? He's fantastic in bed. Although, it does make for a bit of a dilemma because your new husband—who is also my friend, by the way, a dear, dear friend—doesn't share. Should I talk to Carlos? He and I came to an accord once that was divine and—"

"Pearl, have you lost your mind?" Damali yelled, shaking her necklace with both hands and splashing water all around. She wasn't sure which part of what Zehiradangra had said flipped her out the most. Most likely all of it.

"Yes, yes, I know," Zehiradangra said calmly. "Carlos is enough to handle alone without adding Cain's prowess into the equation. You would need a lot of rest and—"

"Z, talk to me about *Lilith*!"

"Oh . . . her," the pearl said, her tone still nonchalant. "She's only temporary, because he could not stand another day in his condition. But he is planning to come to see you. He needs you in the worst way. I believe he has become obsessed."

"From where?" Damali screamed at the submerged pearl, her face hot with sudden rage.

"From Hell," Zehiradangra murmured calmly. "Do not worry. After he sat in his father's throne and he satisfied himself with her body, I most clearly received the impression that he was simply resting to summon the strength to come for the real object of his desire—you. But he did have a nice family reunion, and I was oddly happy for him. His grandfather received him well and—"

"What!" Damali was on her feet, stumbling around in a circle before she realized that she had taken the pearl out of the water. She dropped to her knees quickly, her mind frantic, and dunked the pearl back under the surface. "Oh, Jesus, Pearl, are you sure? You saw all that? Positive? You have to be very, very clear about what you're telling me."

"Now, Damali," the pearl cooed, and then made a little tsking sound. "Why would I tell you something false about my dear friend? I make no judgment about the choices any of my friends make, and only disclose what I see them do. Cain and I have shared many trysts, much energy, and wonderful dialogue and debates. I am a part of his psyche in energy ether form . . . well, at least the Light-bearing side of him. But he is getting dimmer to me now, which makes me sad." The pearl dropped its voice to a conspiratorial whisper. "Back in the old days before all sensation was lost, he and I even shared the full color spectrum embedded in glorious sound. I am very connected to his sexual side, too. But if he keeps up his liaison with this very dark female entity, soon all threads of Light to his core will disintegrate, and I will lose my connection to him."

Before Damali could ask another question, the pearl began to cry. "Oh, Damali, don't let my friend leave me like that. His mind used to be sterling silver. His passion, white hot metals. Exquisite! I cannot bear such a loss. Can't you have just a brief little affair with him for me, to infuse him with what he is about to cast away? For me? He so adores you, and has already tasted your blood, I know—"

"Pearl, you have to pull it together," Damali said, panicking, her mind locking in on the last thing the pearl said. Cain had tasted her blood. "He bit me before, and now all of a sudden, Carlos is acting weird and so is his old line brother, Jose. Carlos bit me after Cain did. What's the connection, because Carlos never bit me like that in his life or death, soooo—"

"They're all connected," the pearl said, sniffing. "I don't understand what this has to do with the real problem at hand. Cain and Carlos had the same father, Dante. Cain was made from seed, Carlos from Dante's bite, but there is a link, just like all the ones that came from the same line—like Jose, who is more like a distant cousin—are related."

The thoughts were whirling through Damali's head so fast she was seeing double as she stared at the pearl. Adrenaline was spiking in her system at record levels, making her limbs shake.

"What time did Cain actually take a stroll out of Nod?" Damali asked.

"Oh, about an hour after sundown. That woman, Lilith, came and got him after he'd banged on the shadow alley wall begging her to get him out. Then perhaps no more than an hour later, he sat on his father's throne, and that's when she . . ." The pearl began sobbing again. "I don't like her!"

"Pearl, don't cry. I will slay that bitch, trust me."

"I am so glad we're friends, Damali," the pearl said in a shaky voice, still sniffing. "I think your solution makes me happy. Tell Cain I send my warmest regards when you see him."

Damali stood and stared out at the ocean. This was a level of insanity that she'd *never* banked on. Her oracle was a nutcase, her husband was getting Chairman throne-spikes from below, and her Guardian brother was linked so closely to Carlos that he'd vamp-mate-marked Juanita! Queen Eve, the mother of all mothers, was going to have a coronary, if she hadn't already. The Chairman's throne had a new ruler, which meant the Vampire Council was back in session. That put Yonnie and Tara in immediate harm's way, not to mention Gabrielle. Who knew what crazy entities Cain would install as councilmen? Some of the ones she'd seen in Nod could come out during the day and still had souls, for Christ's sake!

All she had done was plan a quickie wedding in three days, and leave for four *short* days to try to have a honeymoon, but *noooo*. One week, seven teeny blips on the giant cosmic clock, and all hell had broken loose. Couldn't a sister catch a break?

Meanwhile, there had to be a yawning breach in the veil over in Nod, which meant hybrids either called by Cain, or simply on their own volition, could come spilling over the void any day or night. Sealing the tear would mean first finding it to inform Ausar to get more shields, but with Cain on the darkside, fat chance of that— before, while he was just a horny being of the good side was bad enough. Then there was Lilith. That bitch. Oh, my God . . . she would slaughter her!

Damali turned back to the house, slowly trudging toward it. So, girlfriend finally got what she'd wanted; an apexing male Neteru in Dante's chair, and a chance to ride him all night. If Cain was in Dante's throne spiking Old World male Neteru, it had to be one helluva ride!

"She didn't deserve that one, yo!" A bizarre combination of anger, pity, and jealousy was threatening to make Damali irrational. Just the thought of Lilith laying Cain made Damali want to scream and go to war.

True, it didn't make sense, but that's where she was—ready for hand-to-hand combat. It was a matter of honor. Cain was many things, among them a complex being that she'd really liked, all madness notwithstanding. He was a twisted friend.

But Lilith doing *a Neteru*? One of *theirs* from the side of the Light? Lilith driving a stake into Eve's heart by finally getting to her queen sister through her son? That tall, refined, handsome, *sexy,* intelligent hunk of passionate but crazy protoplasm fucked Lilith? "That bitch!" Lilith took a musical and military genius and broke his ass down in his own daddy's throne? Just cut off the hands of an experienced healer and converted his power to raise the dead into black lightning destruction? Actually turned Cain over as a door prize to Lucifer to get her own trifling ass a get-out-of-jail-free pass on this millennium Neteru team's watch?

"I'll kill you!" That whore had used *her* as bait to make that being filled with so much positive potential to go dark, pitch black, enough to give up his empire in Nod . . . and then make it look like his devastation was all her fault? "Oh, hell no!"

Galled beyond words, Damali spit on the beach as she walked. Fury had put the acrid taste of metal in her mouth. Where was her Isis? When she'd been with Cain, yeah, he'd been nuts . . . but still the brother was cool as long as he was over in his kingdom and had that to rule.

She couldn't even think about the things Zehiradangra had told her. She didn't have to; she could feel it as the pearl spoke the stone-cold truth. Cain's suffering and need to be in her arms had made them ache. But he would have never gone there and been so caught up in a love-jones had Lilith not been constantly thinning the veil between them, working her mojo, plotting and scheming and sending instant airborne messages to him saturated with every lust-filled mirage she could create with her succubus, skank-ass illusions.

The way Lilith had run her seduction game had been smooth, she'd give her that. Damali shook her head as she walked, making her locks slap her shoulders. Girlfriend had been the one to use the airwaves, courtesy of her deranged husband, to send her voice over the cosmic Net to torture Cain—that much she knew in her soul. Then Lilith had let that poor bastard twist.

Stomping in the sand as she walked, Damali's eyesight blurred from repressed rage. Lilith had hit him with sensation the moment he'd tumbled into the gray zone . . . a half-vamp Neteru going through changes. Lethal cocktail primed for disaster. She'd seen Carlos wig under those conditions, and he hadn't been locked up for centuries. And the way this was set up, every Council Neteru would be conflicted, divided. Like they said, every woman knows her husband, and Lilith no doubt knew Adam's weak spot, 'cause girlfriend just did the cha-cha on it.

Damali stopped walking and stared up at the house once she'd reached the front steps. What was she gonna tell Carlos? She had been the carrier of Cain's vamp virus to him, right at the throat. For all the drama Carlos had brought to her door in the past, he'd never dropped the beginning of the cold-blooded Armageddon at her feet.

If Cain was doing Lilith on *Dante's throne* last night while linked to Carlos, *no wonder* he bit the bullshit out of her in the throes. And mild-mannered Jose just got swept up in the male vamp passion tornado by extended lineage. She wondered if Yonnie had practically flatlined Tara yet. Yonnie was all vamp and no doubt a power surge had run through that brother hard enough to have him speaking in tongues. Half the squad of serious warriors was gonna feel the fallout of this crap.

Red-blood-running meat au naturel made sense—feed then . . . Damali didn't even want to say the word when thinking about her and Carlos, or even Jose getting with Juanita, for that matter. But it was a feed then fuck then fight vamp paradigm rush going on for sure. The scenario ran through Damali's mind in an endless dark loop.

Cain would have to feed for strength, then fulfill his next core desire, and if he met the Devil face-to-face while doing his wife, who knew what had ultimately kicked off? The only saving grace and reason Juanita could do sunshine now was because Jose was working with blunt edges. Damn! Carlos was right. This time, she could only blame herself. She should *never* have allowed another male vamp to bite her for *any reason*.

Damali closed her eyes and wrapped her arms around herself. There was no damage control option here. This was one of those times a sister just had to fall on her sword.

"Hey, baby," Carlos said, coming to the front door. "Just checking on you. Folks wanna know what you want for dinner. Better make the most of it, because tomorrow it's back to drawing straws for chores. But today we get served." He smiled and strolled down the steps, and then stopped. "D?"

"Walk with me on the beach for a few. I ain't ready to go in the house."

Carlos looked over his shoulder. "Cool." He ignored several suggestive grins behind him. "You look like something's spooked you. After everything that went down," he said more quietly as he neared her, "maybe the sun and exertion isn't a good idea."

Damali just began walking and didn't speak until they were several yards away from the house. She then began kicking sand as she walked along the shoreline, wanting to be well out of earshot of the team when Carlos started yelling. The man would go off. Correction. Her *husband* would go off.

"Baby," she said, putting her hands behind her back as she kept her eyes on the ground and continued walking farther from the house. "See, what had happened was . . . uhmm . . . remember that thing with Cain?"

Carlos stopped walking. "Yeah. That motherfucker try to contact you while you was out here alone?"

"Not exactly." She peered up at him.

"How exactly?" Carlos said, folding his arms over his chest and glaring at her.

Damali sighed. "Remember I love you when I tell you what I'm about to tell you."

"What happened?"

Damali took a deep breath and then began her rapid-fire explanation while wildly gesturing with her hands.

"Cain busted out of Nod with Lilith's help and went to Hell and took his father's throne, and he's now the new Chairman and may have cut a deal with Satan, and since he's a hybrid, he can do daylight and can make babies, but he also took a teeny, weeny, sip of blood from me—that time, you remember when you said it was cool, so when he sat in the throne, he got a rush, had to eat, then he did Lilith in Dante's throne, that's all you were feeling, baby. Zehiradangra told me it happened last night while we was in bed, and uh, that's the reason you bit me so hard, like I said, baby, it wasn't you—there was a reason, and y'all are sorta linked, by way of both being Neteru brothers, until his silver burns all the way out is my guess, but the Chairman sired him and bit you, so that links you, which also hit Jose last night—'cause he bit the living bullshit out of 'Nita—I healed her a little while ago."

Damali gasped and sucked in a huge breath to keep rolling. She spit her words out like they were being sprayed by a semiautomatic, and they came out even faster as Carlos's eyes went solid silver and his furious gaze began melting sand on the beach when he looked away.

"Oh, it was bad, Carlos. Juanita, had blood-clot-type femoral nicks, but I got it all even though I was tired. She'll live, will just be sore. So, we probably oughta tell the team that this isn't a drill. Vamp Council is back in session, time to go huntin'. You should probably check on Yonnie, too, because if you felt it, then he definitely is in his lair losing his mind—we should just be sure brotherman has enough black bottles to hold him over . . . uh, Cain was younger and stronger than Dante, so all you brothers are gonna feel a big jolt from his coronation."

Damali sucked in another huge breath, her eyes wild and her hair practically standing up on her head. "So, that's what happened. Well, I'd better get back to the house to tell Inez I just want a salad and, like, eight hours of sleep. Cool?"

"Do. Not. Move." Carlos walked around her, circling her with his hands behind his back, a look of such rage in his eyes that it made her close hers.

"I know you're angry and upset, baby, but—"

"Pissed off at that bastard does not *even begin* to describe where I'm at, D," Carlos said in such a quiet rumble that she wondered if the ocean had gone still.

Damali opened one eye. The only saving grace was the fact that Carlos had said his rage was directed toward Cain, not her. Still, she wasn't ready to release her breath. She'd seen her man mad before, but *never* like this.

Carlos dragged his fingers through his hair and tilted his head, coming to a stop before her. "You mean to tell me that while we were on our honeymoon," Carlos whispered, his voice increasing in decibel word by word, "that bastard got out of Nod, did Lilith, and took *Dante's* throne?" He shook his head and looked off into the distance for a moment, trying without success to summon calm. "We're now double linked by what happened out there in Arizona when you let him bite you, is that what you're telling me?"

"Now, Carlos, baby, you have to be rational," she said, backing away from him and talking with her hands. "He lost the whole contest and we got married, so he was apexing and needed some real bad—you've been there yourself, and uh, Lilith was available, since I'm married now," she said, flashing her ring as evidence, "and I wasn't nowhere but with you, right, so, what I guess he figured—"

"Do. Not. Justify this in any way, shape, or form, Damali!" Carlos hollered. "I got a blood taint from that motherfucker through you?"

"No, no, no, it's not like that—there's a lot involved and it's more complicated than—"

"Than what?"

Sand and wind were beginning to form a turbine of energy around Carlos, sending shells and debris in a stinging cloud around them. He had to calm down before he had an aneurysm. The rational side of his brain, the side that was currently frying, knew that it wasn't Damali's fault. After all the bullshit he had done in his life, and all that she'd tolerated from him, he couldn't by rights go there. But the very male part of him, admittedly the irrational side at the moment, wasn't feeling the shit. The thing that was making the whole twisted scenario nearly impossible to process was the fact that he'd never brought anything foul home to Damali! For all his bullshit, he never had her eyes going gold from a were-demon-contracted virus, or dropping fang from a dragon nick!

Carlos closed his eyes, fury spikes making him need to count to ten. He could feel Damali peering at him. Her beautiful brown eyes were filled with worry, which only channeled his fury toward the real source of his anger—Cain. This time he'd gone too far.

"But, I can explain how—"

"No! Don't tell me shit," Carlos said, whirling on Damali. "Don't try to explain why his ass is crazy—none of it. You are *my wife!*"

The moment the tide lapped the shore, Carlos flung out his arm and a sonic boom hit the wet sand, sending a backward tidal wave into the confused surf. Family was on the front steps and heading their way in a panic.

"Yo, yo, yo, y'all!" Shabazz shouted.

The moment the older Guardian shouted, Carlos turned, stopping the family meeting in its tracks just by the expression on his face. "This is between me and *my wife,*" Carlos said between battle-length fangs, and then made a square with his hands in the air, sealing him and Damali in a huge, translucent black box.

For a moment, she didn't breathe. Maybe she couldn't. She had seen him angry in her time, but never like this—at least not when she'd been the one in the wrong. She could see family nervously watching them through the blackish-silver energy seal, but not even the sound of the surf penetrated into the enclosure. Her heart was beating off tempo, making her slightly faint as Carlos stood in front of her trembling with rage, his chest heaving with sudden breaths of fury.

"Now, let me get this straight, Damali," Carlos said in a low rumble. "This horny, apexing, gotta-get-with-my-woman motherfucker busts out of Nod, using Lilith as his crowbar, goes down and gets a power hit that *I* feel . . . that *all* my boys feel, and because I am unnaturally linked to his ass through a blood transfer that *my wife* did with him . . . a willing, throat nick laced with seduction all in it—a fucking pleasure nick, I drop fang on *my wife* . . . in bed . . . on *our honeymoon,* and I can't shake his tie to me now until I take his head off with my blade. Is that what you're telling me, bottom line?"

"Sorta," she said quickly. "But there's more to it than that, Carlos. More important things, and uh, it actually happened before we got married, 'cause, baby, you *know* I would never, *ever,* in a million years go there—we were having problems when it happened, and baby, I love you, you *know* that, so let's not go back to the past, let's look to what we have to do together in the future, and uh—"

"Before we go to the future, such that it is," he said, now studying his nails coolly. "Let's look at the repercussions of what you just told me, okay?" He glanced up at her, his eyes creating unnatural warmth on her face.

"All right," she said quietly. "Okay."

"Fact number one. Had there been no blood exchange between you and Cain, whatever his ass did would not involve you or me at home. It would just be a job, like any other vamp assassination, which I would gladly do." As he stared at her stricken expression, a part of him mellowed. "I've done this type of shit, myself. Maybe that's why I'm so pissed off, D. Not at you, but at the whole damned thing."

Carlos shook his head and rubbed the tension out of his neck. "I know how dangerous it is. Remember, I've had warrior angels all up in my grille about some dumb shit I did, not knowing the repercussions. So, I'm not casting aspersions on you, baby, but I wanna kill this motherfucker in the worst way. You have no idea."

When Damali drew a breath to speak, Carlos held up his hand. "And, because it was your blood in his system and you are a queen, the Neteru Queen's Council's newest made, I am sure they are feeling some fallout from this."

Carlos nodded when Damali gasped and covered her mouth. "Yeah. Eve. His mother. He took your blood with him down into that throne." Carlos walked back and forth and punched the translucent wall.

"Hey, hey, hey," Damali said, holding up her hands in front of her chest, becoming defensive. "Like you said, you did it, too, and survived. You sat in Dante's—"

"Do not try to justify this! Like you would *always* tell me when I messed up, it's time to face it, come clean, be honest about everything that went down, and then come up with a strategy," Carlos bellowed, pointing at her.

They stared at each other, seconds ticking away like a time bomb had been set. He refused to allow his thoughts to descend into suspicion. *Please, God, don't let her have actually slept with Cain.*

Damali's gaze narrowed slightly. "I didn't," she said, quietly. "I thought we'd been over that."

Embarrassed by her charge, Carlos sent his gaze toward the sea. "None of your queens was my mother; none was tied to the energy umbilical cord that never ceases."

"It'll be all right," she said, her calmness grating him.

"I know what the fuck I'm talking about," he muttered, his tone surly. "Even when I was all vamp and on the Vamp Council, black blood exchanges even among the demon realms was disallowed, and ya know why?"

"Why?" she whispered, already knowing the answer, but hoping he'd calm down as he talked.

"Because blood is a carrier of DNA and life-force energy. So, if a vamp exchanged with a werewolf, let's say, that vamp would not only have a problem with daylight, but would be locked up and only come out and feed during a full moon . . . and if said foul vamp bit another vamp—which is the way of that world—then they, too, would become polluted. Works the same way in reverse. It would give the were-demon access to open season on the night, regardless of the phase of the moon, for as long as that blood was running through his or her system. That's why the old Chairman didn't play that shit, D. I cannot believe you've put me in a position to finally agree with Dante!"

"Oh, baby, I'm so sorry," she said, rubbing her palms down her face. "That's why he didn't eat . . ."

"What!"

Damali hung her head and spoke in a soft voice. "Z said Cain didn't eat, I guess, or do an energy infusion to replenish himself after I left him sealed in Nod . . . and, uh, for seven days he was over there and refused to do that while he was apexing after a battle and—"

"Oh, shit . . ." Carlos walked back and forth like a caged panther. "That's what sat in the Chairman's throne? And to add insult to injury, vamp for vamp, given my old council rank and his current one with royal lineage to Dante and beyond, he's stronger than I ever was in the Dark Realms. Did you ever consider that, given his age and his rank as the second male Neteru ever made, Cain might have even outranked me until he went dark, while he was in the Light? A motherfucker with a power-sex-glory jones like that, holding a half-tank of your blood in him?" Carlos stopped pacing and stared at her. "We're even, Damali. I've practically stopped your heart with my mess in the past, and this one, baby . . . damn. You had better *never* say anything to me about *anything* like this again in this life or the next, Damali—and I promise to do the same."

"I won't," she said in a shaky whisper, willing herself not to cry. She had never heard Carlos tell her something so profound in such a forthright manner with the level of hurt in his voice that it contained right now. She was used to his old games, those old sly moves of his— but an all-out admission of how he felt . . . the man might as well have *blatow* flat-blasted her.

"He knew what he was doing, you know that, right?" Carlos stared at her as she kept her gaze lowered.

Damali set her shoulders hard, planted her feet, and lifted her chin, her eyes meeting his outraged silver gaze. "Yeah, he knew what he was doing," she said flatly. There was no point in being anything but direct. "Blood is a tracer element, too, and carries a scent."

"He's coming for you."

"I know."

"Battle bulked like a motherfucker."

"I know."

"Good. Glad you know. Then get the team ready for the brawl. By the time it's all over, fifty-fifty odds you'll either be a widow or a wife—can't call the outcome of this one, baby." Carlos walked away from her, shaking his head. Silver sweat from the angry outburst streamed down his temples, made his T-shirt cling to him, and had dampened his hair, leaving a shimmer to his skin.

"You know this is gonna start the war of wars, right?" Carlos's voice had dropped to a warning decibel that made the sand rumble beneath her feet. "It was an excellent move on Lilith's part, I'll give her that."

Damali's heart rate increased as she watched Carlos's mind begin to work on the problem, instead of what she'd done wrong. But she kept her lips tightly sealed, lest she add the wrong bit of information at the wrong time in the wrong tone. Nefertiti's lessons were not a waste.

"First off, I need to warn Ausar, if he isn't already aware, and my generals are gonna have to get Adam's head right." Carlos closed his eyes. "Me and Yonnie are gonna have to talk, for sure. That brother is a sitting duck for a very bad situation that's about to bring him down. We're gonna have to tell the team we're being tracked by a heat-seeking missile from Hell with our names on it."

Carlos opened his eyes and glared at her. "But, for the sake of this marriage, I won't go into the details about how Cain can pinpoint us like we're on fucking radar. We've gotta move out while he's underground and plotting his next strike. The only thing that's buying us time is the fact that he bit Lilith, which dilutes you in his system, since he's gone dark, and after so many years being over in Nod, after what I felt last night, I'm pretty sure that he's working real hard to make up for lost time."

Carlos walked away, serving Damali his back as he took in two long, cleansing breaths. He loved this woman's dirty drawers, and she'd finally put him in a position not only to feel what she'd felt in the past, but to experience it. It was so wild and so unintentional on her part that he almost laughed. The Light definitely had a sense of humor—as above, so below . . . fair exchange was no robbery. He turned and looked at her. Nothing was coming between them, not even his anger about an old lover.

Damali's eyes glittered with unshed tears. "I didn't do this to spite you. You know that, right? It was messed up how it happened."

Carlos let out his breath hard and came near her, wanting to hug her as much as he wanted to draw a blade on Cain. "I know, baby. But we also know that he's no fool, and won't let an opportunity of getting tail pass by for more than twenty-four hours. However, he is a vampire, and Dante's throne makes it near impossible for even a well-laid, well-fed entity to simply walk away from that . . . my guess is, we have a small window while he gets his head right. Ask me how I know."

"I have to tell the queens," Damali whispered.

"Yes, you have to tell the queens," Carlos said in a weary tone. "You have to go to them and run it down all the way to the bone so your backup understands the gravity of the situation. Straight, no chaser."

Damali nodded. "I know." She sighed as more hot tears of remorse filled her eyes. "I never meant to do this to Eve."

Carlos's shoulders slumped as he rubbed the tension out of the back of his neck again. "It's fucked up, but the whole part about letting Cain out, or hurting Eve, you didn't do." He looked up at Damali and shook his head, the muscles in his jaw working. "Lilith lured him to you—knowledge from a connection to him still flows both ways, so I can feel it. The airwaves are her and her husband's device. She got him all jacked around and on a mission to get you. That part I can accept. He made a decision to take a throne because he couldn't stand being bested by me—that's his old weakness, jealousy of his brother. You didn't do that part, he had it in him . . . and the bastard was empire-building when we met him. So here, Nod, Hell, whatever, that's from his father's side. You ain't got nothing to do with it. Don't take that on and go tripping about that while we all need your head to be right."

"Then . . ." Damali let the words trail off as she saw a new dimension of her husband that she had never seen.

"Then what am I angry about?" Carlos said in a weary tone, still staring at her, but now with eyes that were slowly becoming a normal brown again. "I'm angry that you let him nearly seduce you because you were so angry at me. Probable cause, regardless, that's how I feel. You let him bite you and carry your sacred blood in his veins and feed off that in his head, when your blood carries a beacon. You're *my angel,* and your blood is like a supernova in one of our systems . . . can track it through freaking dimensions, girl. And I'm pissed off beyond—" Carlos stopped speaking and walked away again to place both hands on the translucent wall.

He dropped his head and sucked in several breaths to steady his voice. "Damali, I have done a lot of shit, I'll grant you that. But I *never* got with an entity because I thought they were better than you or because I wanted to hurt you by going there. Don't fling Juanita in my face, either, because what went down with her wasn't me. I know that betrayal cut to the bone . . . yeah, now I really know it. But I'm not gonna revisit that discussion again as long as I live, Damali—just like I'm never gonna speak on this Cain thing again." He turned his head, craning his neck to stare at her. "Fair?"

Damali nodded, her voice quiet. "Fair."

"Then just like you had to get the betrayal out of your system, and get how you felt off your chest so you could finally either let it go, pack it away, or whatever, then I'm asking for the same courtesy."

Again, she nodded and spoke quietly. "Fair."

Carlos nodded, set his jaw hard before speaking, and then looked away again. "All right. Then, lemme say this. Here's what's fucking with my head, D. You went into that whole vibe with Cain wanting me to get messed up by it. Mission accomplished, sis. A part of me is still not right about that, and I thought I was, but him being able to send a throne jolt through me now that I'm clean from the old life . . . not in our bed. Not in our marriage. Not on our honeymoon while I was making love to my wife."

Carlos closed his eyes and his voice sounded like it was miles away as he spoke in a low echo within the box. "The blue-white Light of us joining in holy matrimony might have made him temporarily blind to you, but by him carrying your blood in his veins, his transformation became partially mine. All that pent-up rage and raw lust in him flowed right into me and made me handle my wife like an animal. Still fucks me up."

"Oh, God, Carlos, I am so sorry," she whispered, tears falling without censure this time. "I *swear to you*, I never knew that what I thought was one feed bite to send him packing with enough energy to go home could ever be harnessed like this . . . or could ever affect you like this. If I had known it could have future ramifications, baby, I wouldn't have done it—not even angry." Damali stared at Carlos's back. "I wouldn't have hurt my husband like that," she said quietly. "No."

"I know. That's the bitch of the dilemma. I know you didn't know and I know why he bit you, blah, blah, blah. Yeah, I know where we were at when it happened. The relationship was messed up for a lotta reasons." He glanced up from the sand he'd been staring at and drew in a shaky breath. "But now, as head of the household, where I go, what I do, is linked . . . Jose, Yonnie, and a whole lotta people in between. I'm not talking about ruling anyone, I'm talking about my energy has to stay pure. Can't get all jacked up. What if I had made you pregnant while that was running through me? Shit . . . what if you're pregnant now, as my wife? Would it be his or mine, or some whack combination of both?"

Damali's eyes widened and she walked away to the far side of the box.

"Yeah. My point exactly. That's why I'm bugging, 'cause it ain't about aborting just 'cause we don't know, is it? And it's not like we can find out, can we—even if it presents fangs, still could be mine, right?"

"Carlos," she said, her hands shaking as she held them up before her. "I'll get Aset to scan me with the Caduceus, honey. I didn't know, didn't even think about—oh, shit."

"Cain isn't sterile, and is unlike any other vamp that ever took that throne other than me. We weren't using anything. Why would I think I had to, now that we're married? But his energy was riding with mine on the airwaves or vice versa last night. You wanna make a baby from a damned near vamp rape or the way we did in Australia?"

She bit her lip to stifle a sob and then closed her eyes.

"I agree. I liked the Australian method much better myself. However, that said, this is the kinda so-called macho shit a man thinks about, *a husband* thinks about, when his wife brings him news like this. I love you, Damali . . . You talk about cuttin' a motherfucker's heart out?" Carlos's voice remained a low, fatigued rumble as he glanced around at the sand by his feet. "I know I had one when I came out here, but damn if I do now. Was already wondering if our genes were still compatible . . . hoping we wouldn't run into a fertility problem with my fangs, your wings, hey. But I was hopeful . . . we made a kid once, even while I was dead, so figured we had a shot at it one day. Just hadn't added in a possible third party by way of blood with us in bed."

"Baby, don't . . ." Damali whispered, his image becoming blurred by tears that dared not fall.

Carlos pushed away from the box and came to Damali and touched her hair. "It ain't your fault, in total, that Jose is linked to me, or that Yonnie is, either. I'm not saying that . . . so whatever happens to them or whatever they do, you don't own that. I do. They're *my* boyz."

"I don't see how you can say that," she whispered and went into his loose embrace. She held him tightly and pressed her cheek to his chest, her words becoming thick as she swallowed hard. "You were clean and I—"

"Nah. Let's just be honest, all right? I'm as mad at myself as I was at you. The only reason they're linked at all is because I took a tumble into a throne from the jump. I became a vamp while you were straight, pure white Light. So, if we get technical about it, then hey, a little topspin from Cain affecting everybody through his link to me is another cosmic spanking for even sitting my ass in his daddy's chair in the first fucking place. If I hadn't been down there, he could have bitten you, carried your blood, but I wouldn't have been a vamp, or had any resonance off the throne for him to tap. I played myself, he played you, we both got played . . . and Lilith fucked all of us around real sweet. Game over—until we run it again."

"Baby, I'm sorry," Damali said in a thick whisper against his chest.

Carlos nodded and wearily kissed the crown of her head, and then let the black box barrier drop as his shoulders relaxed. "Yeah. So am I."

CHAPTER FOUR

Cain reclined in his new throne, sprawling in a sated, lazy stretch. His long, black silk robe flowed over the clawed marble throne footrest and his billowing sleeves casually draped the arms of it. His silk belt hung askew, and he didn't bother to adjust it as the black corded tie precariously dipped when he reached for his golden goblet to refill it with blood. His eyes had normalized to their original intense brown gaze beneath heavy lids as he assessed Lilith across the Vampire Council Chamber.

"You want a cigarette?" she asked with a sly smile, smoothing her black gown and sauntering to the door.

He chuckled. "No. That is one vice that I do not own. It pollutes the blood."

She turned and smiled at him. "Then, by all means, please don't." Her voice had come out in a low, sexy murmur. "You look like a huge, satisfied lion. I love your hair. It comes alive in my hands like tentacles . . . did you know that?"

"I can accommodate that fantasy, if you wish . . . perhaps after I eat. Saber-toothed tiger hybrid Greek hydra?" He laughed quietly and shrugged his mane of thick locks over his shoulder, eyeing her.

"You would do that for me?" she whispered, moving back toward the council table.

"No. I would do that *for me,*" he said, peering at her over the large goblet as he took a generous sip of fresh blood. "But the results would be the same. Stupefying."

She began to round the table, and he arched an eyebrow, giving her pause.

"I have to eat."

Lilith stopped walking and stared at him, confused. "The table runs perpetual blood now. What else is it that you need?"

"A steak . . . rare . . . unmolested by spices . . . running blood. I had that on my mind last night, but the primary hunger had been power and you."

"You can *still* eat human food?" She weaved a bit and caught her balance on the edge of the table.

His smile widened as he inhaled her shock. "There are some things still necessary if one from our realms wants to sire in the flesh. Didn't Dante share that with you?" Cain chuckled. "Perhaps it had been so long ago that my father forgot how."

Lilith snapped her fingers without taking her eyes from Cain's and made a charcoal-seared slab of meat materialize on a gold platter before him. Manipulating her fingers in the air, Lilith made a two-pronged gold fork appear between them, and she sent a dagger into the bloodied steak with a glance.

"Thank you, my dear," he murmured and leaned forward to inspect her offering. "From the stock of fattened calves?"

"London's best, grade-A, human stock . . . the cows have all gone mad. Or would you prefer veal?" Lilith came to his side and then slid onto his lap, handing him the fork. "Name a country and I can bring you a whole child," she cooed.

"This will do. . . . The young ones are more tender, but the bulls have more adrenaline and testosterone in them," he said, leaning around her to cut off a sizeable hunk.

"So wise," she said, melting against him and kissing the underside of his massive jaw as he ate. "What else can I give you right now, lover?" she added in a sexy whisper, writhing in his lap.

"Fallon," Cain mumbled through another mouthful of meat, and then he slurped blood from his goblet.

Lilith immediately slid out of his lap and strode across the floor as Cain watched her. She took a wide-legged stance, closed her eyes, and clapped twice, opening a large chasm in the floor between her and the pentagram-shaped table. Cain continued to eat, unfazed as sulfuric plumes swirled up from the fractured floor. Bored by the floor show, he occasionally tossed bits of fat and gristle up for squealing bats to fetch from the air.

Dozens of Harpies swarmed out of the yawning floor, and they eagerly huddled around Lilith's legs.

"Retrieve Fallon Nuit," she commanded in their language, and then she craned her fingers until they became talons.

A black arc zapped from her right hand to her left and soon her soot-covered fist was filled with a damaged, dead heart and broken fangs. Harpies scampered across the floor toward the huge, black-marble, throne-room doors that had been repaired. Bleating screeches made the doors quickly slam open, and the Harpies took off across the bridge that led to the Sea of Perpetual Agony. Now she'd ransomed his attention; Cain sat forward watching with guarded interest.

Lilith smiled as she cradled Fallon Nuit's injured heart with both hands, blowing a steady stream of black breath against it, warming it, massaging it, as she sauntered across the chamber and laid it in the center of the council table. She then set a broken jawbone and battered fangs to either side of it.

"Of all that is unholy," she whispered, cupping handfuls of blood. "Of all that is undead and unclean, I regenerate you from the ashes of incarceration," she whispered, slitting her wrist and adding her own blood to the table's darkening elixir. "From the line of lines, from the first vampire ever made, you have been granted a reprieve to again claim the night by the imperial throne's new heir."

Nothing happened. The heart lay dead and unchanged.

"It will work," she hissed, glancing at Cain and then back down to Fallon's withered black heart. "It is a delicate transformation."

"Fail and you are surely fucked, and not in a way that you will enjoy."

She glanced at him, nervous sweat beginning to form on her top lip. Returning her black, glowing gaze to the heart, she flicked away the dark perspiration with the tip of her tongue through her fangs.

"I call the power of all dark covens! The power of female darkness to bring forth dark life! Envy, jealousy, rage . . . spite, vindictive evil, treachery—I own you! I am your master, your consort, your root of scorn! Hell hath no fury the likes of which we can rent! Havoc, I am your lover."

Nonplussed by Lilith's ineffective theatrics and annoyed, Cain finished his meal and wiped the golden plate away from the table with a sweep of his arm, sending it, along with the fork and dagger, clattering to the floor. From the corner of his eye he watched bats swoop down to claim the remains while battling rats that had rushed in to challenge them for the spoils. The squealing aerial contest was more interesting. He leaned forward and made a tent with his fingers in front of him, watching the dead councilman's heart.

"Rivera even neutered him," Cain said in an amused tone. "Unbelievable."

Concentrating harder on the task, Lilith didn't respond. Dark beads of sweat had begun to form on her brow as her hands strained to arc enough power for another jolt of black magic. "I'm depleted. I used a lot of energy . . . may need to feed again before I can—"

"Fail me, and you fail my grandfather," Cain remarked calmly. "Take your pick on which of us you would like to disappoint. Me or your husband, or both?"

Lilith grabbed her goblet, refilled it, and took several deep swallows from it, then set it down hard. Her dark gaze became a black laser as she focused again and intensified the charge within her talons until blue-black smoke began to rise from the center of the dead heart.

As though a black, charred seam was being sewn, the edges of the gaping hole in the center of the damaged organ began to sizzle and knit back together. The moment the wound was sealed, Lilith gently placed her left hand beneath the heart and regurgitated the blood she'd fed on to cover it in a murky, bloody casing.

The sound of her Harpies' screeches and horrendous wailing jerked her and Cain's attention toward the chamber doors. A smol-

dering, slimy, shuddering body was in their clutches. Only its flesh remained, all evidence of skin burned away. The Harpies' wings were
covered by molten ooze and their scrambling, gray-green, gargoyle-
like bodies were splattered with black gook. Like an army of over-
sized ants, they ferried the twitching form forward and then
unceremoniously dropped it at Lilith's feet, looking up at her for approval.

Rounding the table, she held the heart in cupped, blood-dripping
hands, and then dropped to her knees.

"I will you to live again, Fallon Nuit . . . master vampire . . . made
councilman under Dante's rule, now beholden to the bidding of his
heir and son by seed, Cain."

Setting the heart upon the torn-out section of chest that could be
seen beneath the black, static-charged casing around the lifeless form,
she nestled the heart where the rib cage had been gored. Lilith stood
back, lowered an index finger in a hard point toward it, and sent a
steady stream of black lightning into the heart, driving it back into
the body.

Within seconds the static coating around the body sizzled, lit in an
angry plume of sulfur, and then began to recede from the feet up until it was gone. Beneath it lay a still, naked, unconscious male form.

Hastening her efforts, Lilith went to the table, grasped the broken
fangs, put them into her mouth, and went down on her knees again.
She grasped the long, damp, flowing onyx curls at the top of the un-
awakened vampire's head, forcing his mouth open, and kissed him
hard, spewing his fangs and blood into his mouth.

The body beneath her shuddered, arched in pain, then drew a sudden gasp. Lilith moved back as the vampire on the floor dug his nails
into the marble, opened his red gleaming eyes, and wailed. Lilith was
on her feet so quickly she almost trampled one of the Harpies. She
snatched a goblet, filled it fast, and brought it to the agonized vampire.

"Drink the sweet elixir of life, Fallon," she urged, holding his head
up as she poured a slow stream of blood into his mouth until he was
strong enough to sip from the edge of the goblet.

Tears ran down his face as he greedily drank, blood running down the sides of his mouth and over his chin as he tried to take it in too quickly. When the goblet was depleted, he looked at Lilith, his eyes still seeming disoriented, and snatched her to him, tearing open her throat at the jugular. But she didn't struggle and only smiled as her eyes slid shut.

"Yes," she whispered. "That's it, take it right from the vein and regenerate."

Cain smiled as he watched the process of the frail nude body gain in weight and density. The sunken chest soon filled out to a perfect, smooth, broad marble-cut structure. A once-wrinkled abdomen that showed skeleton beneath gaunt skin became the well-defined torso of a warrior.

Limbs that had been mere withered twigs bulked to add sinew and definition. Hooked, wretched hands and feet gracefully extended into their original, natural, manicured form. Eyes that had been ugly orbs within black sockets transformed into a handsome pair of eyes framed in thick, black lashes. Bronze skin replaced the unnatural death pallor of ashen, green-tinged decay, and the rank smell of rotting flesh vanished, chased away by the masculine pheromone carried in the ingested blood.

Lilith looked up at Cain from the floor when Fallon released her, breathing hard and confused. Cain nodded toward the body beside her on the floor with a half-smile, noting the erection.

"He is a councilman and a new ally. Service him."

Fallon Nuit lifted his head, his gaze briefly locking with Cain's as Lilith mounted him. An echoing moan bounced off the chamber walls as his head dropped back from the intense pleasure.

"So that you always know where your first loyalty should lie," Cain murmured in a low rumble while watching Lilith make tears run down Fallon's cheeks. "*I* negotiated your release. *I* was the one who had you fed. It was *I* who commanded that you receive awakening pleasure, not pain to torture you again."

"Yes!" Fallon yelled, practically choking on the blood that Lilith offered.

Cain glared at Lilith. "Stop moving until he pledges his loyalty to me in Dananu."

"Done. Your service is mine," Fallon said, gasping in Dananu the moment Lilith stopped her sultry thrusts. His gaze fractured between Lilith and Cain and his glowing eyes held a plea within them. *"Tell me your bidding, Your Eminence,"* Fallon said in a strained voice between his fangs when she began to pull away from him.

"Bring me Carlos Rivera's head on a stake," Cain said, standing to round the table and stare down at the entwined couple. "I want his heart, first . . . torn out of its housing anchor by anchor until he goes insane from grief. Then, execute him."

Fallon's expression went rigid as he stared up at Cain, dug his nails into Lilith's arms until they bled, and flipped her onto her back in a hard roll. He stared down at her, a low growl erupting from his throat as he spoke. "I will fucking *destroy* him! I know his every desire and his entire line's weaknesses."

Lilith's spine elongated and her spaded tail emerged, twitching, before it wrapped around Fallon's waist. She licked her lips as she glanced up at Cain and tilted her head.

Cain nodded and swept back toward his throne. "Finish him off, and do not take long. He and I have business to discuss."

"Yonnie," Tara gasped, "I must regen. I have to feed. You'll flatline me. Outside the lair, the sun is still—"

He crushed away her kiss, unable to stop moving against her. Tara's once silky brown hair was becoming brittle in his hands and streaks of gray had crept into it, yet he couldn't stop.

"We have to eat, since early last night you haven't fed, just this," she said, her voice a stuttered wail.

"Take it from my throat," he growled between heaving gasps.

"You're already depleted," she said, panting, and beginning to shudder from the dangerous blood loss. "If I siphon you—"

"Do it!" he commanded, beginning to dematerialize again to drag her to the vanishing point. "If I flatline like this, who gives a damn?"

Carlos walked toward the house, his eyes on the stricken team that had fanned out on the beach. He extended his right arm to his side and the gleaming blade of Ausar filled his fist. "Meeting," he said flatly. "Seal it in a prayer, Marlene."

Damali jogged behind him and tried to call the Isis to her, but only a small tingle of spent energy crept along her palm. Carlos never looked at her as quiet panic overtook her. He just sat down heavily on the wide, low steps. The family backed up and stood waiting for an explanation on the beach, all eyes holding a mixture of deep concern and panic like hers. She neared Carlos, glanced at the family, and then sat down beside him very carefully.

"I suggest you all sit down before you fall down," Carlos said in a flat, surly tone, ramming his blade into the sand at his feet. Then he looked up at Jose. "After this meeting, you and I need to have a conversation."

Juanita's eyes widened. Damali simply closed hers.

Lilith stood over Fallon and bent to offer him a warrior's grip to stand. He was on his feet in one lithe move and gave her a gentlemanly nod.

"It's good to be home," Fallon said with a half-smile.

"Glad to have you back, Mr. Councilman," she said with a smile, and then sashayed across the chamber to stand behind his throne.

Fallon gave Cain a grand bow. "Thank you . . . and eternally at your service."

"Not to spoil your sensual rush," Cain said with a chuckle, his icy gaze appraising Fallon's nude body from head to toe, "but I want you to note the name that is still etched at the top of your old throne before you relax in it."

Fallon slowly turned his gaze toward the throne that he'd once cherished, and neared the table. "No . . ." he whispered, his form bulking to battle readiness. "Treason!"

"Now we talk," Cain said with a gloating smile. "You and I had the same reaction."

Total disbelief engulfed Fallon's expression. "The Chairman's throne? Surely you jest?"

Cain shook his head slowly, all mirth dissipating from his face. "I ripped the top of my father's throne away upon seeing it, and have shared your outrage."

"I stand before Cain . . . Cain of Nod? Dante's lost heir?"

Cain leaned back in his throne. "Indeed."

"I shall go to New Orleans and raise an army at your behest—"

"Monsieur," Cain murmured in French to further taunt Fallon. "New Orleans is in ruin. The French quarter gone . . . mud."

"Non . . ." Fallon whispered, stricken. "My beloved New Orleans . . . *non.*"

Cain issued Lilith a disparaging glance as Fallon Nuit took a wobbly step forward to brace his hands against the table for support. "For some reason, our Dark Lord's ire had been stoked to biblical proportions and he was very displeased."

"Even the graves are no more?" Nuit whispered.

"Anything near Lake Ponchartrain and beyond . . . hundreds of years of history decimated. The crypts that were topside, opened to the sunlight and were swept away when the levees broke."

Nuit lifted his chin as tears burned away from his eyes, and the shock of it all made the red glow flicker down to normal brown.

"Have a seat and reclaim your old title," Cain said calmly, nodding toward the throne. "You and I have shared the same devastation . . . have the same goals, *oui*?"

"Oui," Fallon murmured.

"Très bon." Cain leaned back and sighed. "I want an audience with the Amanthras." He stared at Fallon, who had not moved. "I like the way my father operated through their form in the Garden."

Fallon smiled a half-smile. "Their mating balls are legendary. They can last up to six weeks in the swamps of Levels Three and Four."

"So I've heard," Cain said, leaning forward on his elbows, studying Nuit. "But I do not have six weeks. I am, however, rescinding my father's old edict of no black blood exchanges. He was a purist who hated hybrids. That is why of all those vanquished councilmen I could have raised, I raised you." Cain pushed away from the table and stood. "My father was set in his ways and did not understand the need for progress. If we are to align forces with the other realms for the offensive, preemptive strike I intend, then our bite must know no bounds." He walked toward Fallon and clothed him in a black robe. "You understood this principle, thus I understand your eagerness for a coup. But be very clear that although I am Dante's son, I am *not* Dante. Daylight is not my obstacle. In that regard, I take after my grandfather." Cain leaned closer to Fallon as shock widened his gaze.

"While I was gone, they *bedded* the millennium Neteru to make you a daywalker?" Fallon's awed question trailed off as he slowly dropped to one knee and his voice became a reverent whisper. "Cain, you have my eternal loyalty and it would be my honor to accept your daylight strike."

Cain walked away from Nuit in abject frustration. "No. They never succeeded in that quest," he said, renewed fury roiling through him until his fangs crested. "My father failed, and the huntress took his head off at the shoulders."

Fallon stood slowly, his jaw going slack. "Damali assassinated *a chairman?*"

"Manipulated by the heretic, Rivera," Cain corrected, his eyes blazing black. "I had her in my arms, able to sire . . . and yet he had so compromised her soul that she would not drop the silver shields within her. I would have made her a dark angel, a female version of my grandfather's image . . . completely fallen and corrupted to sire at will . . . her soul mine, her progeny the greatest this empire has ever seen—black winged majesty. But access to my heirs was snatched by Rivera's treachery. However, there is still time. I want her back."

"You had her *in your arms?*" Fallon ran his fingers through his hair, his eyes beginning to glow again.

Cain spat on the marble floor. "Naked, writhing, climaxing, and ready for penetration, but she would not sire with me. Even after I bit her, because of him."

Fallon stumbled backward to hold on to the table again. "You've tasted her blood?"

"I am the direct descendant of the Dark Lord—of course I did!" Cain stared at Nuit for a moment and then closed his eyes, his nostrils flaring, ignoring Lilith's low, jealous hiss. "She willingly gave me her throat in the woods by her family's home. An entire Guardian team in the house, her lover about to commit suicide as he stood on the back porch. You have no concept . . . and for seven days I starved to keep that undiluted, sweet, fragrant elixir in my veins until it was impossible not to feed. I thought surely after that seduction bite she was mine, and siring would be imminent." Cain opened his eyes. "I must have his head on a pike!"

Storm clouds of sulfur began to gather in the ceiling as Cain swept away from Nuit to alight his throne. "I want hybrids to increase our mobility: were-demons, Amanthras, succubae, and incubi, anything from our realms and within my old armies of Nod on this mission. Black blood exchanges, human turns at record levels," Cain shouted, pounding the table and splashing blood under his fist. "I want his heart in ruins. His family decimated. Any and all Darkness within them brought to the surface of their beings one cell at a time! I want all that he held dear razed to the damned ground! Every footfall that he has taken tracked and erased from the planet. His Neteru essence washed away in a tide of blood!"

"*Neteru essence,* Your Eminence, what travesty do you speak!" Fallon said, dropping battle-length fangs. "He is no longer vampire?"

"He went into the Light!" Cain bellowed, sending bats into a frenzy above. "He married her in a *cathedral* in *broad daylight*—using a *Covenant priest* and the bond blinds us to where she is! He is backed by the Council of Neteru Kings!"

"Married her!" Fallon shouted, and then stormed away from the table, black smoke trailing him and streaming from his nose. "Not a vampire mate union? In a what! He has even inserted himself onto a Neteru Council of Kings?"

Lilith nodded and folded her arms, her eyes narrowed to gleaming slits.

"You heard me!" Cain shouted, pointing at Nuit and standing before his now-smoldering throne. "Much has transpired since your incarceration. Double jeopardy! My father's head. One Chairman— the very beginning of our lines. My replacement, another Chairman, slain by the sword in Rivera's hand! Our entire Council of Masters wiped out in Australia during a treacherous plot! Legions of demons and Lilim, slaughtered wholesale. The damned scattered; *The Book of the Damned* abducted and sent into the clutches of warrior angels!"

"*Warrior angels* colluded with him to take our book hostage?" Fallon leaned in toward Cain across the table. "How can this be, Your Eminence? Never in the history of Darkness has such a foul series of events beset our empire—"

"Then that *sonofahumanbitch* takes the blade of Ausar, my Neteru bride, my empire in Nod, and marries her. Redress this injustice with me or return from whence you came, Nuit!" Cain thundered, making small rocks begin to fall around them.

Fallon Nuit stalked toward his old throne, his head held high, and spit blood on Carlos's name etched in the high, black marble back. "Give me a moment to draw my old powers unto me, and then, my ally and commander, consider it done!"

Carlos left a stunned family to walk into the golden obelisk that appeared as he shouted Ausar's name. Jose would have to cope. There was no time for a long discussion; it was about motion. In and out, and raising an army. Ausar met him in the brightly lit hallway wearing a session robe of white Egyptian cotton tied with a golden sash.

"Cain—"

"We know. We are in session as you speak." Ausar stopped walking and put a heavy hand on Carlos's shoulder. "Before you go in to the archons, several realities must be discussed."

"I am so down for whatever, you have no idea," Carlos said in a low rumble, meeting Ausar's steady gaze.

"Adam has stood in your shoes. When you go in there, as you make your valid complaint, do not rub his nose in it by belaboring the previous offenses of Cain against your wife."

Carlos rubbed his jaw, rolling his shoulders. In truth, he'd been so upset that he hadn't considered that. "Aw'ight. I hear you."

"No. Get it out, now, with me in this antechamber, and then go in there like a true general asking for the resources you require and formulating a strategy for us to win."

Carlos closed his eyes and allowed his head to drop back. "Ausar, man . . . while I was with *my wife*?"

"Of what violation do you speak?" Ausar whispered through his teeth, causing Carlos to stare at him.

"He had her blood in his veins," Carlos muttered, sending his gaze to the large gold and alabaster Neteru Council of Kings doors. "When he took Dante's throne last night . . . It was the last night of my honeymoon." Carlos reinforced his grip on the blade so tightly the steel quivered. "If she's pregnant, if his energy rode mine . . . if I die battling this bastard this lifetime, I'll come back a thousand times to kill his ass again and again!"

Ausar briefly closed his eyes and paced away with his hands behind his back, then returned to Carlos. "Now you understand why Dante never came topside again during Adam's reign, and even feared to attempt to do so after Adam was in spirit. All of us had a price on Dante's wretched head for his offense against Eve in our brother's household. Then when Dante did resurface from the bowels of Hell, our Neteru Council of Kings received high angelic commands to stand down. Obtaining *The Book of the Damned* was viewed as more of a priority than an ageless personal grudge. Our brother was denied for the greater good, just as he and his wife's dignity were preserved in the old books—for the greater good—by leaving out the unfortunate circumstances of Cain's heritage. It would have shamed them. Know that we are all eager to avenge Adam, and now your cause also."

"It wasn't Damali's fault," Carlos said, eyes blazing. "The way this went down . . . It was so foul, man, there are no words."

Ausar's nostrils flared as blue-white flames licked their edges. Dropping his voice to a private, angry murmur, he kept a steady gaze on Carlos. "He violated the sanctity of *your marriage bed*? This I did not know!"

Carlos nodded, hot tears of frustration glittering in his eyes. "Man, how can I leave her, though, if this twisted shit plants? She didn't know. Damali thought she was just with me . . . thought it was over and done with between them, you feel me? I sensed it, she wasn't lying—the look in her eyes told me all I needed to know . . . she was blown away. My wife is so shook she couldn't even call the Isis into her grip. And, the more I think about it, even if I kill Cain's ass, he might still have the last laugh and I'll have to raise his heir." Carlos drew in a shuddering breath. "I don't know if I have it in me, man."

Ausar touched Carlos's shoulder. "This, too, was Adam's dilemma. He loved Eve so deeply that he refused to split his house asunder. *That* is strength."

"No," Carlos said, shaking his head. "*That* is pain, my brother." He drew in a few more breaths. "Watching some other man's kid growing in your woman's womb . . . watching her eyes looking down at that child with love but never fully able to look directly into yours again. Having some foul shit snap in that kid's psyche one day, 'cause you ain't his biological daddy—and then try to step to you after all those years, in *your* house, about *your wife* being his mother, and try to run your shit?"

Carlos began to pace, shaking his head in disbelief. "Then you can't slay the little motherfucker, because it will kill your wife—but you gotta take his bull? Oh . . . hell . . . no. I ain't the one. I can't do it."

He stopped and looked at Ausar hard. "It would have been different if she already came to me with a kid; I wouldn't have had a problem with that, and would have been ready to take a bullet for it like it was my own. Wouldn't have cared if another brother and her got together before I came on the scene. That shit happens every day on the planet. Even if we had broken up, and then had gotten back together, and something had gone down while we were apart—okay. Fine. Shit happens, and it ain't the baby's fault. She's mine; the kid would be, too. But the way this bullshit went down . . ." Carlos shook his head. "I can't deal."

"If she sires a blend, the queens will never allow her to purge her womb, you know that," Ausar said in a gentle, philosophical tone. "What if it's half yours and half his, a fusion?" Ausar waited patiently as Carlos slowly lowered his blade in shock. "Damali will not be able to get Eve's permission to end her pregnancy, and how would she be able to stand before that great queen that has gone through no less and make such a request? If there's even a cell of Cain's DNA in whatever Damali conceives, it will be wholly Eve's grandchild, regardless of what men think. Just like it will be wholly your wife's child in your wife's eyes. So, before we enter the meeting, you have to become very clear about how far you will go and where your personal line is. We all know where you're at—we have lived this heartbreak with Adam for thousands of years."

"How did Adam deal with this, make it right in his head day after day, night after night, man?" Carlos raked his hair and stared at Ausar for answers.

"You will have to ask him that yourself, in private. His demonstration of this level of inner strength has earned him my deepest, most profound eternal respect. I don't know that I could have adjusted to said circumstances . . . so I cast no aspersions on your indignity. This conundrum has been a private riddle to me for years, but I can only imagine that my brother focused on the fact that the child contained half of his queen and thus made his peace with loving her and the child as one. Your alternative is to walk away from her and become a solo male Neteru with your own team, which we can arrange, devoted to ridding the planet of evil. Your teams would only have to come together whenever a major planetary disaster strikes, like the one we are challenged to address now. I don't know what other choice to present to you, my brother."

"I can't leave her." Carlos looked away as his voice faltered. "I can't even envision life without Damali."

"That is your strength," Ausar said in a quiet, firm voice. "You love her. That is your advantage. Cain lusted after her. That is his weakness. Use it."

Carlos reinforced his grip on his blade, sniffed hard to swallow away the tears he refused to let fall in the king's presence. "All I can think about is the fact that the bastard broke down after seven short days—a fucking week, man, and went dark. He already had it in him. I told her! But I waited for her for five damned years and never touched her."

When Ausar simply let out a hard exhale and nodded, then closed his eyes, Carlos began walking in a tight circle. "I was there when she virgin-ripened, and was full vamp, and never violated her."

Speaking in a low rumble through battle-length fangs that had slowly lowered, Carlos's eyes went solid silver. "Three months in the damned Mexican desert, wounded, clerics all around me and then quarantined in a safe house run by the Covenant, I waited for her to come to me . . . and now . . . once she's *finally* my legal wife . . ."

"We know," Ausar stated and opened the door. "We stand with you."

Every king around the archon table stood as Ausar strode into the room with Carlos at his side. Adam cleared the table and grasped Carlos's arm in an old warrior handshake as Carlos tossed his blade to his left hand and grasped Adam's forearm.

"First Dante befouls my household, and now attempts to siege my young Neteru brother's household through his son, Cain?" Adam rumbled, staring into Carlos's eyes. "Unleash the dogs of war upon the planet, my fellow Neteru kings. Avenge me and my brother, Carlos, in one war."

"I have given you our collective outrage and power, powers that would have taken you years to refine," Hannibal said in a booming voice. "Did you receive my transmission last night, two hours past sunset?"

Carlos tore his gaze from Adam to stare at the towering Hannibal. "Two hours past sunset?"

Hannibal rounded the table as the other archons passed concerned glances between them. "Indeed! I sent all the outrage in a white lightning jolt to thunder through our archon table directly to you, brother. It was pure battle fury with solid-silver-encased knowing so that it might not be intercepted by the pirating thieves of the airwaves."

"Did you receive it?" Akhenaton shouted, drawing a rumble of dissent from the large gathering of kings. "It represented eons of our knowing and cannot be—"

"It could have cancelled out the other issue," Ausar said in a cryptic manner, looking at Carlos and giving the other kings his back. "A moment of private conference with our brother." Ausar stepped around Adam and body-shielded Carlos from view. "Open a direct telepathy channel to me."

"There are no secrets between archons," Adam raged, walking back to the table fuming. His white meeting robes began to billow out from him as blue-white static lifted his long African locks off his shoulders.

"When it is a matter this delicate, there need only be one archon source of conference," Ausar said evenly, glancing over his shoulder at Adam. "I know *you* can respect that."

Adam looked away and held his peace, the muscle in his jaw pulsing as Ausar turned back to Carlos.

There is a chance, Ausar said mentally, gazing at Carlos with his hand on his shoulder, *that part of what you felt came from Hannibal's strong transmission of power.*

I'm praying to God that's what happened, Carlos mentally shot back, *but it was a battle bite, man . . . one that wouldn't even seal in the morning.*

Ausar stiffened, tilted his head, and stepped back from Carlos. *A battle bite . . . your queen took a—*

Don't even say it. Carlos sent his silver gaze beyond the pillars toward the Valley of the Kings. *It had to be dark energy,* he said in his mind after a moment. *That ain't me by a long shot.*

No, Ausar assured him, bringing Carlos's gaze back to his by the calm thought. *But our brother Hannibal is sheer strength and has one of the most significant warrior minds ever created. However, as furious as he was last night, he does not own province of a battle bite.*

Is that why I couldn't heal it—couldn't pull out of the siphon and close the wound? Carlos's eyes widened as he became more distraught. *Look, man, that brother is a destroyer. . . . Hannibal isn't a healer. You see where I'm going. I could have . . .*

Yes, yes, I know, Ausar said in a fast mental projection.

And if I battle bulked and dropped fang on Damali like that, then that was Cain's shit—not Hannibal's! Carlos's mind shouted.

"Breathe," Ausar said out loud, drawing curious stares from the other kings as he held his focus on Carlos.

"Perhaps you both need to approach the table," Solomon said in a cool tone, his gaze raking Ausar and Carlos. "If what you are discussing has enough import to put our young brother in a position to nearly pass out, then—"

"Let me handle this," Ausar said, not turning away from Carlos.

"Then be quick," Adam thundered, beginning to pace. "Time draws nigh, and every second is a lost advantage."

Ausar simply held up his hand to stop further commentary from the table as he mentally addressed Carlos. *Young brother, if there was a collision of forces, at best, Hannibal's war rage may have cancelled out a potential fusion siring. If the two energies passed each other, one thundering into you like dominoes, one after the other . . . then it is a game of chance. Dice. Your energies would vacillate at a very inopportune time. Neither side can see into the holy union, and as long as you are married, either side can only send what we had toward you, hoping that it would adhere. But, if you were one heart, one mind, one spirit, one flesh at the time . . . God only knows what damage we have done.*

"Oh, shit!" Carlos said, walking away from Ausar. "I'm wounded? Lost the ability to heal a fallen warrior because of this shit," he said, trying in vain to protect his and Damali's personal business using a verbal diversion. "I'm going into the potential fucking Armageddon wounded?" He looked at Hannibal as confused stares met him from the group of kings. "Man, what was in that power hit?"

"Everything from our centuries of battle tactics," Hannibal said proudly, lifting his chin. "A blast of pure, righteous fury infused with warrior skill and strategy profound."

"While I was on my damned honeymoon, man? Are you crazy!" Carlos couldn't help it; the truth rushed out before he could censor it. His wife was in an unknown condition and might be carrying a fusion of him and his archenemy, or worse. "I cannot fucking believe this shit!"

Carlos drove the blade of Ausar into the marble floor and approached the archon's table, suddenly realizing that the power blast hadn't merely closed off his ability to seal a bite or heal a wound, or had simply made him too aggressive—it even went beyond the devastating possibility of a fusion. The significance of the jolt that was sent from the kings was written all over Hannibal's face.

As Carlos's mind raced, he wasn't worried about experiencing a loss of a specific Neteru ability. It became too clear that he and all the kings feared that the sudden lightning rod of war might have inadvertently done permanent, irreversible, internal damage to Damali. Carlos's mind instantly latched on to the image of her standing in the bathroom telling him she was bleeding silver. He was trembling with frustration as he stared at silver-lit eyes that held new uncertainty. "What could happen to her under those conditions?"

Akhenaton closed his eyes. "Hannibal . . . brother, brother, brother."

Hannibal sat down slowly like he'd been punched. "Young brother . . . my deepest regrets . . . had I known . . ."

Solomon leaned forward and made a tent before his mouth with his hands. "This is a problem. Is she injured?"

"I don't know!" Carlos shouted, veins standing in his neck and temples. "Why didn't you wait until I came home, summon me here, and do it here?"

"You were unavailable . . . we could not see you for a brief time," Ausar said quietly.

"I had just gotten married! Where the hell else do you think I would be other than with her?"

"This occurred during heated debate amongst the inner circle," Hannibal admitted, his voice low and deadpan. He glimpsed Adam. "Tempers flared, testosterone rushed, and we forgot that you had eloped. Our apologies."

"You *forgot*? Treated me like I was absent without leave, when you knew I was getting married? Now you're telling me, *our bad*? Oh shit!" Carlos rubbed his palms down his face.

Adam sat down slowly with a thud as Ausar began to pace. "In our intemperance and battle fury," Adam said quietly, "we acted prematurely, perhaps."

"Acted prematurely? Acted what?" Carlos was leaning across the table, sputtering. "Fix it now!"

"Female fertility issues rest in the province of Eve," Adam said quietly, "and lately, given the circumstances before us . . . my wife is not herself. We govern war and paternity, not those things maternal, as you know."

Carlos let out a hard breath, his gaze locking with Adam's. His palms were flattened against the table, glowing white when he splayed his fingers. "Then get the paternity straight," Carlos said between his teeth. "If she's able to carry and is carrying, y'all better fix this bullshit with the quickness."

Adam stood slowly and spoke in a quiet rumble. "There is a paternity question? From whom?"

"Cain," Carlos said in a lethal mutter. "Don't do me like this. Put healing back into my hands and my bites, if I'm on my way to war . . . but before you do *another* thing, you get it right with D."

Murmurs of dissent broke out among the gallery of kings behind the major archons.

"Paternity can only be guided prior, not after conception," Solomon said in a calm voice filled with remorse. "While your petition stabs our collective conscience and has not fallen on deaf ears, young brother . . . you must believe that we hear you loud and clearly. There is only One above who can change destinies to such a degree. Wars against evil demon legions and building righteous, powerful leaders are our charge . . . but on some things we cannot intervene. We do not own such powers. Even the angels tread lightly on the subject and must get official sanction to make an in vitro change like that." He glanced at Adam, who looked away. "If we had this ability, we would have exercised that option eons ago."

"Fix this shit," Carlos repeated, his gaze going to each of the older kings at the table. He walked back to the blade that had been driven into the marble and extracted it with one deft pull. He looked at Ausar. "I got your transmission—translucent box, positioning troops up on a ridge rather than waiting to be slaughtered on a beachfront hacienda. That part I got, along with maps and formations in my skull driving me crazy. How to ride a blinding stallion like it's a nightmare. How to use falcons to fuck up a Harpie tornado. Throw multiple shields and blue-arc oceanic waves backward to drown battleships. Got it. Tried a few out on the beach a little while ago, I was so pissed the fuck off."

Carlos made a fist and allowed it to glow white hot as he stared at it with a searing silver gaze. "Energy ball; put a sonic boom war cry on this and it's nuclear—right?" he said in a quiet, disgusted voice, still staring at his fist for a moment before looking up.

"But do not," Carlos said, his voice dropping to a dangerous energy pulse, "*ever* send me no crazy war shit when I'm with her." He looked up at the kings and then landed an angry gaze on Ausar. "Fix this. Respect *demanded* as a Neteru among you."

Ausar nodded and slung an arm over Carlos's shoulder, taking the fury ball out of his hand and diffusing it. "We shall endeavor to do what we can. You are not injured, only strengthened. The healing will return shortly. But it may be advisable for you to have Damali scanned by Aset for signs of any permanent harm."

"I will confer with Eve on your behalf," Adam said, his gaze going off into the distance.

Ausar tightened his hold on Carlos's shoulder in support. "We may have to draw counsel from the queens on this matter, if not healing by the Caduceus," he added, glancing around and receiving slow nods. "However, our primary mission here at this summit is imminent war."

Damali sat on the front steps of the hacienda with the entire Guardian team staring at her. She could feel their questions like a heat rash covering her skin. Weakened by the double healing, the argument, and something else she couldn't describe, she was so exhausted that she could only watch Carlos deliver a very-edited version of what had gone down. There was nothing to say. He'd kept it short and sweet. Guardians had sat on the sand one by one, seeming as though the air had been knocked out of them.

Her husband had delivered the state of the union in full battle bulk, and then called Jose to his side to walk down the beach. Moments later, Carlos had left Jose standing on the shore appearing numb as he evaporated into a golden obelisk—blade in hand.

Juanita's eyes still held a hard edge of betrayal in them and didn't soften until Jose returned and pulled her into a hug.

"I had to tell him," Damali said quietly, staring at Juanita's back and searching Jose's eyes.

Juanita nodded and kept her face pressed against Jose's shoulder.

"Good looking out, D," Jose said, quietly. "Thanks."

"What happened?" Marlene said, her radar snapping on, but Damali held up her hand. "That," she said, nodding to where Jose and Carlos had been on the beach, "was personal. Let it rest. He just wants Jose to be careful, since he has some vamp line in him. With Cain's energy whirling at Chairman Level, anything crazy could kick off."

Jose nodded, and Juanita turned to finally glimpse Damali with a silent thank-you in her eyes.

"I have to go," Damali said, standing with effort. "He went to the kings; I have to consult the queens." She glanced around the team. "Y'all pull out all the weaponry, get strapped, all seers' radar up. Everybody's personal guard up; sensory capacities at the ready."

She waited until nods and battle-ready gazes met hers and the disgruntled band of warriors began to stand and go into the house. Silent terror was threading its way through her system, though. Each time she'd tried to summon her Isis, she got only a small tickle of current in her palm.

Hastening to the water's edge, Damali focused on the surf, trying to get the violet pyramid to open. Nothing. No juice. It was as though she was a dead battery. Damali glanced over her shoulder and tried to signal Marlene with her mind. Nothing. No telepathy? She covered her mouth with her hands. Her system had never been this fried in her life. Part of her wanted to dash back to the house and get Marlene to open the pyramid. The other part of her knew it would freak Mar and the entire squad out if they thought they had a Neteru down.

Damali touched the large diamond in the center of her collar with two fingers and spoke in a low, urgent whisper.

"Aset, hear me. I must come to you, but you have to get me. Cain is loose."

CHAPTER FIVE

Chaotic, swirling interdimensional winds gathered Damali into a maelstrom the moment the violet queen's pyramid opened and she stepped over the threshold. Crash-landing in a giant marble hallway, she was caught by two hands just before she hit the ground.

"Whoa, whoa, whoa, young queen," Nzinga said, holding Damali upright.

"Cain—"

"Yes," Aset said in a quiet rush, cutting off Damali's words. She motioned to the large chamber that housed the Council of Queens' meeting oval. "We must have a brief private session before we take this to the table." Aset glanced at Nzinga. "Create a diversion and hasten Nefertiti to my side."

Nzinga stepped away as Aset practically dragged Damali down the large rose-and-gold marble hallway to hide behind a pillar. If it weren't for the frantic look in Aset's eyes, Damali would have been sure her queen was about to kick her natural ass. Old school, outside, one on one.

Damali didn't even get a chance to verbally defend herself or put up a fighter's stand to take the blow. Aset had swiftly grabbed her into a hug and now whispered tenderly in her ear.

"I know, I know, sister, but Eve is beside herself. Do not fear me or the other queens. We have to tell her that you have confirmed her son's Darkness, and thus must execute him . . . but stand behind me and Nzinga when you do."

Damali clung to Aset like she was drowning. Perhaps she was. A hundred emotions slammed into her and threatened to burst out all at once.

"I don't know what to tell her," Damali said. "He's lost his mind."

Aset nodded and held Damali away from her, finally letting Damali go to place a graceful finger over her lips before speaking again. "How are your powers?"

"Weak," Damali admitted. "I couldn't even summon the pyramid."

Aset closed her eyes. "All of us are experiencing a dredge."

For a moment Damali just stared at Aset. "You guys, too? Whoa . . ."

"We work on a delicate, cooperative balance of feminine harmonies and energies," Aset said with a weary sigh. "Eve is the cornerstone of that. She was the first of our kind. . . . Perhaps this is indeed the end of our reign, whereby the first shall be last and the last shall be first. Eve was the first, you are the last. I do not know." Aset began to pace. "Never before has our council been so bitterly divided. Eve accepted our collective decision on the surface, verbally conceding to the will of the group, but deep within her spirit, she is so wounded that even the Caduceus did not repair her suffering." Shimmering silver tears filled Aset's eyes. "He is *her son.*"

Not sure where to begin commentary, Damali dragged her fingers through her locks. "I thought the power drain was from Carlos being so angry at me . . . and from the battle bite, but—"

"Your husband . . . *a Neteru king,* battle bit you?"

Aset's voice held a tone so aghast that Damali cringed. Then the fact that she wasn't supposed to reveal that, per Carlos's request, made her close her eyes.

"Aset, *swear* to me on a stack of every holy book ever written that you will *never* disclose this to any other queen. My husband asked me not to—"

"I bet *the hell* he did!" Aset's golden robes lifted at the hem as fury energy began to slowly whirl down the great hall. "Did your mother-seer clear it out and assist with—"

"No, because I *never* want Marlene to see something like that between him and me," Damali said, grasping Aset's arms and staring into her eyes. "It wasn't him. I healed myself! That, and your powers waning from Eve's dissent, is all that's probably wrong with me. His bite, my self-healing, and your power drain—a bad threesome of events. That's gotta be it. But *this* is *private*."

Aset's resistance energy began to lower, and her gaze locked with Damali's in confusion. Nefertiti suddenly rounded the pillar, breathless, like a woman being chased.

"Queen Sisters, what has transpired?" Nefertiti placed her graceful palm flat to her chest, her gorgeous Egyptian eyes darting between Damali and Aset.

"Please," Aset said, her gaze searching Damali for permission. "Just the three of us, a trinity of privacy and sisterly support. You *must* inform Nefertiti. She, above all, understands male energies."

Damali leaned on a huge pillar and stared at both queens. "On my husband's honor, what happens in the Great Hall stays in the Great Hall. Promise."

Both queens nodded.

"We all know Cain took a throne tumble. He went there of his own volition, which was under very different circumstances than when Carlos went," Damali said, setting the backdrop for the queens to be sure there was no way they'd blame Carlos. "My husband was sent there by angelic command to get *The Book of the Damned*. He was manipulated to go before he was ready by Lilith, who had sent a spiritual attachment to work on his psyche, so he got the directions and messages all screwed up. But his original intention was honorable . . . Cain's was not. Dude went down there on a mission."

"Yes, yes, yes, we know that, child," Aset said, waving her hand with impatience. "But we are *not* about to allow you to stand here and justify domestic violence in our presence or keep something that insidious a secret. That has been the horror of too many women's existence, and is a commandment from On High that we stand united to abolish . . . within the sanctity of marriage, no less? Do not ask me to be a party to—"

"It *wasn't Carlos* that attacked me. It had to be Cain's energy. As many arguments and as much drama as Carlos and I have been through, the man *never* in his life laid a hand on me or tried to hurt a hair on my head." Damali was breathing hard by the time she'd rushed out her defense.

"He slapped you once," Nefertiti said, her eyes narrowing. "Now you are saying he *attacked* you?"

"He thought I was Lilith when he slapped me because she was shadowing my energy—remember?" Damali folded her arms over her chest.

"I don't like the sound of this," Nefertiti said. "Sounds eerily like a woman making excuses for a violent man. Damali wouldn't be the first."

"If you all hear me out, hear the entire story, and then you can make a judgment. Okay?" Damali sighed hard and let her shoulders slump. No wonder Carlos wanted a chance to talk to the kings first!

"All right, child," Aset said, waving her hand with disgust. "Go back to Cain. But if this conversation devolves into Carlos's affront and becomes an excuse, I will go down there myself and slaughter him. No man should abuse a woman!"

"I may be many things, Aset," Damali said, looking the elder queen in the eye and then glancing at Nefertiti, "but do I seem like the kinda sister to let a man beat my ass and then hide it from anybody to protect his sorry hide? If I didn't gore him myself, cops, family, a posse, whatever, would ride or die on the situation, and I bet he wouldn't mess with another sister again."

Nefertiti smiled a half-smile and relaxed. "I think we can bank on that, Aset. Let our young sister proceed about Cain—which is truthfully the crux of her mission."

"All right," Damali said in a huff, trying to get her mind wrested back to the point. She waited until Aset seemed to stand down before pressing on. "So you know now that Cain has escaped, he's biding his time to raise an army of vampires from Level Six where he went, probably also gonna bring out his old loyalists from Nod, while he's at it. And with Lilith in the mix, who knows what other level could get into this pending war."

"Yes, we are aware," Nefertiti said, glancing at Aset. "This is what all the chaos is about. The living Neterus must stop him. He has taken Dante's throne, thus, as a demon now, he must be slain." Nefertiti glimpsed Aset again before returning her regal gaze to Damali. She smoothed her white silk gown. "Eve is distraught, but we stand with you on what must be done. Dear young queen sister, your eyes hold sheer devastation. We understand your loyalty to Eve, and she is our sister, too . . . but we cannot compromise on this. You must slay Cain, no matter your earlier attraction to him while he was still undecided about his loyalties. In Nod, and briefly on Earth with you, he did seem good. But now all that has changed. So, you must do what you must. Kill him."

"I know that," Damali said, looking away. Nefertiti's simplistic statement turned a blade of guilt in Damali's side. She didn't want to revisit the earlier attraction or trust that had allowed her to foolishly let Cain bite her.

"Then why the long face?" Nefertiti asked, tilting her regal head. "Especially if you think he somehow came into your home as vampire illusion and beat you up in the image of your husband, I say gore the bastard."

"The problem may be more complex, Nefertiti," Aset murmured, gazing at Damali.

Throwing her shoulders back, Damali nodded. "It wasn't straight vamp illusion, my queen. That I could have handled, and would have seen right through it."

"I don't understand," Nefertiti said, folding her arms over her chest.

"Carlos and Cain both have a throne connection," Damali said slowly, working out major sections of the twisted puzzle in her own mind as she spoke. "They were both made from Dante, one way or another, and they therefore share the same DNA. They both sat in Dante's throne near or during their apex time, and were both Neteru brothers."

"Yes," Nefertiti said, coming closer. "But . . ."

"It wasn't an outright attack. Carlos *battle bit* Damali, on their *honeymoon*—so you can only imagine when the urge to bite her occurred," Aset said, her eyes holding renewed panic.

Nefertiti covered her mouth. "When?" she whispered, dropping her hand away slowly.

"Last night," Damali said quietly, looking at the floor. "Like Aset said, on our honeymoon."

Nefertiti grabbed Aset's arms. "Last night Cain took the throne! In an apex! With the imperative to sire clutching him in its grip? Heaven forbid this! He isn't sterile like other vampires." Nefertiti's eyes were wild as her voice briefly escalated and then dropped to a horrified whisper. "Eve's son is beyond virile. His mother *is fertility*. His father *owned* the pleasure principle of raw lust. If Cain was dark energy fusing with Carlos while Carlos was physically inside our queen sister—"

"I know," Aset said, her gaze tearing between Nefertiti and Damali. "He could have hurt her internally, and that I can fix if necessary. But as we can see, thankfully Damali stands before us, a bit exhausted from the trauma, but not hemorrhaging. However, my greater concern is that the two males are not so linked that in the future—especially during a battle, Carlos's mind could be compromised by Cain."

"It wasn't Carlos's mind that was compromised," Damali said flatly.

"Aset!" Nefertiti said in a tight whisper, shaking her older queen sister. "Listen to what Damali is saying to you. You said it yourself: 'Her husband battle bit her on their honeymoon—and when do you think this might have occurred?"

Aset opened and closed her mouth as Nefertiti just nodded. Nefertiti let her hands fall away from Aset's arms.

"Oh, daughter . . . I know it was a bit awkward, but it was just an energy fusion of both sexually active males, not a true tryst—and their combined prowess might have left you a bit off kilter. You'll recover your energies very shortly, I'm sure." Aset sighed impatiently as she glanced at Damali, and then back to her upset queen sister. "Nefertiti, calm yourself. This will all change once Damali slays Cain. He won't be able to ride Carlos's old link after that, and I'm absolutely positive that once the vital link is severed, your husband will return to his normal self. There should be no more violent outbursts. What is of greater import is that Cain not be allowed to link to Carlos while he's in battle with Carlos. . . . The bedroom is a lower priority concern, given all we face. Worry about the battle, not the bedroom, is my advice."

"I cannot fathom how Cain's energy could have entered your household to bond so severely to Carlos, though." Nefertiti flung her long microbraids over her shoulder and refolded her arms. "It doesn't make sense. Nothing is that powerful to come between man and wife once sealed from On High . . . that is the ultimate prayer barrier, and not even Neteru Councils can see into that space. The only way something insidious can slither in from the outside to turn one partner against the other is for it to be invited in—and I *know* neither Damali nor Carlos did that."

"Cain had my blood in his veins through a previous, willing, throat offering," Damali said just above a whisper, "and it was still in his system seven days later when I got married and was on my honeymoon."

Nefertiti and Aset's collective gasp felt like the cutting edge of an Isis against Damali's skin.

Damali squeezed her eyes closed and tears wet her lashes. "I have to go into battle and slay Cain, but I don't know how I'm ever gonna make this right with my husband. Nefertiti, what do I tell him?"

"I don't know," Nefertiti murmured. "This is my fault. . . . When I sent you in there to seduce Cain to get back the Caduceus and to seal him away again, I forgot to tell you not to give him your blood. Oh, my . . ." Nefertiti clasped her hands together over her chest. "Does Carlos have to know about the blood transfer? Couldn't we just attribute it all to the dark energies swirling on the planet?"

Damali just stared at Nefertiti for a moment. She could not *believe* her queen just *forgot.* Incredible. Still, she couldn't really get angry about the oversight and lay all the blame at Nefertiti's feet. Unfortunately, she had to take the weight for this one alone, and suck it up and be honest. "It happened before I went in for the Caduceus," Damali muttered, "so it wasn't on you. But none of that matters. I've already admitted it to Carlos and—"

"What would make you do that?" Nefertiti shrieked, causing Aset to clasp her hand over her mouth.

"Why would you tell him?" Aset said quickly in a tense whisper, her luminous eyes wide with disbelief. "He's a man, and doesn't need to know all." She let go of Nefertiti and both queens stood before Damali with their arms folded.

"Because it happened on *my honeymoon,* and Carlos and I weren't using *anything.* . . . He was burning solid gold symbol that went white-hot, okaaaay? So was I. And you know if Cain was at the height of a denied apex, the way I left that brother in Nod . . . shit. Then he took a tumble in *Dante's* throne? Double shit, ladies. You and I know that Cain wasn't shooting blanks when he finally got his groove on down there. And if Cain somehow used my blood as a beacon and then rode Carlos's energy through the preexisting link they had, or there was some kinda DNA mix up . . ." Damali caught her weight against a pillar with both hands. It became blurry as hot moisture built in her eyes as she spoke.

"You should have seen the look in my husband's eyes. I might as well have cut his heart out on that beach. I never want to hurt Carlos like that again in my life, or see Carlos's eyes stare back at me with that incredible disbelief that *I,* of all the people in the world, could do something like this to him." Hot tears rolled down Damali's cheeks and she didn't bother to wipe them away. "That man never looked at me with disgust in his life," she said thickly, a sob brewing very close to her surface.

She didn't look up when she heard the older queens swallow hard, and her voice broke as she told them the truth. "This may sound weak, may sound foolish up here in the Neteru Queens' Council with everything else that's going on, but ladies, I'm being real. . . . If that man walks, I don't know what I'll do."

Damali pushed off the pillar and wrapped her arms around her waist. "Fate of the world?" she said, looking at the floor. "My world just experienced a cataclysmic wipeout. Yeah, I'll go down and battle, whateva. Try to save humanity, yeah, yeah, yeah, but when it's all said and done, then what? I've been to Hell and back for that man, love the ground he walks on. Life without him would be what to me? I might as well be the living dead, soulless, just walking around in a stupor without my soul mate. I can't be carrying nobody else's baby but his." She shook her head and closed her eyes again. "Oh, *my God,* you should have seen his face."

"Oh . . . my God . . ." Aset whispered, rushing to Damali with Nefertiti.

"We have to fix this," Nefertiti whispered through her teeth. "History cannot repeat itself in such a manner." She touched Damali's tears. "If you are carrying, Eve is the only one we can go to in order to get a paternity divination . . . and if she learns that you are with child, her hopes that it is Cain's will make her even more irrational."

Aset nodded, walking in a tight line back and forth, hugging herself. "She will want any part of it to be Cain's, as that will be the last flicker of Light within his being. He may have gone dark, but his future holds the heritage of a Neteru in the Light—and Eve will be on Damali like a wasp to ensure the pregnancy comes to term, that the child is reared in an envelope of total love, and she'll attempt to relive every motherly mistake she thinks she ever made by assisting in the upbringing of this child."

"The marriage will crumble under that weight," Nefertiti said in a faraway voice.

"Carlos is not Adam," Damali said, her voice strained. "He wouldn't stick around long enough for it to be all that, if I know anything about the man. At first, I think he'd try to hold on, but the bigger I got . . ." Damali let her voice trail off as multiple negative scenarios played out in her mind.

"Eve wouldn't care," Aset said quietly. "She would bring all her powers to bear to help Damali raise the child alone. In fact, if I know my queen sister's weeping heart, she would prefer it that way . . . would want Carlos out of the picture in hopes that her son would come around to change for the sake of the new baby."

Nefertiti looked at Aset. "Maybe we could develop a compromise to save the marriage and let Eve raise the child here, so that—"

Damali held up her hand, cutting off Nefertiti's words. "Don't even *ask* me to give my baby up if I'm pregnant."

"I'm sorry," Nefertiti said, her eyes containing so much compassion that tears flowed over her onyx lashes. Egyptian kohl was running down her cheeks and a sob made her cover her mouth with her hand. "Even slaying Cain will not fix this. Yet, we are bound to saving the world at large and never taking a soul . . . and, still, my heart shatters for my sister's personal loss. Aset, advise us."

"Just scan me, Aset," Damali whispered, her tone desperate. "At least let me know now what I'm dealing with so I can get my head right to go into battle. Maybe if I'm lucky, I'll die on the job and that way at least—"

"Don't say that, Damali!" Aset whispered, silver tears streaming down her cheeks as she paced. "Maybe we can send a petition up to the angels? This was larceny, not an act of intent. . . . This young queen didn't know—Cain may have done this through a blood heist, since she never actually bedded him. He broke into a marital chamber using an old blood siphon from before, not one given once our sister got married."

"But they take so long on matters this involved up there," Nefertiti wailed. "The debate over this, and with Cain's dark decision, who knows, maybe they want to teach Hell a lesson that no matter the parentage, free will to go into the Light reigns supreme? We never know how they do things all the way up there, what mysteries are unfolding until they do!"

"Just scan me," Damali said, holding Aset's arm. "I have to know. You healed me before when—"

"I can't," Aset said, pulling Damali into an embrace. "Before when I went in to scan you, all queens stood with me united. Before, I was healing the damage to your womb that Dante's claw created, but I was not going in there to see whose baby it was. The small embryo was not there. If I attempt a scan, Eve will know."

Damali dropped her head to Aset's shoulder. But just as suddenly as she'd done that, all three queens jerked their heads up at the disturbance coming down the hall. Nzinga was body blocking Eve, and yet Eve had deftly rounded her with the other queens on her heels.

"Why do you hide her from me!" Eve shouted, striding down the Great Hall in a billowing swirl of opalescent energy. "I have felt her pulse since the moment she entered our domain, yet I waited for her to come into the oval. Do you think I'm stupid, that I have lost all sensing capacity? Is this how you treat your most grieved sister?"

Nzinga lowered her battle-ax and the other queens parted. Eve slowly approached Damali, her ruby robe flowing in a long train behind her.

Damali stared at Eve's face. Her eyes were red and puffy from what she knew had been unrelenting sobs. Eve's coloring was ashen, making her once dewy brown complexion seem nearly gray in pallor. Even the regal queen's hair that was normally wound up in thick, dark locks was down on her shoulders, and beginning to get threads of graying silver within it. Worry lines creased her once flawless brow, and her eyes had a mad, disoriented look in them. Dark circles gave Eve the appearance of a woman slowly dying from within. Damali made a note to herself—before she took off Cain's head, she'd gore his heart by letting him know just what his foul behavior had done to his beloved mother.

"So, tell me," Eve said, standing in front of Damali with her head held high, new tears of rage slowly filling her large brown eyes. "How will you seduce my son to his death? What is the plan?"

Damali lifted her chin. "I will respect his parentage, the fact that he was once a Neteru, and for the sake of all humanity, I will make it swift and painless. He deserves that, as do you, dear Eve."

Eve nodded. "At least you are honest and have told me to my face, unlike my sisters. I see that your cheeks, like mine, are stained with tears of remorse—for that I thank you. I appreciate that you once loved him."

Damali kept her mouth shut, neither agreeing with or denying the charge, as she stared into Eve's tormented eyes. What would be the point of hurting Eve by correcting her and saying she'd never felt like that about Cain? But it wasn't a lie that she regretted having to execute him.

A slow exhale of defeat exited Eve's body and made her dignified shoulders lower. "I had so hoped that he would cling to your Light, Damali . . . or that in Nod, he would find an angel." Eve swallowed hard and wrapped her arms around herself. "If he had found an angel . . . a healing one, from the Powers group on Ring Six, if not a Neteru queen, then he might have had a chance. If he escaped, and sired with the right female, the Light of what he made would have anchored him to our side and perhaps brought him back to our side of the family." Eve opened her arms out slowly. "Do you not see what I had prayed for? But he only found a Neteru queen who had already given her heart over to another like him." Eve shook her head. "Why couldn't you have chosen my son over Carlos?"

In that moment as Eve stood before her, Eve's beautiful, pained eyes searching hers, Damali knew that everything her elder queens had told her was true. Everything that Marlene had told her about a mother and a son was also true. Pity choked Damali's words and kept them lodged in her throat. She so badly wanted to tell Eve that no woman could change a man that way. He had to man-up on his own and make his own choices, just like Carlos had done—and *that* was why she'd picked the man with superior spiritual strength to be her husband. The physical wasn't the issue; Cain was as fine a specimen as there ever was . . . seemed to have it all going on. But he was weak at the core if you put him in a lineup next to Carlos Rivera, in her mind.

"Eve, there is no way for me to answer your question," Damali whispered gently, watching the older queen lower her arms to her side.

If her heart wasn't racing so fast, she would have pressed Eve's hand to it to send the truth into the elder queen's palm. . . . She would have said, dearest Queen Mother of all mothers, you know you are grabbing at straws. Your son is now a man, and that man made an irreversible choice . . . and now, even as his mother, you can't fix this for him.

Eve just set her jaw hard and looked away. Quiet mourning filled the Great Hall and the other queens respectfully lowered their gazes. Damali knew in her soul that, if no one, *not even the queens,* had been able to detect something that had presented while she was in Carlos's arms, namely, wings—that was something to keep strictly between him and her. Eve was already edging toward the high treason of potentially aiding and abetting her son through weakening the queens' efforts; all that Eve would need to learn is that she did have a little angel in her genes. Now it also made so much sense to Damali why even during the first scan by Aset, this part of her being was always hidden . . . even from her. The situation was beyond volatile.

"Eve . . . I am so sorry," Damali finally whispered, truly meaning it. But it was futile to try to get Eve to come to terms with the fact that her son had most likely gone primarily dark years ago.

"As am I," Eve whispered, dropping her shoulders. "Then I guess there is nothing further for any of us to discuss."

Suddenly Eve looked so frail, so delicate, like a wilting red hibiscus that would drop its petals and soon blow away in the wind.

"We have to strengthen her, Eve," Nzinga said quietly, gaining nods from the other bereft queens. "She cannot go into battle with her powers waning. It will take all of us standing together and holding the image of her victory as one . . . just like we always do."

"Please, Eve," Joan said softly. "I was a warrior who led men in battles and what is coming for the planet . . . our sister must be strong."

"How can I hold the image of my son's death in my mind?" Eve murmured, slowly drawing away from the group. "I cannot even hold the image of feminine conception in it, much less the death of my own child. No more children . . . the heartbreak is too much for the female spirit. Let the men war until the earth is a black cinder and you may join them in collecting the charred spoils of bone and ash and let your female war cries demand heads on pikes. I will not bring forth new life under these conditions. I am dying from it all."

The stunned gathering of queens watched in horror as Eve slowly strode away, her shoulders bent, her breathing as labored as her wobbly gait.

"Since last night," Nzinga said after Eve had closed herself away into a chamber, "all conception on the planet has ceased. Not even the flowers are reproducing. Nary a gnat has spawned. We don't have to wait for Cain's armies to eliminate life—he can simply stay in Hell for a season and the delicate ecosystem of nature will collapse. He's dragged his mother's heart into Dante's throne with him. Damali, we have never experienced anything so profoundly dangerous throughout the centuries!"

"Send Damali every battle tactic you own and the use of your most cherished gifts, sisters, that she may be victorious. There is much at stake, and too much riding on the outcome for personal grief to sway the results. Our young queen sister is, like Eve, emotionally, physically, and spiritually exhausted. Replenish her. She must continue to fight," Nefertiti said. She cast a loving gaze in Damali's direction, holding Damali's secret and embedding a discreet message of support in her words. "Even though the personal sacrifice is difficult."

"Encircle her," Aset commanded. "Infuse her with all that we have left, even if it is not the fullness of our supply, it is our best chance."

Aset held Damali by the arms and opened her mind to Damali's. A small, glowing violet pyramid began to pulse in the center of Aset's forehead. *Do not despair or lose hope. We will take your petition up to the Powers Angels for mediation. Also, as you heard Nzinga's words—all conception ceased last night. It will be my silver-sent prayer on an urgent wind that it also included you. However, we won't know until your menses. After what we have seen of Eve's frame of mind, I do not want to risk a scan that she can detect.*

Damali nodded. *Neither do I, Great Queen. Neither do I.*

The team knew the drill; everybody fall out and scramble to gather the weapons and necessities within their area of expertise. J.L. and Krissy rushed around the hacienda grabbing laptops and any computer hardware the team might need on the road. Marjorie and Juanita were on weather protection, ensuring that if the team went to cold climes or the desert, they had blankets, tents, sleeping bags, whatever could protect against the elements.

Inez was on kitchen detail, stashing K-rations in a box, bottled water, and every deadly piece of cutlery she could lay her hands on. Shabazz, Rider, Berkfield, and Bobby were on guns, while Big Mike, Dan, and Jose were rounding up explosives and projectiles. Marlene was on communications and spiritual shields—her first point of contact was to the Covenant, the second to the telephone network of North American Guardian teams, then the sister packed her big black bag. It was a worldwide call to arms.

The two newest members of the team were runners, frantically going from team cluster in the house to team cluster, responding quickly to whatever the more senior Guardians bellowed for them to fetch. Several times Heather almost bumped into Jasmine and vice versa, and everyone went still when the two collided with an ammo duffle.

"That's it!" Rider shouted. "Out! You two go stand on the porch and watch the freakin' sky for signs of our Neterus coming home, but my nerves can't take another grenade bag dropping."

Heather covered her mouth and jumped back from the army bag so fast that her back hit a wall. Jasmine's eyes had widened so quickly that even Rider had to smile.

"Go watch the sky," Marlene muttered. "If the demons don't get us, our own team will," she said, looking up from the satellite phone she was speaking into.

Both team newbies dashed through the house and ran out onto the steps, and then kept going until they were near the water.

"I thought Gabrielle said we would be safe here?" Heather wailed, holding on to Jasmine's arm.

Jasmine pushed Heather's thicket of auburn ringlets back and stared up into her gray, wondering eyes. "If what has just happened did, then Gabrielle's houses could be overrun by vampires. They'll all have to feed—and she has an outstanding debt with you know who. Gabrielle was always good to us and trying to save us, and no one has called her." Jasmine looked back at the house. "We have to get word to her, or at least get one of the others to try. . . . I think Rider would do it, if Damali and Carlos wouldn't."

Tears rose in Jasmine's pretty, almond-shaped eyes as her petite body filled Heather's arms. Heather stroked her jet black hair and clung to her, looking up to the sky, trying not to sob.

"We never leave our own," Heather said. "We are a part of her coven, and we owe her . . ." But Heather's words trailed off as she tensed and stared up at a darkening sky.

Both newbie Guardians looked up, not sure what to make of the spectacle above them. The crystal clear blue sky over La Paz had been ruptured by several horizontal, dark streaking clouds that looked like the wake of an aircraft going down. It was as though minitornadoes were swirling on a sideways funnel that was headed directly toward them. Without consulting each other, both women immediately broke their hugs, pivoted, and dashed toward the hacienda, screaming.

Mike, Rider, and Shabazz were on the porch first, and they took one glance at the newbies as the others joined them and then looked up at the sky in unison.

"Incoming," Rider shouted.

Each Guardian dashed back into the house, with Dan and Bobby yanking the two newbies in with them. Safeties came off weapons, Mike took a position by a window with an RPG shoulder launcher, and the sound of clips clicking into place as each team member took a position was the only sound in the house.

The blast that hit the beach rocked the house, blowing out windows and sending glass shrapnel everywhere.

"Heads down, people!" Shabazz ordered, covering his position. "Get those two newbies down!"

Heather was breathing through her mouth in short pants, her cheek pressed to the floor. Perspiration rolled down the center of her back, making her tank top skin. But she saw something. Almost too scared to scream she trained her eyes on the doorway down the hall. A fast-moving shadow put her on her feet with a scream. "It's in here, in the house!"

"Stay down!" Dan shouted, gripping the back of her shirt and forcing her to the floor. "You wanna get your head blown off?"

"It's back there in the bedrooms," she said panting. "I saw it under the door when it passed through the sunlight."

"Yo, something went past sunlight, and we've got motion, two o'clock," Dan shouted.

"There's another one," Jasmine shrieked, covering her face and becoming a tiny ball next to Bobby.

"Mike, you on it?" Shabazz hollered from his position.

"Moving fast, two o'clock, ten o'clock, eight o'clock—there's more than one."

"Then blow this sucker," Rider said. He glanced over the back of a sofa and got a nod from Shabazz.

Both team sharpshooters positioned themselves to smoke anything coming out of Mike's blast. Mike stood. A huge demon appeared in the hallway. The rocket-propelled grenade left its housing, and blew out the back wall of the house. An instant hail of bullets followed. A low growl rumbled and that demon's tail could be seen flashing away in escape before five more green-and-black-scaled entities with gold glowing eyes and black wings slipped through the smoke, but didn't appear hit. They moved like lightning, and the salt rings and holy water that Marlene cast in their paths didn't slow them down.

"Get that prayer barrier up, Mar," Jose shouted. "I'm doing hollow point packed with church dirt and these boys ain't stopping!"

Dan popped up, slingshot in hand, and exploded several bottles of holy water at the yawning gap in the house that was ablaze. Six more demons strode through it, seeming puzzled but not injured in the least, before dodging away from the Guardians' gunfire.

"Fall back!" Berkfield yelled, as the entities approached, slipping from protective hiding place to hiding place, and seeming to be able to take a bullet, summarily heal a tertiary wound, but keep advancing. "These boys ain't going down like they should, people!"

Mike was on his feet again, new RPG loaded, and Rider and Shabazz hadn't stopped firing, nor had the rest of the group. Jose scrambled on the floor behind furniture to the duffle bag that had crossbows, yanked it open, and began quickly loading.

"In the heart!" Jose hollered. "Dead aim is the only way!"

Bobby was out of ammo with a dead clip, and he rolled over toward a duffle bag but was forced back by another RPG blast. "Throw me a clip! I'm out," he shouted, panicked.

"Take a hostage," a low, demon voice rumbled through the inferno. "Where is the Neteru?"

Smoke and the danger of structural collapse were forcing the Guardian team into a corner. The fight would soon be on the beach as Guardians broke windows with gun butts and fell back, trying to hold their positions behind flimsy cover. But that option was sure massacre.

A clip was hurled toward Bobby by his father, but as he reached for it, a long tail lassoed his arm, pulled, and he was over the couch being dragged to sudden death. Marjorie was on her feet shrieking with Krissy. Rounds were going off, but Marj dashed forward, her hands outstretched before her, going into the smoke behind Bobby and whatever held him.

Berkfield shouted his wife's name to no avail, and then everything seemed to happen in slow motion as Marjorie released a battle cry, and white lightning ejected from her fingers into the billowing smoke. A thud was heard, whatever had been dragging Bobby retreated, and he jumped off the floor, grabbed his mother's arm, and pulled her back behind the couch. Jasmine and Krissy were sobbing, but Bobby couldn't catch his breath to answer their frantic questions about his condition. His mother had him pressed to her breasts, and there was no fear in her eyes.

"You want my son, you bastards, then you gotta come through me!" Marjorie shouted. "Give me a fucking gun, Richard. I'm going into that smoke to blow their heads off!"

"Truce!" a loud voice shouted with demon inflection.

"We did not come to war but to warn," another garbled voice shouted from beyond the smoke.

"Hold your fire," a light female voice said.

Everyone looked at one another.

"I do not regenerate like my friends. If you shoot me, I will be mortally injured."

"Then state your business," Shabazz hollered, jamming a new clip into the handle of his nine.

"We're looking for Carlos. We need amnesty."

The soot-and-sweat-smudged team passed confused glances.

"Who you be then, sis?" Mike hollered, raising his RPG as the smoke began to part with a form. But he lowered it slowly as a fragile, nymphlike entity with white wings stepped through the soot, slightly dirty and looking suspiciously like an angel.

"Demon illusion," Rider said. "On three, right in the center of her head."

As soon as he said it, a huge half-gargoyle half-male with black and green skin leapt before the nymph and wrapped his wings around her. "Kill her and I will lose my soul up in the godforsaken house—and you call yourselves Guardians?"

Rider looked at Marlene. "Wait . . . did dude just say the name of the Most High, or did I hear wrong? Mike, talk to me."

Big Mike lowered his weapon. "Speak!"

The nymph began coughing and the larger demons stood around her, gently trying to hold her and get her to a window.

"She needs air. She cannot tolerate the ash and soot of an inferno . . . we must take her outside."

The team slowly stood and looked at each other, and then watched the brigade of demons carry the small being, swathed in white like she were a doll.

"Oh, baby . . . come on, breathe for me," the large creature with a six-foot wingspan said through his fangs.

Marlene and Rider and Shabazz just looked at each other.

"I'm a healer," Marlene said, "and we got us another pretty good medic, too," she added, glancing at Berkfield.

"The escape through the barrier was a rough ride, and the distortion of energy may have affected her." The entity looked up at Marlene with normal brown eyes holding deep concern. "Can you help her?"

"Is she an angel?" Marlene asked, folding her arms over her chest.

"At my age I'm way too old to be picking up no spiritual attachment in the streets."

"She's a hybrid . . . part that, part nymph, and the sweetest spirit you would ever know," the entity said, no longer looking at Marlene, but down at the small dirty creature in his arms that was struggling to breathe.

"Marlene . . ." Shabazz said, shaking his head. "At least have them put her down on the beach and back off."

Rider pulled his shirt over his head and flung it to the demon squad. "Lay her down on the sand for our lead medic to work on her. Then you gentlemen would be so kind as to give her like fifty feet."

The large one holding the nymph nodded and complied. "Just make her better."

CHAPTER SIX

Okay, so now, let me get this straight, *Hubert*," Rider said, walking back and forth, raking his hair as the motley group stood on the beach eyeing each other. "There's more of you guys over there in Nod trying to get asylum from Cain, and you want to hang with us?" He glanced at the Guardians that flanked him. "Did I hear right, or am I still shell-shocked and deaf from the blasts?"

The heavily armed Guardian team had given the entities wide berth, training their weapons on the strange creatures before them and taking aim at any human appendage that they thought they could wound.

"The bigger question is, what do y'all eat Stateside?" Shabazz said, gaining a fist pound from Mike.

The large entity that had identified himself as Hubert lifted his chin and seemed offended. "It is true that my father was a flesh eater, but he was from the royal legions of guard demons at the Incan palaces. However, my mother was a sacrificial virgin," he added with pride in his voice. "My soul is anchored on my mother's side of the family tree. Thus I do not pursue my baser nature and I am well educated in all the human culinary arts, *and* spent my time in Nod learning world cultures and foreign languages. I hope that alleviates your concerns."

"His *soul*?" Jose said in a sideline whisper to Marlene.

"And you should be the one to cast aspersions, brother," Hubert said in a huff, his tail beginning to twitch. "I thought Guardian teams of Neteru rank were not besotted by prejudices?"

Jose chuckled nervously and simply stared at the being that looked perfectly human from the nose up. He scratched his head as he peered at something that had mellow brown eyes, but whose skin turned green and black in splotches from the fangs down, bore huge leathery wings, and had a spaded tail that hung out beneath black military fatigues. "Okay, my bad, but the packaging, man . . ." Jose finally said.

"I cannot help that." Hubert looked away as the nymph petted his huge shoulders.

"You've hurt his feelings," she said, her voice a soft, angry murmur of chastises. "Hubert is one of the nicest entities I know." She turned to Hubert when he looked away. "They didn't mean it; I'm sure once you're here a while you'll be able to cover up like we did in Nod so that *ignorant people* won't jump to conclusions."

Hubert rolled his shoulder. "The explosion the witch hit me with still hurts, that's all. I am used to humans like him by now."

"I'm not *a witch*," Marjorie said, her voice tense. "I am a Guardian with earth element powers, *mother* power, mister. And I don't care what refinement and culture you claim to have—touch my son again, and you'll see just how unrefined I can be!"

"I was only trying to get you to cease fire before one of us got hurt," Hubert said, rubbing his shoulder that still had a char mark from Marjorie's blast. "I wouldn't have hurt him."

The team stared slack-jawed as the nymph stood on tiptoes and kissed the huge, muscle-bulked green shoulder, and smiled.

"I can heal it later, all right?" the small, lovely creature said, her skin and wings glittering with pastel opalescent hues under the sun.

"Thank you, angel," Hubert murmured and kissed the top of her baby-blue hair. He looked up at Marjorie. "I am not a monster."

"I'm having an out-of-body experience," Marjorie said, pressing the heel of her palm to her forehead. "That *must* be it."

"Those are wonderful," the nymph remarked, and then looked at Marlene. "Thank you for making me feel better. It was the ash and soot in my lungs from all the bombs."

"Don't mention it," Marlene muttered.

The nymph gazed at Marlene with shimmering turquoise eyes. "Why would I not mention it? What you did was divine."

Marlene briefly closed her eyes. "Help us understand, because we *are* truly ignorant of what's going on right now."

"Well," the nymph said with a sigh, glancing around the weary group. "Some of us believed Cain when he said he wanted peace. A lot of hybrid angels are trapped over in Nod, too afraid or not quite strong enough, energy-wise, to get out on their own. A lot of demon hybrids feel the same way, but think it is safer to just hide with the masses and seem like they are going along with Cain. If they get slaughtered, their fate is much worse than those with angelic parentage, I'm afraid to say. So, do not judge them harshly because of their paralyzing fear; they have more to lose in the long run."

"I can only imagine," Marlene said in a weary voice. "I guess we never thought about it that way." She glanced around the team. "Is a lot of what we've been through in the past starting to make sense to anybody else on the team but me?"

"Mar, my brain is so tired that it feels like it's leaking out of my ears," Shabazz muttered.

"But Hubert is strong, as you have seen, and I wanted to be the first to talk to the one named Carlos Rivera that still has silver burning brightly within him. He can call out those more like me. So can Damali. So we gathered a small band of rebels and drew straws to make an escape. Some of us had to get word to the Neteru before it was too late and any of us coming over the barrier would be exterminated on sight by both the Neteru and Cain. We're refugees, caught in the middle of the war. We've always been caught in the middle with nowhere to turn. It was risky, but Hubert held me in his arms the whole time," she said, beginning to glow. "He is *amazing*. He's been our mentor of languages and philosophy for years."

"How come every time our boy Carlos goes somewhere, he comes back with a lot of drama?" Shabazz said, beginning to rake his locks and pace. "This family is beginning to get real strange looking, Mar. I'm serious."

"I'm thinking strategic advantage, though," Dan said calmly, look-ing at the bizarre but potential allies before them. "They know Cain," he added, locking gazes with Shabazz. "That's a serious advantage. They also know what's over there coming for us; we pretty much know what's gonna spew up from Hell and have been battling that for years . . . but if they hadn't come here like they did, we would have been caught blind-sided by Cain's hybrids' abilities."

"True dat," Jose said. "They didn't drop like they was supposed to, and a daylight firefight is a whole new ball game, holmes."

"Word," Big Mike agreed. "Better to know now than later."

"Aw'ight. Dan has a good point," Shabazz conceded, glancing at the hopeful nymph that hugged Hubert tighter.

"See, it was all in divine order," the nymph said with a swoon. "We meant no harm."

"Two questions, then," Jose said. "How do we know which ones among their group that look like Hubert, are cool? We don't wanna smoke 'em by accident. But I also wanna know how come the basic antidemon stuff didn't work."

"Excellent observation," Hubert rumbled, giving Dan and Jose a nod of respect. "Those of us that have not gone dark and still have a human soul will have the same reaction to things like sacred waters and salts as you would. But the answer to your first question is not so easy."

"Cain lied to us," another smaller Hubert-looking entity said. He was a fawn from the waist down and a winged gargoyle on top, but his eyes were that of a gentle doe's. "Once he escaped, he descended into Hell. Initially, we were excited, because we thought he was so bold, so courageous that he'd gone down there on his own on a suicide mis-sion to start the big war and to clean out the bowels of the pit. We felt his exit from Nod and rushed to his cliffside lair to stand watch at his pool." The entity's voice fractured with emotion.

"It's all right," the nymph said, going to the half-fawn and rubbing his small horns. "Tell them."

"When we got there, his own sphinxes were slaughtered . . . beau-tiful animals." The entity shook his head. "We all stood around his sensation pool thinking that perhaps there had been an abduction of our king, and we held the silver thought thread of his Neteru energy until it snapped . . . then burned away black." Tears now streamed down the entity's cheeks. "We thought he was dead," he said and then nodded toward the other more menacing-looking creatures around him. "So we called in for those that could follow a black line. Hubert and the other rebels bold enough to try followed it as far as they could, and got a life pulse below."

Hubert nodded. "Many of us were holding out hope that he would be what he claimed, a full living Neteru—and we would have followed him into battle against evil demon legions. But he deceived us. If we die in battle fighting for him, all of us are going straight to Hell with no hearing or pardon. That was not the deal. We'd served our time in Nod, and were supposed to fight on the side of righteousness in the final days, and if we died, ascend to the realms of Light." Tears filled the entity's eyes. "He lied to us . . . and we all loved him so. Respected him."

"Yessss," another entity hissed with a strange sibilance to its voice. It had the eyes and scaled skin of a serpent but underneath was human flesh, the body of a man, with wings, and yet it moved in a very fluid manner as it spoke. "The ssssensation tank in Cain's lair revealed much. I was an old friend of Zehiradangra . . . loved her with all my heart. We dragons are loyal and stick together, and I *told* her for yearssss that Cain had an incredibly dark sssssside, but sssshe wouldn't listen. He had thoroughly captured her curious mind, and his prowesssss . . . well, even I had to defer. But he is sssso ruthlesssss that after he caused her death he even gave her body over to his troopssss to feed on as a ssssacrificial offering. I vowed to sssservice whomever his greatest enemy was, and I do believe that would be Carlossss Rivera."

"Now *that's* deep," Mike said, shaking his head. "Cold-blooded."

"While we share your sentiments, we would appreciate it if you would refrain from the gross ethnic slurs and stereotypes," Hubert said, looking at Big Mike hard.

"Hey, my bad," Mike said, raising both hands in front of his chest. "But we been fighting y'all for years, so it's gonna take a minute to get politically correct with the vocabulary."

"You have not been fighting *us* for years," the nymph said in a snit. "You have been, and should continue to fight demons. We," she said, waving her arms before the other interesting members of her group, "are *not* demons. We are *hybrids* with human parents, and we were made before the banish edicts regarding intermingling with pure humans." She folded her arms and lifted her chin. "Some of those who look like me are more deadly than these gentlemen here."

"They've got angels that have turned?" Berkfield just stared at the nymph.

"Yes," the nymph said flatly. "Their wings are often—but not always—gray, or falcon brown, and some are black like a raven's. Just because they are feathered doesn't mean a thing. And why should that surprise you, anyway? The most revered, most handsome, the one with the most beautiful voice fell, went pitch black in his spirit, and is now the owner of a silver tongue of lies."

"Touché, sister!" Rider said. "Damn."

"Correct," the nymph said, seeming vindicated as she walked back toward Hubert and hugged him.

"See, I like her because she's smart," Hubert said, stroking the nymph's hair. "My friends and I might have been tricked to go with Cain, except for one of us that had known Zehiradangra well."

Silence fell between the two groups on the beach as the house behind them burned out of control. Rider looked at the small stash of remaining ammo on the ground and then back at the blaze.

"Why does it always come to this, I ask myself time and again?" Rider sighed and checked his magazine and then put his weapon in its holster. "So now what?"

"We must eat," the nymph said carefully, "and hide until sunrise. Those not hybrid will hunt us down, unless we have a Neteru protector." She glanced around. "Did the female Neteru go with Cain?"

The team passed nervous glances.

"Not to my knowledge," Marlene hedged. "Why?"

"He brought her to his lair, twice, I believe," the nymph said, her gaze lowered, "and he had her blood scent on him. . . . The gossip in the alleys was rife about that. This is why we did not seek her. We had to be sure we had true amnesty." She looked up with fear. "That is why we fought—they fought. They could smell her here, even though Carlos also left his blood beacon in Nod . . . during uhmmm . . . an encounter with Zehiradangra, which also led us to this beach. We were frightened and thought that this could be the female Neteru's lair with Cain, perhaps. It is all so disorienting. His troops are preparing for a full-scale assault, and he will behead anyone suspected of treason."

"Carlos did *a female dragon*?" Shabazz muttered, looking at Berkfield.

"Damali and Carlos *got married,*" Marlene said, cutting a glare at Shabazz and then returning her line of vision to the foreign entities. "All that mess is history. If you guys will help us, we'll help you."

"Fair exchange is no robbery," Hubert said, valiantly sticking out his chest.

"Do all you guys from down there say that?" Rider slapped his forehead.

"It is a very old saying and a revered one amongst our kind. I do not understand your tone."

"Everybody just be cool," Marlene said, becoming exasperated. "Look, our Neteru team is doubly strong because we have two working in tandem. A male and female with perfect-pitch, balanced energy. We need a way to identify you guys."

"If Carlos is like Cain, with our shared DNA from the realms, we could send him images of each face that we know to be a friend," Hubert suggested.

"Well, ya better think of something, because in a serious firefight, it's easy enough to clip your own men, let alone somebody that's got on a uniform, so to speak, from the enemy side." Berkfield glanced around the group. "You just saw what happened. Your noses were off, our eyesight told us what to point and shoot at, so we need an identifier."

"Not to throw water on the ID process, but didn't you say you had a choice?" Rider looked at the assembled hybrids.

"Yes," the nymph said slowly. "We all do."

"Then, permit my skepticism just this one time, team," Rider said, spitting on the sand. "The human heart is fickle. I've been living proof topside that decision-purgatory exists when it comes to that— long story. But what if while we're in the middle of a firefight behind enemy lines, and you suddenly decide that, since Cain is kicking our asses with his Hell troops, then maybe you made a wrong decision so you'd like to make amends. . . . Do you see where I'm going and how this could become a very fucked-up situation fast with you at our back or flanks?"

"I ain't trying to be funny," Mike said, nodding in agreement with Rider.

"My vote," Jose said, "is for y'all to leave a calling card, and when our generals get back, let them put an eye on you. If their senses say it's cool, then we'll work with you. But if not . . . I don't know."

"Then your lead mother-seer can come forward and I can give her my image for Carlos—"

"I ain't comfortable with that, Hubert," Shabazz said, stepping in front of Marlene. "Until one of our Neterus checks you out, you ain't sending a demon transmission up into my woman's head."

"He's right," Marlene said with a shrug. "I don't roll like that with an unknown entity."

Hubert stooped down and tore off a piece of the T-shirt Rider had tossed earlier for the nymph to lie on, slit his arm with a fang, swapped it with the fabric, and flung the bloodied rag to Shabazz. "I understand," he said flatly. "Give that to Rivera as my calling card. This way he can track us, hone in, and send a signal. But our hope is that he has mercy."

"It is getting late and it will be a long and periloussss flight back to the ruinssss," the snakelike entity said.

"We must hide there, where we have family lines, old energy bands that can strengthen us," the nymph said. "We have distant relatives in Tulum that might take us in. Your young initiates can help with div-inations of where Cain's troops might attack. Be safe."

"Hold up," Dan said, looking at the nymph and then at Heather.

"You do not see the energy field about her?" The nymph tilted her head. "It is magnetic," she said, pointing to Heather, then to Jasmine, and finally to Krissy and Marjorie. She tilted her tiny head and a bright smile came out on her small, pixielike face. She wiggled her fingers at Inez and then Juanita. "They all have it. Six of them, plus the one who healed me, makes divine seven—how wonderful!" She lowered her arm and smiled brightly at Heather. "Your specialty is standing stones, isn't it? I have a lot of family that is carved in the stones. Why don't you use your gift more?"

"Whoa . . ." Marlene said, looking at Heather and Jasmine. "If ever there was a time to step up, ladies."

Hubert nodded. "Place the three elder seers in the center of a standing stones formation—they need the power of female three. That one," he said pointing at Marjorie, "is strong and is your druid stone centerpiece." He then looked at Marlene, Juanita, and Inez. "Make the inner circle around the one with one green eye and one blue eye, a true cat clan derivative. Her genetics bear out." He immediately brought his attention away from Marjorie and looked at Heather. "That one . . ." He shook his head and glanced at Dan. "Is she yours? A permanent bond?"

Dan bristled and so did the nymph as Heather smiled and shyly looked away.

"Where are you from?" Hubert rumbled, his voice dipping seductively.

"Scot mother, Ghanaian father . . . both keepers of standing stones," Heather said with a half-smile.

"I am what I am, and DNA being what it is," Hubert chuckled, "but she's *one hell of a witch*." He tucked away a smile as the nymph stomped on his instep. "My apologies. But, er, if you put the very pretty fragile one . . . that delicate lotus flower beside her, and *whew* . . . that one," he said motioning to Krissy, releasing a whistle. "They did not dress them like this in my day."

"Hey, the closer it gets to late afternoon and feeding time for you fellas," J.L. said, unholstering a weapon in a lightning move, "the more inclined I am to be extremely prejudiced."

"Ya got that right," Berkfield said.

The serpentine-looking entity smiled. "It is just that it hasss been a while ssssince we have been out of Nod, and to fall upon a Neteru team with ssssuch an embarasssment of richessss is exssssceptional. He meanssss no harm."

"Truly I do not," Hubert said with a toothy grin, ignoring the bee-stinglike swats the nymph pummeled against his massive torso. "Nonetheless. The three, on natural rock formations, around the center seer who also has Wicca in her line, with the outer magnetic ring of young Wicca initiates, should be able to accomplish a divination regarding which direction Cain's troops will advance from. The rocks are important, because all the stones on the planet were created at the same time, and old ruins are where Cain will form base camps to energy-strengthen his men."

"Like a human lighthouse, almost?" Rider said, wiping his palms down his face. "Now that's wild."

Hubert chuckled and looked out toward the sea. "She needs a consistent energy source though. Use the one with red hair, who is most gifted. Right now, what is within her is latent, until it is charged. This would be a polar opposite of her energy. Dark covens go deep within the caverns to pull this from any number of entities, but I am sure your team would abhor such methods."

"We don't go dark, for *any* reason," Marlene said firmly. "Not even for vital information or extra powers. No black masses, dark rituals, whatsoever." She scanned the group and then looked at Heather and Jasmine hard. "The only reason we allowed them into the Guardian fold was because they came clean, had no blood on their hands, and hadn't done any sacrifices. So, you boys had better come up with another option."

"There is another option," Hubert smiled. "One that has always been preferable for releasing unified energy, but I will defer to my friend's sensibilities," he said sheepishly when the nymph tried to push his bulky form and then punched his arm.

"So you're saying that if we could all stand around like on those beach breakers," Heather said, pointing out to a ridge of black rocks in the distance, "I could warn the team . . . but the problem is, right now I'm as good as a dead car battery?"

"I don't know this 'car battery,'" Hubert said, dropping his voice to an even lower, seductive tone, and receiving another nymph stomp that he ignored, "but you do need a male blast from something that can hold a charge, baby."

"Okay, that's fucking it!" Dan shouted, gripping his Glock sideways and pushing past Shabazz and Rider. Blue-white energy rippled over his skin and static electricity made sections of his blond hair stand up on his head.

Hubert chuckled. "A tactical Guardian," he said with a bow. "My apologizes, Miss. I see you have a worthy *battery* already."

"If Carlos and Damali don't hurry up and get back here . . ." Marlene muttered, watching sections of the hacienda collapse as smoke continued to spiral.

"Why don't you allow the cute one to draw the dragonsss?" the serpentine hybrid asked. "You sssshould have had flagsss all around your fortresss that could come to life. Are you not from the Old World, my lovely, lovely artissssst? Tell me Tibet or India . . ."

"The Philippines," Jasmine said with a shy curtsy, making Bobby spit.

"Clossse enough," the serpent hybrid murmured in a low sexy tone, beginning to seductively sway. "I could ssshow you what Zehiradangra looked like if—"

"I don't think so," Bobby said, stepping in front of Jasmine. "Just tell us what she's gotta do to protect base camp."

"Paint on white fabric for purity," the nymph said, folding her arms and scowling at the leering male entities around her. "Forgive them. Anyway. If you have a tactical Guardian with charged blood that is in harmony with her energies, you may use that. No horrible blood sacrifices and dark spells," she added in a tight voice that made Hubert smile and look away. The nymph shivered. "Eeew . . . disgusting!"

"Like . . . uh," Bobby said, glimpsing Jasmine, "somebody who, uh, is close to her?"

"A wizard would be perfect, especially if he has a magnetic attraction to her." The nymph's voice softened as she glimpsed Marjorie. "It wouldn't take much."

"How close, Bobby?" Marjorie said, her eyes narrowing.

"Friends, Mom," Bobby said, opening his arms. "That's all, for the good of the team."

"Stand down, Marj," Berkfield muttered. "It's a lost cause and a done deal . . . like you told me." He cut a glare toward J.L. "Remember that conversation about having to accept the unacceptable?"

Marjorie walked away and stood by Marlene, fuming. "Fine."

"Just let her draw with his blood onto the fabric and with the right energy jolt . . ." the nymph said, lowering her gaze with a smile, "whatever she draws will come to life to always fight on your side. It might get you through the night, if your Neterus do not return before dark."

"I can sketch anything crazy she wants," Jose said, his tone open and no longer defensive. "Then Jasmine could trace over it with a brush or knife, whatever we can salvage here on the beach. Just dot along the lines I draw so you don't have to take more than a pint from Bobby." Jose looked at Marjorie and spoke in a conciliatory tone. "For the team."

"But she will need her polarities adjusted by a warlock or a wizard," the nymph said, swallowing a shy smile. "It is usually done in a private exchange, but you all probably would not sanction that."

Bobby smiled and looked away as his mother cringed. "Uh, yeah, no problem."

J.L. bit his lip and tried to keep from laughing as Berkfield cast a dirty look in his direction.

"My daughter ain't participating in no freaky luau on the beach, got that J.L.? I don't care what her gift is from her mother's side. As it is, with all this hocus-pocus, the Covenant is probably flatlining! Wait until Father Pat hears about this shit. . . . This is waaay outside the boundaries of organized—"

"You heard that?" Inez said, glancing at Mike and then out toward the sea.

Everyone fell quiet as Big Mike neared Inez.

"No, suga. What is it?" he said, tilting his head like a giant hunting dog.

Inez's gaze became distant and glassy. "It's like drums," she murmured, holding the group hostage with her words. "I can see stuff moving in the stones, like serpents coming alive. I heard it first, and then felt it, before I finally saw it." She shivered hard and wrapped her arms around herself. "It's in some kinda old ruins."

Hubert nodded. "Aztec."

"My baby done seen and heard some shit like in a real vision?" Mike smiled wide and hugged Inez off her feet. "You did it! You heard some mess that even *I* couldn't hear?"

"I'm finally coming into my own, ya think?" Inez said, laughing as Mike swung her up higher in his hold.

"I can't believe it—you actually heard something creeping before me, suga, dang!" He laughed hard and set Inez down with a sloppy kiss, making her giggle. "Plus, you got visions . . . shoooot . . . we can talk about this later, one-on-one. But, uh, I really don't want you messin' with the unknown until we can thoroughly check it out, though."

"Yeah, well, I don't care who sees what, my daughter ain't doing no ceremony on the beach," Berkfield said, folding his arms.

"Nor is my son," Marjorie said, fussing as she glimpsed Jasmine. "No matter what he might have done before, all this sounds too dangerous. Spiritually speaking."

"Yeah, and Heather isn't participating in anything until we know who you guys really are," Dan argued.

"Word," Jose said, glancing at Juanita, then Hubert.

"Shit, you ain't gotta worry about me," Juanita said, holding Jose's gaze. "I don't mess with no spiritual nothin' I don't understand. Been there. Didn't like where it took me."

"All right, y'all," Marlene said in a tight voice designed to reinsert order back into the situation that was dissolving into sure mutiny. "A lot of what we've had to do recently is outside of normal sanctions—dealing with Carlos being one of them, but you see how the Light worked that crazy scenario out. And I can name a hundred other examples. But all of it worked out because we did it under prayer, with guidance, good intent, and . . ."

Marlene threw up her hands. "Lawdy, I don't know. All I'm sure of is we've gotta do something, and these, uh, beings, are giving us something to work with right now. Plus, after that brand-new vision of Inez's kicked in, we oughta try and locate the source of the disturbance. The Aztecs ruled in Mexico, and if you haven't noticed, people, that's where we are—so sticking our heads in the sand and acting like nothing is coming for us isn't an option. Good job, 'Nez. We needed to know that." Marlene glanced back at the flaming hacienda. "Anybody else got any suggestions about how to hunker down, create a fortress on the beach while we wait for Hell's gates to open?"

When no one spoke and the grumbles of discontent subsided, Marlene pressed on. "Okay then. First off, we're gonna have to move waaay down the beach, maybe go find Carlos and Damali's honeymoon villa to hole up in until they get back, because we can't stay here. That place was covered in nothing but white Light from the marriage. If these guys honed in on the hacienda, then anything else will come here as a first stop. Plus, if Carlos and Damali see this destruction, I'm pretty sure they'll instantly scan for us and lock in where only they can see in—their last protected hold up—the villa. We can pretty much guarantee that they'll head toward it and I'll keep a sweeping telepathy channel open for them. We might be remote from the town, and things in Mexico move slow, but sooner or later investigators and a fire company will come snooping around. I just hope we got all the ammo out so nothing blows."

"Then the newbies can, uh, do their protection thing and we'll set up a perimeter," Shabazz said, his tone weary.

Rider nodded and held up the T-shirt rag. "We'll pass on your calling card. Thanks for the info."

"That was some deep science that our team has been trying to crack for days," Jose admitted. "We have all these new team members and gotta get 'em up to speed with the quickness. We owe you on that."

"Much obliged," Hubert said. "You gave us possible amnesty and a potential meeting with your generals. Therefore—"

"We know, we know," Rider said, shaking his head. "Fair exchange is no robbery. Sheesh!"

"How come what starts out as a fairly normal day," Rider said, jumping down out of one of the Jeeps that had been salvaged before the hacienda blew, "never works out that way?"

No one responded to Rider's sarcasm as the team cased the perimeter of the villa, groups of Guardians piling out of Hummers, Jeeps, and Land Rovers on full alert. Once satisfied that the coast was clear, senior team members went in first, all senses keened, and ensured the house was vacant.

"All clear!" Berkfield shouted out the front door.

Immediately hands and arms began moving supplies into the villa in a fast-moving assembly line of bodies. Shabazz's locks crackled and arced a charge, and Rider smiled a half-smile.

"Don't say it, brother," Shabazz muttered with a chuckle.

Rider raised an eyebrow and gave Shabazz a sheepish grin, and then inhaled deeply. "You think our young tacticals are gonna be able to hang in here?" Rider motioned with his chin toward J.L., Bobby, and Dan as he unpacked ammo to spread on the counter with Shabazz, moving away the refuse of half-eaten dinners and dishes.

Shabazz chuckled. "The charge coming up off this joint ain't no joke," he said in a private mutter. "I'm more worried about Jose, though. Brotherman looks like he's about to drop fang up in this piece."

"Well," Rider said in a philosophical tone, sighing hard. "At least there's no sulfur trail in here." He stopped and looked at Shabazz. "Did you notice that about the hybrids? They don't trail warning signals like general, regulation demons."

"I know," Shabazz said, glancing up at Rider. "They've got a more human vibe to them, almost. In the hacienda, I could sense motion but wasn't registering blue-arc from their presence."

Rider nodded and shoved the half-eaten meal Damali and Carlos had left into the trash. "I gotta get to Gabby."

Shabazz nodded. "You call her?"

"Yeah. Since her initiates came, I've been calling every number I had for her. Everything's been disconnected. Last I heard, she was heading toward Vegas to set up shop there, since New Orleans was gone, L.A. was hot. . . . I'm worried, man."

"We'll get Mar on the case, as soon as we get Damali and Carlos home. She can't do a double sweep like that." Shabazz laid a hand on Rider's shoulder.

"I know . . . but maybe since Marjorie is her sister . . ."

The two older Guardians stared at each other.

"Worth a try, but Mar's gotta teach her quick how to open a channel without having it tracked," Shabazz said cautiously. "Feel me?"

"Yeah, I do," Rider said, his shoulders slumping. "You wouldn't wanna make a run with me, though . . . to, uh, maybe go by a lair?"

Shabazz closed his eyes and let his hand drop away from Rider's shoulder. "Aw . . . man . . . I forgot. Tara."

Rider nodded and looked away. "I don't wanna open it to possibly injure her to daylight, but if I can get a word to her somehow . . ."

"Man, listen," Shabazz said. "Me, you, and Mike, we'll ride at sundown. You go to Yonnie's spot during the day, armed, and surprise him, some real fucked-up shit could happen. But the minute the sun sets, we can holla at him with a little distance between him and us. I'm with you. Cool?"

Rider leaned against the counter, his line of vision roving the group that had fanned out and was securing entry points to the villa. "Yeah. That makes sense." Rider dropped his head back and closed his eyes. "I'm between a fucking rock and a hard place on this one, 'Bazz . . . just like old times."

Dan walked beside Heather along the beach, and then slowly slipped his hand into hers. Hot current ran from his palm into her soft fingers and he watched her breath hitch as the blue-white static charge eased up her arm and covered her breast. She flinched and briefly closed her eyes as the static charge circled a pouting nipple, licked it, and then encompassed the other one. Tempering himself, Dan released her hand and clasped his hands behind his back, humiliation scalding his face.

"I'm sorry," he said quietly, watching the sun glisten in her hair. He laughed self-consciously as she fought a smile. "The villa had a serious charge in it, and we were all pumped after what went down back at the hacienda. Didn't mean to get fresh with you. It sorta slipped out."

She glimpsed him from the corner of her eye and kept walking. "I like you, too, Daniel," she murmured, and then looked off toward the rocks. "I know we just met under very insane circumstances ten days ago . . . but it's like I've known you forever."

"I know what you mean," he said quietly as she stood looking up at a long natural pier of huge, jagged rocks that jutted out into the crashing waves.

If she only knew how it also felt like it had been forever waiting for her. Just like Christine had promised, the moment he'd seen her, the ache for Krissy had dulled and then vanished. Heather's eyes and voice literally drank him in during their field exercises, the laughter in the hacienda, and the long, wonderful nights just sitting with her on post talking, learning her moods under the stars. The one kiss she'd allowed had almost brought him to his knees, but there hadn't been enough time or privacy for more.

"You think you can do it . . . I mean, create a human lighthouse up there?"

She chuckled softly and began climbing up to find a flat enough surface for the number of bodies the formation would require. "I don't know," she said merrily, pulling herself up and sensing on her hands and knees. "These are sooo old and so virginal . . . they've never been tapped."

Heather looked at him with an expression that devastated him, but he remained cool on the outside.

"Dan, you have to feel these," she murmured, then looked back down and caressed the stones.

His body lurched and his mouth went dry as he watched her graceful hands hover above the jagged rocks, her lithe body clad in jeans and a jewel-green tank top, her spine dipping into a gentle sway while she balanced on all fours.

"Okay," he breathed out, and touched the rocks, not daring to climb up there with her just yet. But the moment his palms splayed against the rocks, to his chagrin, a blue-static charge fanned out from his fingers and rushed over the rocks, leapt a quarter inch to her hands, and spread over her.

She just looked at him. "Wow," she whispered.

He immediately pulled his hands away and walked into the sea up to his boots, needing distance and to cool down. The throb in the erection she'd given him was pounding in his groin with the same intensity of the surf.

"Uh, listen, about that . . . that was an accident," he said, embarrassed, unable to deny that he wanted to climb all over her like his charge. "But I think it was the jolt those guys were talking about," he added, beginning to breathe hard while keeping his back to her so she couldn't see just how affected he really was.

"That's it!" she said, laughing. "Dan, take off your boots, and walk into the water, and then lean over and touch the rocks while I'm on them."

He glimpsed her over his shoulder, then became mesmerized by her brilliant smile. For a moment he couldn't move. The afternoon sun was behind her, framing her in light, her auburn hair glistened with red, copper, brown, and gold . . . and her small heart-shaped mouth drew him, but her gray eyes practically smoldered with excitement as her new powers began to unfold. His gaze traveled down her body in pure reflex, following her pretty toffee-hued skin down to her tank top, over the swell of her unrestrained breasts to linger on the tight, tiny pebbles that her nipples had become and then raked across her flat belly down her pelvis to then take in the full length of her shapely legs.

"I can't," he admitted in a quiet, gravelly tone, knowing full well what sea-salt-infused water would do to the hard current that was pulsing through him. If he did what she'd asked, and then touched the rocks, she would definitely be offended.

Her smile widened. "But you heard what that green guy told us," she said, laughing. "I have to start my dead car battery. Oh, Dan, I've never felt anything like this in my life!" She sat down on a flat area cross-legged, closed her eyes, and turned her face up to the sun. "All my life I've known I was different, and I was so afraid that I would have to one day make a pact that could steal me away from the sun forever. Then I find you guys, and now I'm learning what I can do for the good . . ." She opened her eyes. "I know it has a hot charge . . . but, I don't mind. If I was going to feel something so magical, I'm blessed it would be with you."

He turned slowly and ran his palm over his hair. "You're not mad that I'm sorta thinking like that about you this soon?"

She smiled and began picking at the nap in her jeans. "It's sorta natural, you know . . . for two people who really like each other and share a lot in common to feel a wee bit of chemistry. Doesn't mean it has to wind up going too far," she said, glancing up at him and then down the beach to the villa that was a half-mile away. "I wouldn't want your family to think that's the kinda girl I am, or lose their respect . . . or yours, given where I came from."

"You definitely wouldn't lose my respect," he said, coming closer to the stones and beginning to unlace his Timberlands. "We all came from some pretty wild places and nobody thinks like that," he said, talking faster as he yanked off each boot and hurled them to the dry sand. "I just wanted to be sure you liked me like that, too—before I sent that kinda charge your way. I mean, if you didn't feel like that, I don't want a weird vibe between us on the team, and uh, *God* you're beautiful, so I don't know how steady the charge would be, because, Heather, seriously, it's been a long time since I've felt a charge like this running through me. If you're not really into me, then I want us to still be cool, after. You know?"

Dan clamped his lips shut and could feel the muscles in his jaw working. The woman had him babbling and he knew he needed to shut up. He'd been down this road before with Krissy and didn't want to get burned again.

"I like you a *lot,* Daniel," she said softly and then leaned forward and placed her hands on the rocks. "You are so precious . . . and the fact that you would even worry about such a thing like that has stolen me away." She shook her head. "Do you know what kind of dark energies I've seen and that I've had to fend off while in Gabrielle's care? I never thought in a million years I'd be able to find a nice guy like you."

He waded into the water up to his calves and kept his gaze on her. "I never thought in a million years I'd find a woman as nice and as beautiful as you to care about me as a friend."

"Then the other ones that passed up on such a deal were crazy," she said, her voice dipping a bit. "You make a great friend."

"This isn't friendship energy that's arcing," he said, honestly warning her. "Even though we're friends."

She didn't move. "I didn't suspect that it would be," she said after a moment. "Sexual energy is the oldest and most natural energy between the opposite polarities of male and female," she said, shyly looking down at her hands. "It's as old as these stones."

Heather glanced up, and before she could draw a breath Dan had placed his hands against the rocks with a hard slap. The blue arc instantly sizzled up the boulders in a blue-tinged coating, crawling over it with a thick charge and then hit Heather so hard she fell backward. Dan yanked his hands away, the current rippling over him, charging his hair, and making him shudder as he began to walk around in a disoriented circle. When he looked up, Heather was leaning back on her elbows, breathing through her mouth.

"I . . . uh . . . didn't know it could—"

"I tried to warn you," he said, panting. "I shouldn't have stood in the water. It was stored up for a long time."

She dropped her head back and moaned as an aftershock of current rippled over her skin again. "Daniel . . . it won't stop. . . ."

His better judgment in shreds, he climbed up on the rocks to try to help her down. But as soon as his entire body slid onto the solid surface, she closed her eyes and moaned.

"Oh, God . . . Dan."

"Okay, okay, I'ma get you off of this charged surface," he said, putting one arm under her back and gently guiding her over the edge of the formation on the opposite side from the villa. "Take some deep breaths, and get out of sight of the house so you can pull it together and won't be embarrassed. I'm sorry, Heather. I . . . oh, shit . . . you feel so good."

They half-fell, half-slid into a sandy crag that was filled with water in a little tide pool between the massive boulders. The blue charge was all over the rocks, all over them, and Dan's bare feet were in the ankle-deep sea. Her palms swept up the sides of his flushed face and tangled in his static-ridden hair as she kissed him hard, her tongue seeking his.

His fingers cradled her head, allowing her thicket of auburn ringlets to glide between them as his arm protected her back. Joined at the pelvis, he couldn't have stopped moving against her if a war broke out on the beach. The long-awaited sensation of her touch dampened his lashes and smothered him as he tore his mouth away from hers to kiss her neck.

"You want to?" he asked in a ragged whisper, kissing her chin, her eyelids and the bridge of her nose quickly. "If not, I understand."

She nodded, her words choking out. "I do. Don't stop touching me. I never felt anything like this."

It was as though something within him had instantly snapped. He tugged at her tank top and her breasts bounced free. His mouth immediately sought the warmth of her cleavage and he closed his eyes and shuddered with a groan. She was gonna do it. *Actually let him.* He covered her breasts with his mouth and his hands, pulling her distended, rose-colored nipples between his lips, feeling the shiver go up her spine as she leaned in harder and sought his mouth.

Afternoon sun and her pulsing body produced instant sweat. His hair was wet now, adding to the charge as they grappled with jeans fastenings, kisses, entwined legs, creating friction sounds against the rocks between gasps. Her snug jeans and underwear were down around her knees and so were his, the feel of her silky, moist mound causing delirium.

"I can't get my pants all the way down," she said on a breathless chuckle.

It was true; her tight jeans didn't leave room enough for him to enter her.

She touched his face and looked at his pained expression and slipped from under him, but not far enough to totally break their physical connection. However, when the charge dipped from her slight movement away, he shuddered hard and groaned deep inside his throat.

"Please don't move," he said between his teeth with his eyes shut. "Don't break the charge," he said into her hair as she turned around and faced the rocks. "Oh, God . . ." he whispered hard into the crook of her neck as he slid against her creamy, smooth buttocks and let his hands trace her hips.

His face was burning and she threw back her head and flattened her palms against the hard surface before her, pushing away from the stones.

"Don't break my jaw on the rocks," she said with a gasp, laughing a little as he flattened her hard against them.

"I'm sorry," he said between deep breaths, and then placed a hand above her head to brace himself and protect her face. He stood that way for a moment, his forehead on her shoulders, remembering that she had never been entered . . . also remembering that she didn't have birth control.

"I'll be gentle," he said, kissing her shoulders and back. "Just for a little bit, and then I'll pull out, okay?"

She glanced over her shoulder with a question in her eyes. "I can't get pregnant right now . . . I—"

"I know, I know. I won't let that happen." He sounded insane to his own ears, knew he was on the border of a promise and a lie. But the charge had him, she had him, the agonized wait for the cosmos to send her had him. "I just want to feel you," he whispered, sweeping his lips against her fevered skin. "Just once," he said, his voice urgent and at the point of begging. "I *swear* I'll pull out."

She closed her eyes and nodded, as his hand slipped between her legs. His gentle caress made her bend over and dip her supple spine into a deep sway the moment his finger slid between her swollen folds and flicked her bud. "I trust you," she breathed out and then leaned back against him and climaxed hard.

Trembling and almost unable to breathe, he held her close and slid against her gently, opening her to be so tightly sheathed that he nearly wept. She might have trusted him, but he could hardly trust himself as he eased himself inside her, sensing, checking, feeling her reaction to be sure he wasn't hurting her. Holding on to the rocks and her waist he moved slowly, her slickness maddening.

"Tell me if I'm hurting you," he said in a ragged whisper into her hair. "I'll stop if I am."

She violently shook her head and moved back against him hard to take him in deeper. That's when he lost it, totally forgot everything he was entrusted with. Blue-arc current sent a bolt of energy down his spine, increased his thrusts, and linked his pending orgasm with hers.

Suddenly he pulled out of her, the humid air knifing him, but instinct and raw desire made her clamp her thighs tightly around him. A slicing contraction caused him to pelt her back with her name, making him move in ragged, jerking thrusts against her wet inner thighs, and then stop breathing as a climax seizure claimed him. Her voice rent the beach with his name, temporarily drowning out the surf, and she wriggled against him, trying to recapture him inside of her. But rather than risk catastrophe, he held her close and simply gulped air.

"We can't," he murmured against her ear, allowing his hand to pet her gently between her legs until she convulsed against him again. "Next time I'll be prepared."

"Okay," she gasped, leaning back against him. A slow giggle bubbled inside her. "Ya think we've charged the rocks?"

Daniel hugged her from behind and dropped his head against her shoulder, laughing softly, breathing into her hair. "I think they're good to go."

Bobby sat on the bedroom floor of the villa pressing a wet towel to the inside of his elbow, watching Jasmine as she lay on her belly. Her intense focus had knitted her lovely brows into a stern frown as she dabbed a toothbrush into a cup and spread crimson on a clean sheet along the lines Jose had drawn for her with a Sharpie.

He swallowed hard as he watched her small, lithe form stretch and work against the fabric. The charge left in the room by the honeymooners was almost enough to make him levitate.

"You know . . . they said it needed a jolt of energy to go with it," he murmured quietly, stretching out on the floor beside her and staring at her until her huge brown eyes stared back into his.

"I know," she whispered, glancing around the room like a thief.

"I haven't seen you in a year . . . and then when you came to the house in Arizona, things were pure chaos. Then, once we got here, I thought maybe we could sorta pick up where we left off?" He smiled, glanced up at the bed, and then down at the floor. "It's real quiet down here," he said, pressing on the floorboards under the Oriental carpet.

She lowered her gaze, a rosy blush forming on her cheeks. "But *your mother* is here, right in the next room. I wanted to in the worst way, but . . ."

"We could have died today," he said, coming closer and kissing her bare shoulder.

"I almost did when that creature grabbed you." Jasmine gazed up at him and kissed him slowly. "But your mother is here."

Bobby rolled over and stood without using his hands, kept his eyes on her, and strode over to the door. "Yeah, I know," he said, locking the bedroom door with a sexy smile. "She'll get over it."

Marjorie and Inez looked up at the same time, their lines of vision meeting Juanita's and then going to the hallway that led to the bedroom.

"Marj, let's you and I go see of we can find some driftwood to, uh-mmm, make stakes?" Marlene said cheerfully, grabbing Marjorie's sleeve and hustling her out of the villa.

Juanita shot Jose a glance that said *Don't even try it*. Dejected, he went back to sorting ammo. Inez went to the cabinets to rummage for grub to feed the team, while trying to ignore the intense sidelong glances Mike sent in her direction.

"Puhlease," Inez muttered under her breath. "After this morning, you must be crazy."

"I'm a Guardian, not a saint," Mike said under his breath, annoyed.

"Just like old times in Arizona," Shabazz muttered, shaking his head while reloading spent artillery.

"Gives me the hives," Rider said, scouring the cabinets with Inez. "Don't these kids know that at times like these, wine is like fruit punch? Damn, where is my old buddy Jack Daniel's when I need him?"

J.L. casually glimpsed Krissy from the corner of his eye. She smiled at him, and then redoubled her efforts to get a signal on the wireless laptop.

"Might get a better signal outside," he said in a slow, sexy tone. "Wanna take 'em outside and go take a walk . . . to uh, see if we can get a signal going?"

She giggled and then glimpsed her father, who was staring at them both, stone-faced. "Maybe later. Besides, we can't open up a wireless signal without a seal to be sure there'll be no demon interception." She kept her eyes on her father and offered him a broad grin. "I'd better stay here and get some regional maps of Central Mexico right now."

"Okay," J.L. said in a defeated voice, blue current suddenly running down his hands to black out the laptop system he'd been touching. He set the system aside and muttered a curse.

"Why don't you go walk it off," Mike said over his shoulder, chuckling, "before you fry another motherboard and get yourself smoked by Berkfield?"

CHAPTER SEVEN

Carlos walked out of the golden obelisk onto the beach, ready for war, blood in his eyes. He had never experienced such profound rage as what was quaking his system right now. But it took him a moment for his brain to sync up with the image before his eyes. The hacienda was in flames, full of spent gunfire, and the burning rubble carried a warning stench into the air. Fire engines and people were crawling all over what had been the Guardians' temporary compound. The faint scent of demon incursion was on the beach. He began running toward the blaze yelling the names of each team member before logic could stop him.

Mexican authorities pushed him back, and then took one glance at the blade he had in his hand, and drew on him. Carlos stepped back, stunned them with a quick energy pulse, and closed himself away into nothingness.

Frantic, he went back to the last place he knew there was a tracer of Damali. He had to contact her, get to her first before her mind broke from seeing that her entire family had been wiped out. Breathing hard, he spun around in circles, trying to get a lock on her and whatever had razed their family to the ground.

Too battle-hyped to filter out friend from foe, the vibrations and sounds coming from his villa meant more than one aggressor was inside. Invaders had already planted flags painted in blood on the beach, demon images fiercely emblazoned on sheets, boldly surrounding his villa with victory flags. It was Bobby's blood! The acrid scent of a huge demon wafted from the infested dwelling. His family's bodies were inside, still warm. A fire had been built—fucking flesh eaters were about to devour his people! Carlos inhaled as renewed fury choked him, the scents blending together to make him go blind with rage. He spit the taste of battle and death out on the sand. The two newest females on his squad had even been violated!

Adrenaline was making his ears ring. A very weak message was stabbing at his mind from Marlene. He became the wind itself, blade raised, the door a flimsy barrier that blew off the hinges before he'd even kicked it. Two hands gripped his sword as he crossed the threshold and then stopped. Guardians froze, hands held midtask, and eyes not even blinking.

Carlos stood still for a moment, silver burning a path across the rug from his gaze, his chest heaving, his mind scrambling to sync-up faces with heat tracers from familiar bodies. Then he slowly lowered his blade.

"You all right, dude?" Rider asked nervously, stepping away from the counter with his hands raised. He nodded toward a bloody rag on the drain board that had demon blood on it. "They left you a phone number and were looking for you, General."

"I thought . . ." Carlos sucked in a huge breath, closed his eyes for a moment, adrenaline still giving him the battle shakes. "The hacienda," was all he could say.

"Yeah, we had a little problem," Shabazz said calmly. "But we handled it, for now."

"In broad daylight?" Carlos said, coming into the villa and then leaning against the wall with a thud.

"Was crazy, boss," Big Mike said. He nodded to Inez. "Get our brother some water. I think this shock just used up one of his nine lives."

"I'm cool," Carlos said, allowing the blade to dangle at his side. "Where's D?"

"She didn't get back from the Queen's summit yet," Shabazz said. "She wasn't in the house when it happened." He shoved a stool away from the counter toward Carlos. "Sit down and take a load off, man. We got some crazy catching up to do before sunset."

Damali gripped her Isis as Aset kissed her gently and escorted her to the edge of the violet pyramid. There was nothing to say other than good-bye and Godspeed as she stepped into the strobe of the purple light. But . . . oh . . . woe unto Cain's no-good, low-life ass for what he had done to Carlos and Eve. Damn what he had done to her. She wasn't half as angry about that as she was about the other more dear hearts Cain had broken.

When her feet hit the beach, for a second all Damali could do was stare. *He had razed her house to the ground with her family in it?* She couldn't even propel her body forward as she watched plumes of billowing smoke rise from the hacienda. Emotions too numerous to sort rocked her mind, colliding fury with core-wrenching grief.

The frantic people who were fighting the blaze blended with fast-moving still-frame images of demons spiraling through the air from Nod, Mike's RPG blast, Marjorie's scream, Bobby being dragged across the floor by a spaded tail. "No!"

Carlos's war scent haunted the air like a thickening fog. She could see Shabazz and Rider emptying clips, Dan exploding holy water vials. Bobby's blood was fresh kill on the breeze. Damali jerked her head toward it; the scent was coming from the villa. She cringed and briefly closed her eyes. They had eaten the poor newbie alive!

Then she inhaled deeply and opened her eyes—Heather and Jasmine had been raped. Damali was shaking her head as rocks, the surf, grunting sounds fused with the image of victory flags planted in the four cardinal points around her and Carlos's villa. Even now she could smell a huge demon's scent coming downwind from there—had to be the one that was feeding on warm bodies pulled from the inferno.

But eleven, twelve entities had ransacked the house. The sand was still vibrating with their energy. A huge one had obviously stayed behind to create a base camp a few miles away in the old honeymoon villa. The reality brought instant insanity. She would slaughter Cain a hundred times over. Carlos had come home before her, and had made his last stand on the beach.

Damali threw her head back and squeezed her eyes shut. There was nothing left to live for. Her family was destroyed, her man killed, all she ever knew and loved. Her Isis was in the air, held by a two-handed grip above her head.

"Cain, *you motherfucker,* come get me! This is war!"

Cain dropped his goblet and stood. Fallon Nuit was on his feet along with Lilith. The three looked up at the ceiling as a blue-white arc of lightning parted the transport cloud of bats in the ceiling and scorched the center of the Vampire Council table. Clothed in armor within milliseconds, Cain rounded his throne.

"She called me," he breathed out, almost unable to speak. He materialized a Black Death sword in his trembling hand. "Fallon, she called me."

Lilith backed away from the table. "She's insane . . ."

Fallon shook his head and smiled. "She's fantastic."

Carlos jerked his attention around two seconds before Mike did. "Damali!" he hollered. "Oh, shit, baby—no!"

Mike was on his heels and then lost him as Carlos cleared the back deck and was running headlong down the beach. Shabazz tore behind them and the other Guardians came to a slow stop as they realized it was futile.

"Damn!" Mike yelled, kicking sand. "She called Cain out when she saw the hacienda."

"By herself?" Shabazz said, gripping Mike bulging biceps.

Rider began walking in a circle. "Kiss my ass! We should have posted something there for her!"

Mike nodded toward Carlos who was frantically searching the shoreline, blade raised, and yelling Damali's name. "*Now,* we've got a problem."

— •—•—• —

A black bolt of lightning had hit her squarely in the chest, knocking the wind out of her, and her back collided with a cavern wall. But being temporarily stunned hadn't made her forget. Battle rage brought her off the wall, swinging the Isis with both hands. She couldn't have ventured a guess about which Level of Hell she was on, nor did she care. They could battle all the way down to Seven and beyond.

Steel met steel and the collision sent a hard quake up her forearm into her shoulder, almost chipping a tooth as she set her jaw.

"Sweetness, let me explain," Cain said in an amused tone, backing up as she advanced on him blow for blow.

"You murdered my entire family!" Damali yelled, and then released a war cry that made rocks fall.

"What? Are you mad?" Cain said, catching her next swing against his black blade, and then quickly wrapping his tail around her arm.

"Let me go, you bastard. I will cut out your heart, rip it from your chest with my bare hands!" she screamed, not caring that he was a lot bigger than she'd remembered and a whole lot stronger.

"Your family is alive," he said in a calm, sensual tone, still holding her arm hard with his massive tail.

She yanked away, the scales scraping flesh off her forearm and leaving it bloody and raw. "Where are they?" she panted through her teeth, ignoring the searing pain.

"On Earth, I suppose," he remarked coolly, now beginning to circle her. "You think I would do something like that to you?"

She straightened and lifted her chin, on guard for a potential lunge. His admission felt like he'd punched her with relief. For a moment she couldn't answer. "Why not?" she finally said and spat, remembering all the other offenses she needed to slaughter him for. "You tore out your mother's heart. . . . Do you have any idea where Eve is now?"

Cain lowered his shoulders and glanced at the demon-skull hand protector of his sword. "She knows." He sighed heavily. "That is regrettable. I imagine she did not take my decision well." He looked at Damali and slowly smiled.

"You *imagine* she didn't take it well?" Incredulous, Damali leveled her blade. "The mother of mothers is prostrate on the floor *of Council*," she shouted. "Her firstborn son is killing her slowly. The woman can barely draw her next breath! Her heart went into that throne with you, Cain. What about this don't you get?"

"Her condition is regrettable," he said calmly, beginning to circle her again. He tilted his head as he stared at her when they took warrior stances and squared off again.

"Regrettable? Regrettable! She is my queen!" Damali took a running swing and scored his chest armor, but he deflected the blow with a defensive move.

"I love you," he breathed out, raw desire in his voice as his eyes went crimson. "You would battle me because of my mother's honor. Do you know what that means to me?"

"You're crazy!" Damali shouted, lobbing three steel-to-steel clashes, but he caught her blade with his and drove it down to the rocky floor and stepped on it, holding it down with his boot.

"Totally insane over you. Devastation, come let me heal your arm. The combination of your fury and blood in here is—"

She pivoted, using the blade as anchor and caught him dead center in the chest with a hard, flat-footed blow. But she backed up quickly when he didn't move and just looked at her with a handsome smile. He removed his foot slowly from her blade and allowed her to pull it away. She backed up farther, putting ten feet between them and glanced around. Okay, she was on Level One, not in too deep.

"You shouldn't have taken that throne," she said, fury still roiling but now mixed with deep concern. This bastard was *waaay* stronger than she remembered. Dante wasn't even that solid, and definitely didn't have the Neteru moves to go with it.

"Are you telling me that your rage was born from your concern for me . . . and for my mother?" he whispered, advancing toward her slowly. He licked his lips and then glanced at her arm, sealing the wound. Inhaling deeply, he kept walking forward. "Damali, you simply render me—"

"Hey, motherfucker—back up!" Damali said, judging the edge of the precipice behind her that yawned into an abyss, and whether or not she could get up onto a boulder fast enough to avoid him.

Cain's gaze narrowed as he stared at Damali's throat. "While I was away, he abducted you with a battle bite?" Cain's thundering voice bounced off the crevices and cavern walls. "Infidel! He forced you to marry through such brutality? I knew you would never forsake me! The union is void! Come to me, my angel, and stop this foolishness. We will vanquish his armies together!"

She was motion. Five boulders up there was a ledge and a wide enough space to battle before making it to an exit tunnel. A shape-shift would be her friend. Then she was out. Only problem was, when she got to the top, he was standing there, and had the gall to reach down and offer her a hand. The bird thing wasn't working, in fact, nothing was. The queens needed to stop tripping and come together, like now!

"Come to me," Cain said in a quiet voice, pulling her up with one strong yank and stopping her wrist in midswing. "You do not want to take off my head."

"Like hell," she said, reinforcing her grip on the blade, refusing to let him see how panic-stricken she was. Then it slowly dawned upon her . . . in her outrage she'd told him that her Neteru Council of Queens had been weakened by Eve's devastation. *He knew* what that meant. She'd been played!

Her wrist felt like it was made of papier-mâché in his hold, and he wasn't really applying pressure. This was *not* how this was supposed to go.

Cain chuckled low in his throat. "You have a wonderful dexterity with words. I love anything that rolls off your tongue. Let me taste it."

She yanked her head back when he tried to kiss her, and he quickly put both of her hands behind her, the Isis scraping the ground. When she tried to lift her knee to go for a groin kick, or alternatively stomp his instep, his tail whipped between her thighs, anchoring them open. Fifteen different shape-shifts raced through her head, every power that she had hummed inside her, but it was like turning the key in a car engine and just getting a click—dead battery. A weak energy pulse arced from her palms, but the Isis caught the charge between them, sending a medium current into the cavern floor. Now she was scared, something she'd rarely been. It was time to bargain.

"Why would you make a deal with the Unnamed One?" she said in Dananu, breathing hard. "He'll rob you, take everything, every beautiful gift you once owned, once it's all said and done."

"Probably," Cain murmured, inhaling her scent in a hard nuzzle against her hair. "But that will be a very long time from now." He closed his eyes and sent craven images into her skull by force. "There is so much that I want to do with you," he whispered into her ear. "Choose one and I will make it so, lover."

She thought about using her teeth as a weapon, but then thought better of it. What was the point? She had to say something, do something, to get him up off her to buy distance. Seconds felt like minutes as he pressed against her befouling her mind.

"Speak to me again in Dananu," he said with a shudder, sliding against her. "I did not *know* you could speak it thus."

"Brother, why you got me all up against a cavern wall like this, huh? Tacky. When I first met you, you behaved like a royal—had wet my drawers, could sing, made me scream 'cause it was so good, and I hadn't even gotten any, for real. But see how one tumble into that throne has jacked you up?"

Cain pulled back to look at her and smiled. "I missed you. Perhaps that is what has made me too eager."

"Well, some homecoming."

They stared at each other.

"Damali, let me say this to you once. I am not the same man you met before. If this is a ruse . . ."

"There's no fraud. I'm scared of your ass now. I wasn't that before," she said in a sexy whisper in Dananu. "What happened to the lair in Nod? It was beautiful. This frightens me. Can't we go there?"

"I have something better downstairs," he said, nipping her jugular. "All black marble. Would you like to see it?"

Go lower into the pit with failing powers? No way.

"Nah, here is fine, but the rocks—"

He crushed her mouth with a kiss and transferred both her hands into one of his, still able to hold her, which was truly disconcerting.

"It's all in your sweat," he said through a ragged breath. "Adrenaline, fight pheromone, rage, fear . . . that and your skin, the way you feel beneath me. I've suffered for you, woman. . . . This time I'm being selfish, but will make it up to you at the next vanishing point."

Her clothes had dissolved with his before she could blink. He'd knocked her head back so hard with his massive jaw that for a second she was sure she'd blacked out. Something seven feet tall with an iron grip had her. She was looking at his old Neteru tattoo blackened in the center of his chest; all silver was gone. The flash of mate-bite fangs made her yank her head to the side with a scream, and he almost bit the wall, but came up furious.

"I forbid it over my husband's bite!" she yelled, going for a battle versus whatever else Cain had planned. "I chose the better man, asshole! No matter what you do, you'll never be Carlos Rivera!"

Her hands were suddenly loose, but not soon enough to block the backhanded blow that sent her sprawling. The Isis went one way, and she went the other. Stunned, she had never had the snot knocked out of her like that in her life. No demon or vamp had landed a blow so squarely. Not even in the Amazon had she been sucker punched and unable to instantly get up. This time she'd heard bone actually snap. Tasting blood in her mouth, her lip split, she quickly tried to stand, but was flattened by a black arc drilling heat into her chest.

"You make me nearly lose an empire, ransom my soul, disgrace my mother, and raise an army for you, and you tell me *what*! *Rivera* is the better man? Bitch . . . I will slaughter you! Will fuck you to death down here! Are you *insane*?"

Gone was the gorgeous hunk with the megawatt vamp smile. Huge wings ripped out of Cain's shoulders, casting a shadow over her in the dim fire-lit cavern. His eyes went from a desirous crimson glow to solid black gleam. Fast-moving ghostly phantoms whizzed by, taking cover as the cavern imploded with a sonic boom and flames. Damali shielded her face to the inferno with her again bleeding forearm. The searing ground against her naked body made her arch in agony and try to reach the Isis and draw it to her, but just as quickly as she did so, Cain's massive body blanketed hers.

"You have tested my patience for the last time, lover," he hissed in her ear. "When I am done with your disloyal, traitorous carcass, you will be vomiting blood and choking on your own womb."

Dark energy was prying her thighs open; the cavern floor was scorching the flesh on her back. She could smell her own skin burning, hear it sizzle. Sulfur fumes were making her choke and gasp, while the heavy male demon on top of her was crushing the air out of her lungs.

A prayer for survival sent silver shock into her mind. If she could just live to fight another day. He'd dropped twelve inches of battle-length fangs and had pressed them to her throat in a snarling threat, breaking the skin. His talons were digging into her forearms as he lifted her hands above her head. An angry, razor-sharp tail swished like a bullwhip in the dense smoke. Something akin to marble, the length and width of a baseball bat, pulsed against her thigh. Damali squeezed her eyes shut. She could feel her jawbone knitting back together from an unknown source the harder she prayed in her mind.

"Angels hear me!" Damali shrieked when her thigh muscles gave out and Cain finally parted her legs. "Protect me from all that is unholy!"

Her voice cracked with a sob, and her wings tore through her shoulder blades as hysteria overtook her. Her back was suddenly cool, and the sulfur began to dissipate. Cain leaned back, his eyes normalizing with confusion. His fangs retracted as he brushed her wild tangle of locks away from her sweaty forehead to better see her eyes.

"No!" Damali kept screaming between the sobs. "Until my body is a limp dead rag I will never concede! Never! Get thee behind me, spawn of Satan! No!"

Cain backed off of her with a pain-filled roar and stood. "You're a Powers? A Realm Six healing angel?" He looked around the cavern nervously. "Down *here*?" He raked his locks and backed up farther, de-bulking and retracting his tail, wings, and fangs. "How can that be?

They do not walk the Earth in human form! There has never been a Neteru blend of that. It is forbidden."

He pointed between her legs and she glimpsed down. Her sex was encased in a solid silver, glowing shield of liquid metal, white-hot heat.

Damali covered her nakedness with her wings, sobbing. "Fuck you!"

Disoriented, Cain stumbled backward. "You speak curses, come here, mate like a lusty human female, even take a vampire lover, but have wings?" He clutched his chest like a man experiencing a heart attack and leaned against a boulder. "I felt it when you were in Nod, in my arms, so close to letting me inside you . . . there was something beneath your skin that I had never encountered. But I dared not believe."

Damali stood, dashed for her Isis, and clutched it to her, her eyes frantically glancing around for an exit.

"Devastation, as an angel in the Light, I cannot take you against your will. But do you know what we could create together?" Cain murmured in an awed rush. "Do you realize what type of being you and I could create, if you'd just stop chasing after that young fool and become my bride? Divorce him now!"

"Please God, send in reinforcements!" Damali shouted, looking up at the endless black ceiling. She raised her Isis over her head. "I need an airlift, an extraction—stat. Warrior angels, one of your own is trapped in Hell. Send a beacon; I've got a crazy big demon on my ass!"

Cain covered his ears and yelled in pain. The cavern filled with light, causing bats and vermin and unseen phantoms screeching for dark corners. Cain stood covered by smoldering wings, glimpsing up as Damali folded away into a silver splinter.

"Concede to me, Damali, or I will raze the planet!" he called after her. "That is my ultimatum!"

Damali tumbled onto the sand, clutching her Isis, her body so sore that she could barely get up. Her ripped tank top and ragged jeans were back on, her wings sealed away beneath her skin, but somewhere along the chaotic route back she'd lost her shoes. She looked up at the villa and saw the team on the deck, gun barrels pointed at her, Carlos standing at the ready with a sword in hand.

He cleared the deck rail in a one-handed jump. Guns lowered. The sky was lit with thunder and lightning in a display that rivaled the Fourth of July. She was crying harder than it was raining by the time he reached her. A torrential downpour and hurricane-level winds made waves slam against the beach in an ominous warning. Carlos hugged her hard and she groaned, and then nearly passed out from the pain.

Carlos half-dragged, half-carried her into the villa with one arm, both of their blades cutting into the sand as they walked. The team parted as Carlos looked at her jaw in disbelief. He dropped his blade where he stood once he truly saw the bodily damage she'd sustained, and he took her sword and angrily cast it away with a loud clatter.

Water streamed onto the floor from their drenched bodies, placing them in a huge, spreading puddle. Their clothes clung like second skin and his eyes searched hers as he studied the large, purple, angry bruise that had begun to make her cheek swell. Blood still ran from her nose, and she sniffed it back. Carlos's eyes darted downward to look at the deep talon gouges in her arms, and then he saw her blade arm and finally freaked. Damali shivered, going into mild shock.

"Oh, Jesus . . . get a towel, some ice, some-fucking-body move!"

He swept her up into his arms and hustled her over to the sofa. The bewildered team moved like jerky robots, bringing the supplies Carlos had bellowed for them to bring while Marlene ransacked her black bag with shaking hands.

"Oh, shit, Marlene, seers, healers, medic! Get over here!" Carlos was on his knees on the floor beside Damali, his palm hovering over Damali's injured cheek, silver tears of rage in his eyes. "Baby, it's gonna be all right. I'ma take the pain, Berkfield is gonna open a vein to clean out the gashes. Mar is gonna do her thing. We got you. It's all right."

Damali groaned as Carlos's hand came nearer to the jaw wound and he ran his fingers over her jugular, seeing where a huge, battle-bite entry indentation had been attempted.

"Oh, my God, I'm gonna cut his heart out," Carlos whispered. "Twelve inches of battle-length from jaw to shoulder."

Damali clutched the center of Carlos's T-shirt to pull him near so she could hide her face against his chest. *Baby* . . . she said in a garbled mental whisper, *I wasn't being arrogant. I thought he had slaughtered you and my family.* Sobs came out before she could pull it together. Humiliation tore through her; the whole team was watching.

"Shhsssh, shhhsssh, I know," Carlos murmured, rocking her as the healers gathered. He buried his face in her hair and kissed the crown of her head.

He kicked my ass, she sputtered mentally, unable to admit the unthinkable in front of the team. *I ain't never been—*

"I know . . . I know. It's gonna be all right, 'Mali. Just breathe, baby," Carlos said, rocking her harder.

What if I can't fight anymore? her mind shrieked, as she became hysterical in his hold. When he wouldn't let her go and she realized how much his strength eclipsed hers, she wigged. "Let go of me!"

She rolled off the couch to a wobbly stand, meeting his bewildered gaze. "I'm still a Neteru," she said, tears streaming down her cheeks. "I will not let some motherfucker just take me like that! No!" she screamed, wrapping her arms around herself. "He had no right to violate me like that! Never surrender, never give up!" She was screaming and looking around for her blade like a madwoman. "My queens left me down there ass-out," she said, covering her mouth with a hand. "How could they?"

"Oh, Father," Marlene said, coming closer and pausing as Damali put her hands out in front of her.

"Don't touch me!" Damali shouted. "I'm so unclean . . . the images, his filthy touch is all over me, Mar. I'm dirty! I need a white bath!"

Carlos was on his feet and he rubbed his palms down his face, sipping air.

Tears wet Shabazz's face. "Baby girl, we'll smoke him, don't worry, ya hear?"

Big Mike left the circle with tears of frustrated rage streaming down his huge, ebony cheeks, and began packing shells. "We ride." He sucked in a huge breath and threw a shoulder cannon to Rider, who caught it with both hands.

"We ride," Rider said, his jaw muscles jumping.

"I gotchure back," Jose said to Carlos, shaking his head. "Not on our watch. Uh-uh."

Inez flung a kitchen blade and impaled it into the wall. "I'm down!"

Several clicks echoed through the villa as every Guardian Glocked-up and slammed in a clip.

"This is family," J.L. said, breaking a stool, and instantly creating a wooden stake.

"Oh fuck no," Berkfield said low. "Not one of my daughters."

"No, *I* wanna kill him!" Damali shrieked, her voice so shrill everyone slightly cringed. "After what he did to me? Throw me my blade."

Baby, how bad? Carlos asked mentally, coming to her slowly. Trying to hold her hands, trying to reason with her and calm her down before she had a stroke.

"He—he—he . . . held my legs open with his tail," she said, looking at the floor. "He's morphed into something . . . twenty-foot wingspan . . . twelve-inch fangs . . . seven feet tall, breathes fucking fire . . . put me on my back naked on an inferno floor—oh Jesus . . ." Damali walked away.

Carlos stood numb, staring at her back.

"I couldn't get away," she said, shuddering and wrapping her arms around herself. She began to shake her head slowly, her voice a shattered mental whisper. *I was calling on Heaven, warrior angels, the Most High, hiccup crying, moved two seconds past two late and he bit the wall . . . and he knocked the taste outta my mouth. I've been in many battles, but I don't think I've ever been that afraid, and all it did was turn him on more— you know the vamp power paradigm . . . but I couldn't even summon enough mental discipline to hold that in check. That's why I'm bugging.*

"Baby, if he raped you—" Marlene said in a gentle murmur, tears coursing down her face. "We can clean you out . . . me and Marj. We'll call the queens, all right, suga . . . please just let me hold you."

Damali turned around, her face crumbling as she bit her split lip. She glanced at her husband's ashen expression and at Marlene and choked back a sob. "He didn't rape my body, Mar," she whispered. "Eleventh-hour escape." Damali closed her eyes and hugged herself tighter and sucked in a deep breath. "He gangbanged my mind."

Cain returned to his throne room, quietly chuckling to himself and shaking his head. Nuit and Lilith stood holding their breaths, awaiting his news. He flopped into his throne and sighed.

"She's the one," he said. "I found her."

Nuit cocked his head to the side in a silent question. Lilith slowly approached Cain with a goblet outstretched in an offering, unsure of his mood.

Cain sighed. "Wow."

"Your Eminence?" Nuit said, visually scanning his body for signs of an Isis wound.

"She's ready," Cain said, snatching the goblet from Lilith. "Her council is fractured, her battle powers waning as my mother's health and sanity declines. Her confidence is broken, her husband in a state of conflict—paternity questions burrowing into his psyche like a parasite. Their team is in an uproar and unfocused for battle." He held up his hands. "Smell this, my allies." He smiled. "Pure fear."

Nuit sat down slowly in his throne. "From the millennium Neteru?"

"How did you inspire such terror?" Lilith hissed, coming closer, curiosity making her foolish.

Cain glanced at her with disdain. "Leave my side or leave your heart in my talons, bitch."

She backed away quickly and stood near Nuit. "My apologies," she whispered.

"Do you think that after mind-fucking a Powers angel I would stoop to you tonight?"

Lilith and Nuit simply stared at him for a moment.

Cain chuckled and leaned forward, greedily slurping blood. "Do you know what one of them can breed with one of us? The ultimate destroyer," he whispered, pleased with himself.

Shaking his head and looking off in the distance, Cain spoke in a quiet echo. "The legend is true. The best kept secret in the universe. The escapee hybrid human angel," he said, now laughing hard. "Only *one* of the Powers angels ever lost discipline and sired with a human before the edicts—only *one*—and that gene had been submerged and hidden for millennia! Do you know how long my grandfather has sought this vessel? It is their side's Holy Grail! And *I* found it, within a beautiful, female Neteru body with gleaming white opalescent wings. I had her cowering beneath me crying out for salvation. That is why I didn't bring her down into our realms too deeply, because I *knew* they would come for her and pull her out if I sufficiently terrorized her while she was weakened by the Neteru Council of Queens' strife. They would scorch the entire pit with Light, in search of her."

He set down his goblet and looked at them hard. "I watched her do a healing that no normal Neteru of her age should have been able to accomplish. I felt the fledgling stirrings under her skin when I held her, each time hoping to bring them forth in passion so that I would know for sure . . . but she was too frightened, and had not enough time to bond to me in blind trust. Then her voice, her perfect-pitch healing words . . . I was almost certain, but I *had* to know for sure." Cain rubbed his chest and again shook his head in wonder. "Even with all my suspicions, seeing it stole my breath. And to think, I had almost bedded her. Had there simply been more time."

Fallon Nuit opened his mouth and closed it, holding his goblet in midair before his lips. Then he took a quick sip of blood and dabbed his brow. "Your Eminence . . . permit my ignorance, and I, of course, defer to your greatness. However, if she is totally afraid of you, how—"

"A trade," Cain said evenly, picking up his goblet and sipping from it slowly. "Tonight, compromise her inner circle. I've nicked her, and my energy is in her household. No doubt her team has hugged her, they will put ministrations on her wounds, and her husband will wipe her tears."

He leaned back and closed his eyes. "Her vampire friends should be waking up soon, and the torrential rains lock the Guardians in—Carlos's energy fractured between battles, his wife, his friends . . . divided loyalties are difficult to rein in . . . when you care. And the sheer beauty of it all is that Heaven can only intervene so much, because she, like those they sequestered in Nod, is *a hybrid*. She was *never* supposed to exist beyond the walls of Heaven or Nod, but they allowed her to, because they knowingly let the carrier progeny of her ancestors escape the banishment zone. *They*, this time, the Light, breached the cosmic laws. I know this, because I used to be one of them—a Neteru with ancient, biblical knowledge."

Cain chuckled softly to himself and made a tent with his fingers before his mouth and shook his head. "I risked it all to find her, gambled everything, and I was richly rewarded tonight. An empire for a larger empire, with a caveat that can stop Heaven in its tracks." He leaned over with a wicked grin. "She is priceless because she still, being human with a soul, has free will . . . and there is nothing they can do about her choice. Put it all on black on the roulette wheel of life and, as they said from your old favorite zone of rule, let the good times roll, my friend."

"Then a trade. A sacrifice," Nuit said with a chuckle, peering over his goblet at Cain as he sipped his blood. "Decisions, decisions. One female body as host in exchange for so many loved ones held hostage. She will go mad."

Cain leaned forward. "She will. She will lose her mind for her queens, for the planet that we will siege tomorrow night, for her husband, for her team, for her mother-seer, and anyone else we can twist her heart with . . . she will lie beneath me with silver tears streaming down her pretty face and will open her gorgeous legs and let me sire. Period. She might not like it, but the point is moot. As long as she says yes and drops her shields to save her family, she can sob and wail the whole time. Who gives a damn? I'll ride her pain like a stallion."

He chuckled and set his goblet down hard. "And knowing there is no choice, that will satisfy my first edict, which was to rip out Rivera's heart by its anchors. Finding him after that to sever his wretched head will be child's play. That fool will probably stand in a clearing, open his arms, and beg me to battle him, once it is all said and done."

Nuit stood, bowed, and turned to leave. "Sunset is quickly approaching; I will prepare my reentry to topside and rest. It is *such* an honor to serve you."

"Let me serve you, as well," Lilith whispered, biting her lip as her dark eyes glimmered with anticipation. "After that encounter . . . I'm sure you require relief."

Cain just stared at her, and then glanced down at his lap, dismissing the power erection that throbbed.

"You said you would do a hybrid. Lion and—"

"I am going up to the were-demon realms, alone," Cain said, standing. "Then I may join Nuit to forge a permanent Amanthra alliance. Alone."

"But you said . . ." she whispered, her voice dejected, yet trailing off as he cast a hot glare that stopped her words.

"Like you have so many, many times, Lilith," Cain said, materializing an emperor's robe and slipping it on. "I lied."

CHAPTER EIGHT

His attention was so divided that Carlos was ready to rip out his hair by the roots. Damali was down the hall in the bathroom with Marlene getting a white-bath full dousing after he'd healed her jaw and Berkfield had closed up Damali's nicks and gashes with sacred blood. His wife was in an emotional place that he'd never seen. The newbies were telling him some insane shit about a huge demon named Hubert, and talking some bizarre madness about prayer flags and standing stone formations.

Berkfield lay on the sofa, slowly recovering from an intense healing session. Shabazz, Mike, and Jose were so amped that it was quite possible he'd have to put bit-restraints in their mouths. The females in the villa were walking around in a stupor of fear and outrage, teetering on the brink of a suicidal, unplanned, go-for-broke, gang-war option. Then there was the not-so-small dilemma of Rider and Marjorie's very real fears that matched his: Tara and Gabrielle were at risk, and so was Yonnie.

Carlos reined in his own emotions and stared at the maps Krissy had provided, leaning on the dining room table with his hands.

"Aw'ight, listen up, people. Here's the deal. Forget the flags—they've blown out to sea. Forget the rocks down the beach, in hurricanelike winds and torrential rains. With black lightning strikes, if you can get up there and hold on, you'll fry."

Pointing to a map, Carlos looked up at the assembled team. "Our options are limited because of civilian populations. When we bring the noise, we can't have a Los Angeles situation go down like it did before, or even a Philly-type firefight. The Pacific Northwest or the Midwest is a possibility as a last resort, although some freaky tornadoes have been touching down in the midsection of the country, too. But the Gulf area, all the way from Florida to Texas has been hammered by hurricanes and devastation, and the last thing those innocent people need is a war. Kids running in the streets while bullets are flying, Hummers rolling down sidewalks like Sherman tanks taking out women, old folks, and babies—shrapnel and bullshit exploding. No."

Carlos pushed back and stood straight, stretching his back. "South America is out, even though we could hit Bolivia, Peru, Brazil—any of the areas that have vast uninhabited regions . . . but is anybody feeling an ambush in the jungle again?"

"Hell no," Mike muttered.

"That's my point," Carlos said, frustration singeing his tone. "We have strong teams over there, but the wildlife that could be used against us is no joke. Anacondas and jaguars and shit. No. Same deal with Africa."

"Been there, done that," Shabazz said, nodding. "It ain't about getting caught in the motherland during a situation like this."

"Same thing with Asia," Carlos said. "We saw Tibet, and India is the same way. Wanna come face-to-face with a were-demon Bengal?"

"Shit," Rider said and sat down hard on a stool. "Europe, then? What do they have over there? Wolves we can handle easier, right Mike? You've sucker punched a few of them in your day and didn't draw back a nub."

Mike nodded. "Yup. I'm down."

"Then, like I said, Europe," Shabazz argued.

"Where, man? Think hard and long about Europe. Anybody remember a little war called World War II?" Carlos said, not being sarcastic. "We go there, and we have the population problem *plus* the fact that Transylvania is a very old vamp headquarters. That would be like kicking off the noise near the Pentagon. You know how cold it gets on the front in some of those Alpine regions?" He sighed hard. "If we take it to colder climates, Canada, Alaska, Greenland, Russia—you feel me—and this thing goes on for months into the dead of winter, we could have bodies dropping from just the cold or falling off mountainsides. And I know nobody is ready to go back to Australia." He stared at the group and walked back to the maps. "We dusted so many masters over there that if they raise one, we're talking possible legions that could get up behind him with Cain to try to smoke us."

Dropping his weight on his hands against the table, Carlos stared down. "Don't even discuss the Middle East . . . old Ten Commandments lands and whatnot. That's ground zero, as far as I'm concerned. Plus, the population is already at war, it's thick with people, and you definitely don't wanna be out there wrangling in the desert . . . not to mention, if we go there, Cain has cellular memory of the area with the ruins on lock for his troops to launch from. That's a stronghold zone for him."

"Then, where, man?" Shabazz said, his voice strained. "We're running out of global real estate, and at some point, we can run but we can't hide. Gonna have to dig in and take a stand."

Carlos nodded. "Ain't about running, it's about backing up to launch a strategic, preemptive strike. We only got a coupla hours until sundown, and before I try to whirl this family outta here on a transport, I wanna make sure we're all in sync. I also need to be sure that I'm not dropping us into an ambush in the badlands, and I have to position us where we can get human resources quickly without having to suffer the elements."

Everybody groaned, muttering frustrated curses of agreement beneath their breaths. Carlos rolled his shoulders, the tension about to snap his spine.

"The darkside can only keep up the winds for a short while. Uses up too much of their energy," Carlos said, rubbing his palms down his face, fighting fatigue. "The storm that's got us currently boxed in from outside ain't coming from Mother Nature. All the deadly hurricanes that hit the States were theirs, not the Light's—that many innocent people caught up in the madness, nah. But the darkside latched on to naturally occurring events. They can't completely jack the weather to use it against us, unless a hurricane was already out there brewing off the coast, which it wasn't. My shields will hold against the sea wall building outside until the enemy pulls back—then we're out."

"Okay, I hear you, man," Shabazz said in frustration. "Where to?"

"It's gotta be Central Mexico," Carlos said flatly. "Warm to moderate climate year round, good hiding places for the team and high-ridge strategic advantages in the Sierra Madre Oriental and Sierra Madre Occidental—we'll have underpopulated towns between those two mountain ranges and we wouldn't have to blow up half of Mexico City, which is like New York. If we stay away from the coastlines, then hurricanes and whatnot won't be an issue, like it would be in the Caribbean. Other than rattlesnakes and mountain lions, the wildlife there is more manageable, too, if it turns."

"Cool," Shabazz said, still sullen like the others. "We'll round up our gear and be ready to roll on your order, man." He glanced at Rider. "Maybe Marj, Krissy, and Heather, with Jasmine, can get a lock on Gabrielle in Vegas . . . last place Rider heard she was going."

"Thanks," Rider said flatly and stood to go look out the sliding glass doors.

"I've been trying to get up with Yonnie," Carlos said in an apologetic tone. "But the darkside's got me blocked eight ways from Sunday. Can't get nothing in or out to any vamps topside. But I'm working on it. Might be able to get a jumper cable connection—Gabby to him, one that they can't block because of her soul ground wire, so we can get Yonnie and Tara inside our net again."

"Appreciate it," Rider said with his back to Carlos.

"Why don't you leave the rest of the loose ends to us, man?" Shabazz said, going to Carlos for an embrace handshake. "Go check on your wife. We got this."

Carlos nodded and released Shabazz's grip, then headed down the hall. Whatever Damali and Marlene were privately discussing, he didn't want to intrude. The last thing he wanted to do right now was further upset Damali; she'd been through enough. At this point he was beginning to realize that, even though he was her husband, he was male—Marlene was a mom, and some things only another woman could fix.

Stopping at the door, Carlos tapped on it gently. He could hear Marlene grunt as she stood, and within moments, Marlene cracked open the door.

"Just checking to see if she's all right," Carlos said quietly. "I won't bother you guys, if she needs some space . . . but . . ."

"Come on in, baby," Marlene said and then hugged him. "She could use a shoulder from you, too, right now."

He kissed Marlene's forehead, thanking her with his eyes, and slipped into the humid enclosure as Marlene slid around him and shut the door behind her, leaving him and Damali alone.

"Hey . . . how you feelin'?' Carlos asked, stopping just inside the door and staring at Damali with concern.

She had on the thick white terry robe that had been in the villa from the honeymoon, and her wet hair was swept up in a towel. Sage smudge, frankincense, and myrrh thickened the mist around her, and shea butter mixed with anointing oils glistened on the little bit of her skin he could see. The terrible bruises were gone, as were the fang and claw nicks, but he knew the bruise against her spirit would take a much longer time to heal. As he nervously waited for Damali to answer, he prayed the old defiant side of her would reappear in her eyes.

But instead of that street fighter, he saw defeat shimmering in her wide brown eyes, and just seeing that made him cross the room and kneel down next to where she sat on the side of the tub. He took her hands into his and just looked at them, tracing the graceful lines of her fingers and the delicate skin over her knuckles. Even though she was a serious warrior, he wished she'd never have to bust her pretty hands up in a demon-brawl again.

"Listen—"

"I already know what you're going to say," she murmured, cutting him off and squeezing his hands. "I'm gonna have to get back into the fight. I just got knocked down, was seeing stars, but I have to get back up."

He nodded, not arguing with her. What made him worry was that while he agreed with what she'd said, her voice and the tone of her statement sounded like textbook rhetoric . . . there was no passion in it, like it came from the heart—and that was the easiest way for her to get seriously hurt again.

"I know," he said after a while, kissing her knuckles. "But it's like . . . I guess, being a quarterback, and getting tackled and thrown down hard—a lot of brothers talk about hearing footsteps in their sleep from defensive linemen. Phantom terrors that are as real as the day is long. So, I want you to give yourself permission to heal in your head, is all I'm saying. I'm not challenging your ability, just saying that you're also human."

She brought his hands up to her face, kissed them, and pressed them to her cheek, closing her eyes. "I love you." She let out a hard breath. "You were right."

"I'm not trying to be right," he said quietly and really meaning it. "Things have gone way beyond that. I'm trying to be your husband."

He watched tears roll down her cheeks from beneath her closed lashes, making them glisten, and he wiped them away with the pad of his thumb, feeling her pain lodged so deeply in his chest that he almost couldn't breathe.

"You know what really messes me up, Carlos?" she whispered through a sniff. "I might be . . ."

"I know." He pulled her to him and hugged her, rubbing her back so she could get it all out. He knew that was the core of it—the fact that after it all, she might be carrying for Cain, if she was pregnant. "I ain't going nowhere."

She balled the back of his T-shirt up into her fists, and he could feel her fighting an all-out sob. He was, too, and just held her tighter, beginning to rock her, trying to come up with something to say to grant her peace. The more he held her, the more he understood Adam's position. What did a tiny little baby have to do with larceny and the schemes of grown beings? There was so much chaos in his spirit that he could barely contain it, and it came out in silent tears against her shoulder that began to wash the dilemma clean in his soul. The only thing he was sure about was how much he loved her.

"Damali, God as my witness, if it's got any of you in it, I'll raise it like my own."

His thickly murmured confession broke the damn loose within her, and hiccupping sobs rained down on his shoulder as they both rocked away the pain.

"I never wanted—"

"I know. You don't have to say it again," he whispered, slowly recovering and pulling back to see her face. "Look me in the eyes, Damali." He waited until she would. "*Nothing* comes between me and you—not nobody, not no bullshit. Nothing."

She shook her head. "Nothing," she whispered, touching his face.

"Nothing," he said, resolute. "Ever."

"He threatened to wipe out everyone I love and care about."

"So, you gonna let him?" Carlos said, working on the defiant ember he hoped was still within her. Knowing Damali well, he went for that insane switch inside her that even Hell couldn't deal with.

For a moment, she just stared at him.

"That punk bastard thinks he's broken your back, baby, just because he made you cry."

Carlos watched her slightly tilt her head and hope coursed through him as he egged her on. "Arrogant motherfucker thinks you're gonna go out like Eve, so upset that you can't deal with possibly taking another blow . . . just 'cause he got you good the first time and you came up dazed, he thinks you're gonna do whatever he wants to appease the beast and let him run you," Carlos added in a philosophical tone, watching liquid fire ignite in Damali's irises.

"I know how twisted men think," he said with a shrug. "It's a power thing. Holler at 'em and beat 'em down, and they'll be so scared they'll do whatever. He probably figures, 'cause you're a queen, like his mother, he can break you like he did her. In fact, because you *are* a queen, it gives him all the more pleasure to make you get down on your knees and beg him not to hurt you—sick, slimy motherfucker that he is. But I don't think holmes is used to dealing with a twenty-first-century sister from around the way."

She nodded slowly, her nostrils beginning to flare.

"You tell me how to play this, baby," Carlos said, deadly serious. "If you're scared of him, ain't no shame in the game. He's bigger than you and stronger than you. If he shook your confidence, that stays between me and you. If you ain't ready to go gansta, pure guerilla on him, then as your husband, you know my position—I'll go out swinging for you. But I just want you to remember, one round in a boxing match ain't the whole match . . . unless you can't get up from the mat."

He hugged her when her body went rigid with silent fury, pleased to see he'd thrown the master switch. "I got your back. If you don't wanna deal, I can dig it. That's why we're a team. If I go down hard, you got me until I can stand, and vice versa."

"He thinks I'm weak because my queens are experiencing a power drain through his mother," she said, yanking back to stare at him.

"So, all right," Carlos said, resuming his philosophical tone, loosening his hold on her to sit on the floor. "They're experiencing a power loss from his bullshit, but ain't there a higher power source, D? One battery that can't nobody drain?"

"Definitely," she said, lifting her chin and glancing away to stare at the tiles.

Relief wafted through him. "Cool, then maybe you just stepped up and graduated to the next level again?" He almost smiled when she snapped her attention back to him. "You always get your lessons faster than me and before me. I'm just learning how to deal with that reality without actin' the fool, myself."

Awe slowly dawned in her eyes.

"Damali, you ever think that maybe the reason the queens never came or their powers were of no use in that particular situation might have been because . . . you got some new serious powers blooming?"

"I never thought about that, Carlos." She stared at him and slowly brought both hands up to cover her mouth.

"Don't you always tell me that the Light always adds, but doesn't take away?"

She nodded, wide-eyed, with her fingers still shielding her lips.

"All I know is, hombre probably didn't bank on that. Doesn't know how my wife will patiently lay like a cobra for his ass and strike like white lightening when he least expects it." Carlos nodded and stood, and then sat down beside her on the edge of the tub, holding her gaze in an intimate lock. "Keep crying. Keep wailing. Keep seeming insecure around him,'cause I know that ain't you, but he don't. Keep begging for the safety of your family . . . and the next time he rolls up on you, slay him."

Damali shut her eyes and stood so quickly, Carlos almost toppled into the tub.

"That no-good, lowlife, sneaky, arrogant demon . . ." she said, walking in a slow, deadly circle with her eyes closed, just shaking her head. "Next time, I'll have a dagger on my hip for the tail." She stopped walking and looked at Carlos hard. "Thank you for the battle bite. I know I can take one, now. And I'm glad he hit me good and hard, because now I know how strong the bastard is—it wasn't a punch, but I can guestimate. I also found out the hard way that as long as the queens are divided, my Isis won't shear his blade. Okay. Experience is the best teacher. So if I call for your sword in a firefight— work with me, and throw me yours."

"Done."

"Shape-shifts ain't working," she said with an angry smile, "I guess because I'm supposed to use my real wings . . . and maybe I'm not supposed to be turning into anything crazy anymore now that I have them and they're fully matured."

"I'll go with the theory." A slight smile crept out on one side of his face.

"Yeah," she said, her head bobbing as she folded her arms over her chest. "No coincidences or accidents in the universe. We're supposed to use *everything*. Every lesson, every heartbreak, and every game that was run on us . . . gotta keep your head in the battle."

He just looked up at her, both proud and amazed.

"I need to meet with Eve . . . maybe give her a little hope to send some white Light down into a brother's chair. If Darkness can subtract, then the Light can add. Whatchu think, baby?"

Carlos smiled wider. "Sounds like a plan."

"Honesty is the best policy, right? With a little diplomatic omission."

He chuckled. "You getting ready to fuck dude up, ain't you, baby?"

"Did I tell you I loved you?"

Carlos laughed and stood, going to her to pull her into his arms. "Yeah . . . you just did."

She watched Carlos slip out of the bathroom and she stood in the center of the tiled space using her hands to make a pyramid. She called to Aset softly, not even bothering to put on her clothes. A robe, wet towel, and bare feet would have to do. Slowly the violet entrance opened, and Damali stepped through it with her head held high. As soon as Aset neared her, she held up her hand.

"I have news for the full oval. May we meet, and bring Eve?"

Aset stared at her for a moment. "Queen Sister, are you sure?"

"Never more sure in my life," Damali said, and strode past Aset.

Damali opened the large chamber doors and entered the Neteru Council of Queens' session room that already had a heated summit underway. All voices ceased as Aset calmly entered the white marble-ensconced gallery behind Damali and shut the large doors with a wave of her hand.

"Damali has recent news from the front," Aset announced.

Eve looked up with anger and released a weary sigh. "So you have come here triumphant." Eve stood. "Then I need not hear the details, now that my son—"

"Cain is very much alive," Damali said, staying Eve's departure. "Aset, can you reveal wounds that have just been recently healed?"

Aset nodded and slowly approached Damali.

"Show them everything that my body sustained in the last few hours," Damali said, unceremoniously dropping her robe and standing nude before an aghast council. "Show Eve how strong her son is . . . I want her to see what he did to me when I went down there to confront him—to tell him to go back to Nod and to convince him that he shouldn't have bargained with the Devil, and I even explained how your soul was crushed." Damali shook her head. "Yes, I went armed and furious, yeah, with indignation, but I also tried to tell him the truth and give him a last-ditch option, once I learned my family was still alive. Look at this. I tried your approach, Eve. Talking. This is the result." Damali set her jaw hard. "And, oh, by the way, when I told him about his momma, he said 'Her condition is unfortunate.' Now get to that."

Aset closed her eyes and turned away as every wound Damali sustained overtook her body. Eve gasped and held on to the edge of the oval table and backed away, but as much as the injuries hurt when she moved, Damali neared Eve to make the point visually sink in.

"Wait until you see my back." Damali slowly turned around and showed Eve and the assembled queens the third-degree burns, huge demon talon welts and gashes, and then opened her thighs to show the thick ropes of black-and-blue marks and raw scrapes where Cain's scaled tail had forcibly parted her legs. Convinced that the queens were sufficiently mortified, judging from the shocked expressions on the regal faces around her, Damali turned her attention back to Eve. "And let me add that I might be carrying for him, dear queen. I could be pregnant."

Nzinga's battle-ax rent the chamber with a whir and came to a clanking stop in the marble door. The Amazon let out such a thunderous war cry that thrones shook and Aset's lions roared.

"I'm going to Ausar about this shit," Damali said, leaning onto the table and staring at Eve. "I was in a battle with your son in Hell, and because you wouldn't stand with me to do what has to be done, my powers waned." She pushed away from the table, fully naked, and folded her arms over her bare, bruised breasts. "But Carlos, being the man he is, said even if I am pregnant and it's Cain's, he would love it and raise it and protect it like his very own."

Eve was on her feet with a strangled gasp. "My son did this to you? Are you certain?"

"Is she on drugs?" Damali said, moving away from Eve to stand by Aset. "Like I wouldn't know who went after me in Hell?"

Eve bowed down and went to one knee. "There is not enough that

I can say to you, Damali, but to beg you to forgive me for any danger I may have put you in. I suspect you want a scan, and to end the pregnancy . . . after this?"

"No!" Damali shouted, drawing confused stares from the other queens. "I will raise it with my husband, if I am carrying for either man." She waited until Eve slowly stood. "But I would not lie to or deceive my husband about it. Carlos deserves better, and the decision to stay or leave based on my situation is his choice. I told him and had to suck it up—had to be *a queen* about it and honorably take whatever decision he personally made about this—and I did. I respect him that much."

Eve nodded, wrapping her hands around her waist. "You would keep it?"

Damali held out her bloodied blade arm so that Eve could see the ravaged flesh better. "Even after Cain did this to me," she said in a low, threatening voice. "Even after he pried my legs open and forced himself between them and made me cry out to Heaven . . . even after he dropped twelve inches of battle-length fangs and told me I'd be puking my own blood and choking on my own womb when he was done . . . Yeah, sis, no problem. Me and *my husband* will raise *your son's* baby, together—and will even let you act like grandma. The baby didn't have nothing to do with it and I won't play those kinds of games, keeping you from the child to spite you. Why? Just because you loved your son so much you forgot that *I* was somebody's child? Now how would *that* seem?"

When Eve cringed and drew away, Damali pranced around the table naked, watching rage implode in each queen's eyes.

"My mother-seer almost went blind when I came home. My husband was almost ready to put his blade to his own throat. Shabazz, who is like my dad, hey, we almost had to thump on his chest to restart his heart. My brothers and other Guardians in the house—they still can't breathe." Damali leaned across the table and stared at Eve until Eve looked up at her. "*I am* somebody's child, too, Eve. It's not all right for you to cover for your sick-ass, twisted son, just because he's yours and let him tear apart a woman and her family. No matter what!"

Every queen was on her feet and pandemonium broke out in the gallery so badly that daggers and weapons were drawn in milliseconds. Aset literally had to send a crack of purple lightning into the oval table and speak with thunder to quiet the council.

"Eve," Aset said, pointing at Eve, "this demands redress! I want *all* her powers immediately restored, her Isis securely in her grip, her seven-stone necklace returned from wherever it was lost at once! Ausar will be notified *by me*—personally—know that. Carlos has done no less than Adam, in this regard, and what has been visited upon Queen Damali's household and personage is an outrage!"

"You got that right," Damali said, and gave Eve her back. She spoke softly to make the room go still, using every stage performance and voice technique that she owned to heighten the drama.

It didn't matter that her wounds were the result of an attempted rape this time and she'd come away with just a severe beating. What mattered was the violation of her humanity—period. So if the queens wanted to jump to conclusions that a rape also happened while she was in Hell battling, so be it. Cain had already done no less by riding Carlos's energy. He'd violated her once on Carlos's wave, and then again by beating her ass almost to death. Determining when each event occurred was splitting hairs, as far as she was concerned. This was war.

"You especially wanna know why, Eve. You know what else happened down there?" Damali allowed her voice to falter. "I am *Somebody's* child," she said, pointing upward and slowly, painfully through the bruises, she unfurled her clean, damp wings.

The collective gasp that echoed through the Neteru Queens' Council could have cut stone. Damali turned around to face them with tears in her eyes that were not a part of the theatrics. Just thinking about it brought it all back full force along with every foul indignity.

"They came out while I was down there!" she shouted, pounding on the table and making the opalescent colors within it swirl. She closed her wings around her nakedness in a hug, silver tears streaming down her face as she railed. "I was on a *dirty* cavern floor under his foul body, ghosts and poltergeists laughing and murmuring like phantom peeping Toms, while that sweating, grunting beast humped me, sliding his tongue into my ear, and sending the most depraved sexual images into my mind! I'm *married*! How can I sleep with my husband again *after that*—with those images in my head? Eve, you tell me! This *wasn't* a seduction. This was—"

Damali tore herself away from the table when the elder queen closed her eyes and covered her face with her hands.

"Oh, God!" Eve wailed. "He didn't!"

"He did!" Damali screamed, feathers flying as she snapped open her wings. "And you know what, you know what! He's threatened my entire family, who I can't protect because my powers are shaky. . . . He'll wipe them out, if I won't go down there and get with him again!"

Eve was up and out of her chair, and she ran to Damali and held both her arms. "Child, my son has lost his mind," Eve said in a horrified, urgent rush. "You *cannot* go down there and allow him to take you like that while possibly carrying our—"

Damali shrugged away. "I don't want him to *ever* touch me again, Eve. I just want to raise my baby in peace . . . and to have my full family there in love and support around me so I can put this horror out of my mind."

What she'd declared was no act; if she was pregnant, it was the pure truth. Thinking about Cain touching her gave her hives. Damali looked at Eve hard. "But I can't do any of that as long as Cain is free to roam to and fro. He's stalking me, and either has to go into permanent lockup, or be put down like the animal he is."

"I say put the bastard down for good," Nzinga shouted across the chamber. "He's dangerous, and if he's after Damali and her family— what if he attacks her while she's very ripe with child, huh, Eve? The bigger she gets, and the further along the pregnancy goes, she'll be crippled to fight him and ward off an attack! He's a demon and would rape her when she was like that and you know it!"

"I shall beg all of Heaven to allow me to materialize in the flesh again to cut off his member, first," Joan said. "*Heresy*, against a heavenly body," she whispered, gaining nods all around.

The Aztec, Asian, and Native American queens stood unified with Joan.

"We will raise every noble Aztec warrior from the crusts of their graves!"

"Every dragon's teeth of Shanghais shall be sewn!"

"Every honorable brave shall ride again like a nightmare on the wind!"

"I will summon Anubis, the scarabs of Amen-Ra, and all the ancient Egyptian entities of old . . . plus will draw the Orishas of Africa to assist, and I will call the winds of Cyprus and sweep a plague into the bowels of Hell so vast that the Earth will shudder!" Nefertiti hollered, her golden robes billowing after her as she paced behind her throne. "I have six daughters! *Six*, Eve, count them—and never in my incarnations have I been so enraged. I do not care that we are not supposed to directly get involved in the Armageddon until we are called," she shrieked. "This is beyond my endurance to idly sit by and witness! Your son violated *an angel,* and my petitions will be heard Above, if I cross the line!"

"Yes, he is not beyond committing this heinous violation again," Penthesileia yelled. "Or are you going to let him make our young queen miscarry your own grandchild or have a *cherub angel* born deformed because Cain beat Damali so badly that—"

"Never!" Eve said, sweeping away from the table. "This time my son has gone too far!" She shook her head and then slowly advanced to Damali. "Let me scan to see if—"

"No, don't touch me!" Damali said, backing away. The last thing that she needed to do was have Eve find out that whatever was possibly inside her wasn't Cain's, then all of this drama would be moot. She also wasn't truthfully ready to know if she was pregnant or not—

and she would definitely pass out from heart failure if Eve's scan told her she was and it was Cain's. Later, after she killed his ass, then she could get technical. Her mind and heart could only bear so much.

Damali stood covered by her own wings, holding herself away from Eve in a challenge. A combination of reality, terror, and sadness filled her that was completely honest. All of it imploded within her at once. It was a terrifying reality that Cain could have busted a sleazy vamp move and planted something in her, and she knew in her heart that she couldn't go through another womb purge. A deep sadness made her close her eyes as the image of Carlos's agonized face entered her mind. The man would actually deal with this for her if he had to . . . damn. She wanted to drop to her knees and weep.

"After all our sister has recently been through, Eve," Aset said in a firm tone, "Damali shouldn't have to endure anyone touching or violating a hair on her head—not even a hug, without her permission. This is the foulest act that can be committed against our kind."

Every queen in the room nodded and Eve slowly backed away.

"I am sorry beyond what you can fathom," Eve whispered. "Please let me try to make it up to you by putting every power at your disposal . . . anything you need . . . the elements, nature, whatever I can do, so that should you find yourself in battle with him again, you can protect yourself." Eve lifted her chin. "In my own grief, I have been blind." Huge tears filled her regal eyes but burned away with rage. "If this is what he has become, he shames me and his stepfather, Adam, a man that stood behind him . . . encouraged him, mentored him, loved him as his own. Adam was a role model of what it was to be a man with honor, and that Cain has become this not only breaks my heart, but enrages me."

"Rage is good," Nzinga said with a scowl. "Better than acting crazy and being in denial."

Eve closed her eyes, balled her hands into fists at her side, and spoke through her teeth. "When I *think* of how I loved that boy! The sacrifices made as only a mother can make them! My marriage always on the precipice! The way I went against my beloved husband for him time and again! He disrespects Adam, and me, and even slaughters my baby boy, Abel . . ." Eve's voice cracked, but no one dared near her as she sucked in a huge breath and squeezed her eyes shut more tightly. "I gave Cain the world, everything in my soul! Now he does this? And now he would violate the woman who carries his seed—*my* grandchild?" She opened her eyes and pointed to the table. "Never! I will kill him myself and put him out of his misery first!"

The entire gathering of queens quickly jumped away from their thrones and took shelter behind them. Damali had found a column to hide behind before the bolt ever left Eve's hand; she could feel it winding up. Having seen that look in Marlene's eyes for years, that mother death stare was easy to read. The table took the charge with a loud crack and a high-pitched whine whirred, magnetizing everything in the room as a yawing color spiral sucked a pure white current of lightning into the center of it. Heavy gold-and-white marble thrones inched forward as Eve held her arm out, her index finger ignited by a four-inch-wide swath of energy.

"You are dead to me!" Eve shouted. "My hope is contained within a thousand lights of Heaven that my grandchild will never be as you! I forsake you! I am no longer your mother. You have brought shame upon our household. I turn you over to the authorities On High! They may do with you what they will!" Eve lowered her voice and intensified the ray as she now spoke in an ending threat. "I shed Light on you with my final prayer of pure essence of mother love—may *God* bless you!"

The table exploded and energy shrapnel went flying. Afraid to peep out once the room nova-lit, Damali waited until sparkling confetti-like color particles began to slowly float down to the marble floor. Eve's wails were a cross between the screech of a woman losing her mind and a piteous moan.

"Heal Damali. Gather the table and assist Eve with the Caduceus," Aset commanded urgently to the others, as the queens began to pull pieces of the disintegrated table back together with tender rays of violet light from their hands. Aset held out Damali's robe with a silent plea in her eyes for Damali to leave, and quickly waved healing green light over her to remove the injuries. "We will take it from here, child. . . . Your petition has been heard on multiple levels, rest assured."

The explosion that hit the Vampire Council table went off like a mortar round. Midstroke, Cain released a were-demon, unable to still mount the lionlike she-beast as a missile ball of pure Light tore through Level Five and kept going. The black forest around him was in white-light flames as though a comet had ripped through the realm. He looked up, mesmerized, to witness white and blue flickering embers clinging to the sides of the cavern. Late sundown filtered into the hole five levels deep and beyond in a smoky gray filter, leaving a trail of screeches and demon screams in its wake.

The entity he'd been holding immediately burst into flames and went to screaming ash. He swiftly transported himself to the narrow bridge over the Sea of Perpetual Agony outside his council chambers, and stepped through the remains of ashen, charred messengers that never stood a chance.

Dead bats littered the floor as he opened the black marble doors. Burning vermin twitched where they lay, sending their putrid stench up in small, smoking funnels. Thrones were scorched. The pentagram-shaped table was a pile of white-hot glowing rubble . . . and his throne was melted down into a tangle of rock as though a nuclear blast had hit it.

Paralyzed, for a moment he could only stare and gape. Had Fallon Nuit or Lilith been in the room . . . or him, they all would have been instantly liquefied. But the thing that stunned him the most was the source of the blast. *His mother?* The facts were incongruent. *His* mother? True, her signature was in the glowing rubble, but *Eve* had rent such destruction?

While it could all be repaired in due time, albeit through the great expense of a lot of energy, that was not the point. That his mother had obviously sided with Damali for some reason and had made him dead to her heart was a significant variable he'd never gambled on. It also meant that Damali's powers, and then some, would be restored.

Cain began to pace; he had to work quickly and redouble his efforts to break Damali's spirit, or all that he'd invested in his quest would be lost. But *his mother* sided with someone over him?

Slight remorse tugged at him as he threw his shoulders back and rubbed his palms down his face, too stricken for fraud. "Damn, Mom," he muttered, still somewhat bewildered by what could have gotten into her. "I'm sorry."

"Did you feel the blast?" Lilith said in a hissing whisper near her husband's ear. "You know what I told you Cain discovered about the living female Neteru."

"Yes," he said in a calm voice.

"What should we do?"

"Nothing . . . for now. Let us bide our time." A pair of red gleaming slits opened and a lazy, bored voice spoke. "My grandson has always suffered from delusions of grandeur." The statement was delivered with a long, weary sigh that escaped into the pitch blackness and then a slow chuckle followed it. "Let Cain do all the work, let him use his armies as cannon fodder to reduce the ranks of Guardians on the planet . . . then I will decide what to do with the vessel. This new development is *very* interesting, indeed."

"Are you pleased with my work so far?" Lilith's voice hitched and she held her breath after she'd spoken.

The slits disappeared in the darkness as the beast closed his eyes. "Yes."

Nuit opened his eyes and sat up so quickly in his coffin that he bumped his head. Disbelieving, he flattened his palms against the black marble crypt covering in the Vampire Council's antechambers to sense for heat. Level Six was now under siege by the Light? What had that arrogant, foolish, bastard done? *Cain was out of his mind.*

Did Cain think that after being the most ruthless master vampire ever made that this pretender to the throne would rule through heritage alone? He'd been a vampire for much longer than Cain could imagine, all the while Cain was dallying in the Light . . . posturing as a Neteru pretender that knew *nothing* firsthand about the insidious politics of the realms! Now this? A direct attack, the inner chambers under siege?

Everything Cain knew was all throne-knowledge, nothing hard-won by ducal rights battles for territory and amassed wealth snatched in hand-to-hand combat. Forging intra-Level demon alliances took years of détente! And now he wanted to lay claim to the huntress . . . a treasure he'd found, cultivated, and had almost captured while she was still a virgin during her first ripening. *Non.*

Fallon Nuit became very still, slowing his breathing to a near stop. He surrounded his coffin with an extra black arc barrier of protection and closed his eyes. An hour until true nightfall . . . he needed his rest to be strong.

"Yeah, I did," Damali said, tugging on her jeans and talking to Carlos in the bedroom while she dressed.

Carlos blew out a long whistle. "The *table* blew?"

"Yep. Eve wasn't playing." She looked at Carlos with a mischievous smile. "Neither was I, okaaay."

"D . . . I just wish I could have been the fly on the wall down there when the Light hit. I *know* he didn't bank on you being crazy."

Yonnie dragged himself to the edge of the bed, and put his hand on the last black bottle in the lair. He weakly turned it up to his mouth, and then offered it to Tara. When she couldn't lift her head to even drink, he gently cradled her skull in his palm and raised it, pouring slow sips into her mouth until her cracked, dry lips moistened.

"Baby, I'm sorry. I don't know what got into me," he wheezed. "I couldn't stop."

She greedily drank with her eyes closed, blood running from the corners of her mouth until she choked. "I was almost gone," she gasped.

"I know," he murmured and gathered her into his arms, gently rocking her. "That was too close. . . . I scared my damned self."

A loud knock on the bedroom door made Carlos and Damali look up. He stood and went to it.

"Yo, what's up?" Carlos stared at Damali as she put her baby Isis blade into a hip holster and grabbed her Madame Isis long blade off the dresser. He watched her put her necklace on like a queen and lift her head, ready to battle.

"Storm's over," Big Mike said through the door. "Wind's let up, it ain't raining, and Shabazz said to tell you now's probably a good time to move out."

"Sho' you right," Carlos said. "Two minutes." He looked at Damali. "You good? You ready to roll?"

She nodded. "Let's do this."

She glanced out the window and groaned. Carlos had his hand on the doorknob but didn't open it, following her line of vision.

"Just what we need. A full moon," she muttered.

"Can we just catch a break?"

Carlos yanked the door open and began walking down the hall, trying again to send a signal to Yonnie with his mind. The weak signal that came back at him made him walk faster.

"We got a man injured in Vegas," Carlos said, turning to Damali and looking at Rider. "We can take a small squad, an in-and-out detail, now that the sun is going down, but—"

"Go," Damali said. "Rider, Shabazz, and you. Half-hour, and it'll be dusk. Then we all have to move as one unit."

Carlos kissed her quickly and looked at Rider. "We gotchure back, man." What he didn't say was that he was barely able to get an energy pulse back from Tara.

"While the winds are down and the lightning has stopped, and we have a break in the rain, we should take a crew up on the rocks to do the lighthouse move Hubert told you about," Damali said, looking at Marj. "Rather than sitting around and waiting for Special Forces members of the team to report back, we can use that time wisely, and can maybe even get a secure beacon out to Gabrielle."

"You sure you feel up to this?" Marlene said cautiously, her line of vision now locked with Damali.

"Yeah, she's good," Carlos said, as Damali's eyes went to his with respect. "Girlfriend is *definitely* back on the block."

CHAPTER NINE

Check your clips," Damali said to the female contingent of Guardians that were headed out the door toward the jetty of rocks down the beach. "Jose, Mike, Berkfield—you guys are on point and holding down the villa."

"No problem, we got this, D," Jose said.

Mike simply nodded and raised his shoulder cannon.

"You got my wife and daughter with you, darlin', so you know I'm on it," Berkfield said, checking the sightline of his M-16.

"Good." Damali glanced around as she and the female squad turned to leave. "J.L., you keep in contact with the Covenant and keep scanning for anything, and I do mean *anything,* that sounds weird. Any type of electromagnetic disturbances, anything from the government units that are friends, geological—"

"I got it, D," J.L. said in a firm tone.

"Me and Bobby are on tactical sensing." Dan motioned to Bobby and tossed him an assault rifle. "We'll be on the roof, watching your backs, while you ladies do your thing and see if you can get a read on which direction trouble's blowing in from."

"I've only got one question," Bobby said, motioning toward the bloody T-shirt in the sink with his weapon. "What do we do if Hubert and his crew show back up? Carlos never said if they were in or out, and neither did you, D."

Damali blew a stray lock up off her forehead in frustration. Bobby was right. With all that had been going on, the issue of what to do with refugee hybrids hadn't been settled. "I don't know," she finally admitted. "When Carlos gets back, we'll do a joint reading on the situation, and let ya know."

"Cool," Bobby said, reinforcing his artillery, packing his vest down with ammo. "Then like Dan said, we got your backs."

"All right, listen up," Damali said as the all-female squad trudged through the sand. "We do this fast, according to the formation Hubert gave you, because I'm getting dead air, no signal. And I want me and Marlene as seasoned vets with the prayer-lock around this. . . . Do *not* allow anything into your heads that isn't radiating white light. Got it? This could be a setup, too, so let's err on the side of caution." She glanced around and received nods of agreement. "Cool."

"I'm all for playing this safe, D," Inez said, her eyes on the horizon. "This shit gives me the heebie-jeebies, and if something huge comes after me . . . girl, I don't know."

"That's just it; this is *not* a drill. Everything you've been dealing with and have learned up to this point is the only defense you've got—so use it," Damali said, making the group come to a halt in front of the jetty. "At any given time, any of us are vulnerable to something bigger, stronger, and crazier than we are. The key is to always fight, especially if it tries to abduct you. Make a stand wherever it comes for you. Don't let it drag you into the pit or a cavern or separate you from the group."

"But if it's stronger and has weapons . . ." Jasmine said, her voice filled with fear.

"It's going to try to kill you," Damali said flatly. "There is no negotiation with it. Your goal is to maim it, kill it, do it before it does you, and run your ass off the second you get free. Do not try to bargain with it, reason your way out, and you have to be in the mindset that its intent is murderous, therefore, no holds barred." She looked at each woman without blinking. "I almost made a fatal mistake because I knew the attacker and thought that I could reason it off me. Not.

Next time I see him, it's mortal combat. I was lucky the first time. I'm not gambling on the next time."

Damali began climbing, and soon the tense group had mounted the rocks with her. All she could wonder was how many women in the world had dealt with the same thing, and never lived to tell about it or rehash options. Renewed fury entered her as she thought about every woman and all the children worldwide that had been found in Dumpsters, alleys, or in their own homes, killed, beaten, or raped by someone they knew. To her mind, what had happened with Cain was no different, and the odds of winning against a huge predator no less dicey. Even going against her own foster father had been the same; the beast was bigger than her, stronger, insane, and the only reason she'd lived to see another day was because she'd lashed out hard, used every weapon she'd had at her disposal as a defense, and tried to kill the bastard where he stood—and then ran.

She sensed for the right position as the group gathered into a loose assembly, knowing full well that fear was a virus, one that predators fed off of and used to make a potential victim hesitate. The thought of getting stabbed or shot or punched was generally enough to make a human being cringe and try to avoid pain. What she had to get through to the group was that if trapped, they *would be* shot, stabbed, punched, or worse, so anyone who found themselves in that position might as well go for broke within any split-second opportunity that presented itself.

"Whew, there's a serious charge coming off these rocks," Damali said, trying to divert the fear rippling through the team and to get the group to relax enough to get the job done. "Enough to light up half of Manhattan. Dang."

Heather offered Damali a weak half-smile after a moment. "Uh-mmm . . . well, I can explain."

"No need," Damali said with a wink as the group formed the correct circles. "It's all good."

Marlene gave her a slight nod. "You ready to put up the barrier?"

"Like old times, Mar," Damali said, growing confident. "Just because something is bigger and stronger doesn't mean you can't lob a good defense. Everything has a weak point, and even if our backup gets here late, we can protect ourselves from an attack."

The women joined hands while Damali and Marlene joined mentally and then focused on white light and said the Twenty-third Psalm out loud. As soon as the barrier was set, Damali could feel a slight current ripple from Heather to Jasmine to Krissy and gain strength as Marjorie stood in the middle of the group, her gaze becoming faraway and glassy.

Juanita's head dropped forward as Inez began to pant through her mouth. The image ricocheted from Marj to Juanita to Inez and then to Marlene and entered Damali's mind. Quick snapshot visions of worldwide ancient ruins filled Damali's inner sight, and soon she could make out large, red, bubbling seawater, as well as horizontal, black funnel clouds streaking the air.

"It's on the move now," Juanita said in a low, guttural voice that was foreign to her.

Heather reeled and Marjorie caught her before she fell. "Hundreds of them," she said. "All focused this way."

Damali broke the circle and turned to see J.L. rushing down the beach.

"Land, air, and sea! Incoming!" J.L. shouted. "Get back to base camp!"

The group scrambled down the rocks as a huge, gray plume whirled past them and crash-landed on the beach with a boom. Guns whipped out of holsters, and a small nymph held up her hands as larger entities surrounded her.

"Sanctuary!" the nymph shouted, and dropped to her knees.

"Hold your fire!" J.L. and Marlene shouted in unison. "Refugee hybrids!"

The largest entity in the small group of hybrids bowed slightly, and spoke, breathing hard. "We felt you access the stones and came to take a stand with you, but you must get Sara into the house." He motioned to the nymph with his chin. "She cannot withstand a battle. She only has love and gentleness in her. I am Hubert and at your command with the others."

"It's getting dark, and we hadn't heard from the Neterus," Sara said, becoming hysterical. "Please don't leave us out here alone."

"All right," Damali said, reluctantly. "J.L., let her inside, but you other guys are gonna have to wait for a threshold pass." She raked her locks, not sure, as she stared at eleven very suspect-looking creatures and then at something that had gentle angel written all over her.

"All right. We understand and can take up a position outside with your men. He will bring hybrids, first," Hubert said, glancing around the group. "Cain is not a full vampire, and has not formally died from the bite—at least not when he was in Nod. If that is still true, he can only make them by seed, not the bite, and the hybrids that follow him are part human. Your normal artillery should stop them. They will also be slower in this density than full-breed demons that have already adjusted to the earth pane's atmosphere."

"That's bullshit, man," J.L. argued, helping Jasmine down. "This afternoon we fired I don't know how many rounds and none of you bought it."

"That was illusion," Hubert said, ignoring J.L. and looking at Damali as the group began hurrying toward the villa. He spoke urgently while he jogged by Damali's side. "We can throw images of ourselves and move with speed like any demon once we adjust to the new density, but if we get hit by a shell, it's a mortal wound. That is why it was necessary to trick you into expending artillery and shooting at what was only a hollow image of us."

"Now *that's* good info," Damali said, jogging faster down the beach toward the villa. "If Cain hasn't had time to amass vampires or other full-breed demons yet, and is on the move in twilight, then whatever we hit we can possibly take down."

"The witch with one green eye and one blue eye is the only one that got an actual hit," Hubert said, slowing to a stop to look at Marjorie. The small team of female Guardians briefly stopped to hear him out. "The ammunition went through illusion mass, giving the appearance of invincibility. But as Cain's forces come into this plane, it will take a moment for that to happen."

Hubert pointed toward the lingering spiral in the sky. "This is why

you can see our entry points, unlike other demons. The distortion between the dimensions of Nod-land and Earth has a drag coefficient of
pure energy reconstituting into mass, and the loud sound like thunder
tells you when beings have exited the other realm to break through."

Mike, Jose, and Berkfield were on the deck, weapons at the ready.
Bobby and Dan had the hybrids within their sight lines, peering at
them through assault rifles.

"Okay, people. We listen for the sonic boom, then unload your
clips," Damali said, motioning for the squad of hybrids to fan out on
the beach. Her mind was screaming an SOS to Carlos to return to
base, but it was as though her calls had gone into a black void.

"We gotta get Rivera back here, D," Mike said, eyeing the motley
group of hybrids and then the darkening horizon.

"Ya think?" Damali said, not meaning to be sarcastic, but her
nerves were shot. She let go of the beacon to Carlos and locked in on
the horizon and then the sea. "All right," she commanded. "I want all
newbies and Sara inside. Mike, you hold position on the deck with
RPGs with Berkfield, with Dan on the roof with mortars, along with
Bobby covering with sniper rifles. Jose, you're on the roof with Bobby,
sniping with automatics. Krissy, Inez, and Juanita, you cover windows,
but keep your heads down. Marj and Marlene, electrify both entry
points. Nothing with fangs comes over the threshold."

Damali tightened her grip on her Isis and then quickly unfastened
the baby Isis dagger holster at her hip and double-checked the magazine on her nine millimeter. "Keep Sara down, behind the kitchen
counter."

"Thank you," Hubert said, nodding to his team to surround the
perimeter of the villa.

But for a moment, Damali stopped. Fear was wafting from the
large entity in waves that almost created pain. It was a disorienting
fusion—wide, terrified eyes and a voice like an English professor with
what under any abnormal circumstances would seem like a warrior
demon.

"Have you guys ever been in combat?" Damali asked, not sure why
she cared or was concerned about their safety.

The entities shook their heads, eyes glistening with panic. She sighed and allowed her shoulders to drop. "Okay, if it gets crazy, fall back beneath the house crawl space. That's the best I can do."

But before any further discussion could ensue, Hubert grabbed the nymph and shoved her toward Big Mike. "Take her. The aerial assault is upon us!"

All eyes were immediately trained on the horizon as Mike caught the nymph and hustled her inside and quickly returned to the deck. Jose scrambled up to the roof with mortars and hunkered down next to Dan and Bobby, everyone trying to get a sense of direction and an enemy head count. Initially it looked like what could have been small specks in the sky resembling a flock of birds, but as soon as Hubert had flung the nymph into Mike's arms, Damali's internal radar picked it up a beat after Hubert's. The specks were fast-moving spirals headed their way.

"Positions!" Damali shouted, dodging behind the deck for cover and holding her Glock at the ready.

Guardians scrambled, hunkering down and taking the nymph deeper into the villa with them. Artillery would only hold up for so long, given the numbers of hybrids that she could sense on the move. It would only be a matter of time before her team was slaughtered. Damali's mind latched on a quick plan: Use nature against things that could bleed half-human blood. The debate in the Neteru Council of Queens' chamber stabbed into her consciousness, but she also knew her queens had as much as said that both Neteru Councils had been given explicit instructions from On High to stand down and to let the living Neterus do this job. However, every threat her enraged queens had hurled across the oval table in a fury, Damali mentally grasped.

Instantly she felt a current strobe down her arm, and she stood quickly and headed toward the beach. "Hold your fire until I give the command!"

She couldn't address the stricken expressions held by the team; now was not a time for them to challenge her command. It was basic mathematics. They were outnumbered, therefore severely outgunned. Shells and bullets could be quickly exhausted and wasted, but there was a rich supply of natural weapons the queens had made available to her. Plus, she knew how Cain would probably play this; her team was expendable, but he wanted her alive and able to mate. He'd try to take her as a hostage to lure Carlos to his death. Damali advanced down the beach, knowing she wasn't the primary target for annihilation, although her family was expendable to Cain.

As the air spirals came into view, Damali held up her Isis and sent out the call to arms. "I call a murder of ravens," she shouted, and within seconds a thick, angry cloud of ravens amassed and headed toward the spirals.

The fast-moving black cloud of birds with razor-sharp beaks flew into the funnels, and within moments, screaming, winged entities began to fall out of the sky with dead birds. Multiple sonic booms of hybrids entering the atmosphere were deafening. Headed on a suicide mission, the ravens zigzagged away, broke formation, and then reconvened to hurl themselves at the airborne invaders again. Smaller, more aerial-agile black bodies went after huge leathery wings, flying right at them like living black bullets in a frontal assault, tearing through the membranes that gave the hybrids flight and sending stunned entities crashing into the waves. Damali watched the sea bubble and quickly ran to the shore, touching her Isis to the water.

"Sharks—U-boats, clean up the carnage! Dolphins—torpedoes! Killer whales—subs! Do not let anything come up breathing!"

Large red bubbling patches spread out in the water as the sea churned and the winds kicked up again. Huge entities riding a black dragon cavalry tried to emerge from the red underwater pits to crest the waves, but lost limbs to slashing shark teeth and were knocked off their mounts by leaping bottlenose dolphins. Huge orcas battled the dragons that were carrying the hybrids, ripping open exposed underbellies beneath the waves and slamming into dragon rib cages like massive, thick-bodied missiles with teeth. Hurricane winds rose as a seawall built, but Damali held the line, grabbed her Isis with two hands, and made a batlike swing that split it in two to send it crashing backward into the hybrids.

"Eve owns the elements, you bastard!" Damali yelled, and sent multiple white lightning strikes from the tip of her blade to fry aerial hybrid attackers that were trying to advance on the villa.

The ground beneath her feet had begun to rumble and she knew the land assault was coming. Jamming the Isis long sword into the sand, she sent an arc of war fury into the earth.

"Insects swarm! Leaf-cutter ants from the Amazon, I call you! Scorpions render deadly! The scarabs of Anubis I summon you!"

Hybrid demons emerged from the sand like they were coming out of a hundred foxholes at once, but the instant their heads surfaced, scrambling insects swarmed over their faces and ate out their eyes, delivering lethal stings to the howling beasts.

The rain and wind was almost too severe to hold her footing, but Damali hunkered down, using the Isis as an anchor and watching in horror as a massive black dragon surfaced too quickly for the seafaring creatures to attack it. Even in the driving rain she could see the black armor and Black Death sword raised that only belonged to one entity she knew. Cain. Behind him came a stronger cavalry, and she pushed herself to her feet with her blade.

"Fire!" she shouted to her team.

Damali fell against the sand from the RPG blast Mike released as it missed the lead entity's dragon and took out the one behind it in a red-and-black splatter of guts. The demon hybrid that had been riding the dragon hurled toward the water, but was saved by a black feather-winged entity.

"Go for their horses!" she yelled over the din of exploding artillery and death cries.

Wounded entities screamed; war horns and hybrid command-screeches rent the air. Machine-gun report from the roof shredded feathers. Bullets flew by her in hot flashes of metal and lethal whizzes. Grenades pelted the beach with canisters of holy water tear gas, making shrapnel from friendly fire an obstacle course that pushed her further away from the house. Black arcs from the sea met white arcs coming from the villa that crackled in the air, lighting the torrential downpour like fireworks. The huge entity wearing a black helmet had made it to the beach.

"Attack!" he yelled.

She knew Cain's voice anywhere. For a moment Damali hesitated. But as soon as she did, she saw four large white patches of fabric rise to the churning surface of the ocean. Jasmine was on the deck with Bobby while Mike and Berkfield covered them. The young Guardians' hands were united, a blue current rushing out toward the seaborne fabric. As soon as their energy touched the water, four large opalescent red dragons with black skeletal lines leapt off the sheets and took flight, headed toward the beach.

"Those are ours!" Jose shouted from the roof. "My drawing with Jasmine's!"

The living-blood dragons added to the aerial assault of the ravens, capturing hybrids by the midsections using severe fanged jaws, shaking them like outraged dogs before flinging them into the water for the sharks. But Cain kept coming, the smaller red dragons no match for the thing he rode.

Too close to Damali to fire a mortar round or RPG at it, Dan and Mike hollered in unison, "Fall back, D! Fall back!"

"No!" Damali shouted when Cain smiled and leveled his blade at her, his dragon snorting and breathing fire. She began running and could feel the heat chasing her down the sand like a laser as she zigzagged away from the flames that scorched and melted sand behind her. The instant the dragon drew a breath she pivoted, turned, and rammed her Isis into the sand to get off a two-handed shot with her Glock nine, blinding it.

The massive beast reared, swinging its huge head back and forth in agony and scorching some of Cain's ground forces as well as those that had reached the beach from the sea. Cain roared in fury and tightened his grip on the reins to steady the flailing creature, but pulled up too hard and caused the dragon to lose its balance to go down hard on one side.

His wing trapped by the struggling dragon, Damali quickly advanced on Cain. But he was on one side of the beast, she was on the other, and a dangerous, razor-sharp, muscled tail, panicked flame bursts, and huge dragon claws made it impossible to scale the thing to get to Cain. However, she could cripple him.

A cut from an Isis blade left a permanent, nonregenerative wound in a demon, living or dead, and she seized upon the opportunity to deliver one the moment Cain's tail lashed under the dragon's to help right the fallen beast. Nearly blind with fury, she yanked the Isis from the sand as she rushed forward, dodging claws and flames and swung.

The chime of the Isis rang out, hybrids in midair attacks and those left on the beach slowed to a halt as their leader yelled out in pain.

"I bet you won't violate me with your tail again, demon!" she shouted to Cain, ill-advisedly moving forward to render a death blow to his dragon by plunging her sword up to the hilt into its heart. Fury had her in a stranglehold. There was no fear, just lizard-brain blind rage. "And when I get this thing up off of you, and cut off your dick," she yelled, so angry that Cain's image literally blurred, "that appendage is going straight up your ass!"

The roar that Cain released knocked her back ten yards, and to her frank awe, he sliced off his own wing and shoved the dragon off him. Okay, now it was time to run.

Mike and Dan's shells cut a path between her and Cain in speeding woofs that exploded behind her as she zipped past the house down the beach, Cain hot on her trail. The arcing black blast that Cain rocked the house with knocked her sniper team off the roof and sent deck-rail-wood shrapnel flying. Mike and Berkfield hit the charred deck flooring and covered their heads. Jasmine and Bobby dove over the rails to the sand below it. Windows blew out, forcing those inside the house covering her with gunfire to duck down and flatten themselves to the floor. Hubert and his team were suddenly forced into hand-to-hand combat with the few remaining demons on the beach as Damali breathlessly made it to the rocks with her Isis in her grip.

She immediately turned on Cain and sent a hot Isis blast into the center of his chest. "You'll never take me alive, motherfucker!"

Sprawled out and only temporarily dazed, Cain's gaze narrowed on her as she jumped down, prepared to confront him in mortal combat.

He tried to summon his black blade to him, but it was in shards, his wing dismembered, and his tail a bloody stump.

"Fall back!" he shouted, and within seconds was gone.

The beach went still. The rains receded, leaving only a smoky battle trail in the sky. The full moon overhead shone brightly.

Damali glanced around and then ran toward the villa to check for casualties. The truth stole her breath: this was just one quick campaign, a battle. Not the war by a long shot.

"I'm not liking this at all," Carlos said to Shabazz and Rider, standing outside Yonnie's lair. "It's full dark, I can sense two vampires inside, Yonnie and Tara's signature, but I've got a blackout to the villa and it's like we're in a dark-shielded zone."

"In and out," Rider said, urging Carlos to open Yonnie's lair. "Do it the old-fashioned way, man. For Christ's sake, just holler."

Carlos nodded and complied, yelling his friend's name at the top of his lungs. "Yonnie! It's family—open up!"

The lair door eerily creaked open. The full moon over Nevada peeked into pure blackness. Carlos's eyes instantly adjusted to the darkness and he lit the wall torches with a silver glance. As soon as the others could see, Rider and Shabazz flanked him.

Yonnie looked up from the bed and hissed at the sight of Rider. But it was obvious that something had gone terribly wrong as Yonnie crouched over Tara's lifeless, naked body. He sought Carlos's gaze, squinting and disoriented, his fangs lowered between a mating bite and battle length. All Carlos could do was stare at Yonnie for a moment. Yonnie's bare chest heaved as though he was unable to take in enough air, and his black silk, drawstring pajama bottoms hung loosely on his hips as though he'd quickly materialized them on with great effort.

"You all right, man?" Carlos asked, advancing slowly.

Rider pushed around Carlos, but Carlos caught Rider by the arm before he could get close enough to have his heart ripped out.

"I don't know what happened," Yonnie said in an agonized voice, growling low in his throat as he stared at Rider, and then brought his gaze back to Carlos's. "She's flatlining, even though I fed her."

"Oh, shit, man! What did you do?"

"I don't know what happened, man!" Yonnie yelled. "Heal her! I can't, and I don't know why!"

Carlos stood with the stunned Guardians near the lair entrance and watched in horror as Tara's eyelids fluttered. She weakly reached toward Rider without lifting her arm, and then murmured his name on a final breath as her hand relaxed against the bed. Carlos jumped back, causing Rider and Shabazz to instinctively do the same. Rendered speechless as Tara's spirit sat up from her body in a white haze and glanced around in terror, Carlos scavenged his mind for what to tell Rider. They had gotten there too late. Carlos reinforced his grip on Rider's arm and blinked twice as he saw a fast-moving white orb stop in front of her, pulse, become Lopez, and take her hand.

"She's not supposed to have a spirit in a vampire body," Carlos whispered in awe. He watched helplessly as Lopez's spirit calmed Tara's distressed soul and began leading her away. He looked at Yonnie, and then at Rider and swallowed hard. "It's too late."

"Tara!" Rider shouted, breaking Carlos's hold before Carlos or Shabazz could intervene. His gun was raised in the blink of an eye, the barrel pointed at Yonnie's chest as Carlos and Shabazz shouted no, and a bullet tore through the air. Gone in a flash, Yonnie was mist. Rider unloaded the rest of his clip, blowing out sections of black marble wall that was behind where Yonnie had been.

"I'll kill that sonofabitch!" Rider shouted, and went to Tara's limp body. He dropped his weapon on the bed as Carlos and Shabazz rushed to her side. Rider swept her up, hugging her lifeless body to his chest. "It's not too late. Don't tell me that shit!"

Shabazz and Carlos put a hand on Rider's shoulder, but said nothing as they stared down at their Guardian brother.

"Carlos, man, if ever there was a time to work your shit . . . it would be now, brother." Shabazz's eyes glistened with empathy and he looked away when Carlos slowly shook his head.

"C'mon, baby, take a breath for me," Rider said, rocking her against him hard. "Take a vein, just wake up, sweetheart." He turned and looked at Carlos. "Make her wake up!" he yelled, becoming more frantic. Rider looked at Shabazz. "Ransack this joint and find a blood bottle so I can feed her! Just don't stand there looking at me! Do it!"

Shabazz kicked away the refuse of bottles beside the bed, and Carlos held Rider's wrist when he reached to yank his Bowie knife off his belt to slit a vein for her. Rider jerked his arm away and worked around Tara's body to slit his wrist, dribbling blood into her mouth. But the blood simply collected between her semiparted lips and ran down the sides of her face.

"She's gone, man," Carlos whispered, his voice hitching in his throat. "He took her too far and—"

"She's not gone!" Rider shouted, hugging Tara to him, tears streaming down his cheeks. He looked away from Carlos and buried his face in her hair, which had gone gray, stroking it roughly. "Not after more than thirty years, she's immortal. A vampire. Tara's not gone, just sick. Help her, man . . . you're supposed to be a healer."

"Even I can't raise the dead," Carlos said quietly, closing his eyes and stooping down next to Rider. He briefly held Rider's bloodied wrist and sealed the self-inflicted wound. "I can't lay hands on her with Neteru silver in my veins. . . . I'll torch her on impact during a healing. Marlene was normal, human, living tissue." Carlos looked at Rider, trying to make him understand, his tone faraway and broken. "She's vampire remains now. No spirit in her to absorb the silver . . . she'll go to ash in your arms like I'd touched her with daylight."

Shabazz yanked a black silk sheet from the bed and tried to cradle it around Tara. "Man . . . let me take her and cover her up," he said to Rider quietly. "She's been gone for over thirty years and you should remember her like this, beautiful. Don't torture your mind and watch the decay. C'mon, man, as your Guardian brother, I'm begging you."

"She's not gonna decay," Rider said, clutching Tara's body to him tighter, "because my baby isn't dead . . . just asleep." He kissed her forehead, which was beginning to wrinkle with age. "You just rest, sweetie, I'ma get somebody to help you. We'll find a good medic. You just hold on."

Carlos stood and backed away with Shabazz to allow Rider to

grieve for a moment alone. He put a hand on Shabazz's shoulder and spoke in a low, reverent murmur to him.

"'Bazz, you have got to get her body out of his arms before the maggots and the grubs infest it . . . and before her flesh starts dropping off the bones. It'll take his mind."

Shabazz nodded and turned Black Beauty around to hold it by the barrel. "You wrap her up good in the sheet, and bring her ashes with us. At least that way the man can bury her under a prayer."

Rider's sobs were so painful that they brought tears to Carlos's eyes. Carlos nodded as Shabazz walked forward, and he looked away as Shabazz approached Rider from behind, then landed a gun butt blow to the back of Rider's skull.

Yonnie's gaze tore around the casino floor as he turned in a panic while seated in a red velvet padded slot-machine chair. The machine's roller was spinning, just like his head, and Yonnie soon glanced down to notice that he was fully clothed in a black designer suit with a crimson shirt. The roller within the slot slowed and came up 6-6-6 and then began ringing as it spilled endless gold coins into the catch tray.

"Seems like tonight is your lucky night," a smooth, deep male voice said beside him.

Still somewhat disoriented, Yonnie jerked his attention toward the voice coming from the chair beside him and then froze.

"Councilman Nuit . . ." Yonnie's eyes widened. "It was rumored that you were extinct," he whispered, but kept respect in his tone.

Nuit smiled and dragged his fingers through the coins in Yonnie's slot tray. "Rumors are deadly, but I have a proposition for you . . . since you now owe me."

Yonnie just stared at him.

"You were too weak to jettison yourself away from the Guardian's attack, *n'est-ce pas*? Who do you think pulled you from sure extinction and strengthened you again?"

Yonnie nodded and slowly closed his eyes with defeat, feeling

Nuit's cool breath waft near his throat. What Nuit could never fathom was he would have gladly taken that bullet. What was existence worth now, without Tara? Eternity without her was his Hell.

"Your councilman is no more," Nuit crooned seductively. "He abandoned you and went into the Light, and yet he couldn't even heal your mate . . . who, from what I could see, even reached out for another man—*a human*—in her final breath. That is weakness, not power, Yolando. Such a travesty is beneath our species."

Yonnie fought the building moisture within his eyes and swallowed hard. Trapped, the only option was to negotiate his way out. "Then, what do you want me to do, sir?"

"Take a throne next to me, elevate yourself under a new leadership, and be my eyes and ears topside to assist against a Guardian team that has plagued our world. These are the same humans who betrayed you. Rivera stood there and watched Tara die in your arms, allowed your eternal mate to go into the Sea of Perpetual Agony, and will bury her remains on hallowed ground so that even the Vampire Council cannot raise her from the ashes again . . . all for the sake of their brother, Jack Rider. You were never one of them, and when it counted most, they left you. Tried to murder you. But I can lift your turn bans so you can make another mate."

Yonnie stared at Nuit, a quiet scheme roiling within him as he nodded faux agreement. Carlos had shown him a lot; Fallon Nuit was stronger at the moment, and there was no sense in getting his heart ripped out on the casino floor.

"Who's running council now as the new Chairman?" Yonnie asked, holding Nuit's smug gaze.

"Dante's son," Nuit said with a sly smile. "You know the legend . . . Cain."

Yonnie keyed in on Nuit's oily tone of jealousy. "I know him," Yonnie said in Dananu with the slightest disdain registering in his voice. It was time to bargain. "I saw him when he came to the Gray Zone as a Neteru king and went for Damali." He allowed the information to fester in Nuit's mind for a moment, also fully remembering Nuit's desire for her as a prize. "He's not one of us, really. He's a hybrid."

"Then, you know his . . . weaknesses?"

Yonnie smiled at Nuit and a quiet alliance was formed. "His, hers, and Carlos's."

Nuit leaned in and smelled Yonnie's jugular, testing for a lie and then sat back appearing temporarily satisfied. "That you do. *Très bon*."

"Yeah, it's all good," Yonnie murmured, extending a handshake to Nuit. "Now hook a brother up, so I can go to work."

Lilith calmly walked through Gabrielle's Nevada condo and sat down in a Queen Anne chair in the living room and crossed her legs. She watched in amusement as Gabrielle worked hard to focus on the dead crystal ball that was set in the center of her dining room table.

"Your powers are weak these evenings. Such a shame," Lilith murmured, causing Gabrielle to turn with a start.

Lilith stood and sauntered over to her and stroked her hair, sending a pleasure shiver down Gabrielle's spine. She kissed Gabrielle's shoulder and began a lazy trail up Gabrielle's neck that made her tense. "I would never hurt you, as long as you're doing my bidding," Lilith whispered against the vein in her neck.

"I . . . I know," Gabrielle said with a dry swallow. "Just tell me what you need me to do tonight."

Lilith's hands trailed down Gabrielle's shoulders, putting gooseflesh on her arms. Gabrielle closed her eyes as fear and disgust fought for dominance over the excruciating pleasure Lilith invoked. She struggled against a gasp as Lilith's hands cupped her breasts and she began to knead her nipples until they pouted to taut pebbles beneath her fingers.

"You're getting so wet," Lilith murmured, suckling Gabrielle's ear. "How long has it been since you were truly pleasured?" she asked in a breathy whisper, sending a phantom caress between Gabrielle's legs until they parted. Lilith flicked her tongue against Gabrielle's jugular until she moaned. "I bet never like this," she said, leaning in closer to trail her hand down Gabrielle's torso and dip her hand beneath her silk robe to part her lips.

Gabrielle arched as the caress found her bud. "Please don't," she said in a quiet, panicked whisper.

"Why not?" Lilith murmured seductively, gliding her finger in agony-producing sweeps against the swollen, slick slit, and massaging it until Gabrielle arched again. "Surely your virginity is long gone . . . and you can't be saving your virtue for a husband." Lilith giggled low in her throat as she inserted her finger gently inside Gabrielle, causing her to clutch the edge of the table.

"I can't concentrate for you, dark queen," Gabrielle gasped, trying to bargain her way out of the situation. "I was trying to contact my initiates for you . . . and . . . oh . . . I was . . . I was . . ."

"We've already found them," Lilith hissed seductively and then chuckled low in her throat when Gabrielle tensed. "Why so nervous?"

"I thought you might be displeased that you'd located them before I had," Gabrielle said quickly.

"You did help us, immensely," Lilith whispered, sending a blinding orgasm into Gabrielle's canal. She laughed as Gabrielle cried out. "Your initiates were our beacon . . . just like your loyalty to Jack Rider and your family was. Now I'm here to reward you with your fondest wish, one that you had asked us for years ago."

Faint, Gabrielle tried to turn to look at Lilith. Tears stung her eyes and she spoke on a strangled whisper. "Please . . . I've changed my mind. I only wanted Yonnie to do that."

"I know," Lilith cooed. "But he has been remanded for other tasks. However, now that Tara is dead, you can take her place beside him as his wife."

"No!"

The strike that tore at Gabrielle's jugular was so violent that the scream never left her throat.

CHAPTER TEN

The carnage that met Damali's eyes made her run toward the villa in a flat-out dash. Big Mike was on the ground panting, sweat pouring down his contorted face as he struggled against a huge section of deck-rail wood that had pierced his abdomen like a stake. The overwhelmed nymph flitted anxiously between Mike and Hubert as she furiously tried to heal wounds, not sure of who to tend to first, her loyalties severely divided.

"Medic! Marlene!" Damali shouted, coming to a hard slide next to Mike in the sand. "Berkfield! We've got a man down!"

Berkfield struggled to rise from the sand, dazed from the blast, but couldn't. On a mission to save a life, undaunted, he tried to drag his injured leg with a compound fracture behind him. He yelled out in pain as the broken thigh bone shifted under his skin.

"Okay, okay, stand down," Damali said quickly, realizing that Berkfield was too weak from his own injuries to help her heal. She gently pressed one hand to Mike's forehead to siphon away the pain, causing him to groan when she touched her other hand near the gaping wound, and then threw her head back, panting. "Where's Mar? I need another healer to go in with me," Damali called out. She opened her eyes and looked down at Mike. "You hang in there with me, Michael Roberts. You hear me, you big ox!"

Inez came through the shattered doors first, screamed, and rushed to kneel beside Damali. "Oh, Jesus, Lord have mercy!" she said, rocking on her knees next to Mike with her arms wrapped around her waist.

"Where *is* Marlene?" Damali shouted.

"She fell down hard and hit her head on the counter trying to body-shield Sara from a black blast. Marjorie is trying to get her up," Inez said, choked. "She was unconscious."

Jose was flat on his back where he'd been blown from the roof. Juanita was hunched over him, patting his face trying to bring him around, while also trying to pick thick panels of glass out of his chest with shaking fingers.

"Don't move him," Damali ordered. "He could have injured his spine from the way he fell—I'll get to him in a minute, after I triage this man who's bleeding out."

J.L. was sitting on the sand, his head leaned back against the villa, his eyes closed and clutching his right arm to his side. Krissy ripped her T-shirt and began making a tourniquet and shrieked to Damali as she realized that the limb had been nearly severed from a black lightning strike.

"Damali! He'll lose his arm!" Krissy screamed, frantically working to stop the bleeding.

"Tie the tourniquet as tight as you can and start working on that man—stat! Focus everything you've got to start knitting tissue back together!" Damali hollered across the beach.

The moment Krissy touched J.L., he arched with a wailing sob. His agony set Damali's teeth on edge and she watched flickering blue static run down J.L.'s body and terminate where the limb had been disconnected to only hang by ligaments and muscle.

"Don't touch me! Please, don't move it!" he screamed, sobbing.

"He's a tactical," Damali yelled to Krissy. "Stop the bleeding! Ignore his cries and work on him if you wanna save that arm! Connect his own energy arc from his upper body to the dying forearm, use your hands as a bridge, and juice him, once you secure the tourniquet. Sit on his ass if you have to!"

Damali's gaze shot around to take note of any other wounded. After the siege, the villa had now turned into a makeshift M.A.S.H. unit triage on the beach. Bobby was being helped to his feet by Jasmine, clearly still reeling from the effects of a hard fall off the deck and nursing a postblast concussion. Dan was out cold with a black smoldering stripe across his chest. Heather was administering CPR, giving Dan the breath of life.

"Get your hands into it," Damali said, pulling more pain away from Mike as she slowed his internal hemorrhaging. "Thump on that man's chest! Get his heart started—he took a black blast!" *God, just don't let Dan have fractured his skull or Jose have snapped his neck or spine.*

Damali squeezed her eyes shut as Mike shuddered, groaned, and began going into shock. "I need the Caduceus," she said between her teeth, turning her face skyward to send her complaint up to Heaven. "To heal my team in battle, queens hear me."

We cannot send it to heal demons, Aset's sad mental voice murmured on the wind. *It is forbidden.*

"What are you talking about?" Damali screamed, now putting both hands on Mike's abdomen. "I am working on my Guardians! Humans!"

Do NOT unfurl your wings before your team, Aset warned. *Not with hybrid demons in your midst. Their legions must NEVER know. It is bad enough that Cain has learned this truth. That's an order from On High!*

Then send the Caduceus!

Your team has been infected by a Level Seven demon genesis. The sacred Staff of Imhotep cannot be utilized in this manner. Once demon energy bonds to its serpents, the Caduceus would be their greatest weapon against us. Heaven forbade me to send it to you, child.

"I don't care what they said!" Damali shouted. "My team is—"

A thick white lightning bolt split the dark heavens above Damali's head and made her and Inez duck down.

The queens wish to help, but we have been given EXPLICIT orders that we dare not violate. You marriage is in jeopardy of annulment for the same reason—just like we cannot send in the Covenant to reinforce you now. Even they are unaware, just like your team is blind to the truth of what you are. Any of those who love you will not do what is necessary should the time come, and could also be corrupted to leak classified information to the wrong side at a perilous hour. Because of free will, as you know, humans are vulnerable to sway and to misguided empathy.

"What the hell are you talking about, Aset!" Damali briefly looked up at the sky. "Don't get shaky on me now, ladies. *Not tonight.*" She returned her attention to her agonized Guardian brother, trying to blot out Aset's voice in order to concentrate fully on keeping Big Mike alive.

You, as a descendent of a Powers Angel—the highest form of healer, second only to archangels, were NEVER to marry or consort with a being that still has remnant traces of vampire demon in his DNA. Carlos is your soul mate and has been reborn in the Light, but after his rebirth, once redeemed and clean, he was to never have taken a dark throne again—and definitely not the most deadly one of that insidious realm. If he had been clean, your angelic lineage would have strengthened him as the strongest Neteru to have ever lived. Your progeny was to be without question a child of the Light.

"Aset," Damali begged, sobbing. "Help my team. Forget about whatever else! We can deal with that later!"

We cannot. I must tell you all now. The recessive gene that Carlos could possibly release from his loins has both Neteru Councils scrambling for an answer. Damali, had we known what was in your lineage . . . Maybe we can beleaguer the point of your love for one another and ask them to save the marriage but render you sterile to one another, by merely canceling out your opposite genes.

"Mike is in *bad shape*, Aset," Damali said through a grimace, pain riddling her body as tears coursed down her face. "Later, we can deal with that later!"

Inez continued to stroke Mike's brow, trying to calm him as Damali worked.

No. You must know NOW! I have only been granted permission for this last conversation.

"Last talk? Aset, you guys are walking away? I have men dying on the beach!"

Queen Sister, regretfully this is the last time we shall be able to directly speak until Heaven draws a conclusion. Communication to us and the Covenant will be summarily terminated. The Covenant will be kept behind walls in vigil, as their impulse will be to come to you to assist you by any means necessary. You will be cut off.

"What!" Damali shrieked, and then quickly leaned in to put her ear to Mike's chest. "His heartbeat is getting erratic." She yanked her attention toward the glimpse of triangular violet light in the sky. "Don't pull this crap on me right now!"

All I can share is that Eve's grief still swaths the Earth with infertility. But even if nanosecond timing allowed Carlos to sire versus Cain before her spirit became afflicted by Cain's descent, the fractals of light still may not have come together in the right combination. We are only now coming to understand this. Our hands are tied, just as our hearts are bound by sorrow. All we can offer is to continue to send you our combined energy from a distance, but cannot materialize with you in battle or in healings from this point forward, dear daughter . . . Queen Sister. Aset's words ended in a sob. *If what you are carrying is the worst of what could be—it could leach into our auras if we are in your density and presence, siphon that very old Neteru energy, and threaten to breach Ring One of Heaven. Then the very Gates of Heaven could come under siege. We have been ordered to wait for a sign. We cannot even allow you to visit our council, until we know.*

Quiet hysteria briefly broke Damali's concentration, sending Mike into a convulsion. "C'mon, Mike, stay with me. Stay with me, man!"

Blood was everywhere as Damali tried to keep one hand near Mike's wound while using the other to feel for his pulse. "He's going into cardiac arrest!" Damali's gaze went to Inez, who was weeping and stroking Mike's brow. "Suck that bullshit up, pound on this man's chest, and keep him breathing while I work, if you want him to live!"

Inez quickly moved into place and kept up the rhythmic CPR, intermittently pressing onto Mike's chest with both hands and blowing into his mouth, while Damali closed her eyes and focused heat around the broken vessels.

Damali, Aset said, her tone apologetic. *We do have mercy. Our tears are yours. But there is a dark energy lesion surrounding your team. Carlos's old alliances are tipping the balance. This is what Heaven waits to witness. The individual choices of you, Carlos, and the team.*

"I can't focus on that right now, Aset," Damali yelled. "If I can't show my . . . then work with me!"

Remove the wood from him, Aset said quietly. *We will assist as best we can from here. If he does not recover, bury him on hallowed ground with full Guardian honors. The kings will send a retinue to escort his admirable spirit to Heaven.*

Damali looked at Inez. It was not about losing Mike. Screw what Aset said! This was her brother!

"I'm gonna have to pull out the deck rail, and he's gonna raise up and holler good when I do," she told Inez in a panting command. "Use your body to hold down his shoulders." Damali kissed Mike's forehead, and tried to still his eyes, which were rolling back and forth beneath their lids. "Mike, I love you," she said, and then grasped the wood, yanked hard, and quickly turned her head when a section of his intestines came out with it.

The wail Mike released echoed on the beach and brought Marlene and Marjorie stumbling to the broken door. Berkfield dragged himself forward, reaching toward Mike before he dropped to the sand, unable to move another inch unassisted. Marlene dashed away from Marjorie, fell, got back up, and half-crawled, half-scrambled to Damali's side with blood running down her temple from her scalp, where she'd sustained a head wound. Marjorie was at Richard's side within seconds.

"Oh, Jesus, Richard," Marjorie said, touching his leg and making him cry out.

Damali's hands were slick with blood as she forced her hand into the gaping wound, shoving Mike's innards back into the hole as Mike cried out again in pain. She ignored his cries, shudders of agony claiming her as his suffering reached fever pitch. He was begging for her to stop and just let him die, but she had to blot all that out with a fervent, mental prayer for him to make it as she worked to save his life. Slivers of wood bit into her fingers and palm as she drew the fragments out along with the internal poisons his intestinal tract was internally leaking into his bloodstream.

The fetid stench of broken bowels and the intensity of Mike's agony put a cold sheen of sweat over Damali's whole body. Inez held down his torso with her own body weight, receiving weak blows to her back as Mike fought in pain to get her off him while sobbing. Marlene instinctively grabbed Mike's legs and began working with Damali's healing in a weakened state. Inez continued to hold him down, dry heaving, trying not to vomit until Mike's body slowly calmed. Damali finally pulled her hand out of his abdomen, her entire body trembling as she rolled over on her side, gasping.

"Seal him up, Mar," Damali whispered through chattering teeth and then slowly pushed herself up to stand after a moment. She staggered forward as she looked at her fallen team. "We ain't losing nobody on my watch," she wheezed. "Marj, get a cup from the kitchen, take blood from Berkfield's inner elbow—other side than the one used earlier today. I'ma work on him, first, so he can help clean up this beach," she said through ragged breaths, "while Marj goes behind Marlene to close up everybody's gashes."

Damali bent and rested her bloody hands on her knees for a second, sucking in air. She glanced around, glad to see that Jose and Dan were finally semiconscious.

Carlos and Shabazz stood on the beach staring at the villa in shock, holding up Rider's limp body. The dwelling looked like it had been shelled with the entire team in it. Tara's disintegrating form was bound in a black silk sheet over Carlos's shoulder, and he let it slide off him to the sand. Shabazz caught Rider's weight as Carlos dashed forward. Damali was lying facedown on the beach with a group of demons and a nymph hostage standing over her. The rest of the team was in varying states of injury grouped around his wife, unable to protect the fallen.

Dirty faces stained with tears and eyes stricken with pure terror looked up at Carlos as he made his way to Damali, calling the blade of Ausar into his grip, and running forward, sword raised, clearly ready to take a demon head. Shabazz eased Rider to the sand and began running, Sleeping Beauty leveled at the closest demon standing near Marlene.

"They're on our side!" Berkfield said in an exhausted croak.

"Allies!" Marlene shouted.

"Hold your fire!" Marjorie yelled, scrambling to her feet to protect Hubert.

Shabazz slowed to a jog, coming up behind Carlos.

"What the fuck happened?" Carlos said, going to Damali but looking at the hybrids with suspicion.

"She healed a near mortal wound that Mike caught in the gut," Marlene said breathing hard, "after expending nearly all her energy in a battle against Cain. Three quarters of the team sustained serious injuries, but she sealed 'em up with me, Marj, and Berkfield—Juanita, Krissy, Inez, and Jasmine didn't do too bad on assist, either. We'll live. So will she." Marlene motioned toward the nymph. "Sara sealed up her team, but they weren't as bad off."

Sara looked at Carlos and then dropped to her knees in exhaustion and awe. "The fabled one."

The eleven demon hybrids that had surrounded the nymph all went down on one knee.

"We are honored to serve you," the large hybrid named Hubert said. "If we die at your side, the Light shall accept us."

Carlos inhaled and Hubert's blood tracer matched the ripped T-shirt Rider had given him earlier. "All right. You check out," Carlos said, ramming his blade into the sand to free his hands so he could gently lift Damali. "You guys wait outside. Sara and the rest of the team go in the house." He stood and looked at Shabazz, and then at Marlene. "Tie Rider to a chair, then wake him up. 'Bazz, me and you dig the grave. Mar, we need you to stand in as chaplain."

Marlene got to her feet with a grunt, her eyes frantic. "Who's in the body bag?"

"Tara," Carlos said flatly, stepping over debris with Damali in his arms. "She didn't make it."

The villa's living room became the recovery ward. Newly healed Guardians rested and sipped water slowly as those less injured tended to them. Damali rested on a stool with her head in her hands, barely able to remain upright, but she'd refused to go to sleep until she knew for sure each Guardian would be all right. But it was the news about Tara that most pained her heart. Rider's bellows from the bedroom simply made her close her eyes as quiet tears fell.

"What went wrong?" Damali whispered, searching Carlos's eyes. "Why would Yonnie do something like that?"

"I don't think he meant to," Carlos said quietly as they both listened to Shabazz trying to reason with Rider down the hall. "It was the look in his eyes, and he'd asked me to heal her . . . but I couldn't. Her spirit had vacated her body before I could even touch her. . . . Lopez came for her." That was all Carlos could say over the thick lump that had formed in his throat.

"Can I pray over her remains?" Sara asked, drawing Carlos and Damali's attention. She looked at Marlene. "Your mother-seer helped us all, helped me. Your team has taken us in, and no matter what your Tara had become, she was your family . . . therefore your loss somehow feels like ours, too."

Carlos nodded. "Yeah, it's cool. Thanks. She could use whatever Light you can send her way. The only thing that's gonna keep Yonnie and Rider from losing it might be knowing her soul really went with Lopez to Heaven and isn't down in the pit."

Damali nodded and grabbed Carlos's hand across the butcher block. "Need to talk to you. Open a channel."

He stared at her. *What else went down?*

She told him in fits and starts what Aset had said, fighting back a sob while looking him dead in the eyes.

They're not annulling shit. He looked away from her. *Nothing comes between me and you.*

Damali nodded. *If I'm not already carrying for you, I might be sterile to you anyway. Aset said something about the council's ensuring that our genes would cancel each other out, which is moot anyway, because as long as Eve is grieving, there is no such thing as conception. But I'm still at risk for a fusion between you and Cain, or your seed could have beaten his to fertilize an egg first by nanoseconds. Even still, if it did . . .* Damali swallowed hard and looked at the counter. *We don't know what we've made.*

I don't want to think about this now. I can't.

Carlos pulled out of the private telepathy and let his breath out hard. "We've gotta move this battered squad to Central Mexico with the quickness, but I'm nervous about moving them in a hard energy whirl until everything has set with their healing for twenty-four hours. Right now, with energy from Nod escaping, a new energy paradigm has to be seeping into the planet—I can feel it."

"So can I," Damali said quietly, staring at him. "If the age-old truth is correct, 'As above, so below,' then maybe things are haywire on the darkside, because it sure is getting strange on our side."

Carlos leaned across the counter and dropped his voice to a tense whisper. "This hybrid energy, if it surfaces in humans, could mean anything. We've eventually gotta go clean out the nests of Cain loyalists in Nod, and let the good hybrids go back there, D. Long term, these refugees can't stay in the Gray Zone. Think about it. How long do you think it would take, if conception is ever possible again, before normal people would have all sorts of combinations with the entities in Nod, and superpowers to go with it—not to mention free will to use that strength? If we help that happen, we'd be going against the oldest banishment edict in the Good Book." Carlos glanced around and leaned in closer. "I'm trying to walk the straight and narrow during these last biblical days, D, for real. Maybe that's why the Light had to pull back from us . . . to see what we'd do, especially since you and I, technically, are hybrids ourselves."

She closed her eyes and allowed her head to drop forward, almost too overwhelmed to think about it all in one sitting. "You're right," was all the response she could muster.

"My other concern is this," Carlos pressed on, squeezing her hands tighter as his inner panic built. "Hubert and company are gonna have to get to Central Mexico the best way they can, because with a team that's dipping in life energy pulse, the added weight of hybrids can throw me off course—which cannot happen."

"I know," Damali said, her gaze now going to Tara's body, which was wrapped in a black silk sheet on the beach. "We need to bury Tara, too. If we get hit again tonight by vamps or weres . . ."

"It'll be just me, you, and Shabazz—maybe Hubert's squad. Everybody else is beat to hell. I'm not even feeling you in the mix, right through here, especially going solo against what just hit this beach."

Damali clasped Carlos's hands and sent the full battle into his mind, showing him the aerial assault, and how the Level One tunnels were used to hide Cain's hybrid army beneath the earth to then bring them up through the ocean in the Bermuda Triangle and Asian triangles near Japan, as well as through old battleground caverns beneath the sand. "I did all right."

He smiled and kissed her knuckles. "You did more than all right. You're one awesome gansta sister. I don't think I could have gotten to everybody that needed healing without losing one," he said in a private murmur. "I love you."

Shabazz's sudden footfalls rang out and made even the weary who were laid out on the floor look up. "Need a purge, people! Brotherman's eyes are glowing."

Carlos jumped to his feet and dashed down the hall with Damali fast behind him. But when they burst into the room, Rider wasn't in his chair. The sheet restraints were on the floor, and Rider was on the ceiling, staring down at them, and snarling. Carlos reached out and instantly contained Rider in a translucent black box that drowned out the curses Rider hurled as Carlos carefully lowered the containment cell to the floor.

"How's this happening?" Damali asked, her gaze steady on Rider. "We healed his last nick over a year ago."

"I know. It doesn't make sense for—"

"Yo, yo, yo, got another man in turn-crisis!" Shabazz hollered from the next room.

Damali and Carlos almost bumped into each other as they rushed through the bedroom doorway and down the hall. When they entered the living room, the team was on one side of the room trying to find weapons, and Mike was on all fours on the other side of it, his jaw slowly and painfully extending in a werewolf transition.

"What's wrong with my baby?" Inez screamed, torn between going to Mike and brandishing a gun.

"Lower the weapon, 'Nez," Damali said, trying to slowly divert

Mike's attention while Carlos arced enough energy to ensnare him in a silver cage with bars.

"When's the last time he got nicked by a were, Mar?" Carlos shouted without turning around, now needing his full focus to hold the cage before him and the black box holding Rider in the bedroom.

"A looong time ago. He sucker punched one and split his knuckles wide open on its fangs," Marlene said in a low murmur that again parted the group. "But not as many times as I most likely took a were-nick or two on the astral plane."

Carlos and Damali pivoted just in time to catch Marlene's attempt to lunge out of an open window. Carlos had her by the tail in a long energy lasso. Guardians dove over the sofa and tried to take cover. Shabazz was shouting for Marlene. She hissed and turned to Carlos, eyes glowing gold, upper and lower canines extended as she growled like the angry jaguar she was quickly becoming. Marlene lunged again, but Carlos silver-caged her, sweat pouring down his face as three draining energy sources held him in the center of the floor.

"Inez," Mike crooned in a low rumble. "C'mere, baby, and open up the door . . . just cross his line with your body and break the energy hold, suga. I don't do silver."

Inez shook her head and began hiccup crying as she turned away.

"Damali, baby, you ain't gonna keep your momma locked up like this, are you sweetie?" Marlene then turned a wicked smile to Shabazz. "Lover . . . come on now, me and you go waaay back, right? Open the cage so I can go eat."

"D, don't listen to her," Carlos warned and he stared at Shabazz. "I need your head right and for you to hold the line, brother."

The Guardian team was scattered around the room in huddles of humanity, not sure which direction to turn. Then Juanita's scream tore through the room. Jose tilted his head and blew her a kiss through fangs, holding her arm hard.

"Oh, shit!" Carlos's eyes sought Damali's for help. Both his hands were tethered to silver cages holding back strong entities, as well as holding a black box in the bedroom. It would only be a matter of time before his concentration fractured or his energy dipped and they'd be out.

They had to get to Jose without killing him, if possible, and if not, blow him away if he went for Juanita's throat. Their team's best sharpshooter was in a black box and had just been pulled off the ceiling—if anybody else took a shot, Juanita would take the bullet. Shabazz could barely hold his gun level, it was trembling in his hand so badly as he watched Marlene fully transform. His boy, Jose, had just dropped fang—but as a weaker vamp, negotiation with Jose was possible.

"Yo, Jose, don't do nothing stupid up in here that'll make somebody have to smoke you," Carlos said in Dananu.

Jose yanked Juanita to him, making her cry harder. He smelled her hair, and traced her jugular with a fang. "I won't hurt her," Jose murmured. "Baby, why don't me and you go find a lair. The night is young."

"Or you could take me," Damali said, creating a diversion. She glanced at Carlos and received his subtle nod. "You know you've always wanted to, right? She'll turn, which could damn your soul . . . but if Carlos is cool with it, me and you can go all night—and still wake up laughing in the morning."

"I'm down," Carlos said, as calmly as possible. "I been missing Juanita, anyway, since you've had her on lock. Fair exchange is no robbery."

"You serious?" Jose said, slowly releasing his hold on Juanita. "You cool with that? Ain't gonna give me no static later?"

Juanita shook her head with a whimper.

Damali stepped forward with a bright smile. "Send her my way, baby," Damali said in Dananu, "and I will blow your mind."

Jose shoved Juanita forward in a hard push that made her fall into Damali's embrace. Damali handed her off to stand by Carlos and slowly approached Jose. She seductively tossed her locks over her shoulder, exposing her neck.

"Lose the silver collar," Jose said, beginning to circle her as the stunned team watched the dance and scrambled out of the way.

Carlos kept his gaze sweeping for any other turns that might begin to materialize on the team, while also keeping an eye on the two cages with the snarling weres and Damali. If Jose hurt her, he'd have to kill him. Would drop him in a heartbeat.

Damali took off the collar, held it out, then let it fall to the floor. She'd expected Jose to lunge toward her, but instead he briefly closed his eyes and licked his lips, nicking his tongue with a fang. She was on him so fast he hadn't had a chance to see her coming. One fist was in his hair, her body behind his back, and her baby Isis to his throat.

Jose chuckled. "Damn, D, in front of family?"

"I like to play rough," she said into Jose's ear in Dananu. "Move, and your head is mine."

Overtaken by grief, Juanita turned, and barreled into Carlos's arms.

"No!" Carlos hollered as the caged Guardians broke free, and Rider scrambled along the ceiling like a crab.

Screams broke out as Mike lunged, landed on the countertop, and snarled down at Inez who was huddled on the floor between the stove and the butcher block. Marlene had taken a feline crouch on the back of the sofa, and was staring down at Shabazz, slowly stalking him. Jose flipped Damali over his head onto her back on the floor, eyes glowing. Carlos sent a split-second containment blast from either hand, sweeping Rider and Jose into a joint black box and Marlene and Mike into a single silver cage.

Damali got up slowly from the floor with a pull from Shabazz. "Anyone who ever sustained a nick is vulnerable. Any of us who had been infected before by the damned are, too. We gotta work fast." She looked at Carlos. *That's what the queens were trying to tell me, but I didn't understand. Our team was somehow infected and whatever swirled up from Level Seven is reversing old wound purges and/or bringing old demon DNA to the fore.*

Carlos nodded, sweating, unable to use the energy to mentally answer her. "Lilith can't heal, though . . . Cain was a Neteru, met this team, and could have sensed or caught the scent of which ones had old demon battle scars or vamp way down in their line. Same deal with our other infections from Lilith's games. A Neteru healer can reverse an energy binding and open it right up like it was brand-new."

Damali nodded as she recalled her visit with the queens and how Aset had just shown her that technique. "I can't purge them all by myself," Damali said over the roars and hisses coming from the cages.

She was so exhausted that she was literally weaving from fatigue and breathing hard as she looked at the newbies. "With the old virus from the damned running through the rest of the squad, none of our healers are gonna be strong enough to go in after a demon nick and not come back with it adhered to their systems and spirits, especially after they just did serious injury healings for the first time on the beach." She glanced at Juanita and Inez, hoping that their sanity held before the old virus imploded within them. "As it is, we're gonna have to douse everybody else, too, just to be sure."

"I can't hold them like this all night," Carlos said, the muscles in his arms bulging as Rider and Jose raked their nails down the inner walls of the translucent black box, bellowing in silence behind the enclosure. The growls that came through the silver cages made him redouble his efforts. A deep wet V had formed in the center of his chest and his legs trembled as he shut his eyes tightly and set his jaw hard.

"Let me help," a small voice said, giving everyone in the room a start.

Sara slipped into the villa through the blasted-out deck doors and neared Damali. "I have worked with purging this type of energy for years in Nod. It is my specialty to bring back the human side and sublimate the darker side. Later, when you are rested and in the daylight, you can make it more permanent."

"We damned sure can't travel to higher ground like this," Damali said, a plea in her voice. She looked around at all team members' eyes. "But we have to try 'cause ain't nobody ready to give up on anybody in our family yet."

"Do what you can," Shabazz said quietly, his weapon now lowered.

Damali and Carlos glanced at Sara and then at the contingent of huge hybrids who stood just outside the battered deck doors.

"She is an expert," Hubert said. "Let her give you back the gift your mother-seer gave her. This is our way."

"Do it," Carlos said, straining. "But she's gotta hurry."

"How you gonna go in that cage, sis?" Damali said, looking at Marlene and Mike, who had begun to square off and circle each other as competing fauna within the same cage.

"I move very quickly," Sara whispered, hesitating a beat before sucking in a deep breath to calm herself, and then rounding Carlos's legs. "The moment I exit the first person, shrink the cage until I do the next, and then you can eliminate it to fully concentrate on only the black box." She looked at Damali. "A black orb will come out of them. Surround it in a silver light sphere and send it toward the sun."

As Sara approached the bars her opalescent body began to disintegrate into what looked like flecks of shimmering, fast-moving dust. The glistening miasma flowed over Marlene, making her hiss and then scream. Yet the moment Marlene opened her mouth, the glittering essence of the nymph rushed down Marlene's throat, causing her to go into a convulsion, and then eventually begin to normalize. Sara's light sparkles immediately came out of Marlene's nose, and Carlos stepped forward to get Marlene's limp body out of Mike's claw range. Damali snatched the black orb that hovered over Marlene's third eye, surrounded it with silver light, blew on it to freeze it, and then jettisoned it with an energy arc from her hands toward the sky.

The team watched in awe as Sara performed the same process on Mike, felling him quickly. Damali swiftly repeated the process of snagging and jettisoning a large black orb that hovered near Mike's right fist, and then caught a smaller, sneaky one near his jugular that was trying to get away. "Five bucks this one came from the vamp he did in New Orleans however many years ago," Damali said as she hurled the small orb into the night sky.

Sara dropped into a small, exhausted pile by Carlos's feet, breathing hard with beads of pearly sweat on her fragile brow.

"The big one," she said, pushing herself up on all fours. "He's really strong like Hubert. He had both were-demon and vampire bites raging inside him, but the were-bite was dominant. I think I got it all."

"You don't have to go in again, honey," Hubert said, beginning to pace. "You should rest."

"That's true," Damali said, lending Sara a hand. "How you holding up, Carlos?"

"Better. A lot better, now that I dropped half the energy load."

Sara shook her head. "The vampire infection is the most toxic and I have to do it tonight, or there could be lasting effects."

Shabazz had gone to Marlene to lift her to the sofa. Inez was on her knees at Big Mike's side, wiping sweat from his dazed brow. Marjorie rushed forward, giving Shabazz and Inez bottled water for the injured.

"Get a purge circle around them," Damali warned, making use of Krissy, Heather, and Jasmine's ability to create a powerful circle of three. "Prayers, salt, holy water. Heads, wrists, soles of their feet anointed fast. Marjorie, you run supplies to 'em while they work and recite scriptures out loud. Man, we need the Covenant, right through here."

The team began moving, but their attention was split between the task at hand and concern for whatever Sara could do to bring back Rider and Jose. Juanita waited near the box with her arms hugging her body, tears standing in her eyes.

"Just bring him back from the Darkness," Juanita whispered.

"Anything he said or did in that condition, 'Nita, know it wasn't from his heart. We had to pull some old strings and open some old wounds to save your throat," Damali said quietly as Sara's energy penetrated the box from a tiny corner that Carlos opened in the top of it.

Juanita just nodded and watched the box, awed and frightened as Jose inhaled the sparkling, floating dust as if Sara was cocaine. It knocked his head back and lowered his fangs to battle-length, bulking his body for a moment, before the fangs gently retracted and Jose dropped to the floor.

But Carlos had to move at vamp speed to get Jose out of there unscathed while Damali quickly caught the dark orb that exited his throat, which was more gray than black with diluted vamp lineage, and sent it skyward. Rider was almost on Jose before Carlos could shrink the enclosure, smelling blood and eyeing Jose's jugular.

In a rage, Rider pounded on the translucent black surface with both fists, eyes glowing a hate-filled warning as he railed. He sucked Sara in by accident, and then suddenly became still, dropping his head back. On his knees, Rider opened his eyes, his gaze going directly past the team to the black sheet that was tucked around Tara's body whipping in the evening sea breeze, then passed out. Damali grabbed at the dark orb with both hands, and it took her several seconds to grapple with it and seal it in frozen silver before straining to send it toward the unseen sun. Carlos dropped to the floor with exhaustion and just lay there for several minutes breathing hard.

Catching Sara in her arms as she rematerialized, Damali kissed her brow. "Thank you, angel," she whispered, nodding for Hubert to cross the threshold to claim her.

What was the point of sanitation barriers at this point? Marjorie must have read her mind because she went to Rider's side to help him while Damali pulled Carlos to his feet.

"We can't move the team now, not until daylight," Damali said.

Carlos nodded, still winded and leaning heavily against her.

"Hubert, with the ultimate trust, we'll give you and your boys some antidemon ammo and some food. Got a coupla steaks in the fridge and some junk in the cabinets. If you have to fall back for your own personal safety, you can enter the villa, but we'd appreciate a night lookout. We can bed Sara down in here on some pillows under a blanket and give her some fruit and sugar . . . if that's what she eats."

"She does, dear Neteru," Hubert said and swallowed hard, his voice filled with gratitude. "How did you know that she eats like a hummingbird?"

"Just a lucky guess." Damali cast her gaze toward Tara's body, which lay prone on the beach, not wanting to know the state of decomposition beneath the sheet. "Try not to let the enemy take her,"

Damali said, in a quiet, faraway voice. "As you can imagine it'll be bad enough having to bury her when Rider wakes up again."

Damali flung Hubert a bag of Red Sea salt from the cabinets, hauling Carlos with her to deposit him on a stool with a thud. Hubert caught the bag with one hand, careful not to rip into the plastic with his talons.

"Thank you, Neteru. Our endurance is made from the night. If full breeds attempt to siege, we will sound an alarm and fight until you are in position, as well as after that."

"Throw the man a Glock with hallowed-earth shells," Carlos said, sweat running down his face. "We all gotta regenerate. Even the humans on the team."

Mental anguish made sleep next to impossible, but the Guardian team's battered bodies demanded it. Chairs, sofas, love seats, the main couch, rugs, anything that would allow someone to lie horizontally for a few hours were pressed into service. Every now and then someone could be heard weeping. Male and female alike; it didn't matter. Acute trauma was no respecter of age or gender. But the privacy of all whispering, crying couples or the sobs of an individual just working things out between themselves and their maker, was thoroughly respected.

Damali and Carlos took turns sitting vigil with Rider. He'd curled up in a fetal position with his head in Damali's lap. She sat that way with him for the duration, humming a low, easy melody, stroking her fingers through his hair with tears dropping off her nose to wet his cheek. The moment she dozed, Carlos would awake to lay a supportive hand on Rider's shoulder, watching the horizon like a stoic centurion, and wondering how in God's name he'd be able to deal if something like that had happened to Damali.

The process was a brutal cycle of heal a bit, cry a bit, tense for possible danger, doze a bit, become philosophical while briefly asleep, only to awake to realize that all of this really did go down . . . then quietly cry some more, just let the tears roll without sound, look over the shoulder and hunker down against panic as hybrid guard demons walked the beach, and then listen to one's body knit, going to sleep from the sound of one's own heartbeat and staggered breaths, thanking Heaven that you'd made it out alive.

Dawn made everyone stir. Moving to an internal, silent dirge, people filed in and out of the bathroom and then went outside to take a seat on the sand beyond the edge of the deck. Church would be outdoors under the sky—the original cathedral. Grateful eyes offered Hubert and his crew a chance to crash indoors on softer surfaces for a few hours. Although, out of genuine concern for the team's most recent fears, he respectfully declined. Everyone knew that the unpleasant but necessary task of burying the dead was before them. All eyes went to Rider as he came out to stand on the partial deck and looked across the beach at Tara's body, which was amazingly still there. Guardians slowly stood and waited for his instructions.

"It's almost full sunrise," Rider said softly. "She's gone but she never even smoldered."

Sara slipped beside him and slid her delicate hand into Rider's. "She won't. When I went inside your body to heal you last night, I felt that you wanted to see her again before you said good-bye. She had a good heart, like you do, and never killed a soul, or fed that way. I begged any angel of compassion that would listen for her not to burn in the sun, given she was to be a Guardian and was turned against her will." Two big tears slid down Sara's cheeks. "It wasn't fair. Come." She looked up at Rider, her expression pleading. "I gave her back her lavender, too . . . just the way it always remained in your sinuses and memory."

Carlos bristled and rubbed the shadow of new growth that darkened his jaw. "Sis . . . the man has been through a lot, and—"

"I want to," Rider said in a quiet, resolute tone, then gently squeezed Sara's hand and followed her.

"I don't know which is worse," Carlos said, his voice reverent as he watched Rider cross the beach. "If he sees her actual remains, it might help him make the separation and finally allow us to put her to rest." He rubbed the tension away from his neck as Damali touched his shoulder. "But if he sees her repaired, sleeping peacefully like an angel . . . smelling like lavender . . ." Carlos shook his head when his voice broke. "It's fucked up either way, even though Sara had good intent."

"We never thought . . ." Hubert closed his eyes.

Marlene turned her back to the beach and covered her mouth with her hand. "He'll never be the same after this," she whispered. "None of us will. She was one of us."

"I'm going down there to stand with him, man," Shabazz said to Big Mike. "Original three."

"Original three," Big Mike said. "Me, you, and Rider."

Damali watched the procession of older Guardians walk to meet Rider with their heads high, shoulders back, dignity and compassion within their strides. One day, if she ever lived that long, she, too, would be going to gravesides with younger onlookers who would be unable to fathom the length and depth of a bond that not even death could destroy. There would be no way to quantify the profound loss with words, or to convey how many years of shared laughter, hopes, drama, and tears linked one to another. It just was. No definition required. You had to be there, experience the phenomena for yourself in order to know that those three older protectors silently wept inside, one for the other, bled the same blood as though it pumped from one heart, one set of veins, sharing the same soul . . . maybe they did.

Carlos squeezed Damali's hand as he neared her. "I know," he said quietly.

"Me and Jack Rider go way back. That's my buddy. . . ." Marlene's voice trailed off as she pulled herself away from the house and walked down the damaged deck steps with care, going toward the standing stones of men.

Marjorie turned to her husband and then looked at Krissy, Heather, and Jasmine, and then finally sent her gaze toward Damali and Carlos. "We have to find Gabrielle. If this happened . . . I have a bad feeling."

Damali and Carlos nodded, neither wanting to give voice to the nagging feelings that gnawed at their guts. They drew closer together as they watched Rider kneel, pull the black drape away from Tara's face, and kiss her lips gently as the breeze blew her long, dark hair. Damali quickly pivoted and turned into Carlos's embrace, shaking her head, unable to watch more, lest she wail out loud.

"Sara made her look like she's just asleep. Lavender is all in the air."

Carlos squeezed Damali tightly and kissed the top of her head. "She is. She just fell asleep on this side and woke up on the other side in the Light." He glanced at Marj. "We'll take an extraction team to look for Gabby after the burial."

Jose was rocking, tears streaming. "The man had to go through this once, and shouldn't have to again. . . . I was just a kid when Tara died at my grandfather's house. Jesus, don't a man with a good heart get a break?"

"Why don't me and you go do the honors, man?" Carlos said to Jose. "It's our turn to step up. We dig the grave this time and let the old-heads fall back and mourn. They've earned that right." Carlos looked at the haggard faces around him. "The original team has been at this war since the beginning, people. But this time, there just ain't no answer and we've all gotta step up like you did yesterday. Soon, we'll be the old-heads, and the ones who come behind us are gonna be standing where we are this dawn . . . wanting to just break down and sob 'cause the shit hurts so bad, watching the ones we love who paid the ultimate sacrifice hurt so bad. The only way I know to repay the debt in full is to suck it up for them, pick them up when they stumble, and do 'em proud. Now let's move out and bury her with full Guardian honors."

Damali watched her husband throw his shoulders back, inhale a shuddering breath, materialize a shovel in each hand, and jump off the deck with Jose behind him. In that very fragile moment, standing near the abyss of living emotional hell, she realized she'd definitely married a king.

CHAPTER ELEVEN

After the battle in La Paz, during true nightfall, while the Guardians healed, Cain sat listed to one side in his throne with his eyes closed. He clung to the armrests to keep from crying out. His face was twisted into a grimace and his entire body shuddered with agony from the shorn-off wing and his dismembered tail, which he hung over the edge of the throne armrest, unable to retract it. A slow, steady drizzle of blood still seeped from the gaping wound, stealing his energy away in minute degrees.

Even though he'd tried to staunch the bleeding by scorching the opening that still yawned with torn gristle, muscles, flesh, and bones, the Neteru symbols from Damali's Isis kept them burning silver to disallow the injury to properly scab over. Glowing brands from each symbol that had sliced through his tail broke through the charred, black flesh, and a steady stream of blood from the severed tail created a pool of muck at his feet.

He heard Fallon Nuit standing nearby with Lilith, and sensed a new vampire presence in their midst. Pride made Cain open his eyes and attempt a kingly repose, but pain won out and he was forced to close his eyes again.

"What do you want?" Cain rasped in a surly tone. "Leave me!"

"Your Eminence, you must feed," Lilith said, her voice a strained murmur as she approached him with caution.

Nuit caught her arm. "He is severely wounded," he said in a tight whisper. "Beware the lion with a thorn in his paw."

Lilith glanced at Nuit and nodded, materializing a goblet into Cain's hand rather than risk being his ultimate source of regeneration. They stood back and watched Cain down the goblet and hurl it away, enraged as his shorn-off wing began to reconstruct.

Unable to endure the agony, Cain hunched forward and clutched the edges of the council table, crying out as a new, damp wing ripped through his shoulder blade as though that section of his body was giving birth. The new wing trembled and slowly extended to give his form balance, and then both appendages were able to retract.

Dropping his head back, Cain panted, sweat pouring down his face, his body wracked with pain. "The tail cannot heal. It was taken by an Isis."

Lilith covered her mouth and looked at Nuit. "I have no remedy."

Seizing the opportunity, Nuit spoke in a gentle, seductive voice. "Your Eminence, this is why I have brought you a new councilman. Upon your orders to reinforce the power paradigm at our throne level, I present to you—"

"I never authorized you to make a new councilman!" Cain bellowed, looking over the vampire that Nuit presented. "Request denied! I alone shall handpick my councilmen."

Humiliation lowered Nuit's fangs as Yonnie stood next to him, waiting. "As you wish. My goal was only to strengthen your inner circle."

"I made you a female master, to also assist . . . based upon the last command you gave us," Lilith said carefully. She sent the image of Gabrielle to Cain and waited for the approval. "There has only been one other female master that was temporarily made, Damali. I thought this one could—"

"She's a common whore!" Cain shouted, grimacing as his tail lost another scab and the bleeding increased. He slowly materialized a black cord of energy around the tail above the injury and created a tourniquet that he tightly pulled with a yell. "Cast her away," he said after a moment, breathing hard through battle-length fangs. "You think a prostitute witch who runs a brothel is any match for the Neterus? You have lost your perspective on reality, Lilith. Did you not witness what only one seasoned Neteru was able to do to an army of my best hybrids?"

"She, like Fallon's candidate for a council throne, is intimately familiar with members of the Neterus and their Guardians," Lilith said in a conciliatory tone. "If—"

"Do not dispute me! My decision is final."

A weak black energy arc singed Lilith's chest, but it wasn't strong enough to do what Cain intended—to snatch out her heart. Lilith rubbed her chest and glowered at him, but kept her tone even and respectful.

"As you wish, Cain."

"May I propose that we give her to Yolando, Your Eminence, and," Nuit said with a deferential bow, "offer her as a consolation prize for the denial of his candidacy to become a councilman at this time?" Nuit looked at Cain and spoke in Dananu now. "We can ill afford for this master to walk away from our table feeling as though he has not been given something rare and of value, *n'est-ce pas*? Perhaps a throne will be in his future," Nuit added, giving Yonnie a promise of that with a sidelong glance. Nuit returned his gaze to Cain. "But he might be mollified by the gift of a female master made by the most seductive female entity of our realms, Lilith."

"So be it," Cain snarled. He closed his eyes after issuing a dismissive glance toward Yonnie. "Give him the whore and get him out of my presence."

Yonnie bowed and backed away toward the chamber doors. "I am honored." Then he was gone.

Lilith refilled Cain's goblet and sent it into his hand, and then waited for him to down it and cast it away again with a crash. "My Dark Lord," she murmured, concern in her voice as she once again glanced at Nuit. "All conception has ceased on the planet. Your continued tether to your mother's spirit has stopped all reproduction."

"I fail to see why this is our concern, or yours," Cain snarled in pain.

Nuit gave her a quizzical look. "Your agony could be blinding you to our realm's longer-term issues . . . if you will permit my assessment for your benefit."

"Speak!" Cain bellowed.

"As we overrun the planet," Nuit said with care, "sooner or later with the human casualties . . . our food sources will diminish. Our goal is to dominate humanity, not to entirely eradicate it in total. If we exterminate it, long term, we eradicate ourselves."

"That is only a problem for full-breed vampires and demons—my hybrids can subsist on other food types."

"Did you not hear me when I spoke?" Lilith said coolly. "*All* conception has ceased. This includes other forms of meat and even grains. With our planned attacks on every continent, how long do you think it will take for us to wipe out mankind? How much of the ecosystem of plants and animals will be burned away as we smite the Earth? What will there be for any of us to eat, full-breed or hybrid alike, if the Earth does not replenish itself?"

"Then what do you propose?" Cain said, still leaning forward with his eyes closed.

Again, Lilith and Nuit shared a glance.

"Your method of producing more vampires has a nine-month gestation period. Making them by seed is too costly, time-wise," she said quietly. "Our age-old gestation period of three nights of death before they rise again is much more efficient. But we still have the conception problem at hand."

Cain opened his eyes and glowered at them both. "My hybrids will regroup and flood the planet. Those are my chosen ones who will surround me as councilmen. Through the seed is the only natural way. Victory will be ours."

"You seem to be forgetting that even your hybrids have no way to reproduce as long as your mother remains in her grieving condition, and her soul linked to yours, Cain," Lilith said, her tone now brittle with frustration. "You must sever the cord and take on the full mantle of your office. Once the cord to Eve is severed, fertility will commence again."

"There is only one way to accomplish that," Cain said, trying to stand, but failed as pain shot through him from his amputated tail. "To actually die and rise again as the vampiric undead, which would make me no more than Dante was, a sterile being, and *that* I will never willingly submit to!"

"It would allow your bite to be the most lethal of all vampire bites," Lilith murmured, slowly edging closer to him. "You could create instant turns, as our Chairman. You could raise an army of vampires with a single night of releasing that dark power, and besetting me, Fallon, Yolando, and his new mate upon the region near the Guardian team."

"And I would be *sterile,*" Cain snapped, his eyes slits of glowing black rage. "My opportunity to sire the greatest of our kind through the vessel that carries the genetic lineage of what would become a fallen Powers Angel would be lost, you foolish, shortsighted bitch!"

"But there is *no conception* on the planet, sir," Lilith said through her teeth in Dananu. "Until you die so that your soul finally parts from Eve's, the point of siring is moot!"

"Your Eminence," Nuit said in a controlled tone in Dananu, "we must be able to feed our troops that are gathering in all realms. From your foray with the Neteru it is clear that we need the combined allied forces of the were-demons, vampires, and the Amanthras, as well as entities residing on Levels One and Two, to break the backs of our enemies. Your hundred-and-fifty-man battalion was wiped out on a beach in La Paz, true?" Nuit sighed and studied his manicure. "Therefore, accepting your true greatness as a full-blooded vampire may be the only feasible solution. Our troops would be fed, as the humans replace themselves after our battles. We would have our victory. And when the female goes into season again as a Neteru, you would still be able to—"

"No!" Cain shouted. "She may have severed my tail, but I will not allow her to neuter me!"

"Your self-loathing sickens me," Lilith hissed in Dananu. "You claim to embrace your father's parentage, the dark side of what you are—death, a demon, the vampire of all vampires, yet you still cling to the side of the living."

"Why don't you ask my grandfather the same question . . . an entity that is not dead, but whom exists in an amorphous state between the living and the dead, able to sire at will by seed, and who also possesses all the dark power of this realm." Cain glared at Lilith, breathing hard when she couldn't immediately respond. "Eve shall recover in time, as will I," he said in snarling Dananu. "Once I do, we can have this conversation again . . . in a way that I'm sure you will regret."

Lilith lifted her chin. "If my challenge makes you act, then it will not have been in vain. My goal is to encourage you into action, and if I must draw the fire of your rage to strengthen you," she said, hedging for her future, "then whatever toll you exact on me for my honesty, I will endure. But I do not think you know the depths of your mother's agony, just as I cannot fathom the depth of your suffering now," she added, motioning to his bloody stump of tail. "It is a spinal injury, Cain. The limb grows right out of our vertebra. The only reason you could still stand to pursue the Neteru to the rocks was because you had fight adrenaline black energy and battle lust raging through you . . . but look at you now that the pain has truly set in."

Cain glanced down at his tail and winced, momentarily preoccupied. She neared Cain, dropping her voice to a comforting whisper as Fallon Nuit moved back to avoid any potential black blast that Cain might hurl.

"Your dark energy meridians have been severed," Lilith said calmly. "Your power leaks on the floor like a bloody stream. You cannot even stand, because the nerves going up your back will not allow you full control of even your legs."

Lilith heard Fallon's mental warning.

Be careful, mon petite. *Even though you are female and what you say is true . . . and although as a woman you can say things to this man that no male could say, be on guard. When he recovers, your words may come back to haunt you and there may be Hell to pay.*

Lilith gave Nuit a subtle smile. *Why don't you withdraw so that I may speak to him more privately? He will not kill me, but will assassinate you where you stand for ever witnessing him in this weakened state. He and my husband are cut from the same dark cloth; I have dealt with males like him for eons.*

"Your Eminence," Nuit said, pulling Cain's glare away from his injured tail toward him. "Allow me to begin rallying your subterranean forces for a night attack. We will stand at the ready for your command so that you may lead the charge of allied demon warriors for the next attack at night . . . once you have recovered. This will give us time to plot the next offensive. It will also allow the warrior hybrids to regroup and stand at the ready for the next wave of daylight strikes. In so doing, we can keep steady pressure on the Neterus and Guardians . . . by night, and then by day, without totally depleting your hybrid forces—so that you will have ample generals to choose from to take thrones once we have claimed victory."

Cain wearily nodded and waved his hand at Nuit. "Spoken like a true councilman. One who is worthy to serve by me." He glowered at Lilith. "Unlike a female who does not understand the fine points of war. You are dismissed. Just inform all our allies to take the female Neteru uninjured and unharmed, when we battle again. But the male . . . his head on a pike."

Lilith waited until Nuit nodded and disappeared. She leaned against the table not far from Cain and folded her arms over her chest. "Without the tail, you're already practically neutered. Let's be honest, since it's just you and me speaking frankly."

Cain released a warning hiss as his talons lengthened.

"If you cannot stand, you won't be able to fuck her to sire. Your tail is as much a weapon as it is a sensory appendage used in carnal—"

"Shut up, Lilith, before I kill you where you stand," Cain growled.

"She knew that when she severed it," Lilith said, undaunted by his threat. "Our tails grow out of the primal meridian and are as sensitive and tactile as what's between your legs."

Cain looked away from her and swallowed hard. "It will grow back . . . perhaps."

Lilith issued a smug smile. "We can possibly create a prosthetic device of black metal so that you may use it as a weapon. Something that adheres to the flesh above the Neteru symbols, avoiding them, but you will never have feeling in it again. It was taken off by *an Isis blade.*" She nodded as horror filled his eyes. "Tell me, darling, can you still feel full sensation in your groin?"

Cain closed his eyes and spoke in a quiet, angry tone. "No. Not completely . . . only at the base."

"Your dick is there, and it works, but you can't fully feel sensation in it, correct?"

"Yes," he muttered. "I will make her mourn the day she did this. Despite it all, there should be honor amongst even warriors . . . old friends, at least, and I cannot comprehend how she could strike such a foul blow against *me* . . . like I was merely a common demon."

"Then, what good is being alive with all these delusions of bedding the female Neteru," Lilith whispered, coming close enough to stroke his cheek, "if you cannot even feel it?" She brushed his forehead with a kiss. "How will you even know that you've ejaculated?" She chuckled and sat back on the table. "Our kind is *ruled* by power and pleasure, the tactile feel of flesh. After this, you might as well pack your bags and return to Nod . . . at least now you'd be able to endure your sentence and the rest of us wouldn't have to starve for the folly . . . Eve's spirit would ease, knowing her son was safely locked away in the banishment zone as you had been for centuries, and the planet would be fertile, unlike you, once again."

He tore his gaze away from Lilith's, his voice now gravelly and quiet. "What Damali committed against me was an abomination."

"Yes, it was," Lilith said in a flat tone. "I am only glad that I had a chance to experience you in your fullness of virility. Now . . ."

"Lilith, do not torture my soul further," Cain said through a thick swallow, his voice a rumbling mutter containing a plea. "Be gone."

"If you allow me to siphon you to death," she said in an evil whisper, "I am an entity of Level Seven that can take your half-life and return you to eternal life."

"Then my soul would be in the clutches of each of the realms," he said, considering her offer. "One false move and my grandfather could scatter me to every Level." He rubbed his palms down his face in frustration. "My soul has harbored sins on every Level."

"True . . . but as the undead, the physical injury you sustained would be no more. She'd have to attack you again and sever the limb once you were a new, full-breed demon, to make it permanent. What are the chances of her doing that again, now that you are aware of her deadly capacities and how much she loathes you? You would have insight into how much she clings to your competitor, who from all that I see now, truly is the better man. . . . Rivera can fuck her with acute pleasure and give that to her in a way you cannot . . . now that you've been terribly injured." Lilith leaned forward and kissed Cain's throat. "Let me heal you, Cain. Then when you awaken to eternal life in my arms, test if I am a fraud by nearly fucking me blind."

He looked at her and lifted his chin. "After I plant her . . . perhaps I would consider it."

"You're in denial, lover, like most men," Lilith crooned, shaking her head. "A female of our devious species would gladly give up both ovaries to rule the world under the darkest night . . . but as a male, you sit here quibbling about what amounts to a vasectomy. You have also overlooked one basic fact."

Cain stared at her with a flicker of rage tempered by curiosity and pain in his eyes.

Lilith smiled. "She may already be planted by your seed . . . from when you took a throne ascension carrying her blood within you and dragging her husband's energy into your father's throne along with it."

Satisfied by Cain's stunned silence that she was making progress, Lilith kept her tone a low, conspiratorial murmur, occasionally glancing around as though Nuit or even her husband might eavesdrop. "Cain, think of the opportunity—you and Rivera were linked as the only two male Neterus to sit in Dante's throne, the only two with a common vampire genetic link that the female Neteru willingly allowed to take her blood . . . the only two men to spark fevered desire within her . . . and if not moments before, surely simultaneously when Eve's spirit went cold."

Cain's eyes widened as he stared at Lilith. A black sword immediately materialized in his hand and he snatched her by the jawbone before she could blink, putting the blade to her throat. "If you are lying, I will behead you," he said quietly, his tone even and controlled.

Lilith only smiled and never flinched. "I have been the harbinger of original demon births for centuries. . . . Why would I lie about how to make the best of them all? *I* was the genesis of original sin, *not* Eve—and history told by men robbed me of my title. That won't happen again, if you heed my advice."

Unafraid, Lilith craned her body around Cain's loosening grasp and leaned in closer toward him, ignoring his earlier threat to whisper mind-bending truths. "The original sin was going against the Unnamed One On High and making a pact with Lucifer, *not* biting an apple in Eden. Men are foolish, as I said, and believed what they wanted. They *needed* to believe that, because they couldn't get to me, and they had to have a female head on a pike thus forever using that misinformed logic to rule women. And fools that they are, ego allowed them to dominate and cut themselves off from the vessels of wise counsel from *their own species*—just because they didn't want to hear the truth of what Eve learned in the Garden . . . just like you're about to do now. Suit yourself." When Cain's glare narrowed, Lilith laughed.

"What did my mother learn?" Cain said in a quiet, tense voice. "What had she discovered that nearly had her stoned to death?"

Lilith's gaze danced across Cain's and then bore into it. "That we are equal," she whispered. "In match to your male superior brawn, we females have superior reasoning, thus are better strategists . . . with the patience to wait for opportunities in a way that you do not own. One is neither superior nor inferior to the other," she said on a seductive murmur. "Both energies were created simultaneously in the cosmos. We're evenly matched . . . which is why you rushed into battle with the female Neteru owning superior-strength forces, but lost an entire battalion in one afternoon."

"That will never happen again," Cain said, slowly tightening his grip on Lilith's jaw.

"Add a thousand soldiers next time, warriors of might. It won't matter," Lilith hissed, unable to get her words to do more than seep from her lips because of Cain's grip. "She slaughtered you with the elements, nature, and used that as cannon fodder, not her own people—then she wounded you and pulled back, and lived, still whole to fight another day. Had Rivera been on that beach, you would have prevailed. But it was *a smart woman* who knew your every weakness, and employed it to her own means. Like your mother, I hate the new Neteru . . . but I respect the hell out of her. She has proven to be my most worthy adversary."

Cain loosened his grip but kept his blade to her throat, steadily eyeing Lilith to sense for a lie.

"If there is anyone you should trust on demon reproduction and how to survive an archangel onslaught, it is me, Cain. Besides," Lilith said casually, not even bothering to speak to him in Dananu, "it is in my best interest, as well as our realm's, for Damali's potential pregnancy with you as the sire to be a possibility."

Lilith waited until Cain finally lowered the blade, never taking her eyes away from his. "What else would have so enraged your mother that she would have sent lightning down to breach the realms against the edict from On High not to intervene or to begin the Armageddon? Think about it . . . think through the pain and become strategic."

"My mother said I was dead to her," Cain whispered. "Yet there was hope in her fury, the entire council chamber crackled with it. . . . I could feel that wafting over my skin and could taste it on my tongue in the aftermath."

"Yes . . . and if she cast away her beloved son, what could make a mother still have hope, if not the belief that there could still be new life coming after him that is of her flesh?" Lilith caressed Cain's face. "Only a grandchild would inspire that. The Neteru must already be carrying for you, my love . . . so die to the agony and rise up from my arms to your full greatness."

Cain pulled back and sat on the throne, staring at her. "Until I know for sure, I am not ready to accept your offer."

"Take your time," Lilith said coolly, "as I am sure the shock is great." She smiled evilly and arched her eyebrow. "But consider this.

If the planet is now barren because Eve's grief still holds her fertility hostage due to her continued link with your soul, there will be nothing in Damali's womb to fertilize, if she isn't already carrying your heir. This is fact."

Lilith pushed off the table and began to pace before Cain. "If there are no new conceptions, thus no new births, eventually your demon legions, and even your hybrids that can eat human food, will starve. . . . Starvation creates mutiny in all worlds—not just in ours. Not a single blade of grass currently grows; livestock will begin to drop like flies. There will be no more lambs or fattened calves for the slaughter." She leaned in toward Cain and looked him squarely in the eyes. "There will be no more steaks for your hybrids or blood for your vampire battalions . . . or flesh for your were-demons and Amanthras. There will be a bloody coup. Against us!"

When he didn't respond, she pressed her point. "If Damali already carries your seed, you win. You can end your agony now, regenerate to your full capacity, and abduct her until she delivers your heir. If she does not currently carry, there is no way to impregnate her as long as your mother's spirit languishes by being tied to yours. . . . Your suffering will then be an unnecessary travesty that also depletes the natural resources of the planet, thereby eventually cascading your armies into starvation. Ask yourself why, Cain. Male ego? Because you'd rather sire by seed than the pure vampire bite? As your lover and top advisor, and as an entity much older than you, who is also thoroughly versed in biblical matters, it is my role to pose the hard questions. And as a good ruler, you *cannot* allow ego to rule you and cause you to make fatal tactical errors that will subordinate reason."

"I never wanted to be like Dante," he said in a quiet, tense whisper, "with dead, black seed spilling from my loins. I never envisioned such a conclusion."

"You've made other children while you were trying to repent and stay in the fucking Light—so get over it." Lilith waved her arms about. "They went on to make you a proud poppa and did good deeds. So what? That's history. Now you've gone dark, and a new era is upon us." Lilith stroked his groin when he looked away from her. "Can you feel that?" she asked, already knowing the answer.

"No," Cain whispered, and glanced down at her hand and then at his bloodied tail. "However, there is another way."

Horrified, she stood and turned her back to him. "You wouldn't. The pain . . . is beyond what even we can tolerate in our realm. Don't do it. Don't ask me to be a party to that."

"Stand at my side," he commanded quietly. "When I go into shock, I will need an immediate black blood transfusion. It is the only way to carve out the Neteru symbols that will disallow regeneration over them."

Lilith whirled around on him; her fangs lowered to battle-length, and spoke in Dananu. "If you die, my husband will murder me. Therefore, make it worth my while to assist in said travesty."

"A Chairman's seat—mine, if I do not survive . . . the first female to occupy one, which should give you enough insurance through power to avoid your husband's wrath up to, and possibly beyond, the Armageddon. My throne will courier the message to him that I did this of my own volition, in fact, it will convey that I commanded it and you could not stop me," Cain said in Dananu, his voice beginning to labor from his injuries and the verbal test of wills with Lilith. "And should I survive, I'll grant you a councilman's seat. Again a first. But if you betray me by allowing me to unnecessarily perish . . . my throne will echo the deceit to my grandfather with a direct blood tracer to your whereabouts, if you ever try to sit in it and claim it through fraud. That is my final offer."

"If you do the insanity you propose and live through it," Lilith said with her back still to Cain, "with your soul still tethered to Eve's you will send her spirit into arrhythmia! Do you know how many times she and I have battled?"

Lilith turned to face Cain and came in closer to him to put a firm hand on his huge forearm. "Why do you think it always ends in a stalemate?" Lilith's voice became an urgent plea as she went into a flurry of Dananu. "As much as I have wanted to end that bitch's worthless existence, for the empire and the food sources her fertility provides, even I have never dared smite her so severely that she might perish. I beg your clarity of thought on this." She looked at his throne and shook her head. "Your offer is enticing, but what good is ruler-ship over a dying planet?"

"I have thought about all of this while you have presented a poignant argument that I respect," Cain said calmly, now holding his bloodied stump of tail. He grimaced as his grasp became more firm and he leveled his black blade over his injury, a hand-width above where Damali's blow had severed it. "If I survive, a healthy feeding will repair the limb no longer beset by the Neteru's incision. My mother's spirit, if she survives, will be severed from mine after the shock separates us."

He glared at Lilith when she closed her eyes. "As my familiar, gov-erned by the edict of my grandfather, I command you to feed me and regenerate me once this is done. If you let me bleed out and die to ac-complish your shortsighted aim, then his wrath for not following my direct command be upon you."

Cain waited for Lilith to stare at him and nod.

"I cannot disobey a direct command from you and you know that."

"Very well," Cain said, breathing hard as the pain from just hold-ing the damaged limb nearly made him pass out. "Summon the black blood from Level Seven and have it waiting."

Cain took a deep breath and raised his sword as he pressed the thick, dripping section of his tail against the throne armrest hard. "Good-bye, Mother," he whispered through blurred vision. "May we forever be separated that you flourish again in fertility." With all his might he swung, cutting off another hunk of his tail, and the cry he released started an avalanche within the Vampire Council Chambers.

A meaty thud of flesh hit the floor as his body went into convul-sions and the blade fell from his hand. He scrabbled at the throne as he slid to the floor, sobbing in agony, vomiting bile, and then clawed at the black marble beneath him. Harpies filled the room in battle readi-ness, thinking their leader was under siege. Cain's piteous death wails made bats scream and cover their contorted faces and beady, red gleaming eyes with their wings. Bulked, armed cavern messengers broke into the chamber and turned away the moment they saw and understood.

Lilith dry heaved and dropped to her knees beside Cain. The agonized pounding from his fists against the marble floor began to open small fissures under his hand as she sat on his back facing his tail and grasped his flailing limb in her arms, almost unable to subdue the appendage.

"Do it!" Cain hollered, tears streaming down his face. "Mercy in your withered soul, woman—do it!"

Her body thrashed back and forth with the powerful jerks riddling the tail in her arms as she rode Cain's writhing form. In a serpent-quick strike, she sank her long fangs into the blackened flesh of his opened wound, causing Cain's body to buckle, arch, and his cries to topple thrones. But she held on, eating away at the flesh until it was bloodied pulp, creating a valley around now-exposed tailbone with a thin margin of scaled skin surface to hold blood around it like a challis, then spewed black blood into it and sealed it shut.

She sat that way for several minutes as Cain thrashed, holding his tail upright so the black blood could adhere, and didn't release him until the flaps of outer skin began to seal over the exposed bone.

Moving quickly, she rolled Cain onto his side, using all of her strength as she shoved a sobbing sovereign into a feed position. She slit her jugular and allowed her thickened black blood to ooze into his mouth, but Cain was so pain-dazed that he almost couldn't swallow it. He convulsed once, and then dropped his head, unconscious.

"You brilliant . . . arrogant . . . fool," she murmured, standing and staggering away. Lilith wiped her brow, depleted. "If you live, I think even your grandfather would be proud."

Yonnie swept into Gabrielle's Nevada condo and rushed to her crumpled body on the dining room floor. "Oh, baby . . . not you, of all people," he whispered, gathering her up in his arms and kissing her forehead.

Her terrified eyes snapped open, and he knew that Lilith or the Chairman were the only ones of his realm that could deliver an instant-turn bite. He dared not send an SOS to Carlos with the air-waves totally compromised at this juncture. As he watched Gabrielle's first crest of fangs lower and her body begin to tremble with new vampire awareness, he held her to his throat.

"It wasn't supposed to happen to you, or like this," he said, gently stroking her hair. "Feed only from me or the bottles. They violated supernatural law, and this was the same way Carlos broke out. You haven't been dead three nights yet—there's still time."

"What's happening to me, Yonnie?" she shrieked, becoming hysterical in his arms. "I . . . I . . ." Pain stopped her words as she wailed and began tearing at his pants and ripping off his clothes.

"Feed," he said gently, rocking her body against his. "That'll stop the burn. It's the only way. Then, as your friend, I'll do you . . . and will explain everything later."

Sara gently held Carlos's wrist as he and Jose began digging a grave for Tara in the sand. "Last night we all went through a lot, and experienced physical, spiritual, and emotional pain that will take a very long time to heal. Do not make a decision in haste to put this all behind you."

The group's weary attention focused on the small being who stared up at Carlos with wide, shimmering, turquoise eyes.

"Neteru, take her body with us to be buried on true hallowed ground," the nymph said quietly. She continued to stare up at Carlos when he didn't immediately respond and she squinted in the sunlight, covering her eyes to shield them. "Please."

The team looked at Carlos and Jose, and then everyone looked at Rider.

"It's only fitting," Rider said quietly. "I'll carry her, now that Marlene anointed her and said a few prayers over her."

"She'll disintegrate in the bright light within the whirl," Carlos said in a gentle voice, sparing everyone, especially Rider, the grim details of what that really meant. This was exactly what he'd wanted to avoid—just having to come out and say it. The heat of a transpo energy whirl would unmask all of Sara's good deeds of making Tara presentable to the family.

"Neither you nor your family should have to endure that," Hubert said, knowing what Carlos had failed to disclose. He walked over to Carlos to place a hand on his shoulder. "Let me carry her. I do not travel by white light, but by an energy current that's been trapped between dimensions. It's not as . . . harsh."

Damali nodded and came to stand beside Carlos. "Let them do it," she said in a quiet voice. "There's a convent in the state of Morelos, Mexico, not far from where the team will be."

Carlos leaned on his shovel and stared at Rider for a moment, and then looked at Hubert. "We're going to Morelos, the smallest state in central Mexico and staying just outside of Morelos's jewel city, Cuernavaca, which is thinly populated—to avoid as many human civilian casualties as possible. That's like ninety kilometers from Mexico City, which is a quick whirl so we can get supplies fast without a problem."

"We will not be traveling together?" Hubert looked to Carlos and then at Sara. "I thought we would travel in tandem?"

"Hubert, it is best that we . . . deliver her to hallowed ground and then follow the Neteru team to the safe place," the nymph said in a near whisper. "If my work becomes undone . . ."

Hubert nodded and stroked Sara's hair. "You are wise. They should not see that. My apologies. It is just my concern for the members of my group who are not as strong."

"We got your backs on this, and you won't get to where we're going and find it locked to you, *we promise.*" She looked at Carlos as he and the team nodded.

"We don't roll like that," Carlos said. "At this point, you're family. Especially carrying one of ours. If you want to guard her here on the beach, let me get the team to higher ground, then I can come back and carry Tara myself. However you wanna do this, man, so you're comfortable."

"That would waste valuable time," Hubert replied, releasing a long sigh of relief. "We trust you."

"Good, because we trust you, and we're not gonna just up and leave you guys this morning," Damali said, looking at Hubert with openness.

"I trust them," Sara said, looking at each member of the small, ragtag group of hybrids. She turned to Damali. "How will we know which house is the safe place, though, especially in a new land that we do not know? The way we look, we could frighten humans and they could attack us."

"You'll know the fortress Carlos picked by the silver signature we'll light that sucker up with—me and Carlos will be throwing a protective aura over it and prayer barriers from Marlene," Damali said, slipping her hand into Hubert's and giving it a supportive squeeze.

"Structurally, what will we be looking for, so we will be sure to reconvene with you quickly?" Hubert asked, seeming a little unsure.

"It's an old stone castle that Carlos found . . . which just so happened to be vacant, and I'll take that as a positive sign and location, since the kings helped him divinate it from their war table," Damali said as she glimpsed Carlos and smiled sadly, quietly acknowledging their shared memory of doing battle in a castle a couple years ago. "High stone walls, gun turrets, iron gates, but completely modernized and for rent, if you can believe it," she added, shaking her head.

"I'll take care of the paper trail," Dan said with confidence. "We're just a vacationing band on hiatus."

"Cool, work it out," Damali said, leaving Hubert to kiss Dan's forehead. "At nine large a week, it's fully furnished with Old World antiques so everybody can get cleaned up and take a load off and get comfortable for a few hours. It comes prestocked with food and top-shelf liquor when we get there, privately sleeps more than twenty with king-sized plantation beds, linens, the works . . . has multiple bathrooms, and came with a staff . . . which we'll dismiss with full pay for the month and tell them we have our own people—which will be Hubert's crew, as a good cover."

"Nine *thousand* dollars *a week*?" Berkfield looked at Marlene. "After we blow it up in a miniwar, what's the insurance rider on that puppy? As it is, the villa and the hacienda are toast . . . and that's gonna—"

"Richard," Marjorie said in a weary tone, "Dan will work it out."

"I got it, don't worry," Dan said with a half-smile—the first one the group had seen since the previous night. "I'll call in ahead for clothes to be delivered . . . can tell 'em everybody's sizes and have everything sent up from Cuernavaca, the closest town. I'll be sure to get some wool ponchos and, uh, something Hubert's crew can wear."

"Look up Casa Del Cuernavaca for my man here before we go, would ya, J.L.," Carlos said. "I want a floor plan printed out for each team member, and Hubert's squad, too, so you know the layout before we get there."

Carlos turned to the other Guardians. "Trust me on this, we've all been battling hard and righteous and this may seem trivial, but this is for the spirit. The one thing you gotta take care of when battling is your head. I got this straight from Ausar—water your horses before they drop from mental fatigue. If your mind is right, you can get through whatever happens to the body."

"That ain't no lie," Shabazz muttered.

"It's a welcomed break, man," Big Mike said. "Thanks."

"I got you, brother," Carlos said, trying to buoy the nearly broken spirits gathered on the beach. "Can't always get nice accommodations, but when you can, ya gotta do it to give your soul a break. So, for *all* our morales, I found us this sixteenth-century jewel, which combinates to the number seven . . . lush exterior gardens, strategic mountain view, Mexican antiques, huge Jacuzzis for battle-weary bones, fireplaces in each bedroom . . . stone floors and walls that absorb a silver charge real nice—bounces it off like laser security systems, near lakes and the silver market—which I'll explain in a few. But the thing is, after what just went down, we all need to get our heads right before we throw down in a firefight again."

Rider pounded Carlos's fist, his expression stoic. "Sounds like a good place for an after-funeral repast." He sighed hard and walked away to stand alone. "Just tell 'em to stock Jack Daniel's and Marlboro Reds, would ya?" he said to Dan under his breath as he passed him.

"I got you, man," Dan said and swallowed hard. "Anything you want."

Damali glanced around at the team. "Hubert and company will be safe. No neighbors for miles, and we get a good view of the surrounding valley and cities. Carlos honed right in on it, and I trust his judgment."

"I'm beginning to feel a little better about this odyssey, hearing that news," Berkfield said. "But after we get Tara properly buried and the team settled in with supplies, me, Carlos, and maybe Shabazz can take a quick whirl to Nevada to go get Gabrielle."

"Done," Carlos said, nodding. "You were reading my mind, brother." He looked at Hubert. "Your aerial landmark is the Tlahuica ruins. The smoking Popocatepetl volcano is the most active joint in North America that threatens everything within forty kilometers of Mexico City. I'm laying odds that Cain will send up night forces from there, since Damali and our squad kicked his hybrids' asses last evening just before sunset, so you get back to us as soon as you can."

Not wanting to just come out and tell Hubert to dump Tara's body on the closest hallowed ground that could be sensed and haul ass back to the group, Carlos tempered his words for Rider's sake. But the message got through to everyone, even Rider. Waiting for Hubert's squad and the Guardians to absorb the information and nod, Carlos gave explicit instructions, quietly worrying about Hubert's navigation abilities.

"The other ruins you can use as an aerial landmark are right in the center of Cuernavaca—that's the Teopanzolco ruins," Carlos said, drawing a quick map in the sand with his shovel. "There's another ruin under the Palacio de Cortes, and you can see part of it sticking out through the more modern palace. Then there's Coatetlco, which is the one with a ball court and small temple pyramid on the western side of Morelos, and another one twenty-six miles south of Cuernavaca called Xochicalco. In the older Nahuatl language, that means 'place of the house of flowers' circa seven hundred to nine hundred A.D. Any of this striking a bell with you guys?"

"We'll know it when we see it," Hubert said with false confidence. "Languages change, as well as the phonetics used to speak them."

"Aw'ight, maybe my accent is off with the ancient Aztec," Carlos said, now seriously worrying. "Check it out; you've got Tepozteco, a ceramics complex that sits up on the cliffs. It's six hundred meters up from the base of the valley, right above the town of Tepoztlan in Morelos. . . . It sits on a Ehecatepetl, the 'hill of wind,' man, which is also called Tlahuitepetl, the 'hill of light.' You follow me?"

Growing exasperated, Carlos searched his mind for information that could go back far enough to put a glimmer of true recognition in Hubert's eyes. "That one you should be able to hone in on; it was dedicated to Ometochtli-Tepoxtecatl, god of fertility and harvest." Carlos rubbed his hand over his jaw. "But whatever you do, man, don't get boxed in up at Xochicalco—the Quetzalcoatl pyramid in the complex of that joint is four hundred and thirty feet above the valley, a seven numerically, and has a carving of a feathered serpent coiling around the sides of it, and until we know—"

"That'ssss a cousin!" one of Hubert's men said, swaying with excitement. "I know thisss monument. It hassss two hundred and fifty stonessss carved with ssssacred animals."

"Seven again," Damali said, glancing around the group. "I think they'll be fine, Carlos." She shot him a private message. *Baby, I know you're worried, but we've gotta move out.*

Giving up, Carlos spoke quickly. They were losing precious time, once again, and Damali was right. "There's a bunch of ruins concentrated in Morelos, which is why we're going there and taking a cliff-side position for the pending assault that's coming, man. So don't get lost. There's so many ruins in the area that one of the biggest sites is like ninety-three kilometers off the freakin' Cuernavaca-Cuautla Highway. You can't miss spotting Chalcatzingo—'venerated place of the sacred waters,' with the whole rock carving thing going on . . . frescos of the king, the flying man, mural of fertility, the puma, the queen—strong Olmec influence—"

"Yes, yes," Hubert said enthusiastically. "More in my time. Seven hundred B.C.!"

"Cool. We *finally* have a landmark winner," Carlos said with a rush of relief. "Between those sites, if you triangulate properly, you won't be able to miss us."

"We know the region well enough from your description . . . the Aztec ruins. I do not know the name Cuernavaca, but will find you," Hubert said, standing taller.

Carlos scratched his head, sorting languages. "Back in the day it was called Cuauhnahuac, meaning 'near the trees,' high up, brother, elevation five thousand and some odd feet. For human transport, going by car, that's only a forty-five-minute drive from Mexico City, but far enough away to be cool if some crazy shit jumps off. But we'll stay outside of Cuernavaca, like close to seven thousand feet up so we'll have an aerial view. You're gonna need some blankets for Sara, too, because it gets cold at night." Carlos looked at him hard. "Make *sure* you find us . . . you're with us now, and we don't leave our own."

"I will not fail," Hubert said with pride. "We will courier Tara with honor and meet with you upon our return."

"With all the stone ruins and silver around," Heather said excitedly, moving closer to Jasmine and Krissy, "we'll be able to help a whole lot, too. We can send Hubert a beacon to follow and keep vigil until they land at the fort."

Murmurs of agreement rippled through the team.

"Cool," Carlos said, hoping that things would for once go smoothly. "There's a cathedral in Tepoztlan, and next to it is Our Lady of Annunciation Convent that's under restoration, which was established by the Dominicans. You can see the hills and the Tepozteco pyramid from there. Use the restoration activities as your cover, as a lot of work crews have left open ditches and . . ." Carlos let his words trail off. He hadn't meant to mention the word "ditch" so callously in front of Rider, but his nerves were raw.

"There's another convent, too, in Oaxtepec," Carlos said in a gentler tone. "But if you guys get lost, home back toward the National Park in the mountains above Cuernavaca. From the air you'll be able to see seven lakes, and three of them keep water year round, even if the others are dry—remember, seven or three bodies of water. There's also mineral springs nearby, because of the volcano."

"What is a National Park?" Hubert glanced around at his fellow hybrids. "This is a new term, a new word."

Carlos let his breath out hard. "Navigate by math—just *do the math,* man, if you get lost and can't do it by sight and sensors, and if you get totally ass-out, head over the state border into Guerrerro to the town of Taxco de Alarcon, that used to be called Tetelcingo."

"I think you're confusing him," Damali said, beginning to panic. "It's so much information too quickly."

"I must learn quickly, dear Neteru Queen." Hubert looked at Carlos without blinking. "I will remember."

"So will I," Sara said, stroking Hubert's arm. "Sometimes he has trouble remembering things, but I'll stay with him. He has a brilliant mind, but his memory . . . he is a very ancient being and this atmosphere doesn't help him."

"I thought you'd be going with us, just in case there's a midair problem?" Damali said, glancing between Sara and Hubert, and then looking at Carlos.

"I do better at finding places when she's with me," Hubert admitted quietly.

"Pleasssse let him take her ssssooo we all have a prayer of sssurvival," Hubert's serpentlike hybrid friend said. "Without Ssssara, we are doomed."

Carlos stopped and stared at Hubert hard. "Okay, here's a fallback plan if you get lost. Taxco is rich in silver deposits. It's a mining town. Darkside hybrids, and even general-regulation demons can't come up through there." He glanced around the team. "If we get screwed in a firefight, that's our fallback position, too. It's also not far from Ixcateopan, the burial place of the last Aztec emperor after Montezuma II and Cuitiahuac . . . My line brother Cuauhtémoc's tomb is there—also known as descending eagle or plunging eagle, so I'm hoping on ancestral support up in that tip if it comes to that."

"If that's what your gut is telling you, I'm with you," Hubert said. "I can easily see the silver region."

"Good," Carlos said. "Because it's not just my gut alone we're working with. I also talked to the kings and we all agreed. Mount the offensive from a high elevation as far away from populated areas as possible, but near areas that have serious spiritual charge for our side, hence Morelos. My DNA code is landlocked there, so are Jose's and Juanita's . . . Tara's would be, too, along with Lopez's. It's also close enough to keep our eyes on the Popocatepetl volcano, which has been threatening major cities and erupted like thirty-somethin' times since the thirteen hundreds . . . that's an accident waitin' to happen. Besides, I don't trust Cain not to use the chaos of an eruption and human civilians as hostages to a pending disaster to come at us, too, to create a diversion."

Carlos touched Damali's face. "The ground is silver rich; it's up in the hills sixteen hundred and forty-five feet above sea level—which breaks back down to seven, for us. Plus there's major hallowed ground there, baby. For a pullback position, go to the Temple of Santa Prisca on Borda Plaza. . . . If it gets crazy, you fall back there, I'm serious, D. The town is small, has a sparse population, narrow, colonial, cobble-stoned streets that wind up the hill and are good for a contained fire-fight and for hiding Hubert and his gang—if they get spotted out in the open by people—versus open boulevards where a lot of innocent folks could get accidentally shot, plus the ex-convent of San Bernardino de Sena is there, built in the sixteenth century."

"If I do my math, as you say, Carlos," Hubert asked quietly, drawing everyone's attention, "and sixteen becomes seven, on silver-laden soil, within a numerically correct seven in elevation—should we not take Tara there to be protected in the abandoned convent on very old, silver-plated hallowed earth protected by the numbers?"

To Hubert's surprise, Rider slowly walked over to him, hugged him slowly, and said nothing as he tightened the embrace.

One human gesture said it all. The decision was made and all conversation ceased. It happened just that fast.

ᑯ CHAPTER TWELVE

Cuernavaca lived up to its name as the City of Eternal Spring. Carlos hadn't lied. Damali kept her gaze sweeping for security hazards as the team walked through the outer grounds of Casa Del Cuernavaca. Lush bougainvillea ensconced by colorful trees and other blossoming vegetation surrounded the colonial-era hacienda that was more castle than fort. A quiet river flowed through the canyon and nearby natural mineral springs made the place feel almost like paradise. Almost, Damali noted, also seeing the profuse outer gardens that were resplendent with color as a good place for anything crazy to jump out of.

I know, Carlos mentally whispered. *But chill. The team needs this. You need this.*

You also lied about this not being were-jaguar country . . . uh, Maya, Toltecs, Olmecs, Aztecs, land of the puma—or did I get it wrong? Damali gave Carlos a half-smile as they walked.

Yeah, okay, so that was an evasion, but it's better than South America. He chuckled softly as Dan and Mike inspected the Jeeps in the wide, circular driveway. *I didn't want the team to bug, especially going into the rainy season.*

Damali hesitated but then kept walking. *Aw, man . . . mudslides, torrential rains, floods—Carlos, come on, now . . .*

In the evenings and nights, June to October . . . what can I say? That's why I asked Dan to secure a lot of ponchos, boots, and wet gear.

Damali inwardly groaned. But what could one do but deal with it?

Paradise came with a price: rain. It was a necessary evil to go along with brilliant, subtropical flora. The moment the thought crossed her mind, Damali stopped and briefly held on to Carlos's arm. There was so much that seemed constant and that one took for granted that it also seemed almost impossible for those things to simply no longer exist.

What if there was no rain . . . and after these blooms fall, no more were born? Have you noticed that there are a lot of blooms on the ground?

Carlos nodded. *Another reason why we came here. The team needs to know that they're fighting for this—not just big, dirty, congested cities crammed with humanity, but the little things that mean everything . . . like the entire cycle of life. This. Take one insect out of the food chain, then the thing that eats that perishes, and the thing that eats that thing becomes extinct, and so forth, like huge, standing stones of dominoes crashing the whole system.*

"That's deep," Damali said quietly as they began walking. "People definitely have to see what they're fighting for, to keep the image fresh in their minds."

Carlos just nodded as members of the team followed them inside. They walked through the massive foyer that rose in impressive Moorish arches above hexagonal-patterned stone floors. "I want the floors mopped with colloidal silver so if anything puts down on 'em, they'll fry. Same with the stone walls."

"Cool," J.L. said. "I can get up to the ceiling with Jose and we can hit exposed beams, the chandelier, and over all the windows, doorjambs, and vents."

"Better split the joint in half," Bobby said, gawking. "Me and Dan can take the west wing, you guys take the east wing, or you'll be at it all day long."

"Cool, just work fast, y'all," Damali said as they passed heavy Baroque-style furnishings in the parlor.

Heather lagged a little, making the group come to a halt. Her gaze silently roved over the massive mahogany mantle above a huge stone fireplace and lingered on the heavy crimson velvet tapestries and drapes before becoming consumed with the fine, ivory-hued, silk-embroidered seating. She allowed her palm to gently caress the ornate woodwork of each sofa, teakwood end tables, and Queen Anne chairs, and then she got down on her hands and knees and touched the fibers in the thick, multihued Turkish rug.

Pressing her hands to the stone floor, she glanced up quickly to find the team curiously staring at her. "I was drawn," she murmured. "This feels like . . . a master's lair."

"Oh, shit!" Dan shouted, beginning to walk in an agitated circle.

"The girl is on," Carlos said with a sly smile. "No further comment."

Damali shook her head and chuckled. "Tell me this isn't—"

"Yeah, yeah . . . okay, people, chill. It used to be mine a very long time ago. Familiarity breeds contentment," Carlos said with a widening grin. He watched shoulders around him begin to relax. "I had bought it for you when I was in the life, and put it on the market—of course," he said, giving Damali a sheepish sidelong glance. "But after the joint I saw in Australia, my pride wouldn't even let me show it to you. Humans bought it, so don't worry. This never passed through another vamp's hands."

"Carlos, man," Shabazz said in a cautious tone. "You ain't backsliding on us again, right, brother?"

"Naw," Carlos said, chuckling. "This isn't an ego move, it's a strategic one." He allowed his line of vision to go around the anxious group. "How much sense does it make for me to take y'all somewhere in the blind? I know this joint like the back of my hand, every crack and crevice in the walls, every vent, and every pipeline and basement access point. The windows and skylights have leaded beveled glass with metal running through them—so they can be charged. Get the ladies on that. The pipes are old lead pipes, not PVC, so they can be charged. Mar, you and Damali are on subflooring and exterior wall barriers. Pull the garden hoses out and spray the exterior walls . . . after you bless the house tanks . . . and make it holy water." He looked at Shabazz, Berkfield, and Mike. "I want a cleric to do a walk-through and then the fort walls sprayed. Find us a local parish priest."

"I feel better," Marjorie said with a tense smile.

"Marj, this used to be my house," Carlos said with a wink. "*Mi casa es su casa,* literally, as they say, and I wanted you all to be somewhere that you could really rest until it was time to rumble again."

"The man is making a serious point," Marlene said, her eyes glancing around to the long, polished dining room table in the adjacent room that could easily seat twenty-five guests. "Me and Shabazz were sorta worrying about all the dark corners and back stone stairwells, plus all the glass windows with no way to seal them properly at night."

"We can always stand at the top of the steps and throw a bucket of water down them, and sweep 'em off, old school, Mar," Damali said, smiling. "This joint probably has multiple escape routes and secret passageways throughout the house, if Carlos bought it." She gave him a glare with a smile as she arched an eyebrow. "That's a benefit for our side. Anything that tries to run behind us inside the house will torch as soon as it materializes or tries to set a foot on the floor."

"The dark corners are for us, people—our ambush if the house gets sieged, and it's hard to burn down stone. . . . I hate new construction," Carlos said, resolute as he folded his arms. "I learned from the best on both sides."

"I'ma give you a hug, my brother," Mike said, pounding Carlos's fist.

Hidden agenda? Talk to me. Damali shot Carlos a knowing glance.

This will also rub salt in Cain's wound and piss him off, which will hopefully make him come at us sloppy again. Last time we did his lair, this time, he can do ours.

Excellent. Damali smiled. "I like it."

"The sooner we get the house swabbed down, the sooner y'all can go take showers and rest," Carlos said, feeling a sense of relief wash through him as the family visibly relaxed. "The casa is shaped like a big **H**. Center hall on the second floor has eight bedrooms, each with its own private bath . . . huge beds, feather-down mattresses and comforters, towels, whatever. Everything you need is in there. Dan's got supplies on the way so you'll have clothes and whatever else you need. On each wing are also two bedrooms, for a total of four—making twelve altogether. The west wing has a library between the bedrooms, and on the east wing is a conservatory and study between them. I was thinking about claiming one of the ones on the east side, for me and D . . . and maybe Shabazz and Mar . . . since that section of the house leads to a tower."

"Works for me," Shabazz said. "Us old-heads need to be on point, first, and maybe Hubert and his crew can take the other wing that has a tower, near the library, since that's his thing, and he and his boys can man the towers like gargoyles."

"That's where I was going with it, 'Bazz," Carlos said. "Put the newbies in the middle, with senior squad flanking them in the center hall—sharpshooters in rotation up in the towers."

"Cool," Jose said. "Y'all heard the man. The sooner we get supplies in and this joint protected, the sooner we can all crash."

"Then, if everybody is cool," Carlos said calmly, "while I've still got some energy, me, 'Bazz, and Berkfield can make a run to Nevada."

Rider looked at the threesome. "On this one, I'd like to come along, fellas."

"You sure you're up to it, man?" Shabazz asked with concern. "It's an in-and-out job—we go get Gabby and then come home."

"I need to do this," Rider said, checking his weapon clip. "I don't wanna stand around useless with Jack Daniel's calling my name."

The moment they entered the condo, the hairs stood up on Carlos's neck. Shabazz's locks crackled with static charge, and Rider hocked and spit. Berkfield was the first to move, holding up his hand, his detective instincts keened.

"Don't touch anything," Berkfield said as they slowly advanced on guard.

"There's blood everywhere," Rider muttered. "This ain't a good sign." He inhaled deeply and his attention shot to Carlos. "Your boy's signature is all in it."

Carlos didn't respond but advanced to the dining room table. Rider was right. Yonnie's definite blood signature was in the room.

So was Gabrielle's. But something else was wrong. He touched the dried blood-splatter on the table that had thickened and crusted over, and then bent to sniff it better. He looked up.

"Yonnie was here . . . but so was Lilith."

"Lilith?" Berkfield whispered. "I thought we flat-blasted that bitch in the Himalayas."

"Me, too," Rider said, rushing over to the table to deeply inhale the scent.

"Yonnie was here, but his signature is slightly altered," Carlos said in a far-off tone, thinking.

Old scent patterns near Yonnie's blood formed a maze in Carlos's mind. The male scent he'd detected didn't jive. If there was one vampire he *knew* was dead, it was Fallon Nuit—he'd neutered the bastard with his own hands.

"Lilith was definitely here, and so was Gabrielle," Carlos finally said, then walked away from the table and looked out the window.

"He killed her, too?" Rider said, crossing the room quickly to grab Carlos by the arm. "He murdered Gabby!"

"Don't jump to conclusions, man," Carlos said, forcing calm into his voice. "You know how this goes. Everything you see ain't always what it is."

"Why are you *still* protecting that motherfucker after what you saw him do to Tara with your own eyes, Rivera?" Rider shouted. "The woman wasn't even in the ground yet, and he—"

"Hold up, man," Shabazz said, coming between Carlos and Rider. "All we got is circumstantial evidence on both counts, now that we know Lilith is loose. That's important info, and you know I loved Tara, too. She was one of us, so I ain't siding with anybody that could've done her. But you also saw some foul shit slam the inner team—us old-heads, right? I saw my own woman go were-jag with *my* own eyes, man. But I also knew something beyond that was wrong. Get a grip."

Rider lowered his weapon and began pacing while dragging his fingers through his hair.

"That's true, Rider," Berkfield said. "I'm no psychic, but I didn't have to be one to see Marlene, Mike, and Jose . . . *and you* turn back at the hacienda to know something went way wrong. That shit still gives me the heebie-jeebies. So, I'm going with two possibilities as a cop theory, all right?"

Rider begrudgingly nodded, standing down once both Shabazz and Berkfield had spoken. "Only because you weren't his friend and are both married men, I'll hear ya out and won't cap that sonofabitch on sight."

Carlos let the dig pass, knowing where Rider was. He kept his mouth shut, but gave Berkfield the go-ahead with his eyes.

"Okay," Berkfield said, rubbing a shiny spot on his bald scalp. "First theory goes like this. Whatever made members of our team flip was caused by an evil outside agent—Lilith, possibly the same one that made Yonnie accidentally flatline Tara. If so, the man is somewhere eating his own heart out right now . . . and I'd lay bets on that being why he can't send or receive messages from Carlos."

Carlos nodded. "A Level Seven communications block, just like they'd blocked all vamp turns before—seen it done."

"My point exactly," Berkfield said, his eyes on Rider's. "Yonnie may be a lot of things, but he never struck me as stupid."

Rider turned away from Berkfield to stare out the window.

"If dude figured out before we did that Lilith was on the loose," Shabazz said, going to Rider and putting a firm grip on Rider's shoulder. "And knew Lilith was somehow in cahoots with Cain to break this family's back, then he went to protect the only one in the fold who was outside the net—Gabby."

"I think that could be part of the answer as to why you guys picked up three scents and three vibes," Berkfield said slowly, casing the room and looking at the toppled chair. "Here, she's sitting at the table trying to do a crystal ball divination to get info to warn us through Heather and Jasmine . . . something blows in and scares the bejeebers out of her, and she stands quickly, the chair goes down. Hopefully it was Yonnie in his right mind and trying to get to her fast. Lilith comes in, walks in on 'em, and there's a struggle. . . . Yonnie gets her out of there in a black, master vampire's cloud. Blood is everywhere, but Gabby is somewhere recovering. The girl knows how to purge a vamp nick, running the joints she used to have."

Carlos just looked at Berkfield for a moment. Shabazz and Rider's eyes burned against his skin, waiting for answers. What he couldn't immediately bring himself to tell them was if Yonnie had rolled in there and Lilith had ambushed him and Gabby, then there should have been tracers of black blood from both demons—and no master vampire would have come out on top against a Level Seven entity . . . not to mention that Gabby's blood had Lilith's turn-bite saliva in it. The woman was most likely dead or dying from a serious bite with no going back.

"Yeah," Carlos finally said after a long pause, walking away raking his hair.

"That makes sense, right?" Berkfield asked, pressing for a more conclusive statement from Carlos.

"That's what you should tell Marjorie when we get back," Carlos said in a sad tone. "Krissy, Bobby, Jasmine, and Heather need to know she's probably somewhere with one of our people."

"You didn't say that with a lot of confidence, brother," Shabazz muttered and looked at Carlos hard. "I'm feeling a weird vibe coming off you, man."

"I ain't got a lot of confidence, right through here," Carlos admitted. "Since all of us are working from theory."

"So, let me ask you this," Rider said in a tight voice. "Since we're not sure if Yonnie's system has been purged of a Lilith influence, especially since he didn't have the benefit of a healing nymph going up his nose. . . . Ya think at least we should bar him entry to the castle, until we know for sure—or is it me?"

Carlos nodded and closed his eyes. There was no getting around it until he knew beyond a reasonable doubt that Yonnie was stable. "Sho' you right."

Her lower back felt like someone had been beating on it with a hammer. Adding to the body aches and fatigue, her forehead thrummed with a nagging headache behind her eyes. Damali slowly made her way to the huge stainless steel and white walled kitchen to find a gathering of women already there. Elbows leaned on the large, center island, and Spanish-tiled counter. Weary heads were bowed over cups of red raspberry teas and tinctures. Marlene was working the stove. Lights danced off large copper pots and pans that hung overhead, making Damali squint.

"I brewed a big pot," Marlene said. "Want some?"

"Yeah," Damali muttered, and dropped onto a vacant stool beside Inez.

"You all should have seen Dan negotiating for *supplies*," Marlene said with a smile. "Usually Marjorie handles *that* kind of shopping, but under the circumstances . . ."

Damali looked around at the fatigued, ashen expressions. "Everybody came on at the same time?"

"Girl . . ." Inez sighed, sipping her tea. "Marlene has been trying to tell us about how in tribes and close family units, every woman in the group's cycle syncs up at the same time, but this shit is ridiculous."

"Like we need this right now," Juanita said with her eyes closed.

"You ain't sensitive to light, or nothing?" Inez said, giving Juanita a fishy glance. "I ain't trying to be funny, but right before the hacienda burned, Jose bit the shit out of you."

Juanita just held up her hand. "Don't start the drama while I'm PMS-ing, 'Nez. You *will* get your ass kicked today."

Damali groaned and accepted a cup of tea from Marlene.

"It was so much simpler when there was only one ovulating female in the house," Marlene said, glancing at Marjorie.

"Tell me about it," Marjorie said on a weary sigh.

"I'm just glad I'm not pregnant," Heather whispered, and then crossed herself as she took a sip of her tea.

Jasmine, Inez, and Juanita followed suit—Krissy looked out the window with an expression that said, *Thank you, Jesus.* Damali just looked down into her cup, staring for answers.

"I can't really rest, though," Juanita finally said, glancing at Damali. "Lemme be honest, sis. I'm scared."

"I feel you," Inez said, oddly agreeing with Juanita. "I don't think I'ma ever be right after seeing Mike change into a . . . a thing."

Juanita nodded. "Shit, let him sleep in the room with Jose. I'd rather be in a room with you until I know if they're gonna flip out again, or what."

Inez pounded Juanita's fist. "I ain't trying to play."

"All right, ladies," Damali said, jumping into the discussion. "Maybe that's not a half-bad idea. But I don't think it'll happen again . . . something kicked off that was abnormal, and—"

"I should have been covered," Marlene said in a tense voice. "Just like I should have married Shabazz a long time ago."

The group went slack-jawed and nobody moved for a moment. Marlene stood by the sink clutching a teacup between her hands so tightly that Damali hoped it wouldn't break. The group stared at Marlene, new awareness filling them as their matriarch broke down and cried.

"As many clerics as we've been around, as many priestesses in every culture that 'Bazz and I were around, and we never formalized it under a shield . . . don't matter what religion. Those astral visits wouldn't have been possible, nor would those old nicks have been able to break through . . . if . . ." Marlene's words trailed off as she looked at Damali for answers. "There's a shield to the union, isn't there? A special something you can't see with the naked eye—doesn't have to do with paperwork, it's the holy union, right?"

Not sure how to answer her mentor without divulging too much, especially when the other women had turned to stare in her direction, Damali chose her words carefully.

"Mar, there's a light that the Darkness can't see through within a union that's prayed over. But if one of the partners breaks the bond and lowers their energy around the marriage somehow, it can still get in to wreak havoc. You're right, though . . . it's not about paperwork, per se, it's the ceremony, the holy ritual in whatever faith you claim that puts the seal around the couple. It can be just you, your partner, and a cleric or judge, whatever, a witness—it's saying the words to each other in an affirmation of commitment that does it, I suppose."

"I knew it," Mar said quietly. "I poisoned—"

"Kamal was from the side of Light, though, Mar. Remember that," Damali said, trying to help Marlene deal. "Guilt is negative energy. Don't you always tell me that?"

Damali stood and gave Marlene a tender smile, then walked over to hug her. The nervous females on the team needed to see that she wasn't afraid of any were-demon jumping out of Marlene or turning her into a jaguar. Fear was poison, just like guilt, and jealousy, and everything else of that nature. They had to be a cohesive unit to survive another attack.

"Well, I for one think we should all just go ahead and get married," Krissy said, looking at her mother. "Dan is already talking to people quietly about doing life-partner wills, anyway."

Damali hugged Marlene closer and shut her eyes. What else could go wrong? Possible demon incursion outside the fort; half the squad on the rag and armed inside the fort; a group of hybrids AWOL without a good navigation system and carrying the fallen; senior Guardians on a rescue-and-recovery mission to parts unknown in Nevada; a clerical and Neteru Council headquarters comm. blackout; a potential outbreak of old purge wounds making everybody jumpy; and now a team of male Guardians about to be descended upon with marriage ultimatums. Mutiny was in the air. New flowers weren't blooming. Lady luck had thrown up her hands, leaving her as the only female other than Marlene who didn't need feminine hygiene products. There was no justice. No wonder she had a headache and lower back pains.

"See what you started?" Marlene chuckled sadly with a sniff, shaking her head. "The brothers are really gonna love you for this one."

He hated returning to the casa without better answers, but sometimes the bullshit just went down like that. Carlos briefly hung back on the wide sweep of front steps and kept his eyes straight ahead as Rider walked inside and poured himself a shot of Jack Daniel's. Shabazz had supposedly peeled away from the small squad to finish unpacking supplies and to assist with barriers. Although Carlos was pretty sure that the main reason Shabazz was laying low had everything to do with not wanting to deliver really bad news. It was somebody else's turn this time.

That left Berkfield as the decided spokesman. Gabrielle was, by rights, his sister-in-law, and his wife, Marjorie, would take the news poorly . . . as would his daughter, Gabby's niece, and Bobby, Gabby's nephew. Jasmine and Heather had also both loved Gabrielle dearly.

Sucking in a deep breath to steady himself, Carlos entered the hacienda and followed the sound of Berkfield's voice. He stopped briefly and stared up the wide antebellum-era staircase that curved off in separate directions, wanting sleep more than his next breath. But he had to go into the kitchen. As one of the team's cocommander-in-chiefs, it wasn't about not showing up for the postmortem. Rider raised a short rocks glass to Carlos as he passed.

"Two in one day, hombre," Rider said flatly, and downed his drink. "You want one?"

"If I didn't have to fly another recognizance around half of central Mexico to go look for lost hybrids, under any other circumstance, I would have said yes."

Rider flanked Carlos and they went into the kitchen and stood by the door. Marj took the news just as they'd expected, badly. First there was the flurry of questions, which Berkfield tried to finesse to stem alarm that was already there. Carlos watched the man ransack his mind for a way to put the indelicate as gently as possible.

"Well was there a sign of a struggle? Blood? Anything that would give us clues?" Marjorie stood in the middle of the kitchen, her panic-stricken gaze going between her husband and anyone in the room connected to Gabrielle.

"There was blood, Marj," Rider said quietly. "Honey, listen, we're gonna keep searching. All right?" He looked at Carlos when Marjorie slowly brought her hand up to her mouth.

"Yeah, in a few I'ma go out and look for Hubert and company, and as soon as it's dusk, I'll try Yonnie again . . . to see if maybe he might help us look, too."

"There's something else you're not telling us, Richard," Marjorie said, her hand dropping away from her face. "I have a very bad feeling." She spun on Heather and Jasmine. "I want to do a rock divination, me, Krissy, Bobby, and you guys. Right here, right now, we go touch some stones or something, however that works, and *find my sister.*"

"I want you to rest, first," Carlos said in a very calm voice. He could feel Damali's gaze boring into him. "None of you will be strong enough to protect yourselves and also pull info while you're this wrung out. Lie down for a couple of hours, then do it."

"But in two or three hours, the trail will have gone from warm to ice cold!" Marjorie shrieked. "And whatduya mean, protect ourselves? If they've got my sister—"

"Honey, we'll find her," Berkfield said, going to Marjorie to hug her.

"When I think of all the time we missed not getting along or understanding each other, and then, this past year, we made up . . . but time ran out," Marjorie said, beginning to sob. "Richard, I can't lose her now—we didn't have enough time. I won't waste another minute not looking for her."

Berkfield rubbed Marjorie's back as her tears started a cascade effect from Krissy to Jasmine, and then Heather. Clearly overwhelmed, Berkfield gave J.L. the eye and rare permission to take Krissy upstairs to calm her. Jasmine and Bobby were a mutual wreck and left the kitchen in tears, holding each other up. Shabazz had come in the back door to flank Rider. Mike's supportive arm over the shoulder guided Rider back to the dining room bar. Jose sat stunned between Juanita and Inez, holding both of their hands.

Tell her, Damali quietly urged. *It's rippling through your skin, Carlos. The look on the rescue squad's faces, baby, says it all. Marjorie isn't stupid. Her instincts are dead-on.*

We got there too late, D. Carlos looked at the floor. *I picked up a turn in the blood. Lilith was in the mix.*

Damali's gaze narrowed with rage. *Ain't she always!*

Yeah . . . which would make Gabby a master, if what I think went down, did. With Tara gone, Yonnie's probably got her—but I'm blocked to send or receive from him. I picked up his tracer there, too.

Damali placed a hand on Carlos's shoulder. *Then you better also tell Marjorie and anybody who ever loved Gabrielle . . . or Yonnie . . . that the barriers are up against them until we know whether or not their blood hunger is under control. Don't have Gabby come to a window, Carlos, or Yonnie for that matter, and whisper to their loved ones. This team can't take it right now.*

Carlos let his breath out hard and squared his shoulders. "Marjorie, honey, look at me," he said in a firm, gentle tone. He waited until Marjorie lifted her head from Berkfield's shoulder, and he stared into her teary eyes. "I picked up a turn scent while we were in there."

Marlene's gasp from across the room rattled his skeleton.

"I should have seen it," Marlene whispered.

"You were spent," Damali said, trying to stem any additional hysteria. "That's why Carlos is right; all the seers have to rest for a few hours and recharge their batteries."

"This . . . this turn scent," Marjorie said, blinking as quickly as she spoke. "Carlos, what are you saying?"

"I'm saying that, this evening, if Gabrielle shows up at a window, a door, or calls to you from a vent . . . unescorted by a Guardian, even if she's with Yonnie—you *do not,* under *any* circumstances, let her in this house. We clear?"

"Oh, my God." Marjorie's voice was a lifeless whisper.

"Berkfield, you get it straight with everybody that went out of this kitchen in tears. I want all of you in the same room, barriered-up," Carlos said. "This is the hardest part for the family and the new turn . . . night one."

"My sister *is dead*? You know this?" Marjorie broke from Berkfield's hold and stood in front of Carlos with her hands wrapped around her waist, shifting from foot to foot. "How do you know?" she said, her eyes pleading, and then she suddenly flew at Carlos, slapping his chest and shoulders, as though trying to swat away the ugly truth as she screamed at him. "She could just be abducted! You won't maim her with a stake or cut off her head—I won't allow it! She might be fighting her way to us! She's a witch—she can see into a crystal ball and would have escaped! Yonnie wouldn't do that to her.

He's family and wouldn't make her the walking dead, Carlos! It's a lie!"

"Marj, no," Berkfield said, struggling with her as she fought him to slap Carlos again.

"Let her get it out," Carlos said, taking the blows as Marjorie broke Berkfield's hold when he tried to move her away.

Damali blinked back tears and swallowed hard but didn't move. "She has to get it out and be clear now, because if she sees her later . . ."

Jose pulled Juanita's head to him and rubbed Inez's back as tears streamed down her cheeks.

"It's the truth, Marjorie," Rider said, coming back into the kitchen with Mike and Shabazz. His calm delivery made Marjorie go to him and leave Carlos. "I was there, Marj. I smelled what I have learned over the years . . . is what it is."

Rider set his drink down on the side counter and opened his arms. "I loved her, too." When Marjorie barreled into his arms, Rider stroked her hair. "But if you see her tonight, sweetheart, for the love of your children, don't let her in. We all have to be strong."

Damali stood outside on the front steps with Carlos and touched his back. "Com'ere. You look like you need to lie down before you fall down." She pulled his rigid body into a hug and rubbed his back. "Baby, why don't you go rest . . . save it for tonight."

"If I lay down right now, I'm so beat I might not get back up."

"I'll stand watch."

He kissed her head and kept his eyes on the sky. "I gotta go get Hubert. He's lost. I can feel it."

"Me, too. But give him an hour—so you can get an hour. Do that for me?" She looked up at Carlos. "Just stretch out on the couch and I'll bring you some water, something to eat . . . you need fuel. Everybody does."

"Maybe for a half, on the sofa. Then I gotta go."

She touched his face. "How's your head?"

Carlos closed his eyes. "Fucked up."

"I'll meet you in the living room with some spring water and OJ, and some fruit and whatnot. . . . You need to get something with sugars in you. I'll watch the sky."

He was so tired that he was practically staggering like a drunk by the time he reached the sofa and fell down on it face-first. There was no way he could argue against Damali's point. Rest was imperative, or he'd be slow and sloppy, and could put the entire family at risk.

But preternatural heat in the room made him push up and look around, readying for something to attack. Adrenaline shot through him, even though he was running on fumes. When a gold obelisk opened in the room, Carlos almost shouted.

"We need to talk," a disembodied male voice said.

Immediately recognizing Adam's familiar baritone, Carlos was up and off the sofa in a flash. He slipped into the golden light as it closed away, and was face-to-face with Adam in a distant glen he didn't recognize. Renewed energy washed over Carlos as he stared at the more senior Neteru king.

"I am not supposed to be here, but under the circumstances, Ausar was gracious enough to turn a blind eye." Adam paced, his white and gold court robes billowing behind him. "I need a personal favor. My sons, Abel and Seth, cannot be involved. They could jeopardize their pure light by doing vengeance—even on behalf of their mother's honor." He stopped and looked at Carlos hard.

"I got you, man, if it has anything to do with slaughtering Cain's foul ass, you know—"

"That goes without saying. We have discussed that ad nauseum. I need to get word to your Neteru Queen, Damali."

Carlos folded his arms over his chest to keep Adam from seeing that the request had sucker punched him. If anything else had happened to Damali . . . "Aw'ight," Carlos said in a tense voice. "What's the problem?"

"Last night, Queen Eve went into a violent seizure." Adam's voice hitched. "My wife is in a coma. The other queens are at her bedside, sitting vigil. Aset tried the Caduceus, to no avail. We were wondering if we could ask Damali whether or not . . . anything happened to her womb? We cannot fathom what could have stricken Eve so badly, and without her consciousness pulsing, we have no way to find out. We began to wonder if the sudden loss of a grandchild could have killed what was left of Eve's hope."

Tension wound its way up Carlos's vertebra. "Naw, Damali's all right. She didn't get injured that way. I can ask her for you and send word, if you'll accept a transmission, but she didn't purge her womb or sustain a mortal injury like that."

Adam let out a heavy breath and rubbed his palms down his face. His complexion was ashen as though his spirit had been tortured without relent.

"Thank you, brother. I had to ask. That's the only thing I could imagine that could have Eve so distraught. Her energy literally went into arrhythmia and then began to sputter out." Seeming as though he was on the verge of losing his mind, Adam raked his long locks with his thick fingers and looked off into the distance with tears in his eyes. "Do you realize what will happen if her energy completely folds in upon itself?"

"World annihilation," Carlos said in a gentle tone, "but more importantly, you will die a thousand deaths and still won't be able to get over losing her."

"Yes," Adam whispered thickly. "What could have traumatized her so completely, after all she's already been through?"

"Sometimes it's just the final straw, man," Carlos said, staring at Adam, remembering the times when Damali had been close to that state. "It's always the emotional wounds that never completely heal with women."

"And men, too," Adam said quietly, searching Carlos's eyes.

"Damali cut Cain pretty badly on the beach. She sliced off his tail and left a quarter-part stub. . . . Maybe he bled out, and that's what Eve is feeling?"

Both men stared at each other for a moment.

Adam slowly shook his head. "His death in Darkness would have simply severed the cord . . . then there would be a period of grieving when all fertility and replenishment would be slow, but it wouldn't have sent her into a seizure. This much both councils are sure of."

"Then, let's be honest and speak as men," Carlos said, holding Adam's gaze. "You came here to ask me to take a day trip down to Hell and see what's up, right?" He hung his head back and closed his eyes. "Just give it to me straight."

"World annihilation is my paramount concern and—"

"I said let's talk as men," Carlos said, straightening and coming in close to stand before Adam. "No bullshit between brothers! I'm down, but I need to go strong. I'd do that for your wife, but I'd expect you to do that for mine, one day—we clear? Not because of a debt but because *we're brothers*."

"Understood." Adam grabbed Carlos's arm in a warrior handshake. "Any day, any night. We just need a map."

Carlos tightened his grip on Adam's massive arm. "I know my way in and outta Hell like I know the back of my hand. Just gotta lower your vibrations." He released Adam's forearm and stared at him. "You ain't never been where we have to go to do this thing—ain't pretty, hombre. Ain't the Garden of Eden by a long shot. You down?"

Adam lifted his chin higher. "Given Eve's condition, we have just cause, and the realms of Light will sanction it. Ausar cannot go, but would. He is coruler and should I perish—"

"Me, you, Hannibal. Small squad," Carlos said, cutting off the senior Neteru King. "We step to that motherfucker, Cain, old school. Let's ride."

Damali slowly set the tray down on the living room coffee table and stared at the empty sofa. She closed her eyes and let her breath out hard. "Oh, baby . . . what did you go and do now?"

"What is his condition, Lilith?" Nuit said as he slowly entered Cain's inner sanctum.

He looked across the flaming moat that surrounded the ailing monarch's high crypt pedestal. Cain was sprawled out on his stomach in his massive black marble bed, black serpents twining around the solid gold posts, hissing for Nuit to stay back. The black silk sheets were glistening not only from the flickering glow of wall torches, but black blood seepage. Nuit glanced up at the nervous warning bats that clung to the crevices in the vaulted ceiling, teeth bared. Harpies sat sentry with their muscular arms folded over their small barrel chests, anxiously shifting on side altars. Two pit bulls lay at the foot of the bed and had looked up at Nuit with a snarl.

"Still unconscious," she finally said, walking away from Cain's bedside to go stand by the door with Nuit. "He's in a coma, and I tried all night to raise him."

Both she and Nuit looked up at the vaulted ceiling at the same time the bats screeched and began flying.

"Move the Chairman to Level Seven. Do it now!" Nuit yelled, and dashed out of the room.

The white light spiral that Hannibal hurled hit the Earth's crust so violently that it took the entire Neteru Council of Kings to prevent a tsunami in the Mediterranean Sea. Three silver stallions thundered into the abyss that parted the water, their wings razor sharp at each feathered edge, nostrils snorting blue-white fire, gleaming hooves crushing demons by the hundreds as blades took heads in passing. The moment the black cavern closed over, all light was extinguished. Laserlike eyes cut a swath in the darkness as hooves crushed rock and then silver, armor-clad blurs spiraled down into the void.

"Don't touch down in the tar pits!" Carlos yelled over his shoulder. "Keep those steeds airborne!"

Giant serpents immediately uncoiled and began to drop from the wet foliage overhead as stallions of Light pivoted and tried to find a way in wide enough to keep them airborne.

"Put down in the mud! Not the swamps!"

Thick-bodied Amanthras hissed at the invasion and striking fangs made horses perilously rear. Stomping serpents, the war horses galloped forward, but the hind legs of Hannibal's steed became tangled in a nest that anchored its back legs.

He was off his mount in seconds, desperately using a Claw of Heru to clear his horse's legs. Silver blood splashed and singed the writhing coil, making cinder at the bucking stallion's feet. Serpents foolish enough to bite the steed went to instant embers.

"Leave me if you must!" Hannibal shouted.

"Like hell!" Carlos shouted back. Then he felt a presence coming before it materialized. "Overhead, at your six!"

Hannibal pivoted, swung his blade, and severed the throat of a multiheaded hydra. Adam rushed in, his horse stomping the agile serpents that lay screaming on the ground near Hannibal. In a lightning-quick move, Adam glimpsed a thick-bodied threat above him, and caught the belly of a fast-moving black reptile that whirred pass them with the tip of his blade, spilling entrails on the three-man squadron. Hannibal remounted and spurred his steed forward. Black maggot rain and wriggling pests burrowed into the horses' wings, making them shriek in pain and take off in lopsided, frenzied flight.

Carlos held on tightly and wrapped the reins around his fist.

"No! Use your legs! Only to steer—keep your hands free for weapons!" Adam called out.

"Duck!" Carlos shouted, and pushed his horse into a low underpass. "Three men! The barrier guard ain't no joke!"

The moment Carlos spoke, a huge black head the size of a minivan lifted from a border-pit abyss between Level Four and Level Five with the swiftness of a cobra. Its dripping fangs were longer than a man's body and there was no way to judge its true width. Instinct kicked in, and Carlos's shield of Heru became a discus.

The serpent swayed, snapping first at Adam and then Hannibal, but reacted too late to dodge the gold blur with a silver edge. The shield went right through its throat. The Amanthra's jaws were still open when its eyes turned to embers and the head fell into the pit. The explosion that followed sent the three warriors into the wall, their horses' chests pelted with shrapnel. Stunned for a moment, the team watched their mounts struggle to right themselves. Each man slowly got to his feet to protect his steed from quickly approaching adders, praying that all three horses could stand.

Carlos motioned with his blade, breathing hard. "It blew the doors off Level Five. Were-realms—big cats will come first—gotta fly through."

Hannibal checked his mount, steadying his injured stallion. "Easy, easy . . ." he murmured, looking at the damaged wing. "He's lame."

Adam dismounted. "We won't leave him down here to suffer."

Hannibal touched the whinnying horse's nose and then backed away, gripping his blade tighter.

"Yo! Hold up! Can it still fly?" Carlos's horse was prancing in an agitated circle. "Nothing down here goes to waste—they'll eat it."

"The horse cannot carry my weight," Hannibal said, his tone flat with grief.

"But topside, you can heal it?"

"Yes, Brother Rivera. Topside all is possible."

"Then send it in first as a decoy. The big cats will try to attack, and send a flood backward looking for the rider—chaos theory, man." Carlos extended his arm and pulled Hannibal up onto his mount behind him. "We've got maybe sixty seconds before that hole seals over again and another border guard comes up outta that pit."

Hannibal nodded and whistled through his teeth, pointing the way with his blade toward the wide void between Levels. His horse backed up, took a running gallop over the edge of the abyss, and flew through the Level breach on sheer faith, listing to one side. Just as it crossed, two more Amanthras the size of the one they'd just slaughtered sped across the damaged wall blocking the opening. Adam and Carlos released shield discuses at the same time, splattering the three riders with demon guts as they rushed to the narrowing hole and made it through.

The screams of Hannibal's horse shot adrenaline through the other stallions that instinctively followed the sound and entered the fray. Although the animal might have been injured, it fought like a knife of lightning, using its sharp hooves to stomp low-crouching were-jaguars and panthers, slashing at predators with its blade-sharp good wing.

Carlos rode hard to bring his steed next to the frightened mount. It calmed and became more centered as soon as Hannibal jumped off Carlos's horse onto its back.

"Away, demon!" Hannibal shouted, slashing at snarling beasts.

Adam caught a were-lioness in a two-handed swing, taking her head off clean, but the momentum of the leaping body knocked him off his steed. The male was right behind her and stalked forward with a roar. A shield in one hand and a blade in the other, Adam round-house kicked away a were-jag, breaking a fang off with his boot, gored the were-lion behind him in a hard, fast pivot, and then spun to throw his discus to sever in half the one stalking Carlos. Hannibal rode up to Adam, pulled him up on his crippled mount, and trotted his horse next to Adam's.

"You need to ride with me," Adam said through deep breaths, helping Hannibal onto his stallion. "Just like before. Let your stallion fly first, then we follow."

Hannibal nodded, panting, and slapped Adam's shoulder, both men looking at Carlos.

"This way," Carlos said, wiping burning demon splatter out of his eyes, breathing hard.

The sound of werewolf howls filled the cavern as they rode through the gravel pit of bones and skeletal remains. Just as they'd expected, the portal to the next Level was covered by an army of were-wolves and all manner of were-demon manifestations, legions deep. Hannibal's steed had turned back, desperately trying to keep airborne over the snarling mass of muscle-bodied demons. Without needing to speak, three Neteru minds synced, three blades touched to become one, blowing a white light arch into the rock solid wall, showering blue-white energy sparks against it and sending were-demons screaming away from the deadly light.

Carlos and his fellow warriors were through the other side in an instant, but flight within the initial entry to Level Six was impossible. The vamps had designed the passages to be narrow enough to allow only vamp mist and bat tornadoes through. Even a seven-foot warrior angel wingspan would find an obstacle here, so a thirty-seven-foot silver stallion wingspan didn't stand a chance.

The stallions put down hard, avoiding stalactites and stalagmites. Carlos turned to Adam and Hannibal.

"Messenger demons will fill this area in seconds. Scythe bearers. You got me? The bats are still stunned from the light. If they fly at you, use your eyes. Light is the deadliest weapon down here; the vamps move too fast for the blade or the discus unless they're right up on you."

Adam and Hannibal led their mounts behind Carlos, weapons ready. Hannibal turned just in time to duck from a scythe swing. Knowing messenger vamp energy patterns like the back of his hand, Carlos sent a white-light charge at the seemingly invisible space from the tip of his blade, lighting the entity up and charring it. But the quick flash revealed how many more of them were behind it. Thousands.

Three minds met, a black wall went up.

"Charge it," Carlos said through his teeth.

Instantly, silver light radiated off the black translucent wall, and flashes of burning messenger demon bodies combusted behind it, sending up dank plumes of billowing smoke. Turning away from the carnage, the three-man squad grabbed their stallions' reins and ran forward, blades raised. Bats had recovered and were beginning to dive at them, and the Neterus and horses pivoted in a circle looking up with silver laser sight, sending the flying vermin into crags and voids in the cavern, burning and screeching. Huge sentries dropped down before them and hurled black arc energy that made each Neteru warrior raise his shield. The force from the black blasts backed them up ten yards, but as soon as there was a break in the ray, the shields belched it back as cinder-producing white light.

Forging ahead, the Neterus ran as the ground beneath them suddenly heated up. Choking sulfur spiraled to attack them. The bottoms of their boots began to smolder and the armor they wore began to sizzle their skins. It was nearly impossible to keep the horses grounded as their silver hooves began to melt and anything metal began to heat, causing the animals to rear in pain and confusion.

"Hold up. Not further than this." Carlos stopped at the edge of the narrow stone footbridge and leaned on his knees, breathing hard. "Blast chamber doors. All I've gotta do is sense the power in there, then we're out."

"We must ride across the bridge to—"

"The horses won't last three more minutes," Carlos said, leveling his blade at Adam. "We came for info, not a head, much as we all want one. These motherfuckers on Six are smart. Thirty more seconds and you'll be stripping your armor!"

"Blow the doors," Hannibal said, and looked at Adam hard.

Again three blades touched and the Vampire Council Chamber doors blew off the hinges to fall into the molten Sea of Perpetual Agony below. Screams from the torture pit were deafening, forcing the Neterus to cover their ears. Using seconds and his old ties to a throne, Carlos scanned the chamber, his laser line of vision leaving a deep scar on every throne as it passed. But he hesitated when he saw the one name he never thought he'd see there again: Fallon Nuit.

"Okay, we're out!" Carlos shouted, backing up, mounting his stallion with the others, and pointing his sword up in a three-way, hard clang of metal.

Bloody, dirty, and covered with ash and demon slime, the kingly Neteru team came to a thud landing in the hills of central Mexico near Popocatepetl volcano.

"He's injured," Carlos said, trying to calm his horse as he dismounted. "She severed his tailbone at the midpoint, which is like cutting off half a man's dick."

Hannibal winced then shook his head. "I like your wife's style. Befitting of a queen."

"Yeah, the problem is, they're desperate now. Raising old, previously exterminated motherfuckers like Fallon Nuit."

"But . . ." Hannibal said, his voice trailing off as he sucked in deep breaths of clean air. "He was killed by an Isis blade."

"Yeah, but I found out much later, and so did she, that unless you behead the bastard, they have a workaround going on down in Hell. This is where Lilith comes in. We were aiming for the heart only, before we knew. Learned a lot going up against Lilith before. Girlfriend had been all up on the table and in Cain's throne with him. No telling what deal she cut or why. He definitely fucked her, though, and made a deal in Dananu—which, by itself, would be enough to send Eve into apoplexy. I didn't get the full lowdown; just that Cain and Lilith were working as a team."

"But if Cain was severely injured, surely he will die from the mortal Isis wound." Adam's silver gaze sought Carlos's for confirmation, but Carlos shook his head.

"I have to give it to him, the man's got heart, even though he's nuts. He's attempting to rule the vamp empire and beyond with hybrids, but doesn't wanna be the walking dead. Rather than die slowly or take an instant turn strike, he tried to stop the Neteru blade burn by cutting above where Damali sliced him." Carlos hocked and spit, trying to get sulfur out of his sinuses. "They did a black blood spell on him, and he passed out from the pain. He's in a coma. So he ain't dead, just fried, and while still linked to Eve, she felt the trauma. That had to be what sent her into a seizure."

"We should have killed him while we were down there," Adam said through his teeth, looking at the volcano.

"Yeah, we should have, but Lucifer would have come up himself just to see what crazy bastards tripped into his wet dream. One living Neteru and two more of the spirit, the first one ever made in the capture, too? Are you crazy, man? We hit 'em so hard and so fast that Harpies hadn't even had a chance to swarm. Without backup, we're lucky to be standing out here in the daylight. As it is, we're all gonna have to get a good purge done, the horses, too. Everybody got nicked and cut the fuck up. So let's just chill and count our blessings."

"This is truth, Adam. We must be rational. We have collected vital information and now know the genesis of Eve's condition—thus we know better how to focus healing energy toward her," Hannibal said, cleaning off his blade against his huge, bare thigh. "While we all have a valid grudge," he added, looking up, "the goal of this swift mission was information, not vengeance."

"We needed to send a permanent message—"

"We did, brother. We just let Hell know that if they mess with our queens we'll come down there, riding hard, and blow the mother-fuckin' doors off the hinges—will drop demon bodies without blinking. My brother, this was an *awesome* drive-by, if I do say so myself."

Carlos petted his horse's shoulder, which was a full arm's length above him. The panting stallion nuzzled his hair gently and whinnied, flapping its wings and still snorting and frothing at the mouth. "Nice ride, too. But even you gotta go to the shop and get detailed after that thunder run." He looked at the ash and splatter that covered his horse, then patted the large silver stallion on its heaving side and leaned on his blade. "They let us use these in earth-plane battles?"

"No," Hannibal said with a smile, checking over his horses. "These haven't been released from Ausar's stables in centuries."

"Shame . . ." Carlos said, walking up to Adam. "I'm not making light of your wife's condition, I just wanna be real. When you guys go back, now I have a serious problem."

"I think I can persuade the Council of Kings to, uhm, intervene when it becomes dire," Hannibal said, glancing at Adam.

"Thank you," Adam said. "We will—how do you say—watch your six."

"Appreciated," Carlos replied, suddenly feeling every blow and every blade swing. "Could use a lift home, an energy boost, and a cleanup before *my wife* sees me like this and goes ballistic. Things are real tense around *la casa,* feel me?"

"Yes," Adam said, his tone still frustrated. "I just wish we could have brought an end to it all while we were so close. My hope is that Cain dies quickly from his self-inflicted injuries." Adam spit. "Demon bastard."

"True dat, but I wouldn't bank on it," Carlos said, spitting again. "And now, since fair exchange is no robbery, no doubt they'll send us a nice message in return once Cain recovers. I've gotta prepare for that, and I'm letting y'all brothers know now—don't jerk me around. I'll be expecting some backup from you guys. Even got some hybrids that escaped from Nod working our side of the yard. So if you see 'em, don't smoke 'em."

"Send us their images, so we are clear about your allies," Hannibal said.

"We missed our opportunity," Adam said, and spat again. "Damn!" He looked at his blade and tightened his grip on it. "One swing at that foul demon's head and my wife would have been free of him for all time."

"First off, she'll never be *free* of what he was to her; she'll maybe at best just be able to accept the loss in time. You need to get with that, once and for all, man." Carlos looked at Adam hard. "Second off, Cain wasn't just sitting on a throne waitin' on our little visit—if a Chairman is injured, they'd have dude in so deep that his lair headboard is probably leaning up against a Level Seven wall. Nah . . . You're talking a Council-level vamp breach, and you boys ain't exactly sanctioned to start the Armageddon." Carlos raked his damp hair with his fingers. "Shit, the way we bum-rushed that joint, we probably just did."

The moment Carlos entered the house, she felt him. Damali ran into the living room and stared at him hard. He dropped to the sofa.

"Where have you *been*?" she said in a tight, worried voice and then stooped down beside him to stroke his hair.

He couldn't even lift his head from the sofa; his bones felt like jelly. "Just open a channel and watch the video. I'm too tired to tell you about it right now, baby."

CHAPTER THIRTEEN

After what she'd witnessed flashing beneath Carlos's lids in full Technicolor, Damali ran through the house searching for a tracker. Her thoughts scrambled as she tore across the floors, momentarily forgetting that everyone was upstairs. She'd dashed past the dining room so quickly that it took a second for her eyes to sync up with her brain. Whirling around in the kitchen and about to run up the back staircase, Rider's presence at the doorway startled her.

"Hey, hey, hey, where's the fire?" Rider asked, toting a bottle of Jack Daniel's.

"I need a tracker. Meet me outside in five minutes," Damali said, practically hyperventilating. She glanced at the bottle of liquor Rider clutched and paused. "How's your nose?"

"Good as ever," he said calmly, his gaze assessing her from head to toe. "D, what just happened?"

"We have to find Hubert," she said quickly, but not ready to fully divulge the fact that three Neteru kings just blasted the doors off Hell and stuck a sword in a hornet's nest. "Carlos has to rest so he can whirl us out of here if there's a serious problem," she added, trying to cover the tracks of her panic. "With Lilith on the loose, Hubert and his people are sitting ducks."

"I'd take a bullet for him and Sara, after what they did for me, kiddo, you know that. But, if you don't mind my saying, you look like something just spooked you. Something recent, like two minutes ago. What was it?" Rider folded his arms over his chest and waited.

"Fallon Nuit is back. Carlos and I saw it. They raised him and gave him a council seat."

"Okay, Houston, *now* we have a problem." Rider was in motion, and dashed into the dining room with Damali on his heels. He grabbed a pump shotgun.

"We have to get Jose," Damali said. "His nose is vamp-locked to the bastard, plus we'll need a fluent interpreter, since we're going deep into central Mexico as an extraction squad for Hubert."

"He's in the garden."

Damali didn't ask why, just headed that way in a flat-out dash.

They ran outside, leaving Carlos fast asleep on the sofa. Jose was prone on a stone bench beneath a tree dozing in the early afternoon sun, but sat up quickly when he heard Rider and Damali's footfalls. Rider tossed him the pump shotgun and he caught it with one hand. Jose was on his feet.

"What's going on?" Jose's gaze ripped from Rider to Damali.

"Take a walk with me, Jose, and get into a Jeep," Damali said, not walking but running ahead of him, too frazzled to spell it all out.

"An old friend is back with Lilith, stirring the pot," Rider said. "We've got family out there who got lost. We'll fill you in as we drive."

"I know you guys are tired," Damali said, driving like a maniac, while talking a mile a minute. "If y'all were upstairs asleep, I would have gone alone but—"

"It's cool, D," Jose said, cutting off her apology. "Juanita put me out of the room to catch some shut-eye with Inez, of all people, because she's still scared I might turn—and Mike didn't have it in him to argue, so he just crashed alone. I wasn't really asleep anyway. Had a lot running through my mind."

"Yeah, don't we all?" Rider said, keeping his eyes on the road and tensely monitoring the precarious hairpin turns Damali made as they sped down the narrow mountain passage. "Might be good, though, if we got there in one piece."

Jose glimpsed Rider when Damali didn't answer. "They could have landed anywhere if they were off course, D. There's miles of ruins."

"I'm heading toward Taxco, the silver city," she said, gripping the wheel tighter. "My gut tells me that Hubert would home in there if he got nervous and got turned around . . . because the silver deposits would be his beacon—sorta like a landing strip for him. Once on the ground, their natural instinct would be to head toward the convent and try to hide on hallowed ground to make it through the night."

Finding the partially renovated Convent of San Bernardino de Sena was relatively easy within the sleepy little town of Taxco. Just as Carlos had told them, quaint colonial houses dotted pristine, narrow streets paved with cobblestone that spiraled up in steep inclines rivaling San Francisco. Silver and flower vendors and small outdoor cafes competed with tiny stores and bodegas, while local workers went on about their daily routines, unimpressed by a few straggling tourists.

Damali pulled the Jeep behind the convent, out of view of the main thoroughfare. The decision to leave the pump shotgun in the vehicle was agreed upon without words. Jose and Rider quietly concealed it, and kept their shoulder firearms hidden beneath zipped jackets. Damali's Isis could be called to her palm, if necessary, but the fervent hope from everyone in the group was that it wouldn't be needed for a while.

"How you wanna play this, darlin'?" Rider asked as they walked around the building and up the convent's front steps.

Damali glanced at Rider and Jose. "Let me go in first and see if I can speak to the sisters about a recent request for last rites and a burial. . . . Then, Jose, you interpret for me if they don't speak English. Tara is my sister. That's both the truth, in a way, and our story. Uh . . . I'll say she got sick, also the truth, and went into a coma and the doctors didn't know what to do, and she passed. That's also the truth, and

I won't have to get in spiritual trouble for lying to nuns. Then while I stall, I want your noses on Hubert and Sara's trail."

"Sara is deep into our sinuses, hon," Rider said. "She flew up our noses like fairy dust, remember." He smiled at Jose and shook his head as he released a weary sigh. "And Hubert's blood on that T-shirt is an unforgettable experience for a nose."

"We got it, D. Work your magic," Jose said, pushing open a huge wooden door for Damali and standing aside.

It was eerily quiet as they entered the sanctuary and echoing serenity surrounded them. Brilliant sunlight filtered in through timeless stained-glass windows, draping the weathered mahogany pews in a wash of color. Small white votive candles set in red glass holders flickered on a rack, the scent from burning wax mingling with the thick scent of frankincense.

Rider pulled out a wad of bills and shoved them in an alms box as they passed. "Forgive me, Father, for I have sinned greatly in my day," he said quietly. "Just let my baby rest in peace. I loved her."

Jose and Damali hesitated and bowed their heads for a moment of silence out of remembrance for the dead. They then watched Rider empty his pockets, knowing his next prayer was for Gabrielle.

They all looked up as a small, elderly nun calmly strode toward them, her black-and-white habit flowing as she took dignified steps. She stared at them with kind eyes, but there was a light of excitement in them that made the group stand very still. Tears streaked her weathered face, and when she opened her mouth to speak, initially no words came out.

"Children, be the first to share in a miracle," she said in a flurry of Spanish that Jose interpreted for the group. "I am Sister Louisa. An angel has come to us here in the mountains. . . . Her name is Sara."

Damali almost fell down and she squeezed Jose's arm hard. "Sister, may we see her?"

The nun shook her head and struggled with English, seeming frustrated that she had to wait for a translation delay. "She came out of the sky in a streak across the heavens," the nun said, casting her gaze up, and then making the sign of the crucifix over her heart as she closed her aged brown eyes. "She said she was from a long line of angels of mercy, and asked our mercy to properly anoint and bury a young woman who had tragically fallen ill. She told us that this beautiful woman that she gave us to care for was never to have perished so young. . . . God had work for her to do that was left undone."

"Where did the angel go?" Damali asked in a near whisper, also hoping that Hubert and company had enough presence of mind not to scare the daylights out of these dear sisters by showing themselves.

The elderly nun opened her eyes. Her entire body was trembling as she spoke. "The tiny angel with changing hair color and eyes asked if she could stand watch for three days and three nights in the bell tower," Sister Louisa said. "But she wanted no one to come to her as she prayed for the salvation of the world. She said there were others with her, twelve in all, and she begged our promise of complete faith and privacy. After witnessing such a miracle, she asked that we turn our backs and close our eyes, and we felt them pass by us . . . huge beings with large wings we heard, flying all around us as we dropped to our knees and wept."

Tears of rapture coursed down the nun's face as she stared at Damali and pressed a shaking palm to her breast. "She said the young woman's family would come as a sign . . . she described you, your different hair," the nun said, touching Damali's cheek as though to be sure Damali was real, and then she looked at Jose. "And she said one from our land—a . . . I don't know the word, this Neteru? But we did not question her. We *dared* not offend her grace."

Damali and Jose shared a look, knowing the nun had mistaken him for Carlos.

"Sister Louisa," Rider said in a quiet voice. "May I see the woman the angel left, then . . . if the angel is gone?"

"You are her husband, *sí*?"

"Yes," Rider whispered through a deep swallow. "I was her husband."

The nun rushed up to him and hugged him. "The angel cried so hard as she left her body. . . . She said you loved her so much that she sent up prayers to the Mercies. She begged us to keep this vigil for a man with a good heart. We have, my son. We have, and always will."

Seeming embarrassed by her sudden emotional outburst, Sister Louisa pulled back from Rider and tried to collect herself after apparently forgetting that touching a man was not done. "Come," she told the group. "Our order is small, and twelve sisters surround her with intercessory prayers now until it is time to commit her to the earth and the Lord's care."

The nun walked away so quickly that the small team of Guardians almost had to run to match her short strides. She swept through a huge, carved, wooden archway and motioned toward the cloister that knelt on crimson velvet cushions between mounds of flowers that surrounded a small altar. Twelve praying nuns remained steadfast with their eyes closed and never looked up at the intrusion as their mouths moved in silent litanies and their blind fingers moved rosary beads.

Tara lay prone on a high stone bench just beyond the altar under a statue of the Blessed Virgin. Tara's body was draped in hand-embroidered white linen that had a large crucifix stitched into the center of it over her heart. The nuns had surrounded her with fragrant blooms and her hair spilled across her shoulders in a silky, peaceful wave. Three tall silver incense stands flanked her, sending spirals of white smoke into the vaulted ceiling above. Her forehead glistened with anointing oil, and her peaceful repose put tears in the Guardians' eyes.

"They brought her through the spiral whole," Rider said in a strangled whisper and went to Tara's body before anyone could think to stop him.

He laid his head on her chest and simply shook his head while stroking her hair, causing some of the flowers around her to fall away. "I still can't believe it," he said in a quiet sob. "Wait for me on the other side. I'll marry you in Heaven." With a shuddering breath, he pulled back and then kissed her forehead, and eyelids, the bridge of her nose, and her mouth. He cupped her face as he stood up. "Not even God loved you more than me," he whispered. "Take care of her, Lopez."

Damali bit her lip, crying so deep inside that she had to bear down hard to keep from wailing. The nun stood between Damali and Jose weeping so furiously that the older woman simply gathered their hands up within hers. They watched in agony as Rider's palm dropped away from Tara's cheek in defeat, and he straightened his shoulders, made the sign of the cross over his chest, and backed away from her body.

Rider turned away slowly and then froze. The look on his face made them drop their clasped hands and stare. Damali quickly wiped her eyes, sure that the blur from her tears, her private hopes, and the light was making her see things. The nun backed away, repeatedly crossing herself and then dropped to her knees. Jose rushed forward with Damali as Rider ran to the bench. The threesome stared down, watching Tara's lashes flutter.

Tara's lips parted and a quiet exhalation left her body with one word—*"Rider."*

Damali and Jose had to hold Rider up. Bleating, hiccupping male sobs filled the sanctuary as he gasped for air and repeatedly shouted his dead lover's name from where he stood.

"Tara!"

Rider broke his team's supportive embrace and made the twelve murmuring nuns drop their rosaries to gape as he rushed to Tara's side and held her face with both hands.

"Baby, don't leave me. Wake up," he said, crying hard. He looked up at the ceiling. "I believe all things are possible in Your Name, bring her back, please, God."

Rider's frantic gaze returned to Tara, his hands and whole body trembling. "In the name of mercy, come back. I'll give up every sin," he said, choking. "Will fight a hundred more battles . . . just name it, let her breathe."

She coughed. Five nuns passed out and several screamed. Then Tara gasped and reached for Rider's hand. Disoriented, Tara began sobbing. Rider gathered her up in his arms and started rocking her. Transfixed by awe, Damali and Jose couldn't move.

"Ring the bells!" the senior nun shrieked. "We have witnessed a miracle!"

Damali spun as several shocked nuns tried to stand. "No. The angel is in the tower. You'll hurt her. Remember her warning."

Stunned sisters stood paralyzed, not sure what to do, fervently crossing themselves and weeping as they watched Rider gather Tara up in his arms with the linen draped around her. His face was buried against Tara's shoulder as he carried her toward the door.

"I'm taking you home, and I'll take such good care of you from now on, I promise."

Damali shook Jose out of the awe trance he was in. "We have about five seconds to rush the tower and go get Sara and crew," she whispered quickly. "Let me talk to the nuns so we can get out of here before they call the Vatican. Move, man!"

Jose began running, not sure which direction to go in. Rider was still sobbing by the door with Tara in his arms. Nuns huddled in weeping groups of rapture. Sister Louisa was clutching her heart, appearing faint. It was pure pandemonium.

"Dear sister," Damali said, gathering the older nun's hands within hers and talking quickly. "She was only in a coma and we thought she was dead. It's a miracle, for sure, and the angel said she would keep watch. But now that mercy's been rendered and your prayers have been answered, you *must* let the mysteries of faith further unfold through quiet grace. Please bear silent witness and tell the townspeople *after* we've gone, or they'll want proof, will try to investigate, and may even try to take this woman from her husband to study her. You cannot be a party to that travesty after . . . uh . . . seeing an angel."

"*Sí, sí,*" Sister Louisa said, sobbing. "Go in peace, my child. We will chronicle what we have seen and protect your secret until you have safely passed from gawking spectators. Our lives have been touched by the Hand of God."

"Sara rides with us," Damali told Hubert, gunning the Jeep engine. "Follow the vehicle in a low flight pattern so you don't get lost again." Damali careened away from the back of the convent before Hubert could answer. Her mind was too jumbled to process the fact that only he and the serpentlike hybrid ever showed themselves. The most she could do at the moment was to glance up intermittently into the rearview mirror to be sure Hubert's sky streak was following them.

"There was so much to see," Tara whispered hoarsely, over Rider's shuddering breaths.

"Don't talk, let me get you some water, some food," he murmured, holding her tightly against him in his lap.

Jose sat in the backseat, staring out at the passing scenery. Sara kept a hand on his arm to be sure he was all right. Damali stepped on the gas, but even through her panic, she drove with care. This afternoon she was carrying precious cargo, a nymph and a miracle.

When the Jeep pulled up to the casa, Damali careened it into the driveway and brought the vehicle to a stop with a screeching jolt. She was up and over the door before anyone else could move.

"Everybody on their posts!" she shouted, barreling through the front door of the hacienda. "Situation hot!"

She ran back outside to see Rider on a bench under the trees, gently rocking Tara against him while stroking her hair.

"She didn't want to go inside . . . just wanted to see the sun," Rider said through a garbled whisper.

"I haven't seen daylight in over thirty years," Tara whispered hoarsely.

Rider just gazed at her as though she were a mirage, something fragile that might disappear and leave him.

"Water! Bring her some water!" Damali ran to get it, realizing that she was yelling like a crazy woman, and nobody in the house could probably hear her.

Jose met her on the front steps with bottles of spring water in his hands. A loud sonic boom behind the house told them Hubert had landed. Sara sat at Rider's feet, looking up with a serene, sparkling gaze. Disoriented Guardians filled the courtyard, roused by the blast and Damali's yelling. Team members rushed forward, half-dressing, trying to maneuver weapons, and dragging Carlos with them. Hubert and one hybrid jogged to a stop and gathered around the bench with the others. For a moment no one spoke as they watched with reverence as Rider accepted an opened bottle of water and gently helped Tara sip from it.

"Whoa . . ." Carlos murmured, wiping the haze of sleep from his face with both palms. "D, did you . . ."

"No, no—I don't know how to do something like that!" Damali said in a quick whisper. "I can't raise the freakin' dead. Ya crazy?"

"It was beautiful," Tara said quietly, cupping Rider's face. "Lopez came for me and pulled me away from Fallon Nuit's jaws."

"Fallon Nuit?" Marlene said, elbowing through the group and squatting down to hold Tara's hand. "Baby, talk to us." She looked up at Rider and then back to Damali and Carlos.

Carlos's jaw pulsed with anger. "A simultaneous bite from a councilman layered right over the top of Yonnie's to flatline her. The Chairman did it to me over Fallon's. That's probably how he knew how to do it . . . set my boy up and almost made Tara—"

"They raised him again?" Marlene asked quickly, cutting Carlos off. She dropped Tara's hand and stood.

"Yeah, long story. I'll fill you in later, main thing is Tara is back. And we also know Lopez is where he should be," Carlos said, still amazed to see Tara in the sunlight. "But, how did she come back?" He'd seen a lot of miracles in his time, but this one beat all.

"There was a bond so deep," Sara said quietly, now looking at Rider and Tara. "A love so profound . . . that when I went into Rider to purge all the old wounds he'd sustained, each and every one of them was from their love. His heart and her heart were tied together as one, since they were so young." Sara drew a shaky breath and wiped her eyes. "I come from a long line of Healing Mercy Angels on my mother's side. My father was a Spartan soldier who found mercy and let prisoners bound for death go. I went to them, first, and they appealed to the Mercies in the Rings Above. That allowed Tara's body to be preserved in death, even though she had been a . . ." Sara censored her words and reached up to squeeze Tara's hand. "Even though she had been gone for so long."

The little nymph stood and kissed both Tara and Rider on their cheeks. "I did not know that the Mercies were so moved that they went to the Powers and the Powers wept at the story," she said, giving Damali a quizzical glance. "Only a few times in history have they reversed a fate like this." Sara covered her mouth and spoke in an awed voice between her fingers. "When Hubert got lost, he sought the silver land . . . and it was built in a seven elevation. Then twelve good sisters prayed with us on high ground. I kept hoping and asking that Heaven spare just this one Guardian who was robbed of her whole life. I didn't do this all by myself."

"Forever indebted," Rider said softly, touching Tara's cheek with trembling fingers. He traced away her tears with the pad of his thumbs, unable to say more.

"You give us all hope," Marjorie said, swallowing hard. "There's a chance for Gabby, too . . . even Yonnie, then. Right?"

"One can only hope at this point," Carlos said, still too awed to comment further. "I don't know . . ."

"I saw my whole family, tribes of tribes of ancients," Tara whispered, staring up into Rider's bloodshot eyes. "And there was this bright silver cord coming out of my chest that none of them would break by crossing through it. They said the choice to go back was mine . . . and when I touched the cord I saw your face, heard you crying, and heard every prayer you ever said for me. I held on to that lifeline, pulling on it, hand over hand trying to reach you to tell you that I was all right and was in a place of peace. When I opened my eyes, you were standing there." Tara used her graceful fingers to sign over Rider's chest. "Man with a good heart, I never left you, and never will."

Damali slipped her hand into Carlos's as the team dissolved into tears around them. The emotional impact of what they'd all just seen left everyone spent. Slowly people filed into the house, old grievances and pet peeves with each other were left buried in the courtyard. Each team member then hesitated and stood at the bottom of the main hall staircase and watched Rider take Tara up the steps to rest as though he were carrying his new bride over a threshold.

Hubert and his reduced team anxiously gathered around the two

Neterus as the other Guardians wearily found a private space to contemplate it all.

"Those of us who stayed are honored to be with you," Hubert said, drawing Sara to his side.

"Those who stayed?" Carlos said, looking at Hubert's much smaller crew and then Damali.

The hybrid that resembled a serpent dropped to his knees and clung to Carlos's legs. "Do not forssssake ussss, because of the others. I am Ssssedgewick—of good lineage. My mother was a serpent deity in Thebes, my father a palace high priest."

"Come on, man, get up," Carlos said, becoming uncomfortable as Sedgewick clung to him and began crying. He helped up the distressed serpent and held his arms firmly. "Nobody is putting you guys out. What happened to your squad? Were you attacked?"

"No," Hubert said, shame filling his voice. "That cowardly little son-of-a-satyr, Odefe, used us."

"The fawn, or half-fawn?" Damali asked, trying to piece together the information.

"Yesss. Him. Traitor," Sedgewick hissed. "He wanted to get away from ssserving in any campaign."

Damali and Carlos looked at each other.

"Do we need to hunt him down? Is he gonna be a problem, since nine of your crew went south with him?" Carlos asked, releasing Sedgewick's arms and looking at Hubert hard.

"No. He doesn't want to fight for either side," Hubert said in a huff. "We later found out, while discussing it in the bell tower, that he and his friends only came along to get out of Nod. The moment they saw the green hillside, they ran for it. All they want to do is eat, drink, and be merry . . . he's probably cornered a doe by now and mounted one, if I know him well."

"Great," Damali said. "Just what we need. A bunch of horny hybrids on the loose up in central Mexico trying to nail any creature walking." She let out an impatient breath. "Any of them dangerous, like flesh-eaters that could go after local humans for dinner?"

"Better question," Carlos said in a flat, annoyed tone. "Can any of them lock on to us here and cause a problem by guiding the wrong side of this war to us?"

"No," Sara said in a sad voice. She turned to Hubert and placed her hand on his chest to calm him. "They're afraid of their own shadows and would not be able to stand on the silver ground if they took a life. They do not want to fight with Cain's army and do not want to fight with yours. They just want to hide and enjoy the fruits of peace once it is all over."

Hubert growled and lifted his chin. "They are not prepared to sacrifice anything for anyone, not even themselves . . . and they argued with me about not just leaving Tara's body wherever I could drop it and running away."

"Now *that* woulda been fucked up," Carlos said, rolling new tension out of his shoulders.

"It is their loss, as they missed witnessing a miracle," Sara said. "Yes, it was daunting and frightening to approach the nuns, and what is before us is also terrifying, but if we should perish in the service of the Light, then all was for a worthy cause."

"I couldn't agree more," Damali said, stooping down to stare at the nymph and then hugged her. "Girlfriend, you were awesome. But I want you guys safe, not perishing, okay?"

"You are magnificent, too. Much more than me," the nymph whispered into Damali's ear. "Your secret is safe. We can always see our own . . . your prayers helped."

Damali kissed her forehead and stood quickly. Carlos gave Damali a look, but said nothing.

"Only Hubert and Sedgewick of the rebels had learned the way out of Nod and how to find you, because they were the only ones brave enough to go into Cain's lair to access his pool. The last image we had was the beach hacienda that Cain had seen. Beyond that, the pool holds no more images, so none of the other hybrids know where you are. The good ones will be too afraid to come out, not sure where Cain's loyalists will be or if humans will panic and slaughter them on sight." Sara gazed up at Carlos. "If we die with you, we will go to the place Tara was. I am not afraid to go there."

"Nor am I," Hubert said, lifting his chin.

"Nor I," Sedgewick concurred, straightening his back.

"Our goal is not to lose anybody," Damali said, looking at them all hard. "Not one. Got it? You just saw what losing one person did to us, and you're family now. So no heroics. You keep your heads down in a firefight. I want everybody to grow old and live a long time and to one day die peacefully in their sleep—that's been my prayer from day one."

"But if duty calls, know that we stand with you," Hubert said with pride. "That was what we thought the others also wanted, which was the only reason we allowed them to travel with us . . . that their lives would not have been in vain, and they had served mankind with self-less courage. When we all expire, the Light will then take us home. But that smarmy group of malcontents . . . they can only think of themselves, and care nothing of the fate of the world! I cannot believe the years of debate on this, how we all espoused such lofty goals and to have it disintegrate into mere rhetorical rubbish when the final hour came."

"All right," Carlos said with a heavy sigh. "Why don't you guys get something to eat, then we'll show you to a great room with a view so you can rest. Maybe later, if you're up for it, you can man a tower and our guys can show you how to shoot a gun or an RPG without blowing your foot off."

"Very good," Hubert said. "And my sincerest apologies that my human side makes me inept at sky navigation. But I am strong."

"Hisss eyessssight issss not so good, but if he sssees a location once, he isss very reliable," Sedgewick said, slapping Hubert's back.

"Uh . . . one last question," Damali said, leading the strange new addition to their family into the kitchen with Carlos. "Do you and Sara want your own room, or should I bed Sedgewick down alone?"

Hubert smiled as Sedgewick's eyes widened in terror. "Thank you for your consideration, Queen Damali. However, Sedgewick is afraid of the dark, and my relationship with Sara is strictly platonic. She is my best friend."

Lilith leaned against a cavern wall and spoke quickly to a Harpie as she gouged a talon into her abdomen. She shuddered and closed her eyes as she dragged the sharp claw down her lower belly, and panted as she reached into her body to extract her womb. Speaking through her teeth as sweat covered her shaking body, she weakly extended her hand, which contained a slick, black organ.

"This contains an empire," she wheezed. "Guard it with your life. Courier it to a surviving hybrid and tell them to secret it away in Cain's palace in Nod."

The Harpie squealed and snatched the bloody organ from Lilith, clutched the quivering pulp to its breast and then protectively folded its wings around it. But the creature tilted its horned gargoyle head in a question as its beady little eyes narrowed. The Harpie screeched and made a face, pointing upward with a hooked claw.

"I know, I know, dear one," Lilith gasped, weakening as she walked deeper into Level Seven. "The Light in Nod will not harm it. My womb will burn away, but Cain's seed combined within my egg will not. It may be the last time we can cultivate dark Neteru seed from our sovereign while he still has a living soul, if he does not recover. Should he expire, we will have to make the decision for him and deliver the eternal bite. Do not worry as you fly to locate a hybrid warrior. Level Seven is impervious to daylight, just as Cain's soul layer will make what you carry impervious to the dreaded Light of Nod. Cain's legacy should live on. Just as mine shall. Have the hybrids find a host womb for the crown jewel of our empire in Nod."

Lilith pushed off the wall and staggered deeper into the pit. "Fly now with haste! The deposit Cain made into me is only forty-eight hours old. My womb was of no use, and could not hold a fetus to term . . . but a healthy female demon hybrid's can. Be gone!"

Damali sat alone in the kitchen with Carlos, listening to the faucet drip. They sat that way quietly for a long time; him watching her sip her tea and nosh on fruit, her watching him take an unsteady sip of Jack Daniel's every now and then as he polished off a burger.

"You all right?" she finally said.

"No," he said calmly. "You?"

"No," she said, and sipped her tea. "I don't even know where to begin."

He lifted his short rocks glass and clinked it against her mug. "My point exactly."

"They're not ready for battle," Damali murmured, staring down into her mug.

"You talking about Hubert or the team?"

"Both," she said, glancing up to hold Carlos's gaze.

"I know," he muttered, slowly rolling his glass between his palms as he looked down at it. "Nobody is. Not even me or you."

Damali reached across the table and held Carlos's hand, which made his eyes finally meet hers and remain there. Her fingers caressed his platinum wedding band as his moved her wedding and engagement rings with a gentle touch.

"Talk to me," she murmured.

Carlos paused and let out a heavy breath. "D, after I saw how tore up Rider was, and then Tara coming back and before that, how shook Adam was about his wife . . . Berkfield about Marj, and the way Shabazz was quietly wigging about Marlene's temporary turn . . ." Carlos sighed hard. "Yonnie is all fucked around out there somewhere by himself with pure Hell on his ass, and nowhere to turn, and I can't even grant my boy sanctuary until he checks out. We've got Gabby out there screwed, and can't help her. Plus, now, every man on this team has something more precious than his own life to lose, even the newbies. And Hubert, for Christ's sake, has a hybrid angel to worry about. The man is shitting gold bricks about going into a firefight, no matter what his big ass says."

"I know," Damali said quietly, squeezing Carlos's hand hard. "Maybe it'll make everybody fight harder, when the time comes."

"That's just it," Carlos said, reaching across the counter to cup her cheek. "They'll fight hard enough to die quick. They'll take risks in a panic, their minds divided . . . and when it's all said and done, we can't raise 'em all from the dead, baby. None of us know how or are even probably supposed to, if we did. The Tara thing . . . we just got lucky. Had a lot working with us combining the thing right. But we're gonna need a whole lot more than luck with Cain, Lilith, *and* Fallon Nuit as a councilman coming for us. This bullshit is insane now."

Carlos pushed a stray lock behind Damali's ear and dropped forward to lean his forearms on the counter between them, and then looked out the window as the early evening sun splashed pink-rose-orange color against the azure blue mountain clouds.

"Seems not so long ago," she said in a gentle voice, "that it all seemed so much easier back then—and even just saying that sounds crazy, if you think about it."

"You should have seen Adam's face, D. The man, a seasoned warrior king, was ready to burn to death in his own armor and die down there to avenge Eve's heartbreak. Sloppy. That troubles me, baby."

Carlos's gaze slid away from the horizon to look at Damali. "What worries me the most is *everybody* on the team is right there, including me . . . so emotional about what was done to one of our own, each nursing a deep, personal scar that we're all *right there,*" he said, pointing on the counter hard. "Just where Adam was today. Not good."

She didn't know what to say to him. All of what he'd said was true. The subject that was too tender to discuss was also in the room with them like a leering phantom that could turn into a poltergeist at any given moment. There were two approaches she could take: a silent hug that would simply allow the thing to fester within her husband's soul, or she could flush it out into the open and make it bleed . . . but without knowing how to heal it, that didn't seem like the best option.

"Did you get any rest today?" Carlos finally asked, obviously needing to change the subject.

"No," Damali said quietly, now staring down at her lukewarm tea. "I'm glad you got a few hours, though."

Carlos nodded. He'd gone back to twirling an empty rocks glass between his palms. "You should lie down for an hour or two before sunset, at least, especially if your back is bothering you and you have cramps."

"My back is bothering me from body blows and tension," she said just above a whisper. "Everybody else in the house has that problem except me. That's what your nose is picking up."

She watched Carlos's gaze seek the window and then the sky for redemption that he didn't need to request. The question was valid, just as his hopes that she wasn't pregnant by anybody right now were. Yet she could also feel a thin thread of a prayer lingering, a prayer that she was carrying for him wrestled just beneath the surface of his skin. Deep conflict was shredding him to death. The muscle in his jaw pulsed as she watched him fight within himself. It would be the toughest battle he ever waged, possibly a fruitless campaign that might very well have no victory one way or the other.

She stood and came around the counter to give her husband that silent hug he so desperately needed but couldn't ask for. This evening the decision was made clear as he enfolded her in his arms and held on to her for dear life: the wound would just have to fester a while longer. He didn't want to talk about it and she respected that.

CHAPTER FOURTEEN

Carlos patrolled the halls of the castle, watching the sun go down as Damali slept. He could hear other Guardians stirring throughout the expansive structure, hoping they were braced for whatever was yet to come.

There was something calming, almost comforting, about the stillness that surrounded him, walking the old stone floors just remembering. This time he was careful not to pine for the past, just to observe it and give that history proper detached reverence in a personal requiem within.

After all he'd seen there was no doubt about the incomprehensible power of the Light. Yet after all he'd seen there was also no question about the lengths evil could go to break a human being's back. One by one, the Darkness had come for them all, using each person's deepest fears to twist agony into living souls. How Fallon would come at him was a nagging question. If anyone wanted to exploit his deepest fear, Lilith, and then Cain, had beaten Fallon to the punch. In that regard, Fallon was late to the party. Carlos smiled.

Maybe the worst had been done to him. Then again, maybe not.

Bottom line was, the Light had shown the Darkness that it was indeed a force to be reckoned with. Although he still didn't quite understand why all of Heaven, with every Neteru warrior available, wouldn't just blow a hole into the pit, shine a bright light down into it, and be done with the madness—having seen miracle after miracle, he checked that question at the door. He was not only living proof that the awesome was possible, now he was a living witness. Rider was upstairs with a woman in his arms that had been dead for thirty years.

"Damn . . ." Carlos murmured to himself, occasionally glancing up as he strolled the vacant halls. "Y'all are awesome."

He quietly walked up the wide center stairs and pressed his hands against the large bay windows at the landing, spreading his fingers between the beveled glass panes. As though seeing the results for the first time, he watched heat from his living body fan out against the cool surface, remembering when he was dead and that was the only way to touch what was now his wife. But he was alive now. Tara lived again. Heaven obviously heard prayers and delivered tangible answers. One just had to be able to see them. What wasn't he seeing?

Carlos rested his forehead against the glass and breathed deeply. "Please don't let her be carrying for Cain . . . not for my sake, but for hers. It'll break her heart—will rip it up and spit it out." He pushed away from the window. "I respect your decision either way, though."

Come what may, he kept telling himself as he pushed back from the glass and just looked at the mountainside beauty that was fading. . . . It was all happening so subtly yet so fast while people down in the valley went on about their daily routines unaware, oblivious to the ticking clock that had stopped. Beyond his personal worries, lush hillsides would soon be dead and brown. Streams and oceans would become big, blue bowls of stillness. Skies would lie dormant, no birds taking flight, or gnats to stir the air. Life would stop moving to the natural rhythms that had been a constant on Earth since the dawn of time. Not a single baby would suck in that first gulp and cry out to tell the world they'd been born.

Suddenly the magnitude of what they faced as a challenge slammed into him. He knew the mission, the issues, but still his own personal dilemmas had been paramount. Hubert's words, as well as those of Adam tortured him. When they'd been so close, the desire to survive had made him pull the small team out of the bowels of Hell to live to fight another day. Now he wondered if that was the right thing to do. What if the greater test was to go out in a blaze, sever Cain's head, and restart the stalled cosmic clock?

"I don't know," Carlos said, now walking the second-floor halls with his fingers laced on top of his head.

A familiar voice made him stop and slowly drop his hands away. The female voice was calling to Rider from outside. Mike met him in the hallway.

"I know, brother. I heard it."

Mike already had a weapon in hand. "Your call. After seeing Tara's situation, you want me to stand down, or what?"

Damali opened the bedroom door and jogged to meet them in the observatory. "I heard Gabrielle."

"I know. She's out there going for Rider, first." Carlos looked at Mike. "You're gonna have to help Berkfield hold Marjorie down and assist with the rest of 'em. Don't shoot, yet, but I don't think Gabrielle's situation is the same as Tara's."

"The hard part is gonna be convincing her family of that," Damali said sadly. "Okay. It's started. Time to get everybody up."

Mike ran down the hallway with Damali and Carlos knocking on doors. Guardians spilled out into the hallway still exhausted but ready. Carlos cocked his head to the side with Mike and Damali as the faint haunting voice begged for an invitation into the casa.

"Everybody in the same room," Damali said, running down the steps with the team to get the group to convene in the living room.

"You swab all those fireplaces?" Carlos asked, looking at Dan.

"Uh . . . we think so," Dan said, glancing at J.L., Bobby, and Jose.

"Yeah, I'm pretty sure we did, man. Jose and Bobby were working with us and then Jose got called away to make the run to get Tara and Hubert and his crew," J.L. said as all eyes went to Jose and Bobby.

"I was working on the wings and—"

"Oh, shit, which ones, Jose?" Carlos shouted.

"You were on the east side with J.L., right?" Bobby said. "Me and Dan were working on the west side, I think."

"Never mind! Neteru team only," Carlos said, losing patience by the second. "Just me and D, 'cause we can take a nick." He glanced at Damali and she nodded. "Me and you, both wings. Newbies, start a sagebrush and frankincense fire in this room. Mar, set up a salt perimeter around the living room." Carlos's blade materialized in his grip.

Shabazz drew his weapon. "I got a lock with Mike and Rider—three seasoned guns in the house with hands free to point and click." He looked at Berkfield who was body blocking his wife. "You got your hands full. That's just as important."

"Sara, you stay on Hubert's hip and don't leave his side. You, too, Sedgewick," Damali said, materializing her Isis in her hand.

"Rider . . . don't leave me outside in the cold," a disembodied female voice said way too close for comfort. "I'm scared, lover. I thought we were at least friends?"

Damali, Carlos, and Mike turned toward the large living room windows at the same time. Tara closed her eyes as Marjorie stood.

"Marjorie," Berkfield said slowly. "Sit down. If you don't, I'll have to body slam you into a chair."

"Gabrielle could have a chance, just like she did," Marjorie shrieked, pointing at Tara. "Give my sister a chance. Tara had been dead for thirty years and came back! You even trusted Tara around our children when she had fangs!"

"Way different situation, Marj," Carlos said. "And I'm sorry about that, more than you know."

"Marjorie . . . Marj . . ." the eerie voice cried out in an echoing wail. "Please don't let them hurt me. I just want to come in and talk to you. Or you can come outside the gate so I can explain. *Please . . .*"

Marjorie covered her mouth as Krissy began to cry.

"Can't we just talk to her?" Krissy said, holding the sides of her head. "Maybe she's like the others?" Krissy suddenly broke down, sobbing harder. "I can hear her inside my mind. I'm so sorry, Aunt Gabby!"

"J.L., stay with Krissy and sit on her if you have to," Carlos said quickly. "Dan, you're on Heather," he added as Heather broke down and reached toward the windows. He looked at Bobby and Jasmine.

"I got 'em," Mike said. "Y'all have a seat and Uncle Mike will be cool."

Inez moved closer to Marjorie. "I'm a mom, too, so let's talk about what's at risk tonight. Focus on my voice, not your sister's, okay, baby?" She stared at Marjorie until she sat down. "Let these people work, they haven't let us down yet. If there's a way to save her, you know they will. If not, we've all gotta let 'em do what they've gotta do."

"I've been there, Marj," Marlene said in a gentle tone, "and it was my daughter. I know where you're at, but you've gotta hold the line." Marlene glanced around the group. "All of you who are deeply connected to Gabrielle, start saying a prayer, any one that you know, and it'll help block her out of your minds."

Juanita rounded the back of the sofa and stood behind Bobby and Jasmine. "Right now, she's not your aunt or your mentor. When she becomes that again, we can let her in, but not now." Juanita nodded to Mike. "I'll work this detail with you so you can keep your hands free to shoot if you have to. Everybody will be cool, won't they?" Juanita rounded the sofa, folded her arms over her chest, and gave Jasmine a hard grit. "Won't they?" She waited until Jasmine nodded but looked at Bobby's defiant face. "Let a vampire in here, boy, and I will personally kick your simple ass."

"Rider—she's calling for you. How's your head, dude?" Damali said as Rider stood and cocked back the hammer on his weapon.

"Never better, sis," he said, moving around to cover Tara and to potentially assist Berkfield with Marjorie. "Breaks my heart and hurts like hell, but I'm *real clear* where I stand. Said my prayers and had 'em answered earlier today. Ain't too much of nothing she can say to me to make me open a door to let her in."

"Cool. Now listen up," Carlos said. "The master vamp call is strong. She has to try an entry point from the roof, since she can't cross the courtyard or the thresholds and windows. Mar and Damali put up energy and prayer barriers," he added, glancing at Marlene and Damali, "but we were all maxed out at the time. Who knows how strong the barriers were when they rimmed the casa. And if our mop team accidentally missed a spot due to fatigue, that means we have anywhere from two to five holes in the roof. So, while me and D check for a possible breach, you all stay in the ring set up here. If Gabrielle gets in without an invite it's gonna get hectic. Watch the ceilings and walls that are painted and aren't stone—the ones we didn't mop down. We clear?"

"Let's do this," Damali said, motioning to Carlos with her chin. "I heard her in the east wing, but for all we know, she could have been throwing her voice as a diversion."

"Very good, Damali," the voice said, but now it had manifested just outside the window.

Everyone turned to stare in horror as a contorted, ghostly pale face came near the glass but didn't touch it, hovering in the air just beyond it. Her body floated above the ground, avoiding the protected dirt. Gabrielle's once clear green eyes had been replaced with angry, red glowing orbs that had sunken in with deep, dark rings under them. Her mouth was filled with long, glistening, feed-length fangs. She smiled and crooked a razor-sharp fingernail at Rider.

"Look at her," Marjorie gasped in a choked whisper. "Oh, God . . ."

Gabrielle's hair was again raven black and no longer the natural, vibrant auburn it had been. The brittle tresses moved as though a supernatural wind disturbed them. Rider's shoulders dropped in personal defeat as Gabrielle's pale green silk robe hung loose and flowed on the evening breeze, exposing her voluptuous, naked form. Marjorie stood but didn't move toward her. The young initiates covered their faces and wept as Krissy and Bobby turned away.

"Don't blow the glass, that's what she wants," Carlos said, going closer to the window.

Then suddenly, Gabrielle became beautiful. Her old coloring was back, as were her green eyes and auburn hair. She floated on the breeze like a mermaid, her voice that of a melodic siren's. Carlos motioned for Damali to cross the barrier and head for the steps.

"She's changing back to what she was," Marjorie whispered through her tears.

"No. The one you saw before was her," Carlos said, running past the group. "What's outside the window is an illusion. A placeholder for the one that just breached the house."

Reaching the top of the steps as one, Carlos and Damali went back-to-back, blades raised. A slight energy distortion rippled on their skins coming from the east wing, and both Neterus spun to meet the threat. Carlos's silver line of vision caught the outline of the creature scampering along the painted walls sideways like a crab.

"Don't make me kill you, Gabby," Carlos said in a low, warning.

"We're giving you one chance to get out of here," Damali said, leveling her Isis. "We need you on our side, even if you've turned."

"I bet you do," Gabrielle said, instantly materializing. She growled low in her throat and crouched on the wall in a spider's hold, tilting her head from side to side. "But I'm a master, sis, and I need to eat right."

Gabrielle lunged, but another unseen entity collided with her midair, making her fall to the floor and begin to sizzle against the stones where she fell. She screeched curses and went to a painted wall smoldering, clinging to it like a treed cat. Yonnie materialized and covered her before Damali and Carlos could advance.

"I told you, never family!" Yonnie said through a hiss. He looked at Carlos and Damali and trapped Gabrielle against the wall in a black holding arc. "I got two seconds to tell you this, then we're out." He strained against Gabrielle's struggle as she twisted under his dark energy hold. "Lilith made her, not me."

"That's right!" Gabrielle screamed. "You're not my maker and I'm a master, too! I need to eat real food, not venison and whatever weak blood you have running through your veins!"

Yonnie's gaze went to Carlos. "I'm older, but she's learning fast. Once she feeds correctly, she'll be stronger." He turned to Gabrielle and reinforced his hold. "But you were given to me in council. Lilith and Nuit turned you over as my prize for not accepting a council seat—so I do have power over you, bitch . . . and I said no family or humans!" Yonnie looked back at Carlos with hope in his eyes that the message was clear.

Carlos and Damali both nodded. Yonnie had given up serious information while subduing Gabrielle: he had declined a throne, Gabrielle was a master, Lilith and Nuit were in cahoots with Cain, and Yonnie was on their side but possibly being monitored, so had to speak, in riddles. Much had been said in a few short sentences.

"Good," Yonnie said, staring at Carlos and Damali. "Seal up the main fireplace on the east wing. That's where she got in, not the west side. That's the only breach. And don't forget the basics. You've got masters and councils coming at you. Say *each name* in the barriers. A general prayer won't do it." Yonnie looked off and cocked his head to the side. "I gotta go. Watch your back and the rains. That'll wash down the walls and the gate."

"Oh, shit . . ." Damali said on a quiet breath.

"Thanks, man. We gotta talk later." Carlos looked at Yonnie and for a moment they said nothing. "Tara crossed over into the Light."

Yonnie nodded and briefly closed his eyes. He sealed Gabrielle's snarling mouth. "I didn't kill her."

"I know, man. Get outta here before it's too late and you get caught."

Yonnie hesitated. Carlos stared at him, tension roiling within.

"Am I losing my mind, man?" Yonnie asked in a barely audible whisper. Awe threaded through Yonnie's tone. "It's like I can still smell her, actually *feel* Tara's pulse." His stare bored into Carlos. "But that's crazy, ain't it, *hombre,* 'cause you woulda told me if I shoulda known she was still around, right?"

Carlos sighed. "It's a very long story about the Light thing, man, and I promise to—"

"Blow your ass away if you ever come near her again," Rider said low in his throat as he entered the hallway holding a rocket-propelled grenade launcher.

"Oh, shit . . ." Carlos muttered, blocking Rider's shot with his body as Yonnie snarled.

"I shouldn't have found out like this—not from, of all people, you," Yonnie hissed between his teeth. The accusation in his glare was lethal. "Not from my blood brother."

Carlos briefly closed his eyes. "We ain't have time for the details, man—"

"Rider, please," Damali said, her voice strident.

"Kiss my ass, darlin'," Rider said as he hocked and spit. "If he came for her tonight, this whole house can go up in flames first."

"I didn't come for her," Yonnie said in a low growl, circling around Carlos without touching the floor to accept the open shot. "Until two seconds ago," he added, blame flaring in his eyes as he glanced at Carlos, "I didn't even know she was alive." Yonnie squared his attention on Rider. "But the only reason your heart isn't lying on the floor from a black charge is because with me, right now, she'd be in mortal danger." He issued Rider a withering look. "However, one night . . . we'll get back to this conversation, just me and you, motherfucker."

"I'm sorry, man," Carlos said quietly.

Yonnie glared at him and said nothing. Rider cocked back his weapon and headed down the stairs without another word. A fragile peace had been reestablished. The scary question was, for how long? Both Neterus waited for the tension crackling through the hallway to dissipate.

A whirling funnel cloud filled the hallway and spiraled hot ash plumes toward the east wing and was gone. Damali and Carlos ran behind it and stood before the large fireplace in the conservatory, working furiously to lay barriers. There was no time to dwell in feelings and emotion, much less discuss all of that.

"You heard what he said about the rains," Damali murmured, keeping her voice low so family wouldn't overhear. They had to stay focused and close the breach. It was as though both she and Carlos had silently agreed to deal with the Yonnie problem later.

"I know," Carlos said, his eyes haunted. "That means the interior of the casa is the only safe place. Even if the roof, outside walls, exteriors of windows, gates, and pathways are open—we still have the fireplaces sealed, every vent, pipes, doorjambs, floors, and most walls. The hot zones, if anything gets in, would be the second-floor hallways along the walls. But wherever we have stone enclosures, we should be good."

"Then we'd better let everybody know where to go if it gets hot," Damali said, looking at him. She could tell this thing with Yonnie was tearing Carlos up. Her husband wouldn't be right until he could make his best friend understand. "This break-in could've been a disaster . . . me and Marlene were so tired when we put up the barriers, I don't know. Rain shouldn't be able to wash that away, just the holy water layers." She kept her conversation to what was necessary.

Carlos slung his arm over her shoulder as they walked back down the hall. "We're all beat down, neither of you really got a chance to rest."

Damali briefly stopped walking. "They can get images through a weak barrier, even if it holds against their actual physical manifestations—which can be almost as damaging." She didn't even want to risk a guess. So much had already devastated Carlos, although he'd never outwardly show it, she just hoped they could all simply make it through the night without further incident.

Carlos only nodded and began walking again. She was right. The dark side could send an image between two Guardians and have them blow each other away. Or they could send in something to torture a weary soul that could possibly break a Guardian down so hard he or she would be near suicide. When they reentered the living room, Carlos sat down hard in a chair, leaned his head back, and shut his eyes.

"We found the hole," Damali said without judgment in her tone. "East wing, conservatory fireplace got missed. No blame. Me and Mar were fatigued, too, so our barriers weren't as ironclad as they should have been, either. But we did find out Yonnie is still on our side, but he's compromised."

Damali eyed Rider when he bristled and took her time filling in the team on exactly what had transpired in the hallway, as well as the dangers of illusions being cast inside the house.

"That's the thing, though, D," Bobby said when Damali was finally done. "If we see something that seems real manifest, how do we know not to shoot?"

"That's gonna be a real issue for the newbies who can't sense through the panic. Ask me how I know," Shabazz said. He allowed his gaze to evenly rove over the team. "That's how I lost ten years of my life in the joint, when I was just coming into my own and didn't know it—felt a presence, turned on it, and shot clean through it and dropped my boy in an alley. I took the murder rap. In a stone castle like this, we could hit one of our own with a ricochet. So everybody's gotta be on point, even though you only have seconds to make a decision."

"Everything that's solid has a pulse," Damali said, nodding in agreement with Shabazz. "If it's illusion, it won't. That's why it's gonna be very important for everybody to get real still, and get *real* cool in their heads, so your sensory awareness is at peak performance. Everything, not just your eyes has to guide you, if something rolls into this house."

She looked at Heather, Jasmine, Krissy, and then Marjorie and Bobby. "Because Gabrielle is linked very closely to y'all, and we're in a stone structure and you have Stonehenge-type energy, plus know wicca, if you see her, and you all are in the right space in your heads—focused—you can subdue her with the power of three. Literally, you can put her in an energy cage, which is what I suggest if you wanna save her."

"All right," Marjorie said, drying her face. "The tactical Guardians should be able to sense if what we're seeing is illusion or not, and we can contain her."

"And throw her out of the house," Marlene said in a flat tone, "then seal up where she got in behind it."

"Maybe we can bring her onto our side at some future point," Carlos said, sitting forward and rubbing his hands down his face. "But you might have to start getting used to the idea that it might not be possible. She didn't look good up there at all . . . like her mind is in the wrong space, you feel me?" He looked at Marjorie. "Who knows what they did to her, or what hidden things she had in her soul that they're twisting?"

"Yes, I agree. A soul *is* a terrible thing to waste, *n'est-ce pas?*" a melodic male voice said, putting everyone on their feet. "Carlos, long time, *mon ami.*" Low, rumbling laughter filled the living room and then a deep sigh echoed that raised the hair on everyone's arms. "Damali . . . gorgeous as ever, *cheri,* you still captivate me . . . now more so than before, since you have been such a very bad girl."

"On guard," Damali whispered to the team. "This is not a drill; Council-level threat."

The lights in the house went out, the team took formation in the darkness, all weapons drawn and facing the ring, backs touching the hybrids and nymph in the center. Only moonlight and Carlos's silver gaze lit the room in a bluish-white light.

"Why don't me and you take this outside, Nuit?" Carlos said, needing the entity to speak again to get a bead on his direction, or to tell if he'd been able to get into the house. "Like old times?"

"Gladly," Nuit said. "I have been waiting to neuter you like you tried to neuter me. Fair exchange is no robbery."

Don't go out there, Damali said urgently in her mind. *He's not in the house. It's a bluff.*

Hadn't planned to, but needed to know where the bastard was, Carlos mentally replied, fangs beginning to lower.

"But perhaps Cain beat me to the punch," Nuit said and laughed cruelly. "Our new Chairman does have a way with the ladies, and has obviously positioned himself well to geld you. Right between your wife's legs."

Carlos tightened his grip on his blade. "Meet me outside."

"Don't let shit talking take you out of the right headspace," Shabazz warned.

Carlos rolled his shoulders.

"Yes, Rivera, take advice from a seasoned Guardian whose woman has been indulging in trysts with were-jaguars . . . I suppose you married into that family and abide their lusts—like mother-seer like daughter, *oui?*"

Big Mike caught Shabazz around the waist before he could break the circle.

"We're both outside, man," Shabazz hollered. "Me and you can step to that motherfucker pronto!"

"That slimy bastard will use whatever he can to try to taunt you out of the house—don't let him win like that," Damali said, her face burning with rage. "It's not working. Don't let him play you."

"Ah, but you love to play, *cheri* . . . and you play so well," Nuit said on a breathy, sensual sigh. "Lilith shared a little insight with me, *ma petite*. I didn't know you had it in you. Had I known, I would have raised myself from extinction to experience . . . *this* . . . "

Instantly Damali's voice filled the room and the walls lit with images of her and Cain. Guardians cast their eyes to the floor to avoid seeing it, but the floor lit, and when they closed their eyes, their lids fluttered as they fought not to see what was careening beneath them. Damali's voice came back to haunt her in sense-around-sound, "He hurt me so bad." She cringed as she saw Carlos's sword lower a fraction.

"Don't close your eyes, *ma petite*—you were ravishing," Nuit crooned, as he made her voice crescendo.

"Oh, this is complete bullshit," Juanita said, her voice slicing through the room and making Damali's attention jerk toward her. Everyone stared at Juanita. "I'm a team-seer, and I would know, asshole. But I guarantee you, Damali ain't neva rolled like that! Our Neteru has more class than that, and she ain't do no freakin' Cain, okaaay," Juanita yelled at the ceiling, one finger pointing. "So how you gonna come up in here with some tired crap like that and try to get all up in our heads, right 'Nez?"

"That's right," Inez hollered toward a wall. "I been knowing my girl for how many years, bitch? Puhlease. Take that tired shit somewhere else to somebody who's tryin' to hear it, 'cause we ain't!" Inez slapped Juanita five.

"Interesting," Nuit crooned. "You have your team well trained, I see."

"It ain't about being trained, you piece of shit," Juanita yelled, stepping beside Damali, Glock in hand. "It's about knowing my girl. We don't care what you show us, she's still the one and you ain't, *bitch*."

"Really?" Nuit said in a dangerous tone. "You don't care what I show this team? Then would you like to go with me for a trip down memory lane to Arizona, *bitch* . . . when Carlos was not himself?"

Sudden panic glittered in Juanita's eyes. Jose raked his hair as Carlos's gaze sought the window. Damali fought with everything in herself not to cringe.

"Stand down," Damali whispered. "This is my fight. You'll get hurt if he goes there."

"Aw, fuck him!" Inez shouted, trying to divert the image-attack away from Juanita and Damali and toward herself.

"That's right," Krissy yelled. "What a slime ball. We're not impressed. Team knows all about Arizona—nobody but you pigs on the Darkside to blame, so what of it?"

"Ah . . . the youngest member of the team finds courage. This is truly a group hug moment," Nuit said, chuckling in a sinister tone. "But I wonder if her father will be able to focus on shooting me and not one of your young, male Guardians, Damali. Should I show her daddy what a naughty girl she's been? Or should I tear out your team philosopher's soul by detailing your mother-seer's secret life?"

"If her father can't focus," Marjorie said in a clear, strong voice, "trust me, you bastard, her mother will."

A slow applause filled the room as a quick flash of Krissy in J.L.'s arms hit the walls.

"You sonofabitch," Tara said evenly, standing from the couch. "Even when I was a full vampire, I didn't want your foul ass. . . . You couldn't even pull me as a Master, you were so vile. I *hid* from you."

"Tara, Tara, Tara . . ." Nuit said, clucking his tongue. "Your current mate will blow you away and then blow his own brains out, my love, if I run your vanishing point images across the wall."

Tara turned away and hugged herself, trembling with rage.

"I thought not," Nuit murmured seductively. "But to have your death on my hands would upset my newest protégé, Yonnie, and I cannot have that. So shall we call it a draw, *ma petite,* for now?"

In a split second, Damali glimpsed Krissy and Juanita quickly, noting that the blood had drained from their faces. Marlene and Tara's eyes glittered with a level of rage she'd never seen, but their stone expressions said it all. Like Damali and the rest of the team, they were trapped. Each woman's personal pain became shielded behind a steely, outward grit. Only Inez was left standing, but who knew what Nuit had up his sleeve for her and Mike . . . perhaps the baby? Damali prayed not. Every male Guardian's jaw pulsed with unspent rage, but no one wanted to draw their woman's deepest secrets to the walls.

"This is between me and you, Fallon," Damali finally yelled, exasperated. She had to make it stop, draw the fire to herself, and spare the team. But in doing that, she'd sacrifice her husband's peace of mind. Damn!

"I love it when you use my first name . . . but they baited me, so now they're hooked."

"Leave them alone!" Carlos hollered as a sordid variety of team images splashed the walls. "You got beef with me and Damali, then bring it to us."

"Then tell them to *shut* . . . the . . . fuck up and to stay out of it, Rivera," Nuit said evenly.

"We got this," Damali said, her furious gaze going around the team. She mouthed a silent thank-you to everyone who'd tried to help and then briefly shut her eyes, so angry that her ears were ringing.

The fact that Juanita was trying to right all the wrongs of their shared past by having her back against an unknown threat made Damali want to hang her head, but also need to butcher Nuit at the same time. Of them all, Juanita and Marlene probably had the most to lose. Then again, who was she to say? Humiliation was ripping out her guts as the previous images returned to haunt *la casa*. Her best girl, Inez, had jumped to her defense. Her old team pet peeve, Juanita, had shown sudden courage, an unspoken thank-you for having her back when it mattered most. Tara put her psyche in harm's way. Even Krissy and Marj had stepped up, and yet the most humbling aspect of all this for Damali was she was guilty as charged. Everything Nuit showed was the stone-cold truth, in stereo. Carlos would wig if she didn't lose it first.

"I didn't know the brother had it that bad, dayum," Carlos finally said, in an unusually calm voice, and then forced a brittle laugh to follow his statement. "That's all you guys got down there is one of

Cain's old wet dreams? Pitiful." He rolled his shoulders and pointed his blade to the floor, leaning on it. "'Bazz, man, that's all they got. Punks."

The team began to relax from Carlos's statement. Unity was key, salvaging his wife's dignity and a little of his with it was a prime directive. Nobody needed to know that what they were seeing was true.

"A wet dream, you say?" Nuit murmured, laughing. "You're either delusional, or she really played with your mind, *mon ami*. You know very well I cannot project a Neteru image unless it's true."

Increasing the intensity of the visual invasion, Nuit added sensation into the textures of sound and sight, and slowly the scent of Cain's and Damali's sweat filtered into the room.

"In your own backyard," Nuit whispered over the carnal sounds. "She gave him her throat." He jettisoned the image onto the walls with Damali's pleasure-stained expression and gasp. "In her bathroom . . . the studio," Nuit murmured on another thick exhalation. "But in Cain's lair, that is where you were truly neutered, my friend. Cuckolded. So, yes, do step outside so we can finish old business between us."

Damali almost shrieked from the horror of seeing that deeply intimate encounter played out on the casa walls before her husband and the team. She wanted to cut off her own hands as she watched them trail down Cain's back and cover his ass, pulling him to her as she arched and wrapped her legs around his waist.

Dying a thousand deaths where she stood, she was helpless to stop the image of her lying in another man's arms within a king-sized, solid-gold bed hitting high notes . . . a massive back working against her arch, sinew rippling beneath broad shoulders, her fingers clinging to them . . . unfamiliar hands touching her, caressing her, stroking her hair as her fingers tangled in his waist-length locks. Her words, "I don't care," made her turn away quickly as though she'd been slapped. The fact that Cain never entered her that day or any day and the encounter had been interrupted was moot.

"I'm going outside," Damali said, about to break the line, but Carlos caught her by the arm.

"Uh-uh, since it was just a lie," Carlos said, looking at her with solid silver eyes, and then glanced around at the stricken team.

She relaxed, understanding, but humiliation roiled within her so thickly she wanted to vomit. She watched Carlos fight the urge to battle bulk. His lip was bleeding from a nick from his own fang.

If I can hang, you can! He turned away from her and stared out the window.

"Okay, man," Carlos said in a falsely bored voice. "You done with the floor show? I'm not impressed, if that's all you got to show me. Fuck you."

The images stopped and Nuit paused. "I guess to have sloppy seconds is better than not having her at all?"

"Why don't you take that noise somewhere else? I thought you had something worth a damned battle," Carlos said between his fangs, trying to regulate his breathing.

"Well, if you can live with her being pregnant by our Chairman, then I guess we can all go home happy," Nuit said with an evil chuckle.

The gasp that was drawn by several female team members finally made Carlos bulk.

"It could have happened in the woods in your backyard, or that wonderful morning in the studio, or most assuredly in his lair . . . *mon ami,* I just didn't want you to be cuckolded into believing it happened while on your honeymoon—you know how women can lie . . . mother's baby, father's maybe, they always say. And, since you *are* a Neteru king, as a gesture of respect between royalties it is only fitting that you be duly advised." Nuit sighed with contentment. "I suppose you have been tutored by Adam to take the honorable approach. But I wonder how you will feel as you watch our leader's progeny swell your wife's belly . . . will you still attempt to make love to her while Cain's seed grows within, or abstain? Curious dilemma, *oui*? But I guess you did wait for her all those years to have your unspoiled—"

"I'm coming out there to kick your ass for talking shit about my wife, not because you got truth to your game! So when I lop off your fucking head," Carlos said, breaking the circle and walking into the foyer snorting silver-blue flames, "know that, you lowlife, ass-kissing, sonofabitch!"

He was through the door and over the wall in a blur before anyone could stop him.

"Hold the line in here!" Damali shouted, going around the outer ring of the circle, arcing a blue-white energy barrier around it.

"Don't open the door, D," Shabazz yelled. "Carlos went through it, but you can't pass through without causing a breach. We got newbies in here, and Nuit's lies don't mean shit to us, baby girl. Hold the line!"

"Don't let history repeat itself, *cheri,*" Nuit crooned. "Your father lost his life in my arms because he was arrogant and thought he could battle me alone. Your mother, like you, allowed her vanity—pride, her shame over what people might think about her husband's liaisons with me to keep her from wise counsel. So, listen to the tactical Guardian." Nuit laughed a low, cruel laugh. "Stay in the house and let that young fool battle for your very tarnished honor."

Torn and trapped by the responsibility around her, Damali released a battle cry and drove her Isis into the floor. She looked at the eyes of older team members that were filled with worry, and the stricken expressions of the newbies, and knew in her soul that one of the Neterus had to stay with them for the moment.

Carlos landed outside the castle gates and the moment he did, a black blast came at him as Nuit materialized. His shield caught it and he cut a swath through it with his sword and sent a solid silver beam into Nuit's chest, sprawling him out in the dirt. Nuit was on his feet in seconds and took a defensive stance and smiled.

"Much stronger, I see?" Nuit said with a sly smile, and then vanished as Carlos lunged, his blade chiming in the air.

"Let's do this shit to the finish!" Carlos hollered, so angry that his vision blurred.

There was no answer, just howling wind. He returned to the house breathing hard and needing very badly to kill something.

Although his first impulse was to walk straight up the center steps and close himself off into a room to calm down, Sara's voice held him in the foyer, and then he remembered the team. He had a lie to protect.

"Neteru!" Sara called out again. "Is that you, are you injured?"

Carlos walked back into the living room and the lights came back on. Tears of frustration made the lights dance, but there was no way in Hell he'd let them fall. His heart was beating so hard inside his chest that all he could do was suck in deep breaths of outrage. His blade arm was trembling with the unspent desire to take off Fallon's foul head and he cast his shield to the floor so hard it stuck into the stone vertically. Adrenaline made his ears ring and the fight burst kept him pacing for a few seconds as his system slowly normalized.

"Punk motherfucker wouldn't stand his ground and fight! He did this shit and told a buncha lies to try to get us all outside where we could be attacked, or to get one of us to open a door or a window to come for him or shoot at him." Carlos wiped silver sweat away from his brow with the back of his forearm.

"You have been injured, Neteru," Sara said quietly. "The team has, and Queen Damali. Let me heal this and take it from your mind. I can take back the illusion."

"Work on the others first, us Neterus last," Carlos said, and rammed his sword into the stone floor. "I need a drink."

What he couldn't tell the helpful nymph was that she could take it from the others, as they'd only perceived Nuit's illusion attack as a lie. But the truth could never be siphoned from a mind, especially once it was locked in Neteru silver. The moment Sara went into his or Damali's heads, she would know, and then wouldn't be able to cleanse that foul shit they'd just been shown.

"Pour me one, too," Shabazz said, and held out a glass for Rider.

Rider held up his hand. "I'm going straight, even if this ain't the night to do that." He looked at Tara. "Made a promise."

Shabazz nodded. "Anybody else want a round, while we're at it?"

Sara hesitated. "I'll be drunk by the time it's over."

Shabazz set his glass down hard with a sigh.

"Work on him first," Marlene said quietly and turned away to stare at the fireplace.

No one spoke as Sara made the rounds, and slowly but surely, bodies relaxed. Winded, she gathered her iridescent particles and sat down on the sofa with a wobbly thud.

"I could only dull the images as one quick blur of knowing, and what you'll all feel is that you had been attacked about the subject, but the details will be vague." She looked at Marjorie. "I also tried to give you strength against your sister's calls, the others in your family, too. That's why I must be so tired."

"You did a lot in the last day or so," Damali said carefully, monitoring Carlos's back as he faced a window knocking back Jack Daniel's. "His mind, as well as my brain is on fire right now . . . maybe you should rest and later you can worry about us?"

"But . . . you were the ones who needed it most," Sara protested, trying to stand.

"Hubert, make her rest," Carlos said, glancing at Damali over his shoulder. "She's been through enough. If she goes into my head, the shock might kill her."

The team gave Carlos a puzzled look, but accepted what he'd said. Damali turned away and walked to a far window with her arms wrapped around her waist.

"They're trying to come between me and you, you know that, right?" Damali lifted her chin as she stared out into the darkness.

"I know that!" Carlos shouted, and sent his rocks glass crashing into the wall behind her.

Damali didn't flinch. The team didn't move. Sara covered her mouth and then allowed her hand to fall away.

"I have a different kind of balm, one that doesn't require me going inside . . . since I'm so tired," Sara said, patting Hubert's arm so he'd let her go to the Neterus.

"I don't need balm, just some space for a minute!" Carlos hollered, and then crossed the room and yanked his blade and shield out of the floor. "I'll be in the west tower on watch. Y'all do whatever."

Sara inched toward Damali and took her by the hand. "Can you make me some sweet tea? I need energy."

Damali nodded and looked at the team. "Hold the line," she said in a hoarse voice. "We'll be back in a bit."

She moved like a robot as she tried to remember how to make tea. Her entire body was numb as she opened cabinets and stood before the stove fighting back tears. No, she would not cry. She brought the small, porcelain teacup with seven heaping teaspoons of sugar in it to the nymph with shaking hands and set it down on the counter.

"I'll put an ice cube in it so it's not so hot," Damali said. "Thanks for taking that away from the family. In fact, thank you for everything."

Sara patiently waited until Damali went to the refrigerator, pushed on a door panel, and ice dropped into a napkin. Fascinated, her wings fluttered as Damali slid the ice cube into her teacup.

"These inventions are marvelous," Sara said with a delighted squeal, and then carefully lifted the cup that looked like a bowl in front of her face and sipped the sweet tea. "Perfect. Thank you."

"Inez likes her Kool-Aid like that, her iced tea, too. Tons of sugar so it's almost syrup," Damali said in a far-off tone. "Marlene says it's not good for you. Lotta things aren't good for you, but seem like they are at the time. Don't ask me why humans go there." She turned away from the nymph. "Catches up to you in the long run, though."

"Why don't you have some, too?"

Damali shook her head. "If I put anything in my mouth right now, I'll vomit."

Sara was up out of her chair and had crawled across the center island counter to touch Damali's shoulder. "I know."

The simplistic words delivered with a tone of compassion made Damali turn and stare at Sara. Tears fell in earnest and Damali wiped them away quickly.

"I . . ." Damali sent her gaze to the mosaic tiles on the counter, the textures blurring like an out-of-focus kaleidoscope as she stared at them.

"You don't have to explain," Sara said in a quiet voice. "Cain is a very convincing and sensual creature. I thought it was a lie, but then realized once I got inside each team member and couldn't thoroughly erase it . . ."

Damali closed her eyes. "There was a lot going on at the time, Sara. I don't expect you to understand how this happened, and . . . just help Carlos deal, if you can. I'll always carry the unfortunate memory, but I never wanted him to ever see it like that."

"I came to give you the balm of self-forgiveness," Sara said, giving Damali a hug from where she knelt on the counter behind her. "It is one of the greatest mercies and I do not understand why people rarely employ it. They seem to be able to forgive everyone else's flaws and humanity, but their own . . . and the more powerful the individual, the greater the leader they are, the less likely they are to forgive themselves if they stumble and fall." She pulled back and stared at Damali. "Do you not yet understand that forgiveness is divine?"

Damali nodded and swallowed hard, covering the nymph's hands with a soft caress, but couldn't speak.

"Women are the worst at this, mothers even more so," Sara said with a sigh. "It took a very long time to work on Marlene and Marjorie just now. Guilt, after you have already asked for your transgressions to be pardoned On High and have learned to never commit them again, is a nasty toxin. Those two ladies practically had me flat on my back when I was done."

Damali bobbed her head as more tears fell, but her vocal cords were frozen. *What can I tell my husband, Sara? I so don't wanna be pregnant right now. Not under these conditions, and I really don't know how to forgive myself about any of it . . . most especially Carlos seeing all that Cain did.* Damali paused and gathered her next thoughts in with a shuddering breath. *Even if I'm not, the damage has been done to Carlos's psyche. He'd accepted that I could be, understood how it might have been possible, but the details . . . oh, God, the details, he didn't need to see—especially not in front of the whole team.*

"You cannot control what a demon entity will do," Sara said softly, sliding around to sit next to Damali on the counter with her legs dangling. "So, don't take on that guilt. Also, as I went into your mother-seer, I learned that Carlos had such misunderstood encounters, too—which you ultimately forgave."

Damali chuckled through a sniff. "Yeah, but let's be honest. Most men aren't enlightened enough to see it that way. I know where you're going, but that's a dead end, Sara." Damali glimpsed the nymph from the corner of her eye. "Plus, when I first found out, I didn't handle it all that well, either."

Sara smiled. "I know. But this conversation isn't about him or how he will react. I came to give *you* the balm of self-forgiveness." She swung her legs back and forth while looking at Damali. "He will take it badly, and for a very long time, unless he can accept a healing. But I have a secret for you that may make you smile."

Damali turned around, stared at the nymph squarely, and tried to keep from passing out. Sara leaned in closely and glanced over her shoulder like a tiny thief and then cupped her hands to whisper in Damali's ear.

"You're from the line of Powers Angels—the ultimate healers, just under archangels." Sara sat back, her wide eyes sparkling.

Damali's shoulders slumped. "Oh, yeah, that." Disappointed didn't even begin to describe the emotions that bottomed out in her stomach. She thought Sara had some real news—like she wasn't pregnant or maybe she was and it was Carlos's.

"You do not understand, do you?" Aghast, Sara sat back.

Feeling foolish, Damali shook her head. "No, I don't."

"Guilt is blocking you. Forgive *yourself* and then your body will heal the problem." Sara shook her head when Damali's eyes widened. "That is step one. 'Physician, heal thyself.' I know Hubert told me who said that—I cannot remember all his lessons, but I know this saying is true. *Then,* you can heal your partner. Nobody can do this but you, Damali."

A very slow smile came out on Damali's face, and she laughed through the tears, scooping the nymph up off the counter and hugging her until she squealed.

Carlos stood out on the tower watching storm clouds gather far off on the horizon. Even the sky was pregnant. Everything in him told him to just let Nuit's bullshit go. But try as he might, he couldn't. He'd thought he'd known Adam's pain before, until tonight. The images he'd seen in the living room would kick his ass until the end of time.

"Man . . . how did you do it?" he said quietly into the night air, wondering how to wrap his mind around any and all of it.

A sudden presence behind Carlos made him spin and turn to meet it armed. He was the last being on the planet that anything wanted to fuck with right now.

Rather than Nuit standing ready for a tower duel, Adam leaned against the stones looking very concerned. Carlos ran his senses over the king and then stood down, once sure it wasn't a vamp illusion.

"Thought you guys only showed up with an obelisk. That's a good way to get yourself smoked," Carlos said, and lowered his blade.

"This is an unauthorized visit, and I had to pull some strings. You haven't seen me tonight," Adam said, coming closer.

"Cool. Ain't seen you," Carlos said, giving Adam his back and returning to his previous position of leaning against the stones to stare out at the night sky.

"They are nervous from our previous attack," Adam said coolly. "They were testing for fissures in your fortress by sending a new female master who is still weak but has ties to your family, and then Nuit's illusion attack. If they were strong, your castle would be under siege by now. Therefore, take that as a sign that they needed to regroup."

"Good info, thanks," Carlos said flatly. "Appreciated and duly noted."

"But they did find a fissure to get in," Adam said, coming beside Carlos, leaning on the wall next to him, and joining him in staring at the sky.

"Yeah, I know. People were exhausted, missed a fireplace in the wing by the conservatory. But we got it sealed now. Thanks for watching our backs."

"That is not the fissure I speak of," Adam said with care. He waited until Carlos looked at him. "There is another one that could imperil you all."

"Talk to me," Carlos said, pushing off the wall.

"The one between you and Damali. If the heads of household are not united, all is lost."

Carlos let his breath out hard. "We're cool. The team got their brains cleansed from that foul bullshit Nuit showed us. I let it go."

"I thought you said we were brothers, and you would do for my wife, thus I should do for yours?"

"Yeah, well . . ." Carlos looked away again.

"I needed help," Adam said plainly. "I couldn't do it alone. Do you imagine that Dante never showed me his dalliance with Eve?"

Carlos looked at Adam and lifted his chin.

"He showed me everything, time and again, in excruciating detail . . . and as my wife became heavier with his child, he tortured me with it until one day I feared I might wrap my hands around her pretty throat for hurting me so."

"Damn . . ." Carlos murmured. "I never went that far with it in my head . . . didn't think it all the way through that far."

"They will come at you like this for years, brother. Every time you heal the scab over, they will slice it open. On your anniversary. Each time you try to lay with your wife. They will open the wound and make it bleed like a black aneurism in your head."

Carlos rubbed his palms down his face. "I can't live like that. Seeing it once was bad enough . . . but—"

"Then ask me!" Adam shouted. "Ask me for help so I can do for you what Ausar did for me."

The two Neterus stared at each other.

"Help me, man," Carlos finally whispered. "I don't wanna carry this."

"It will hurt," Adam said, coming to Carlos and placing his wide palms on either side of Carlos's head. "I cannot block your knowing of events that are true, only siphon away details and nuances you never needed to see . . . and from there your block must come from your spirit, so they can never implant that in your silver psyche again."

Carlos nodded and closed his eyes. "Do it . . . get it all out. It can't hurt any more than it hurts right now."

A black translucent box surrounded them, stilling the night. Particles of silvery flecks began to glow within the walls until the entire structure lit with a blinding, blue-white glare. Carlos threw his head back and wailed as agony stripped from his mind surrounding Adam's fingers with black, snakelike tentacles that he drew to him and squished between his fingers. Sobbing, Carlos held on to Adam's shoulders as the last of it came out through his eyes, his ears, his nose, and his mouth, choking him and making him gasp.

Adam dropped the box and hurried Carlos over to the edge of the tower. "Get it out. It is poison," he said, slapping Carlos on the back as he vomited bile over the ledge.

Panting, Carlos turned and leaned against the stones, sweating. Clear tears ran down his face, and he kept his eyes shut tightly, shuddering.

"The next time they attempt it, do not be so consumed with curiosity to know the details or rage at your partner that you allow them to show it to you," Adam warned. "Use the translucent box to block it from both you and her, or even your family, should they be near as a device of humiliation. Never allow this useless information back into your home." He held Carlos by the shoulders. "Knowledge is power, but without wisdom it is deadly."

Carlos nodded. "Thanks, man." Wanting to return the favor he looked at Adam. "Maybe if you bring Eve's other sons around her . . . the spirits of Abel and Seth, it might help? *Your* sons. Your blood. Understand?"

Adam hugged him in a warrior's hold. "Good advice that had not been considered. Thank you. Rest while they rest their armies. Be ready when they are ready. Go take care of your wife. And remember, you did not see me tonight."

"I never saw you tonight," Carlos said, still winded.

He only told the team as much as they needed to know: there was a small window of cease-fire, for now the house was secure, everybody needed to eat and rest. He went to find Damali who was sitting alone in the kitchen sipping tea, rubbing her back. Without words he relayed as much as he'd told the others and simply took her by the hand and guided her up the back staircase to the second floor, and into their room. Space. A moment of sanctuary was all he could offer her.

Her expression was confused as she watched him cross the room and go into the bathroom to brush his teeth and splash water on his face. He climbed onto the bed and lay on his side.

"Go wash your face," Carlos said gently and closed his eyes, patting the place on the bed that would allow him to spoon her body when she returned. "Then lie down so we can get some sleep."

She stood in the middle of the floor for a moment, not sure. There was nothing she wanted to do more right now than to find that spot that was theirs alone . . . that warm, comforting, protective, fetal-position spoon with him behind her and his arms around her waist, making the world go away. New tears rose as she thought about how she'd believed that place was gone forever. One brutal image and that haven was blown away. It was such a fragile little ecosystem within their private universe, a slice of Heaven on Earth that had been ruined by demons, illusions, and lusts.

When Carlos had left to go up into the tower alone, he was a different man. The change was unnerving, but she chalked it up to emotional fatigue. Her face felt tight and crusted by tears, she needed to pee, and her back was killing her. Maybe after they'd both gotten an hour or two of real rest she'd be able to talk to him. But Carlos's expression was so peaceful that it was almost frightening.

Damali hurried into the bathroom and splashed her face with fresh water. The sound of the running tap increased the urge to pee to the point where she was practically dancing as she stripped down her jeans. But as she sat down on the toilet she stared into her underwear with dashed hope and then closed her eyes. Her period still hadn't come on.

She finished quickly and washed her hands, wishing she could go back in time. Almost afraid to face Carlos, she slipped out of the bathroom and hesitated. It wasn't that she feared he'd try to harm her; she just didn't want to see that look on his face.

Carlos opened his eyes and gazed at her as she stood just outside the bathroom door. He flattened his hand against the comforter. "You gonna lay down?"

Damali allowed her eyes to drink him in, fusing the memory of him inside her mind. The ivory sheets, the large, comfortable bed, and his peaceful smile . . . that's what she ultimately wanted to remember when he left her for good. No matter what he'd told her before, after Nuit's invasion and what he saw, she knew it was only a matter of time before her husband walked.

Suddenly she felt soiled, and the light-hued sheets too clean for her to lie against next to him. Damali hugged herself and tried to steady her voice.

"I'm all dirty from fighting and whatnot, and need to get cleaned up before I lay down," she whispered.

"I'm all dirty and funky, too," Carlos said, pushing up on one elbow. "Com'ere."

She shook her head. "I'd rather not."

"Please," he said quietly. "I wanna talk to you."

His eyes held an expression that she couldn't turn away from. It said, *baby, it's gonna be all right.* She wanted to believe that in the worst way and her legs moved slowly, bringing her forward until she reached the bed. She slipped up onto the high mattress and turned away from him, glad that he pulled her into their old spoon.

His arm went around her waist and his nose nuzzled her hair. "I love you," he whispered. "No matter what. You'll never be too dirty for me to hold you like this."

She couldn't breathe; his words were tearing her up inside. "I never meant to bring any of this to you . . ."

"I miss us, D," he said into her hair on a thick swallow. "I miss feeling your heartbeat through your back against my chest. Miss babying you in the tub. Miss laughing together. Miss arguing about dumb shit. Miss just . . . everything. Don't let him take all of that away, too."

She covered Carlos's arm as it rested against her stomach and closed her eyes. A big tear rolled down the bridge of her nose as she stroked his hand and felt it slowly capture hers within it. His warm breaths were ragged from not wanting to cry. If ever there was a time to apply the balm Kamal had shown her years ago, it was now . . . she needed to restart a dying man's heart, problem was, hers had nearly stopped beating the moment Nuit had violated their minds.

"You wanna take a bath and get this soot off of us?" she asked quietly.

Carlos just nodded.

She turned and kissed him and he pulled away. Hurt sliced through her like a razor. But he smiled and touched her lips with his thumb.

"I was so upset that I threw up in the tower. I ain't gonna lie. Didn't want you to taste that. Lemme brush my teeth."

While his admission was honest, and designed to let her know that he'd pulled away for her benefit, it broke her down inside to know that what he'd seen had made him vomit. Quiet trauma was making her shiver as Carlos swung his legs over the side of the bed and came around to grasp her hand.

"Let's take a bath and wash this foul shit out of our systems." He issued her a sad smile and gently pulled her to her feet. "You start the water, I'll brush my teeth, and we'll start brand-new. Okay?"

"I have some white bath salts from Marlene . . ."

"Dump the whole bag in there," he said. "We both need it."

She nodded and followed him into the bathroom, and began preparing the water. It seemed so indulgent to take this time away from the team, but if he was sure there'd be no more incursions for a while, it also seemed like a necessary thing to heal their minds.

"It is," Carlos said, not turning around as he brushed frothing lather in his mouth. He spit and spoke with his back to her. "As the team leaders, if we're all messed up, the whole house is messed up. This bath isn't a luxury, it's a necessity. Think of it that way, D. This is a purge."

"All right," she whispered, watching the water turn milky white from the sacred substances she'd added, and she breathed in the fragrant steam that had begun to fill the bathroom.

Slowly calm filled her as the water rose and she said nothing as she watched Carlos walk out of the room and return with three small white votive candles. He set them on the edge of the tub and lit them with care, and then took his time crossing the room to set down the book of matches on the sink. His process of handling all of this was blowing her mind. He stood by the door and took off his boots, and then carefully set them over the threshold as if to say, that was then, and this is now, everything before stays outside this room. He then calmly stripped and folded his dirty clothes over and set them outside the bathroom on top of his Timberlands.

"Come on," he said, turning off the light. "Get undressed and leave it all outside the door. We've got healing to do."

Feeling somewhat modest, she edged past him and followed his same ritual of undressing. He didn't look over her body as he normally did once she was nude, but kept his eyes on hers and took her hand. When she tried to look away from him, he shook his head no.

"Uh-uh. You don't have anything to be ashamed of in front of me. I'm your husband."

She nodded and fought new tears and tried to blink them away as they walked to the tub. Again, he shook his head.

"Let it out. Forget pride. We're gonna have years in front of us that we'll both be laughing and both be crying about. Nothing hidden between us, okay?"

He helped her into the tub with tears streaming down her face and sat so that they could look at each other while her legs gently draped over his, submerged. He took up the natural sponge that sat on the tub's edge and lathered it with the vanilla-scented white bar that had been newly delivered when the supplies came in. He said nothing more as he swirled soap against her throat and shoulders, and gently soaped down her arms then over her breasts.

Giving her his hand, he motioned for her to stand before him without a word, and leaned up to kiss her belly, then washed down her abdomen, over the swell of her hips, tenderly lathering her mound, and then caressed each thigh as he worked down her legs. He placed her hand on his shoulder and lifted her leg to wash her foot, kissing the instep of it as he placed it back in the water to do the other one.

"Turn around," he said quietly, and then began to work his way up the backs of her calves when she did.

He lathered the back of her thighs, and over her buttocks, and then stopped to press a slow kiss into the Sankofa tattoo at the small of her back. The sensation drew a quiet gasp and she felt him shift to kneel so that he could reach higher on her spine. When his hands gently clasped her hips, she slid down to kneel in front of him, but his hands only continued to lather her back and shoulders and neck.

"Sit all the way down so I can rinse you off," he whispered against her ear, making her shudder just from the low, sensual timber of his voice.

For a moment, she couldn't move. The warm seal of him against her backside, and feeling that his body had responded to her, had begun to heat a slow ember between her legs that she thought had gone out. But this was his healing and she complied, sliding down his thighs, feeling the thick sinew in them behind her arms.

It was so quiet, so peaceful, with only their breathing and the slight tinkle of the water being disturbed echoing around them that it was jarring when he turned on the tap. His hands cradled the sides of her head and his kiss landed at her crown. She closed her eyes as he cupped warm, fresh water into her hair and then gently began to massage the mild, fragrant soap into her scalp like a soft caress. As he took up each individual lock and rolled it between his palms gently, she almost moaned from the current of desire he sent into her hair until it arced with blue-white static . . . then he washed it all away with fresh water from the thundering tap.

"Keep your eyes closed," he murmured against her neck, kissing it gently. "I need to wash your face, and don't want you to get soap in your eyes."

Ever so carefully he lathered his hands a bit and just used the pads of his thumbs to make gentle circles over her forehead, sliding down her nose, avoiding her eyes, rounding her cheeks, then gliding his touch under her chin, to caress down her throat. Leaning forward with her snugly between his legs, he reached for the tap again, rinsed his hands off, and gently pulled her to lay her head back against his shoulder while he drizzled clean water over her face until the soap was gone.

"Keep your eyes closed," he told her again, and turned her to face him. Then he kissed the water away from her eyes and took her mouth in a slow, soft kiss. When he pulled back his breathing was labored. "Now it won't sting. You can slowly open your eyes and tell me what you see."

She followed his instructions to the letter and opened her eyes with care. Through damp lashes she saw solid silver staring back at her. He traced her eyebrows, his eyes searching hers, as he brought his hands up to her cheeks, and then let his palms slide down her neck to her shoulders to her arms. He placed one palm over her heart, the other over his as tears shimmered against the silver of his irises.

"I see so much love, Carlos," she murmured.

He nodded and let the tears fall.

"I see acceptance of whatever I am."

Again, he nodded. "Completely. You're my angel."

"I see my husband, who I can't live without," she whispered, allowing her tears to fall without shame.

"I see my wife who I would die for," he said as a silvery torrent wet his face.

"I see a man who I respect and never wanted to dishonor."

"I don't know what you're talking about," he whispered. "That never happened."

He took her mouth under the blue-white mountain moon, keeping one hand pressed against her heart, the other against his. "Can't you feel it?" he murmured as their mouths parted from the gentle kiss. "The silver thread that links us forever?"

The current that ran through her from his hand was like a mild electric charge, lighting pulse points and igniting an inner fire that she was almost ashamed to now claim.

"I feel it," she said softly.

He leaned over and blew out the candles and stared at her in the darkness, his eyes and the moon the only light in the bathroom. "Me, too."

She touched the Neteru symbol on his neck that had begun to glow and followed it with her finger until he closed his eyes and gasped. But he kept his hands firmly pressed against her breastbone and his as she soaped her hands and trailed over his throat and shoulders and then soaped his arms and lathered the exposed portions of his chest.

Gently guiding him, she helped him to his knees without breaking their heart lock as he held the line between them. His abdomen clenched as her hands gently slid over it and then traced his hips, and as she moved lower she could actually see a thin silver beam of light forming between the back of his hand on his chest to the back of the one on hers.

As her slippery hands caressed his hard length, his hands slowly covered her breasts, but the silvery line linking their heart chakras was still there. No matter how she moved to soap his thighs, the line lengthened and contracted to meet her motions, never breaking even as she rinsed him or turned him to do his back.

When he finally turned to face her again, he was breathing hard and so was she. But again, this was his healing, and she wanted to be sure to follow his lead this time.

"The water's getting cold," he said quietly, stroking her hair and squeezing out the excess moisture from her locks. "You ready to dry off and go to bed?"

She nodded yes but could barely speak. The entire surface of the tub had a blue-white charge flickering across it that vibrated with a soft hum. He stood, and it was all she could do not to turn her face into him and kiss him just there. She actually had to close her eyes and take a deep breath not to.

"I don't wanna break the connection," she said, turning her face up to his while still kneeling.

He smiled in the dark. "It won't break. Trust me."

She took his hand and stood. He pulled her close and kissed her hard and then lifted her out of the tub.

"I need to dry you off," he said thickly, standing in a growing puddle of water that their bodies created.

"The charge is better while we're wet," she murmured, kissing his tattoo. "Your aura colors are back."

"So are yours," he said, bending to take one of her nipples into his mouth, producing her soft moan. "It's spilling all over my hands."

Her quiet gasp sent a soft echo against the tiles, and before she knew it, they were in the room, damp on the bed, his mouth on hers. His chest was pressed against her as their tongues danced, and she could soon feel every pulse point of his linked to every one of hers connected by a silvery energy line. Joined as one, his heartbeat synced to hers, his breaths were the same as though coming from one pair of lungs.

They both broke the kiss at the same time, shared the same gasp of awareness and pleasure as they pulled back enough to witness every chakra point erogenous zone united by a thin thread of hue that ran the spectrum. His shudder entered her through each lit point and caused her to shiver with pleasure so violently that it produced a unified moan.

This time when he found her mouth the kiss was ragged, his hands trembling in her hair. His body slid into hers, sending new heat inside her that imploded on impact in her womb before he even moved. This time the tears had nothing to do with pain or humiliation, but profound pleasure. She gasped his name and shut her eyes tightly, nearly insane from the sensory overload. His body moved as though manifesting redemption itself, and she clung to his shoulders for swift salvation.

"Carlos, I love you," she said, choking out the words.

"Baby, I love you," he whispered between each thrust that became more ragged and harder as he fought to breathe.

She was beyond speech and could only wrap her legs around his waist and send her personal truth into his spine with her hands, each stroke down his back a consonant and a vowel, every caress a statement of what he meant to her. Soon she could feel steel packing his jaw when he tore away from the kiss, and sensed his inner battle not to deliver a bite as a thick current of white light lit his spine.

"It's all right," she managed through another gasp, holding him tighter as her wings slid from her shoulder blades and wrapped around him. The instant seizure he'd produced in her was blinding. All she saw was white light.

"Not this time, angel," he said, throwing his head back and then came so hard the silver momentarily left his eyes.

They lay together panting, silver sweat running down his back, staining her wings with it as they both tried to recover. Slowly but surely she was able to catch her breath and retract her wings. By degrees he caught his breath and retracted his fangs and then rolled over to pull her into their spoon.

There was nothing else for them to say. The purge had been completed. For the first time in what seemed like ages, she slept in his arms without fear like a baby.

CHAPTER FIFTEEN

Damali slowly opened her eyes, startled to see dawn cresting on the horizon. It seemed like it had been an eternity since she'd slept through the night, and it was even harder to fathom that she'd done so under the conditions they were faced with now. But Carlos's steady breathing at her back and the warmth of his arm slung over her waist with his body snugly pressed against hers let her know she wasn't dreaming.

Sensing for any trouble in the house and finding no cause for alarm, she slipped from beneath Carlos's loose hold and went into the bathroom to take a shower. That simple luxury added to the inner renewal her entire being required. The warm water washed any lingering foul illusions from her mind, just as the fragrant suds filled her with peace. She took her time with herself, tending the unseen wounds as much as any remaining outer scars. This morning was about healing through the gentle application of body cream and deodorant and balm, and brushing away any remnants of the bitter taste of fury and humiliation out of her mouth. Then she stopped and looked down. Mercy of mercies, her period had come on! Now this morning was also about being grateful that she needed the supplies Marlene had stocked in her bathroom just in case. Making quick work of it, she tore open a box, utilized the supplies, and cleaned up, washing her hands with joy.

Damali wrapped a towel around her and found another for her

hair. She entered the bedroom quietly and watched Carlos roll over in a lazy sprawl and smile at her with his eyes closed.

"Morning," he murmured and then breathed her in. "You took a shower already."

"Yeah, I did," she said, coming to sit on the edge of the bed beside him.

She bent and kissed him. He unwound the towel from her wet hair and looked up.

"You shoulda woke me and I woulda got in there with you," he said with a sly smile.

She traced his eyebrows, wondering where to begin. Part of her was unsure if raising the subject again would be like raising the dead, or if he'd be disappointed that she hadn't conceived for him. He was in such a cool place in his head right now and after last night she wasn't sure how to tell him. She'd just found that spot beside him and curled into a little ball before glancing over her shoulder at him.

But she watched his smile begin to fade as she took too long to contemplate their universe.

"I forgot," he said quietly, and let his hand slip away from her damp hair. "You wouldn't want to mess around again . . . I mean, carrying and all, it probably wouldn't be cool."

He sat up and she stopped him from moving off the bed with a gentle touch. His eyes held silent hurt, but not the blistering agony they had earlier the night before.

"It's not that," she said, taking up his hand and kissing his knuckles. "I came on after last night."

He wasn't sure how to react. If he praise-danced he'd be wrong, and would never live it down. Then, again, part of him was thoroughly disappointed and he wasn't sure exactly why, but he was. At this point, he hadn't trusted his senses, and hadn't wanted to hazard a guess to ask her or offend in any way. Not sure how he felt about the news she'd delivered, he deflected introspection and simply asked about her.

"How're you feeling?" he asked carefully, gazing at her to be sure.

"Crampy, achy, liable to go off about anything," she said with a sly smile.

"You know that's not what I meant," he said with a half-smile. "How's your head?"

She hesitated, not sure how to answer the question in politically correct terms not to offend him. If she jumped up and down and did a jig in the middle of the floor, she'd be wrong and never live it down. And there was still that little part of her that had hoped she was and it was his.

"Conflicted," she said after a long pause. She'd let the statement out on a heavy sigh.

Carlos nodded. "Good word. Was searching for that one myself."

"Yeah?" She touched his cheek and let the pad of her thumb rub against his unshaven jaw.

"Yeah," he said quietly. "Crazy, but I wished it was me."

Damali nodded and a tender smile tugged at her face. "Me, too. That's the only thing that kept me from doing cartwheels across the room."

He laughed and let out a huge breath. "Oh, shit . . . girl . . ."

"Right," she said, laughing as she flopped back on the bed. "Thank you, God, thank you, thank you, thank you!"

He flopped back next to her with a thud. "Damali . . ."

"You don't have to say it."

"Baby . . ."

"I know," she said, laughing and wiping her eyes.

"We dodged a silver bullet this time."

"Yep—go take a shower before I jump your bones anyway."

"You serious?" He rolled over and stared at her with a wide grin, leaning up on an elbow. "A little blood ain't never bothered a brother, ya know?"

"Get away from me, man," she said, smiling and then she burst out laughing. "I'm not trying to tempt fate."

He jumped up off the bed. "Not even, since you put it that way."

She was hungry enough to eat a horse and hummed around the kitchen fixing a huge omelet, scavenging for juice, and acted like she'd hit the lotto when she found some bread and raspberry jam that hadn't been opened yet. Marlene in the doorway just made her hum with more melody.

"Good morning," Damali said in a singsong voice. "You want some tea or something?"

"You okay, baby?" Marlene said, coming deeper into the kitchen. "After last night, I was just checking on you . . . will take some stuff upstairs and eat in the room, but, uh . . ."

"I'm great, Mar," Damali said, pushing the bread into the toaster. She did a little jig and came over to Marlene to kiss her. "Good morning, good morning, good morning."

"Baby, sit down," Marlene said, her eyes worried. "Sometimes things can happen that take a mind to the edge of—"

"I'm not having a nervous breakdown," Damali said, laughing. "Oh, shit, maybe I am."

"What happened?" Marlene whispered, coming very close to Damali and then hugging her slowly.

"My cycle came on," Damali whispered in Marlene's ear.

Marlene's body slumped against hers. "Praise the Lord," Marlene murmured and then yanked Damali back to look in her eyes. "Yes!" Marlene ran around the kitchen like she'd lost her mind, quickly grabbing down two mugs for her and Shabazz and flinging fruit onto a counter from the large bowl as she skipped to the paper-towel rack and snatched one. "Hope springs eternal in the city of eternal spring," she said, making up a little ditty as she gathered up some grub for her and Shabazz. "I'm out. Ain't my business. Y'all have breakfast alone. Bye."

There was nothing like laughter and hope to heal a wound, and Damali couldn't stop smiling as she watched Marlene scamper away so fast she'd forgotten her tea. Within seconds she felt the word get telegraphed to the other females in the house. It wasn't telepathy, but a vibe that permeated the air like excited current. The family was almost whole again, save the loss of Gabby, but maybe even that had potential.

Damali loaded up a small tray of grub with two omelets loaded with everything in them she could find, ketchup, fried potatoes, toast and jam, a whole pineapple and juice, and hurried up the back stairs before one of the brothers came into the kitchen and tried to pilfer her food loot. This was a private celebration.

She banged on the door with her foot and busted into the room like she'd robbed a bank when Carlos opened the door. He was standing there in a towel, dripping wet, and he laughed as he watched her tiptoe over to the table by the window.

"Hurry up and close the door before the noses in the house come sniffing for ready-made grub," she said, giggling.

He shut the door and watched her unload the stash of food and pull silverware out of her back jeans pockets. Her smile was radiant, her giggle infectious, and he found himself laughing for absolutely no reason just watching her set the table in a rush.

"Ta da!" she said, waving her hand over the spread.

"Definitely the best magic I've seen," he said, hurriedly drying himself off and yanking on a pair of drawers and some jeans.

He crossed the room pulling on a T-shirt and sat down in front of her and blessed their private meal. It was a very simple blessing. "Thank you, thank you, *thank you,* Jesus! Amen."

He'd eaten so quickly and so much that he had to unfasten the top button of his jeans just to breathe. The whole house had come alive in the short time that he'd scoffed down his plate, and the noise was comforting—just hearing life happening all around them. And yet all he could think about was time, how ephemeral a thing that was. A few hours ago, life as he knew it was hopeless. A bleak future was before him and tough realities behind him; he'd been trapped between that old familiar rock and a hard place, but this morning, like late last night, he was free.

As he watched the sunlight dance in Damali's still damp hair, catching glistening water drops to shimmer iridescent colors, just like her ring caught every hue of the spectrum, he knew Rider had to be thinking the same thing himself—he was a blessed man. And, yet, what if they'd given up hope? Rider could have put a nine to his skull and missed the future; just as he could have done something so irreversibly damaging that he would have missed this glorious morning with his wife. The same held true for each member of the team. There were times when any of them could have thrown in the towel on their personal brand of hell and not lived through it to get to the other side.

Then he suddenly realized something that had escaped him. Endurance. The team had physical stamina like crazy, and had honed their special powers to withstand the heaviest barrages from the darkside . . . but the emotional core, the things that eroded the spirit, were being heaped on them in record time to possibly get them ready for whatever was coming next. They'd all just built serious muscle in a matter of days—days that felt like years, years that had truncated into seconds, seconds that seemed like forever.

"That's deep," Carlos said, thinking aloud and staring beyond Damali out the window.

"What's deep?" she said, biting off a piece of overly jellied toast.

"Life."

"Okay, Confucius. Elaborate." She shook her head and sipped her juice, chewing.

"Whenever we asked for backup, we got it, right?" he said, the epiphany making him stand. "But, D," he added, now growing excited, "how many times did we actually do that? I mean, ask for help, call in for reinforcements?"

"Whenever it got real crazy, I can recall shouting at the top of my lungs for—"

"That's it! We never asked in advance, always at the eleventh-hour, fifty-ninth minute." He laughed at the simplicity of it and began walking in a circle. "Pride goeth before a fall, girl."

"What?" Damali cocked her head to the side, chewing more slowly.

"You know me, D. I don't ask *nobody* for help, right—unless my ass is in a sling, beat down to the wire."

"Now that's a true confession, if ever I heard one," she said, chuckling, cutting off a hunk of pineapple and plopping it into her mouth.

"But what if we put out an all-points bulletin, an SOS in advance of catastrophe?"

"Now you're talking novel concept, brother," she said, shaking her head.

"I'm serious." He stopped walking and leaned on the table and stared at her without smiling.

"You are serious, aren't you?" She stopped smiling. "Like, we're the Neteru team and—"

"Pride," he said flatly.

She sat back in her chair and gawked at him. "Whoa . . ."

"Yeah, whoa, D." He dragged his fingers through his wet hair. "I'ma say it now. I need help. We need help. I want help. Reinforcements, backup, healers, whatever Heaven can spare to throw our way. I don't wanna lose anybody, or have us go out because we didn't ask for help in advance."

"I need help, we need help," she stated, following his words in seriousness, as though he'd launched a prayer. "I don't wanna lose anybody on our watch."

"Stand up, hold my hands, and concentrate with me in a white light sent to any and all able-bodied warriors in range, then."

Damali stood quickly and wiped her hands on the back of her jeans as she rounded the table and took Carlos's hands. "Wow, baby . . . I never thought you'd be down for something like this."

A lazy, relaxed sense of ease filled the casa, reminiscent of the old days in Arizona. Well-rested and well-fed soldiers hung out on the steps and gardens. A few were conspicuously absent, but no one worried. Music blared from a boom box Dan had scored. Card games and dominoes created raucous trash-talking and bursts of laughter. But the blooms were still dying and no new blades of grass replaced what was beginning to turn brown.

Distant diesel engines made Mike look up from his poker spread and then stand. Carlos and Damali shared a glance.

"Everything cool?" Jose said, putting down his fan of cards slowly.

"Heavy metal moving," Mike said and then went to the front gate. "Yo, up in the towers. Hubert, what's in your sight line?"

"Big things with a lot of beings!" Hubert shouted down. "Like the thing Damali saved us in."

"Jeeps," Jose said, standing and concealing his weapon. "Could be *Federales* or something worse."

"Everybody be cool," Carlos said. "Let me and D put an eye on the situation."

"If it's Mexican authorities, we have to chill," Damali said. "Dan, you got our paperwork tight?"

"Yeah, I'm on it," Dan said, running into the house to get the crucial documents.

"Aw'ight, Mike and senior staff outside," Carlos said. "Everybody else in the house and take a position in case it's a hybrid ambush or demon squad using human helpers. Hubert, you guys lay low until the coast is clear—no sense in setting off a panic, if it's just local authorities. And *nobody* fire unless they shoot first."

Time had again changed the scenario in the blink of an eye. Carlos and Damali stood with Mike, watching a huge convoy roll into the front driveway and other vehicles pull up to block the road. Dan stood in the doorway clutching a portfolio. In the distance motorcycle engines roared. Everyone in *la casa* held their breaths and kept low, waiting.

A tall, built man in his late thirties wearing fatigues jumped down from a Humvee that was loaded with soldiers. He stood six-four and his dark brown hair was barbered into a military cut. He stared at Damali and Carlos from behind mirrored aviator sunglasses.

"Which ones are the Neterus?" he said, glancing among Damali, Carlos, and Mike.

"Who's asking?" Carlos said, scanning the man before him and trying to guestimate the numbers he had with him.

"Hidalgo Cortes, Mexico City Guardian Squad, North American region eleven."

"Oh, shit!" Carlos said and burst out laughing. "*Que pasa,* man!"

"Yo," Hidalgo said, and gave Carlos a warrior hug. "Heard you all were pinned down, had a Neteru team surrounded up here, and we put out a regional all-points."

Damali opened and closed her mouth.

"That you, man?" Hidalgo said, smiling at Damali.

Carlos shook his head. "She was the Neteru first, and is *my wife,* brother."

"Cool. I hear you." Hidalgo extended his hand and shook Damali's. "Nice to meet you. Not every day we get called in like this, sister." He then turned to the assorted trucks, Jeeps, and armored vehicles. "Fall out! Team leaders—approach. ID yourselves by region."

"This is freaking crazy," Carlos said, laughing as Guardians from the casa began to gather at the door and lower arms.

Nearly too stunned to respond to Carlos, Damali watched as buff men and women of every hue piled out of vehicles and stood in the yard before them.

"Esmeralda Cienfuegos—Belize," said a tall, curvy woman with a body toned enough to bounce a quarter off her stomach. She pushed her short, brunette, blunt-cut hair behind her ear and smiled widely as she looked Carlos up and down. "You the new Neteru for the region? Dayum, brother, it'll be a pleasure to serve."

Carlos tucked away a too-wide grin. "Let me introduce you to the other Neteru on the squad, my wife, Damali."

The other Neteru, huh? Damali said in her mind, but had to smile.

"Cool," Esmeralda said. "Your team looks good," she added, motioning toward the front steps with her chin. "Seers, healers, tacticals, a pair of noses, coupla stone workers. Good." She turned to her Jeeps. "Dis . . . *mount!*"

Even Damali stared as she watched the most gorgeous human women with cut sinewlike steel jump down out of the vehicles with duffle bags over their shoulders.

"What's your specialty?" Damali had to ask after the thirty-something-year-old Guardian had assessed her team so quickly.

"After kicking demon ass, I'm on sight."

"Excellent," Damali said, nodding with respect and giving Esmeralda a warrior embrace. "Welcome to the fort."

The next series of introductions happened so fast it made her head spin. Carlos couldn't wipe the smile off his face. He kept sending her intermittent messages each time a new Guardian team leader approached.

Now this is what I call a SQUAD, baby—didn't I tell you to ask, huh? Didn't I?

She tried not to laugh, but the process and the response from a simple shout out was making her dizzy.

"Joe Diaz—Guatemala," a thick, hulking brother said with a chest so stone-cut it looked like if he sneezed his fatigue T-shirt might rip. "Tactical."

"Alana Guadalupe—Honduras," a short, squat woman who looked like she could take Mike announced. "Stone worker."

"Jurado Cordoba—Nicaragua. Audio."

"Call me Salle," a huge, ebony-skinned warrior said. "El Salvador. Tracker."

"Frank Pereira—Costa Rica. Healer, sharpshooter."

"Luis Tunja—Panama. Stone worker."

"Alonzo Salvatore—Cuba. Lover and seer, extraordinaire." He bowed and kissed Damali's hand and then gave Carlos an apologetic shrug. "What can I say, man? She's beautiful."

Carlos laughed. "It's cool, man."

"You need to come down to de islands, mon—after dis," a tall, lanky Rasta said, his rust-colored locks swinging behind him as he approached. "Rockfish, my friends call me dat. Jamaica. I blow shit up and can feel 'em coming from two miles off—tactical specialist."

"We got Jacques Beauxchamp, explosives, seer, coming down from western Canada, British Columbia, as soon as his flight gets in this afternoon," Hidalgo said. "The boys in Bogotá and Venezuela said they'd have our backs, and pull in Bolivia if necessary, and we've got a team flying in from the East Coast U.S., Philadelphia—the Rowdee Black Giants. They're bringing teams from Puerto Rico, Haiti, and the Dominican Republic with them. That covers the threat zone, North and Central America. Heard you all got hammered with hurricanes in the Gulf, which is why the Caribbean teams insisted on being here, too, and the top sections of South America are on standby."

The group parted as motorcycles pulled into the yard, their engines snorting in low-speed rumbles.

A tall, crazy-looking blond guy with hair over his shoulders jumped off an all-chrome custom Harley that had a machine-gun mount and strode forward. He stood at least six foot eight, and had the build of a WWF wrestler. "Duke Johnson, Texas. Specialty is kickin' demon ass and I can shoot the eyes out of a bat from a half-mile in the blind. A little birdie told this ole tracker that something foul was afoot, so figured we'd just come on down and add to the party. Mexico ain't nothing but a thunder run from where we call home."

"Duke Johnson?" Rider shouted, coming down the steps with a pump shotgun. "Duke Johnson! How the hell are ya, man!"

Duke picked Rider up by the waist and swung him around. "Jack-fucking-Rider? The legend lives! Brought you some Jack Daniel's, man!"

Both men laughed as he slowly set Rider down on his feet, walked right past Damali and Carlos, and dropped to his knees in front of the team from Belize. "Oh, Lord in heaven, I know you done heard my prayers!"

"Get up, you old horny toad before they shoot you," Rider said, laughing. "Don't mind him, he don't get out much."

Duke stood with effort, took a bow, and winked at the ladies. "Does it show that much?" he said with a chuckle, following Rider back to the group of squad leaders.

"I'd offer you a bandana to wipe the slobber off your face, but it's in the house," Rider said with a sheepish grin.

"Yeah, well, what can I say? Once a Hell's Angel, always a Hell's Angel . . . let me introduce the boys. Got an alliance. Old pagans and Warlocks riding with us . . . we all came together and got religion, reformed." Duke glimpsed the Guardian team standing on the front steps. "Nice lineup in the house, too. Damn, man, you must be living righteous."

"Okay, people," Carlos said, getting everyone's attention. "We've got like five to six hours until sunset, when we expect Hell to bring the noise. We need to give you the lowdown on what we've seen so far, what we're up against, and get you hunkered down, fed, and your ammo ready to rock."

"I wanna know how many medics we've got in this group," Damali said, walking down the line. Ten hands rose. "With a human head count of what appears to be over three hundred that means you'll be working overtime under heavy fire. I want trenches dug around the perimeter with stakes raised. Everything doused with silver in prep for were-demons. We need a battle formation to flank all sides of the fort." She looked at J.L. and Krissy. "Give these teams maps and show them the fallback position in Taxco—silver ground, if it gets crazy. Any seriously wounded go to hallowed ground at the convent of San Bernardino de Sena, and we can hold up troops in the cathedral next door to that."

"We brought supplies and cases of food, and I know the area like the back of my hand," Hidalgo said. "We can break the teams into specialty formations—seers on radar, tacticals on low-flying incoming and ground assaults, put trackers on recognizance, audios and sharpshooters in the towers."

"Good plan," Carlos said, pounding Hidalgo's fist.

"Oh, yeah, one thing, though," Damali said. "We've got a coupla hybrids with us that under no circumstances should be shot."

"Oh, shit . . . I almost forgot," Carlos said, raking his hair. "Okay, everybody be cool. I'ma call out some special team members who were working both sides for us, and there's a vamp named Yonnie. I'll give you his image in a minute, but Hubert, Sedgewick, and Sara are family. We all clear?"

Murmurs and grumbles of agreement filtered throughout the courtyard as Carlos called Hubert and his crew to the front of the house. The moment Hubert and Sedgewick crossed the threshold, three hundred and fifty guns and several bazookas took aim in a flurry of clicks.

"Okay, everybody chill," Damali said, holding out her arms and standing in front of Hubert. "They saved our teams' asses back in La Paz, and their best friend," she added, coaxing Sara out from behind Hubert's legs, "is part angel."

Duke stooped down and smiled, removing his sunglasses. "Aw . . . now ain't she just the purtiest little thang? Honey, we just a little jumpy about your friends, but we'd never mistake you."

Sara hugged Hubert's leg tighter and hid her face. "They're so big and so scary-looking, Damali. And have so many guns. Can you ask them to back away a little?"

"Aw'ight, you heard the lady. Put away your weapons, you're scaring her," Carlos said with a smile. "She's the top medic on our team, next to Damali, Marlene, and Berkfield," he said, going to Berkfield and raising his arm above his head. "I'll tell you about what flows in his veins when we all camp down and get situated for a strategy session later."

But the rumble from a minivan made everyone stop and turn. Kamal jumped out of the vehicle with Drum and ten of his men.

"I heard the SOS . . . I know this is a North American assault, but we was in the area," Kamal said, looking at Marlene and then at Damali and Carlos. "This is heavy were-jag territory, with all the Aztec and Olmec ruins. Would take a bullet for this team, so figured you could use some men that know the species well."

Kamal looked at Shabazz. The courtyard was so quiet that not even a bird moved in the trees.

"Like old times," Shabazz said with a nod. "Glad to have you, under these circumstances."

"Appreciated," Kamal said and then looked at Carlos and Damali again. "Before anybody gets an itching trigger finger, maybe me and my boys better show them what we mean by specialists?"

Damali sighed and stood in front of Kamal. "He's a seer and a tactical, and knows were-demons like the back of his hand. His team is the best and helped us in Brazil—Amazon country."

"That detail was no joke," Carlos said and then looked at Kamal. "Show 'em the canines, man."

Kamal sighed and then presented upper and lower canines as another round of clicks filled the air and left him staring down the barrels of several guns.

"Might as well show 'em the full shape-shift while you're at it," Damali said on a heavy exhale. "This way the tacticals and seers in the group can know your signature, the trackers, too. I don't want *any* accidents—friendly fire claiming our own."

Kamal complied and his form elongated into a huge jaguar. He brushed against Damali's legs with a low purr and then glanced back at the house at Marlene.

"Don't even think about it," Shabazz said, leveling his weapon at Kamal.

Kamal shifted back and studied his nails. "I'm cool. Just wanted to say hello."

"Oh, man!" Duke said, slapping his forehead. "Anything else we should know about this team before gettin' cozy with y'all?"

Rider chuckled. "Rivera, man, wanna show the man the fangs?"

"What!" Hidalgo said, backing up and shaking his head. "A Neteru? This is bullshit."

"My husband has a long and very interesting history," Damali said with a smile as Carlos lifted his chin, offended. "We met under . . . curious circumstances, but that's my baby. He's all Light now, and the best vamp tracker in the world, I might add. Baby," she crooned, "show 'em the silver, first, then drop fang."

She didn't have to ask. The group's reaction to his lineage was enough to start his eyes flickering. But as he felt the silver heat his irises and overtake them, he bulked, dropped fang, and drew the blade of Ausar into his grip, in case there was still a question, so there'd be no panic issues out on the battlefield.

"Satisfied?" Carlos said, still bristled.

"That is *too* freaky," Esmeralda said, coming closer with her team from Belize. "Man . . . that is some *sexy* shit."

"Ain't it just?" Damali said with pride, going over to Carlos to kiss the underside of his chin.

"I just don't understand women," Duke muttered, scratching his head.

"Me, neither," Hidalgo admitted quickly, still shaken. "I'm glad I saw it in daylight."

Carlos retracted his fangs and debulked slowly, strangely finding the latest rash of comments amusing. Somehow Damali always knew how to diffuse a situation. "I'd better show you my boy, Yonnie, before you smoke a master that's on our side."

"A *master*?" Hidalgo said with a groan. "Aw, man . . . what have we gotten ourselves into?"

Hallowed-earth sandbags got piled in strategic rings well beyond the castle gates, wired with remote, cell phone–activated C-4. Trenches with wooden stake pikes got dug and covered with a camouflage of weathered grass. Catapults were raised at the four corners inside the gates, bearing five-gallon jugs of holy water bombs. Garden hoses became the purveyor of liquid fire connected to blessed water tanks.

Shotguns were loaded with Red Sea salt and silver buckshot. Anointed oil rimmed the fort a hundred yards out, ready to be ignited by the fuse lines laid by the Canadian contingent. Motorcycles swabbed in colloidal silver and loaded down with quick-pitch grenades flanked the house with customized automatic street sweepers soldered between their handlebars for quick maneuver assaults. Silver-edged bowie knives, silver-coated baseball bats, and double-aught, shotgun mounted, silver crossbow stakes had been brought in by the Philly and Puerto Rican squads, courtesy Derrick the Bone Crusher and Galakk the Giant. The Haitian and Dominican squad had made it in with a special shipment of silver-coated barbed wire that had prayer rituals performed over it that no one dared ask about.

The living room and dining room were set up for triage, just in case any Guardian squad members took a hit. The kitchen would be the OR, and the counters and table had been cleared to make room for potential wounded. Marjorie and Sara would take incoming injured with Marlene. Berkfield's blood was siphoned and refrigerated, and he lay inside on the sofa drinking orange juice, ready to give more if necessary.

Sentries of seers kept the towers manned with machine guns and mortars, all shells demon readied with silver and hallowed earth, their eyes on the darkening horizon. Every top floor window of the hacienda had bazooka bearers. The roof had now become the command post of agile snipers with mountain-climbing rappelling gear, able to move into changing positions swiftly. Stone workers had charged the castle wall and exterior of *la casa* so fiercely that intermittent blue-white static could be seen crackling along the mortar. If it rained, so be it. Demons would still fry.

Then, near sundown, it was time to pray.

To the east Muslims knelt on small prayer mats and made their peace with Allah. Buddhists sat in quiet repose, murmuring mantras. Jews knelt beside Christians, each communing with the Almighty in their own way. Shamans walked off into the trees and left talismans. Orisha altars were covered with fruit. Candles were lit in small votives. Incense filtered up from the cardinal points. Each and every combination of devotion was observed, linking all warriors in the single request: Let us win without sustaining heavy casualties. Let everyone go home to their family whole.

"I want a medic in every group on the battlefield," Damali said from the front steps once everyone had assembled. "We need two warriors on each squad to serve as designated runners to bring our fallen in out of harm's way for medical attention. Decide in your units who that will be."

"Both Neterus will be on the front lines, two hundred yards spread between us, to be sure the back and front of the fort are covered. We'll mentally telegraph when it's time to blow the lines to tower seers and catapult commanders. If all else fails and you hear us hollering, just do it." Carlos walked down the steps and glimpsed the sun as it touched the horizon. "Okay, people, it's on—man your posts. Godspeed."

"Godspeed," a unified shout rang out in deep voices, and then the gathering of soldiers dispersed.

This was the part Carlos hated the most, the waiting. Everything was eerily quiet, supernaturally so. As he continually scanned, all seers in a cohesive lock, he also thought about the number of people who had responded to the call to arms. He felt a deep sense of responsibility for them all, knowing that each individual meant something priceless to someone somewhere. Even though he'd just met them and didn't really know them personally, he didn't have to. His family had just grown exponentially and he'd take a bullet for any one of them, just like he intuitively knew they would for him.

"Yo, man," Hidalgo said with a smile as he and Carlos hunkered down behind a wall of sandbags. "Is it true what they say that you actually went down to Hell and kicked some ass underground?"

Carlos smiled a half-smile. "Been down there a coupla times, man."

"More than once?" Hidalgo turned and looked at him squarely now. "No bullshit?"

"I wish I was bullshitting you, brother." Carlos sent his gaze back to the horizon.

"What's it like?"

Carlos gave Hidalgo a sidelong glance. "As bad as they say, and worse. But don't let anyone fool you, the bastards are organized, intelligent. . . . It's chaos but organized chaos—you feel me?"

"I feel you," Hidalgo said, hunkering down again. "The vamps are the worst."

"Definitely," Carlos said. "You got any twisted fantasies, any lies you never told your woman, whatever—you'd better purge it right here in this foxhole, and protect your mind, 'cause when they come, it's a psychological campaign as well as a physical one."

Hidalgo just nodded and fell quiet.

"I heard you and Rivera met in Hell," Esmeralda said, glimpsing Damali from their post. She lay on her belly on the ground behind hallowed-earth sandbags looking through the sight of an automatic with a smile.

Damali chuckled. "In a roundabout sorta way, yeah."

"He all they say he is?" Esmeralda arched an eyebrow and briefly turned to wink at Damali.

"All that and better . . . or worse, as the case may be."

Esmeralda laughed. "You're lucky, sis. In our line of work, it's hard to find 'em like that."

"I hear you," Damali said, checking her clip for the fifth time. "But from what I saw, there's a lotta fine able bodies out there on the field. Let's just make sure we bring all ours back alive."

"Roger that," Esmeralda said, growing serious. "But none of us are worried about not coming home, though." She glimpsed Damali. "We knew what we signed up for when we answered the call . . . we'll still be going home, alive or dead. They say the angels come for everybody who's tried to live right, even on battlefields." She sighed hard and returned her gaze to her weapon. "Besides, all of us wanted to be a part of history, ya know?"

Damali nodded, but the knot was back in her stomach again. More than three hundred new people tugged at her heart and conscience. It was bad enough when she just had her little ragtag group of Guardians to worry about, now she had all these new people who had mysteriously and instantly become friends—comrades in arms.

"The angels do come," Damali said quietly, now watching the sky. "You guys are being written about in the books as we speak."

"You think so?" Esmeralda asked, now looking at Damali squarely.

"Yeah, sis," Damali said quietly. "You be careful out here tonight. All right? I wanna be able to visit you in Belize one day."

"Cool. Just say the word and we'll roll out the red carpet."

Damali smiled and switched the conversation to a topic that would make Esmeralda's brilliant smile and deep, rich laugh come out again. "By the way, since we're talking the mysteries of the universe—how in the heck did y'all get all this gear through however many countries without a problem?"

Esmeralda's melodic laughter filled the foxhole as she flashed

Damali a fluorescent smile. "We knew some people that knew some people, who worked it out," she said with a wink. "The Covenant."

Damali's shoulders dropped in relief as she chuckled. "Cool . . . then it's all good."

A low, barely audible rumble in the distance sent audio-sensors scrambling down the lines into communication positions. Seers locked on the Popocatepetl volcano. Tactical warriors laid their hands on the ground and looked up, nodding. Stone workers watched their divination circles as small pebbles charged and began to move across the ground to show an approaching demon formation. Krissy, Heather, and Jasmine's gazes locked with Juanita and Inez's, broadcasting the sounds and images of awakening Aztec ruins to the team. Stone serpents slithered off walls, carved were-jaguars leapt down and faded into the jungle thicket. Damali's silver necklace charged and the stones within it began to glow.

A bewildered, bleeding half-human fawn ran out of the woods toward the gates. "Sanctuary! They're eating us for fuel!"

Before Hubert could speak, a roof sniper's bullet delivered a single shot to the satyr's forehead. The frontline teams watched the fallen creature's spirit exit his body and get summarily snatched down into the ground by several black claws.

"Not our side, I guess?" Hidalgo asked sarcastically.

"Naw," Carlos muttered. "He made his decision too late."

CHAPTER SIXTEEN

Night-vision goggles were lowered on by those who had and trusted them. Several cold body-shield bracelets clicked on. Anything that the Covenant had been able to scavenge on short notice was used.

All gazes strained to focus on the heavy, sputtering plume that billowed up from the volcano miles away. Soon it became evident that the small glowing red flecks within the smoky ash were eyes, not embers, rising in the black cyclone from Popocatepetl. Dark clouds gathered overhead, and then suddenly burst with black lightning, pouring torrential rains down on the waiting Guardian squads. It was nearly impossible to see through the sheets of rain. Mud made ground maneuvering treacherous. Holy water and salt-ring barriers around the house were washed away, and stone workers reinforced the electrified shields as they rushed down the lines to touch sections of the wall.

Tower Guardians aimed bazookas and mortars at the approaching funnel in a coordinated effort, lighting it up like a fireworks display, dead aim. The cloud exploded and burst into several smaller whirling threats. But roof snipers were having difficulty holding on in the howling winds and rushing water that pelted the house.

Six huge, whirling, angry tornadoes touched down just outside the clearing, uprooting trees and debris to fling it against the fort, but Carlos stood in the gale-force winds and quickly erected a translucent wall to absorb the hurling natural shrapnel.

"I can only hold it until the tornadoes stop, after that, I've gotta conserve energy and we've gotta do this the old-fashioned way," Carlos told his line. "When I drop shields, it's on."

"Drop 'em," Hidalgo said through his teeth. "Gunners, on your marks!"

Carlos dropped shields and the towers released mortars at the swirl of man-sized bats. A direct hit inside one swirl lit it, exploding demon innards for three hundred yards. Huge felled trees and debris caught fire, setting off early hallowed-earth explosions on the outer ring of sandbags.

Guardian troops ducked as wood pieces the size of stakes flew at them. Then the sky grew blacker as a leather-winged aerial assault covered the sky. Machine-gun fire erupted from the roof as snipers and tower guards pivoted to drop anything coming by air. Burning vampire bodies hit the roof and torched on impact, forcing snipers to rappel out of the way. When the Guardians on the ground were able to look up, the landscape before them as far as they could see was covered with legion formations of demons.

"This is looking an awful lot like the Alamo, dude," Rider said as he took aim.

"Depends on your historical perspective," Hidalgo said, releasing a burst from his automatic.

"Catapults!" Carlos shouted.

Whooshing snaps resounded in the darkness to land five-gallon holy water bombs in the middle of legion battalions and burst war demons into blue-white flames. Nuit touched down wearing an all-black, gleaming metallic version of Napoleon's uniform and riding a black nightmare, its leathery wings beating the air with a thud. Its gnarled, yellow teeth and glowing green eyes flashed a warning. Scorching flames flared from its nostrils as its cloven hooves pawed the earth. He raised a black steel curved sword that looked like a giant scythe over his head, spotted Carlos, and yanked his nightmare to rear on its hind legs.

"Attack!" Nuit yelled.

"Cycles!" Carlos hollered as he jumped over the bags. "Kamal!"

The Texas squad slid from the sides of the house in the mud, their choppers eating wet dirt and roaring as they met the first wave of the assault—were-demons. Grenades blew werewolves into cinders as the bikers mowed down anything in their path.

"Fall back," Carlos commanded, slicing his way through a wolf pack, but seeing the mud beginning to slow the riders. The big cats were in the next wave, and too fast for the choppers.

Bikes jumped debris as warriors scrambled to get back to the fort, and then he saw one biker go down on his side, yelling. He couldn't get to the fallen before three big cats descended upon him and pulled him into sections of quivering meat.

Duke turned around and headed back for his man, yelling and shooting, lobbing grenades, insane. Rider was over the wall of sand-bags, running behind Duke, shooting like a maniac in the rain. Kamal caught a were-panther before it got Rider. Duke was on the ground still firing and blowing demon guts out, when a huge werewolf jumped on the center of his chest. One of Kamal's men leapt onto the werewolf's back and freed Duke's hand to yank out a bowie knife and gore the creature's heart. Rider blew the head off the demon that wrestled with Kamal, and he dragged Duke by one arm back over the wall.

"Medic! Get this man a medic, he's been nicked!" Hidalgo yelled, while covering Carlos with heavy fire.

"Kamal, pull back and get your men behind that wall!" Carlos shouted through the din.

Mike lobbed several shoulder-cannon blasts to protect Kamal and his men as Shabazz sent a spray of automatic weapon fire into a newly formulating tornado, turning it to instant cinders. Nuit's ranks broke and flanked the house. Lilith's legions of Harpies were making a run for the back wall, putting pressure on Damali's squadrons. Huge serpents exited the earth and swished through the mud like greased lightning.

Blow the bags! Damali telegraphed in a mental shout.

Ground bags blew, creating wriggling, screaming coal-hot twists of screeching Amanthras on the ground. Harpies ran right over the embers in a gray-green gargoyle leaping mass.

Damali was up and out of the hole, Isis raised. Harpie splatter covered her, driving rain washed it away as she took heads. Small bodies leapt over the trench to cling to the outer wall, only to fry where they clung and fall squealing. Esmeralda sprayed the ground as Harpies poured over a yawning fissure with scythe-bearing messenger demons. Catapults rocked Lilith's formations, and Damali pivoted to see that several Harpies had made it behind the sandbags to attack the Belize and Honduras troops.

"No!"

Racing back to the dug-in Guardians, ammo fire erupted from the hole. Damali jumped behind the bags, stabbing at little bodies with one hand and firing a Glock with the other as she kicked demons away. Esmeralda made swift use of a bowie, slaughtering demons as she and Damali went down the line. Inez and Juanita were up over the bags and had a male vampire in an energy arch, frying him to death. Krissy and Jasmine worked in tandem, blowing back demons and igniting war flags in the towers to send red dragons to assist. Heather worked on Bobby and Dan's artillery, turning gunfire into cold-seeking missiles that always met their targets.

Then one of the men trapped by Harpies behind the bags was overrun. Esmeralda ran forward shouting, "No!" as they clawed out the struggling soldier's eyes.

Before the team could get to him, he jumped out of the barrier and ran blindly into a swarm of Harpies, pulled the pin out of his grenade, and detonated it. Harpies burned in an explosion of human and demon body parts. The blast sent Damali and Esmeralda down into the mud, and when they both got up, more than war was in their eyes.

Damali threw her head back and released a Neteru battle yell. Carlos heard it and fought his way around the side of the house. Nuit's nightmare swooped and dove between the carnage as Damali pitched her gun and advanced with broad, two-handed strokes toward him.

Forced to pull back, he yanked his horse into flight, but Damali caught his mare in the chest with a powerful lightning blast from the

THE WICKED   363

Isis. Carlos was on him in seconds, swung, missed, but severed his leg.
Insane with rage, Carlos lifted the limb overhead and hurled it at scat-
tering Harpies, roaring.

Both Neterus turned back to see the hacienda under siege from the
roof and began running toward it. The Philly team was on the east
wall, swinging silver baseball bats and knocking were-demons into
the spiked trenches below. Bone Crusher got a werewolf on the chin
with a hard swing, breaking off fangs and severing the bottom half of
its jaw, while Galakk the Giant popped up and fired a silver stake to
incinerate the huge beast before it ever hit the spikes.

Demon bodies twitched and writhed in barbed wire as the Haitian
and Dominican squads picked them off where they were caught. Hubert was on a wall with Sedgewick, sending hose blasts of holy water
into funnel clouds that ignited in the night like they'd been hit with
flamethrowers. J.L. and Jose had fought their way to the west side of
the house, fly kicking and round-housing Harpies out of the way. But
a wave of scorpions and adders erupted from the spike pits, making
them have to jump to Hubert's grasp to come over the wall.
Sedgewick covered them with a hose assault and lobbed Red Sea salt
shrapnel on the ground.

Damali and Carlos were up over the wall, and he pulled them into
a cloak to land on the slippery, tiled roof. Straddling it, they fought
back-to-back to give rappelling soldiers a chance to escape. Huge
red dragons from Jasmine's flags gulped Harpies forming in the air.
Carlos's shield once again became a discus to clear one side. Damali's
Isis levied white lightning blasts and scorched the other side free of
any demon claw hold.

"Towers!" Carlos shouted.

"Clear!" the towers yelled back.

"Save your energy," Damali shouted to Carlos. "I can feel it dipping!"

He nodded and turned to stare at the battle scene below. Water
coursed down their bodies as the wind lashed them while they took a
quick moment to catch their breaths.

Gunfire inside the house made the Neterus instantly slide to windows, grab the gutters, and crash in. Jose was yelling outside, and Damali and Carlos ran down the hall to the steps and dashed down the staircases, taking multiple steps at a time.

Marjorie was standing at the door with a pump shotgun. Jose was waving his arms at Carlos.

"Message from your boy!" Jose shouted. "Take it from my head, man!"

Carlos pulled the message as he watched Marjorie advance down the front steps.

She's beyond hope now, man, Yonnie's sad message said. *She's out there feeding on the human wounded and demon blood. Lilith brought her out here, knowing she wouldn't be able to withstand the temptation.*

"Not in my ward!" Marjorie shouted. "I love you, but may God rest your soul in peace!"

Marjorie pulled the trigger on the pump shotgun, the blast knocking her back as she wept. Gabrielle looked up from a groaning Guardian just in time for the shell to blast off her head. Marjorie turned and pressed her face to the open door frame. "Bring in that wounded soldier," she said, sobbing. "We have to clean him out before he turns."

Damali rushed forward, cleared the wall, and grabbed the injured Guardian, lifting him to her shoulders to jog his deadweight into the house. "Open up his throat wound," she told Marjorie and Tara as she heaved the fallen man onto the floor. "Marlene, you got this—it's a double purge. Werewolves got his legs. Sara, don't touch it. Berkfield, you either."

Marjorie and Marlene made quick tourniquets from ripped sheets to staunch the bleeding, while Tara pumped on the man's heart and Damali cut into the puncture wounds with her baby Isis dagger. Carlos saw them from the corner of his eye as he went back to the line, knowing it was already too late. The injured Guardian began to convulse and opened his eyes and presented instant fangs.

"God rest your soul," Damali said as Marjorie and Marlene jumped back to avoid a swipe. His head left his shoulders before he could draw a breath to snarl. "Find out whose team he was on so they can take his body home to his family." Damali bent and picked up the head from the floor, and gently placed it on the man's chest, then pulled a sheet over him. "Say a prayer over him, Sara."

Damali walked out the front door and simply stared at the burning chaos. Gunfire and shouts and demon screeches sounded so far away. She looked at the sky as the rain began to abate and then back down to the battlefield as white blurs went to bodies and whole souls lifted to reach for outstretched, angelic hands.

Wounded were coming into the hacienda by the dozens, flooding the ward. Soldiers limped in with assistance; those carried in, she already knew were mortally hit. She saw Carlos standing on the battlefield, his sword lowered like hers as dawn cleared the area of demon incursion. She knew he was thinking the same thought that now haunted her: They had won tonight, but at what human price?

"How many warriors did we lose?" Damali asked the team leaders as they gathered on the muddy front steps.

Hidalgo looked up with tears in his eyes. "Ten, altogether. A lot of injured. But ten dead. One of mine from Mexico City."

"I lost my brother," the leader from El Salvador's team said through a strangled sob. "He was only eighteen."

"Come here, Salle," Alana said. "We will weep together. I lost two good fighters from Honduras, brother. Be of our family."

The pair clung to each other as Alonzo joined them in a small huddle.

"We should pray this dawn," Alonzo said in a thick murmur. "Cuba has lost three."

"They got Joe," Duke whispered as Rider hugged him. "We'd been riding together for twenty-five years."

"Sam was a good man," Esmeralda said through a thick swallow. "There's nothing to send home, though. Just his dog tags. He blew himself up, rather than be taken."

"That was my man from Jamaica," Rockfish said quietly. "I don't know how I will explain his beheading to his mother." He closed his eyes, crossed himself, and then stood and walked away. "They ate his legs."

"I want every man and woman out of here that sustained a loss or a nick," Damali said, swallowing hard. "The wounds are too fresh, and your spirits are rightfully too broken. While we have daylight cover, you guys pull out and head to the convent in Taxco to heal."

"Damali's right," Carlos said, his battle-weary gaze going around the emotionally broken squads. "You've all paid enough. We would have been slaughtered in here without you, but the price is too high."

"We stand as one," Duke said, pulling away from Rider. "They got us all in the heart, so we go down swinging together."

Mutinous jeers rang out on the courtyard. No Guardian would turn back and they simply covered the dead in hallowed earth, salt, and prayers in a truck and came back to their posts to begin checking artillery.

"The fort is trashed," Carlos said, walking beyond the gates with Damali. "Artillery is low, manpower is beat down. This is suicide for the squads."

Damali nodded. "The healers are spent. Even a new nick at this juncture is gonna pull me and you off the frontlines to purge it, which means they'll be out there alone on low ammo. Berkfield can't give another drop of blood or he'll have to get a transfusion himself."

"I know, and we can't take another assault," Carlos said. "We'll have to draw fire away from the teams, me and you, baby . . . because I can't have another death on my conscience."

She hugged him. "Me, either." In that moment she knew why neither she nor Carlos ever asked for help. It wasn't arrogance but fear— fear of an outcome like this.

Hubert's shouts from the tower made all eyes look to the sky and then forced the teams to scramble for battle stations.

"Get down out of that tower, Hubert!" Damali yelled as the sky filled with hybrid funnels that streaked the clear blue sky with black stripes. "Towers, get down!"

Mortars and bazookas went off and hit several streaks, but the numbers were daunting. Carlos raised a shield over the house as a black lightning bolt flashed toward the casa, and the force of it still rocked the house to the foundation. Tower sentries scrambled to head for the steps and another series of shockwaves blew the front wall.

"I can't shield the towers and the front of the house!" Carlos shouted.

"Black box it," Damali screamed as another bolt tore through the front door and imploded inside the foyer, taking out the main staircase.

"It's too big!" Carlos hollered, and then shifted his position to cover the front of the house.

"It's Cain!" Sedgewick shrieked and ducked down behind the stone ledge, too afraid to run.

"Sedgewick, come down now!" Hubert pleaded over Sara's screams, unable to get to him from the front stairs. He dashed through the house toward the kitchen to reach the back steps, yelling for his friend to get out of the towers, but rubble in the stairwell blocked him. He dashed out to the yard to try to climb up the side of the house, but couldn't hold on as repeated blasts rocked the structure.

Guardians still stubbornly manning their posts to the bitter end tried to save Sedgewick by sending a last mortar blast from the east tower and firing bazookas. Instantly two black bolts hit the towers, exploding them. Hubert looked up to see Sedgewick falling in flames with four men around him.

Damali ran out to the open field and raised her blade amid the chaos. "I call the elements!" she shouted. "Comets and lightning to blow these sonsofbitches out of the sky!"

Meteors began to streak, exploding black funnels. Black lightning met white lightning as she dashed for cover. Damali stopped again, winded from the energy exertion, and raised her blade again.

"Ravens, hit your marks! Bees, swarm and sting! Falcons, find your prey!" She ran and then drop-rolled as a bolt narrowly missed her, and got up running.

The heavens filled with birds as she made her way back to Carlos's side, but the swarms of bees were soon blotted out by a large, moving black blob in the sky that lowered and began to pelt Guardians. Stinging bodies splattered against their faces.

"Take cover!" Carlos yelled. "Biting locusts!"

Squads dashed and hunkered down against walls, vehicles, anything they could find, and covered their heads with rain ponchos to avoid the insect invasion. But the nasty little beasts had red glowing eyes and razor-sharp teeth, attacking any skin they could find like little miniature piranha.

"The bastard knows the Old Testament like the back of his hand, D," Carlos said as he put them under a shield so they could run to shield the others. "New approach. He saw you do that shit on the beach and can go like this all day."

Carlos flung his shield around the remaining squad as Guardians fought the little beasts off them and squashed them under boots.

"I have to get outside your shield to call off the birds."

He looked up as bird bodies began falling, but also bringing down several of Cain's forces. Falcons tore at hybrid eyes, blinding them before dying brave deaths. Ravens pierced wings, making hybrids list and have to land, but got felled in the swarms of locusts. Vehicles blew up all around them as black bolts rained down Cain's wrath from the sky. The swarm of bees Damali had sent attacked black feathered wings and crawled beneath them, weighing them down as they released agonizing stings.

"Let me out," Damali said.

"On three, shield goes down and back up, make it quick."

Damali called the remaining birds back to save them, but battle lust overtook her as she saw the carnage on the ground. Slaughtering several wounded hybrids as she dashed back to the shield, a hail of bullets cut off her path.

Carlos stood. "They're using conventional weapons against us. Oh, shit!"

No sooner than he'd said it, a missile blew out a section of the hacienda.

"I've gotta drop shields—she's out there by herself with bullets flying. This ain't just supernatural bolts, folks. Find cover! Old school, like you was in the 'hood!"

Damali ran a zigzag path and jumped behind a tree. Carlos raced across the clearing and dove behind it with her.

"I'm gonna try to keep a shield around the house," he said, panting as machine-gun fire whirred by them, cutting splinters off the tree. "Gotta give the teams something to cover them. Two more missiles and the house is leveled."

"Do it," she said, hunkered down behind the wide trunk. "I got us prayer-shielded for a minute so he can't see us, but it won't last long behind this tree . . . my focus is split between us and the others. We need to call him out. Psychological attack to make him land and come looking for us. Any ideas?"

"The wedding," Carlos said, gulping air.

"The honeymoon," she said, breathless, and pounded his fist.

"Send that shit live and in living color, baby."

They locked gazes, one mind. Carlos shuddered and smiled an angry smile.

"Yeah, that's the one."

Damali nodded. "Thought so."

A rage-filled war cry rent the air. Two hundred hybrids landed, sending up clouds of sulfur to choke the hacienda-bound teams like it was tear gas.

"Damali!" Cain thundered.

"Now what?" Damali whispered as she peeped around the tree trunk to see a black swishing tail fully healed.

"Oh, shit, the motherfucker healed," Carlos said in a rush, peeping around the tree and then pressing his spine to the trunk.

"You will be a widow today!" Cain roared.

"Okay, let me go to him," she said. "He'll off you on sight, and the teams won't have a shield. We gotta be strategic. He doesn't wanna kill me—just beat my ass real good. Hold the line so our people don't die, and I'll—"

"Do what, baby? You see how huge that bastard is now?"

"Yeah," she said, glimpsing the battlefield. "I remember from the last time." Damali tightened her grip on the Isis. "When I go out there, telepath to the seers to open fire on Cain's hybrids, but not him. Drop your shield long enough to let them get into position. Let me take him, that'll split his focus, and his hybrids can die from bullets, too." She touched Carlos's sweaty face. "You take ten and rest from the shield drain, then come out swinging. Cool?"

"Sounds like a plan," he said, nodding. "On three."

"Three," she said, and then began running toward the clearing. "Cain!" she shouted, and then missed a black arc that singed her blade arm.

Cain threw his head back and roared and took flight behind her. She could hear gunfire erupting from the house, and from her peripheral vision black feathers began to fly as the hybrids were assaulted with sharpshooter bullets. Leathery black wings that had been torn by bird beaks riddled the ground. Grenades were lobbed; the smoke of dawn warfare filled the air. Her people were in position, but she surely wasn't. She narrowly missed an overhead snatch by air, and then Cain landed with a thud in front of her, snarling.

"Not this time, Damali," he said through battle-length fangs.

She missed the bullwhip of his huge, spiked tail by a margin as she flipped out of his range. "It grew back, huh?"

"You incorrigible bitch!" he shouted. "You have no idea how close I am to just exterminating you this morning!"

"Then what good would that do," she said, moving from side to side as he advanced and tried to grab her. "Can't make a baby by yourself, or did you die to come back, lover?"

Damali danced out of the way of a black grip charge and sent one that he blocked. The power that ran up her arm almost knocked her down.

"You wish," he said and cocked his head to the side. "Never."

She sliced through another arc with the Isis.

"You will grow fatigued soon enough; I can feel your energy already waning." He stopped advancing and smiled.

"You can't implant me right now, anyway—your mother is—"

"Severed from me," he said with a low, threatening grin.

"Oh . . ."

A steady beam of white light suddenly entered Cain's spine and made him arch. He twisted and roared, raising his blade and Damali immediately saw Carlos's feet behind Cain's hulking form.

"You got anything to say to my wife, you say it to me!" Carlos shouted, dodging Cain's tail as it thrashed, trying to impale him.

"You will die on this battlefield today!" Cain growled in pain, unable to shake Carlos's hold.

Damali dashed around Cain's body, missed a black bolt and came up behind him to touch her sword to Carlos's to increase the beam.

"Kill their family!" Cain shouted, trying to split the Neterus' focus. "Take no prisoners!"

"Then let's make sure you feel it again for old time's sake," Damali said, lifting her blade and taking off Cain's tail where it met his spine.

Cain's agonized howl rent the air. Carlos swung, but Cain pivoted, and Carlos's blade sheared off both his wings. However, Cain was far from down. The combined attack only seemed to make him angrier as he matched blade strokes with Carlos and pushed Damali back with a black bolt line. Then she saw it happening in slow motion and briefly froze.

Kamal and Marlene's eyes met just once. Marlene stood, AK-47 raised, screaming no. The telepathic message between seers was swift, searing, filled with passion, and tasted of salt tears. Damali licked her dry lips. The transmission contained such a white-hot light that Damali hadn't intercepted it; the message had literally burned across her third eye. But the emotion held within the private exchange made her start toward the hacienda before the reality of Cain's position sunk in. She had to get to the other side of the battlefield!

Three intense words fought for dominance in Damali's mind, carried on the delicate synaptic waves between old lovers, her mind fractured between Carlos, Marlene, Kamal, her team, and the very real threat of Cain.

Kamal's battle roar filled the air but offered Marlene a salt-coated mental caress said through unshed tears, a familiar Brazilian lilt made tense by pending doom. Male truth said hard, fast, no breath or pause—*I love you*. A mother-seer's mental wail, a hysteria-driven call and response caught midthroat, garbled in a mind stuttering with fear . . . not for herself, fear of the inevitable—*please no, not like this!*

Vibrations too thick to ignore even under heavy gunfire drew sight lines between old rivals, warriors on the same team. Shabazz stood. Marlene's eyes briefly closed. Kamal and Shabazz's gaze deadlocked before a shape-shift leap over the wall. Too many shells flying. A semi lowered toward a were-jag ally's back. Bullets squeezed off, casings spent. Hybrid gook splattered as one Guardian brother covered another, respect in tact, regardless of fate. Marlene opened her eyes, tears streaming. Still too many shells flying. *Not like this.* A Brazilian team off the hook, taking no cover, suicide mission, following their leader until the last man stands.

"Marlene, get down!"

A command, half-plea from Shabazz—electrified locks and arms extended, flesh trying to protect flesh from bullets, a body shield the ultimate sacrifice. The intent clear in a man's eyes . . . in his sweat . . . in the blue current running down his raised Nubian locks, coursing down his gun barrel, the most important part of his being could not die on the battlefield. Not today. Her name is Marlene Stone. "Get down!"

Static blue tactical Guardian arcs magnetized passing shells, deflected death's direction by a fraction . . . by a hair's breadth, jumping off Shabazz's dreadlocks, fingertips, white-lightning fury while a woman is caught midair, midlife, midreality between two men . . . men falling, shouting, shooting, ripping out hybrid-demon innards. Bullets, a nonrespecter of name or circumstance, still whiz by in blurs as a daughter screams for them all to stop.

Slow-motion death spiraling from gun barrels, words mentally repeated by both men like a surreal echo sent in millisecond synaptic waves to male vocal cords that never got a chance today to utter what was evident—*I love you.*

Focus momentarily fractured. She'd heard Kamal tell her mother-seer that this was the only way—to die honorably in battle, for her, so that her soul, his, and therefore Shabazz's, could one day rest in peace. They all knew the deal. It had kept them from squaring off for years.

If both men killed each other over Marlene, ascension would never happen, and even Marlene's soul could possibly be damned for participating in the madness until there was blood on her hands.

The word *no* formed in Damali's throat but lodged there, trapped. Marlene's mental shrieking refrains of that same word eclipsed the panicked warning along with Damali's breath. Her mother-seer's pain sent a spasm up Damali's spine, nearly blinding her to the huge predator that she most immediately needed to worry about, Cain. But she fought him numbly, fight instinct lifting her arm to match blows. She went through the reflex blade motions at Carlos's side, consumed with multiple distractions, multiple vantage points of heart-stopping worry exploding in her mind.

Several huge demon hybrids with black feathered wings had cleared the hacienda wall with semiautomatics. Her team was blowing away demons, sending entrails and innards across the field. Kamal's men had cleared the wall to go hand to hand with sharpshooters covering their backs. But Kamal's men were still vulnerable to artillery and had to pull back or die.

"Fall back!" Torn, Damali continued to fight Cain, working with Carlos to cover his flank, but had to get to the casa. She needed to be in three places at once! Then, before she could raise her Isis to fend off another black arc from Cain, Kamal had leapt in a were-jaguar attack to keep a predator off Hidalgo, and was shot in the chest midair by a shell.

"No!" Damali yelled as she saw Kamal's spirit lift from where he lay to go into the arms of a waiting angel. Marlene had stood in the midst of gunfire and screamed, unable to reach the fallen. Kamal's men lost their minds and ran into a hail of bullets on a kamikaze mission, taking leather wings and feather wings with them to their deaths.

Horrified, Damali simply stared for a second, witnessing the entire Brazilian squad be decimated by conventional machine-gun fire and shells. *Not them.* She swung her blade, still fighting in body, but her mind was bludgeoned by the heavy casualties on the ground. She could hear Carlos and Cain battling near her, but she was transfixed as angels scurried around the battlefield in a blur, gathering the souls of Kamal's men.

Carrion warriors fought off the attempts by dark legion collectors to drag Kamal and his men down into the pit. Marlene suddenly stood, continuing to squeeze off rounds, crazed, grief stricken, screaming, her vibrations radiating out a level of pain that stabbed into Damali's consciousness like an Isis.

Ignoring Damali and Shabazz's entreaties to take cover, the older warrior refused, blowing off hybrid-demon heads, splattering guts, standing in the full line of fire unafraid—machine gun in one hand, fighting stick in the other.

Damali felt it the same moment Shabazz did, their tactical senses locked as one while Carlos fought Cain back. She was too far away and too exhausted with too much splintering her focus to freeze time. Seeing a shell whir toward Marlene, Shabazz quickly stood again to protect Marlene and peppered the wall, and then grabbed her and yanked her down before it was too late. Yet it happened so quickly but so agonizingly slow in Damali's mind that she almost blacked out as the shell connected with flesh, tore cartilage, and blew Shabazz's back out.

Damali's entire being had become one with the shell as she'd focused on it, tried to slow it down, tried to deflect it with her energy-depleted mind, to no avail. Once locked on the target, it was impossible to quickly disengage. She rode the shell's searing, destructive metal, unwilling to release it to the course of its fate, unable to break free for a second as it blew through the center of Shabazz's chest and came out his back dragging gore. Damali screamed. She felt his skin tear, his flesh and muscles rip, his vertebrae snap and splinter into shards . . . until she was one with the wet sticky substance of his life being spilled.

Shabazz fell in slow motion, the impact snapping his neck in a hard jerk, large sections of bone and meat and huge drops of blood flying. Damali's consciousness exited his dark body into the battlefield light and drew a gasp. *Oh, God.*

Marlene was immediately prostrate over Shabazz's body, screaming out prayers, calling on all the shaman powers she owned, but his glassy eyes never blinked.

Damali's legs became a blur. Cain and Carlos momentarily stopped battling and backed away from each other, breathing hard. War momentarily ceased as Damali's wings spread in an arc of bright light, ripping through her dirty T-shirt and drawing the full attention of all while she ran. Then her feet were no longer on the ground, her blade was clutched at her side. Dark claws that had grasped at Kamal's men quickly retreated beneath the earth. Guardians fell back and stared in awe as she landed in their midst screaming Shabazz's name. Overwhelmed with grief, she shoved Marlene aside, swept Shabazz up in her arms, and cast the Isis to the ground.

"No, no, no, no, no—not my father!" Damali wailed, rocking Shabazz's lifeless body against hers while the others tried to focus on firing over the wall to keep predators at bay. "Breathe, 'Bazz," she said, pleading against him, covering the exit wound in his back with her frenzied hands. Her fingers met slippery ooze and she flattened her palms against the gaping hole that was gushing blood, wailing harder. "No!"

Hubert ran headlong toward Carlos, seeing Cain pivot to swing while Carlos's momentary hesitation from the heart blow Shabazz took stole his focus. The hybrid dove at Carlos; Cain released the swing. Both Carlos and Hubert simultaneously hit the ground as Cain backed up. Warm wetness oozed down Carlos's legs as Hubert convulsed.

"I died with honor serving you," Hubert said, twitching. "The Light is beautiful."

Carlos jumped up just in time to avoid another swing from Cain only to see that half of Hubert's body was gone. He'd been lying in the valiant hybrid's entrails. This time when Cain swung, Carlos caught his steel against his blade and forced it down, then swung hard with his left fist to sucker punch Cain backward.

"I will kill you!" Carlos yelled, and a bolt ran through his sword and blew Cain onto his back.

Cain's sword went one way, his body went the other, and fatigue from his injuries was draining Cain. Carlos was on him in a heartbeat, but the fallen entity was still strong enough to grapple with the blade that Carlos poised over his chest.

Sara had run out of the hacienda and raced across the grass sobbing. She dropped down by Hubert's body, trying to shove entrails back into his torso and then passed out against him.

Marlene was on her knees beside Damali who would not give up Shabazz's body. She just rocked Shabazz while her team lost it. Neteru Guardians were over the wall with maimed regional Guardians right behind them, every human taking gunfire, and still getting back up as white blurs whizzed by them. Their insane ferocity drove the hybrids back. Mysteriously, hybrid ammunition went off in half-demon hands, grenades exploded as soon as hybrids pulled the pins, full clips didn't fire when hybrid fingers squeezed triggers. When the smoke cleared, two hundred hybrids lay on the ground dead and twitching. Blood was everywhere. Every Guardian had been shot and wounded. Marlene was still prostrate in the courtyard mud near Shabazz, her heart going into staccato arrhythmia.

"Give me the Caduceus," Damali said, her face tilted to the sky and her eyes closed, her bloodied wings enfolding Shabazz. "I'm begging you. Mercy."

The white orbs appeared and only one spoke. "Give him to us," the being murmured. "We will have mercy. He was a good man."

"No!" Damali shrieked, and held her ground. "Not this day, not my father and my husband and my mother—never!" She looked at them squarely and then back up to the sky. "Eve—you see this! Send me the Caduceus."

"Trust us, child," the orbs said in unison. "Heal the others."

Immediately, the Caduceus clattered to the ground. Damali slowly unfolded her wings and laid Shabazz on his back and brushed his forehead with her lips.

"Your spirit is still trapped in your body," she whispered with tears streaming down her face and into his open chest wound. "Please don't leave me, Dad."

She stood and then gathered the golden staff in her hand and opened her wings as she opened her arms. "Mercy of Mercies," she murmured. "Please hear an angel's battlefield cry. Powers Angels of healing, please take my lament up to God. Spare them all, if just this once."

The wounded stared at her, each man and woman gathering up the religious symbol that hung with their dog tags, slowly kissing it in awe. Damali rammed the Caduceus into the ground, too over-whelmed to speak further. Her tears were all that she had left. A blinding pulse of green and gold light made trees shudder and loose bricks fall. The circle of light spread from the base of the staff, over Shabazz and Marlene, glowing blue-white as it began fanning out to the courtyard, covering each Guardian, and overtaking the field for as far as the eye could see.

The white orbs leaned over Shabazz and spread their wings, fever-ishly working. Bullets began to bubble to the surface of wounds in the courtyard and fall from torn skin, slashes sealed, broken bones mended, people wept, and radiant heat and rapture made them fall down and sob.

Carlos could feel the pulse of something rumbling beneath the ground, and he and Cain turned at the same time to look at what seemed to be a nuclear light edging toward them. They ceased their struggle, both getting to their feet to run from what they thought was a detonated blast. But it caught the edge of Cain's foot as it fanned out and trapped him. Carlos tried to get away, but it rooted him where he stood, calming him and filling him with a sense of utter peace.

Carlos turned to see Cain's body writhing in agony on the ground, his cries piteous. He walked back to the felled giant and lifted his blade, but a female hand on his shoulder stopped the beheading.

"Let me do it," Eve said quietly.

Carlos almost fell, he'd jumped back so quickly.

"He was our son," Adam said, shaking his head. "I did love him at one point, too. But my queen must do this to set the world aright."

Carlos lowered his blade as the entire Neteru Council of Kings and Queens made a circle in the glen. They were dressed in royal robes of violet and gold, their expressions grim, as they looked down at Cain.

Eve called the Isis to her palm and slowly closed her fingers around the handle as Cain stretched out his hand toward her.

"Mother, don't do this," Cain said gasping, his body writhing as each wound he ever sustained as a demon opened and bled black blood.

"I love you, son," Eve whispered with tears in her eyes as she walked toward him with the Isis raised. "Let me end your suffering, and all our suffering with it."

"No!" Cain shouted as the Isis chimed.

Eve turned away at the sound of the thud and handed the bloody blade to Carlos, never looking back. "Cain is healed."

The Neteru Councils disappeared in a splinter of gold and violet light without another word. Carlos began running toward the casa and then stopped when he saw Hubert. Sara was lying on the hybrid's chest taking in shallow sips of air. But it didn't make sense. Hubert's body was woven back together, and yet, he still didn't have a pulse. Carlos gathered Sara up into his arms and tried to revive her. She stirred slowly and touched his face.

"We were too late. His soul was eager to end this life and go into the Light. But he will not be mangled even in death." Glistening tears wet her face, and she was dirty and covered with blood. "I will not allow him to be desecrated by Cain."

"I'll take you back to the group," Carlos said, breathing in her pain. "Just hang on, you did too much—"

"No," Sara whispered with a smile. "He's coming for me. I want to go with Hubert. My heart is broken beyond repair . . . I can go because I died trying to save him."

"I know how you must feel, but you're still breathing," Carlos said, trying not to panic.

"I am a Mercy, and what I have seen today has shocked my system," she said in a faint whisper, her voice failing. "Put me on his chest . . . my favorite place in any world. Bury me in with him the same way."

Carlos laid her on Hubert's chest and watched her smile looking up at the sky. "I'm gonna see who's wounded and come back for you. Okay? You just hold on."

Sara said nothing as she reached up and the light went out of her eyes.

Carlos dropped to his knees and brushed the tussled hair away from her face, hung his head, and said a silent prayer. Too many had perished, and this was only the beginning of the big war. Defeat claimed him as he trudged back to the hacienda in search of his wife, numb.

His boots met ash, feathers, and bones. The entire ground was charred like the aftermath of a nuclear holocaust. The sky was overcast from the smoke and remnants of spewing volcanic ash. He looked at the survivors that gathered around the steps, hoping that some of his immediate family made it. But the scene he stumbled upon made him drop his blade from his grip as he walked forward.

Damali sat on the steps, wings spread, with Shabazz in her arms, holding him from behind, Marlene's head in his lap as he groggily stroked Marlene's locks. Guardians that he'd witnessed going down to the ground mortally shot were sitting in the mud in the courtyard, bloodied but not wounded. His eyes tore to the dead-wagon vehicle, doing a laser search, and to his amazement, the dead were whole, not ripped to shreds . . . even the Honduran and beheaded Jamaican warriors were whole. He glanced at Jose, the question in his eyes implicit—did Damali do her thing in time to save Kamal and his men? A brother-to-brother connection was subtly made as Jose shook his head, let out a shuddering breath, and then looked down. No.

"Oh, man," Carlos said quietly, briefly closing his eyes. Not them.

Big Mike was decimated. His line of vision kept going between Kamal, Drum, and the others beyond the wall on the battlefield and then back to Shabazz. Each heavy, quaking breath that Mike released to stave off breaking down held pain so deep that even Rider couldn't console him. There was nothing to say. Newbies sat shell-shocked, eyes staring, faces dirty and bloodied. The Neteru squad was laid out on the ground in small groups, so overwrought that no one could stop the torrent of tears. Then Carlos stared at his wife. The aftermath was profound. Damali's bottom lip quivered as she tried to speak. He put his finger to his lips as more tears streamed down her face. She searched his eyes and a quiet whisper entered his mind.

I prayed you'd come out of the glen . . . Damali said on a choked mental gasp.

That's the only reason I'm still standing, he murmured back, his thoughts caressing hers from where he stood.

I couldn't save them all. She buried her face against Shabazz's hair. *But my daddy* . . .

"I know, baby," Carlos said quietly and came to sit beside her on the steps. "You saved all the ones you were supposed to. Heaven got the rest."

"Lilith, you must help me," Nuit croaked as he lay bleeding out on the floor of the Vampire Council's chambers.

"You were already dead when you sustained the wound from a Neteru's blade," she said coolly, looking at her nails. "I cannot regenerate the limb. It is finished."

"Then stop the bleeding, the agony of it, so I can survive," Nuit begged, beginning to sob.

"Why should I? Maybe Yonnie can help you—he's a master."

Nuit looked up at her as she glanced at his old throne and burned his name off of it.

"No, no, Lilith, I can explain my liaison with Yolando. It wasn't an attempted coup . . . it was a pact, an alliance to strengthen Cain's ambitions!"

"Your armies failed. Your alliances failed," she said, looking at him from Cain's old throne. "Your attempts to sabotage the Neteru team failed, and your ineptitude thus caused my husband's grandson to perish by his own mother's hand. What do you think my husband would do with you, after he was so lenient to allow me to raise you again, hmmmm?"

"Please Lilith, I beg you," Nuit said through his teeth, tears rising to his eyes. "Don't send me to his chambers—*anything* but that!"

"I do feel your pain, as I have been there under less than favorable circumstances. But this I promise. After a month of negotiation with him," she said with an evil grin, "it might help you better endure the Sea of Perpetual Agony." She leaned forward, her eyes narrowed to slits. "The Devil will have his due, and this time you can take the brunt of his fury, not me. I do pity you—at least I was his lover. I had something to bargain with. Do you?"

"No, no, not that, anything, Lilith, I give you my word! We can come to an accord!" Nuit began to drag himself away from the group of Harpies that surrounded him, futilely clawing at the marble as his bloody stump leaked his energy away.

Thundering footsteps made both entities stop bickering as the bats went still. Lilith grasped the arms of Cain's throne.

"Husband," she squeaked. "You're home."

Nuit covered his head and stopped breathing.

"Indeed," a voice echoed just beyond the chambers. "Cain's throne said you won it from him by inheritance rights from your legitimate bargain. This time you did very well for yourself—your treachery knows no bounds like mine, which is why, I suppose, I love you." A deep inhalation rattled the thrones. "But I am outraged to have lost another in my direct line of creation."

"I was just preparing a blood sacrifice for you," she said calmly, looking at Nuit's cowering body on the floor. "The Harpies were about to deliver a traitor in our midst, one that conspired to cause Cain's downfall."

A deep chuckle quaked the cavern. "I know this bastard well . . . he is the same one that attempted a coup against my son, Dante . . . which is why I came this time to collect him myself."

Even the bats and Harpies turned away as Nuit's screaming body slid across the floor leaving nail marks in the marble behind him.

World news said the Popocatepetl volcano was active again, but posed no immediate threat to the cities within its radius. Local papers said that a drug-lord war leveled a villa and hacienda in La Paz, as well as a historic castle in Cuernavaca. The sisters of San Bernardino de Sena swear they witnessed a miracle that cannot be substantiated beyond pure faith . . . they said an angel raised a dead woman before their very eyes. Nonbelievers scoffed at their superstitious awe. But the townspeople of Taxco know that twelve praying sisters and their senior, Sister Louisa, were quietly venerated by the Vatican in a private service performed before the nuns by the Pope.

The angels wept as ten Guardian funerals were held throughout Central America with the Covenant officiating, and all that fought during that fateful twenty-four hours attended. Three courageous hybrids were laid to rest in the ruins, all Guardian teams present, their legacy inscribed in the sacred *Temt Chaas* and books of Heaven as they were guided into the Light.

Ten brave humans who were once bitten by were-demon jaguars in the Amazon were also laid to rest on hallowed ground. Their spirits now reside with the warriors of Light and their children will know them as heroes. The fervent prayers of a sister, a niece, and a nephew, along with those from a man with a good heart, plus the pleas of two young women who'd been spared a horrifying existence to be guided to Guardians by a merciful woman, and the full company of a Neteru team appealed to the Mercies not to leave one of their own. Somehow Light border guards were given the word by an angel named Lopez, who passed it to a spirit named Christine, that there was a battlefield mistake, and in the confusion the preemptive decision was made before hard-hit demons could properly convene. Purgatory was thus breached to take one crying female vampire's soul into the Light to be with friends. That made two additional vampires, friends of the team, that had been spared according to the prophecy.

None of it was a perfect solution or the end of their struggles. This time, it was a draw, a perfect stalemate. But for now, flowers bloomed again, the cycle of life continued, and Guardians could temporarily sleep at night.

EPILOGUE

This is wild, Carlos mentally said to Damali with a sidelong glance. He looked around the huge, nondenominational church and simply shook his head. *I'm never gonna hear the end of it once the brothers wake up tomorrow morning and realize what they did,* he added, teasing her.

Shush, be quiet, we're in church, and this is beautiful, she mentally said with a huge grin.

They can't hear us like we're whispering, you know. I could say any ole thing to you, even get a little—

DON'T even try it. In church, you crazy?

Been awhile, maybe I am. Carlos smiled and kissed her cheek. *Weddings have that effect on me, and seven at one time, hey?*

Damali bit her lip to keep from laughing. Carlos was a trip and the whole thing was a refreshing change. She was so happy this morning that she wouldn't even revisit his married-man barb later.

After a month of burying the dead and eating their hearts out about what they could have done differently, today was about celebration, pure and simple.

Each cleric would have his turn to perform the ceremony in each Guardian's faith, and half of the squad was running up and down the aisle, either walking the ones who went ahead of them down it, or standing in as best man or both.

Rider walked Marlene down, and Mike stood as Shabazz's best man, Imam Asula presiding; Berkfield was crying harder than Marjorie as he gave Krissy away and Dan stood next to J.L. as best man, Father Pat doing the honors. On every couple the Covenant switched clerics. Inez and Mike went with a local Baptist minister, Damali at her side, Shabazz at Mike's. Rabbi Zeitloff performed the marriage rites for Dan and Heather, shouting "Mazel tov!" when it was done.

Under the circumstances, even the rabbi turned a blind eye on the whole conversion thing for Heather, just like Father Pat had done for J.L. at Monk Lin's insistence—time was of the essence, but the elderly rabbi couldn't resist warning Dan that his mother would have a coronary. Bobby was Dan's best man, and Jasmine was Heather's maid of honor, then they flipped the script, changed clerics again, and Father Pat was back on call to marry Bobby and Jasmine with Dan and Heather standing by. The paperwork and licenses would be sorted out later.

Jose nudged Carlos. "I'm up next, man. My tux okay?"

Carlos nodded and brushed invisible lint off Jose's lapels. "You're righteous, holmes. Will be right back with her."

Jose nodded and adjusted his bow tie with a hard swallow. Damali gave him a supportive nod and ran to take her place in the back of the church.

"You ready?" Carlos asked Juanita with a smile.

"Yeah . . . now I am," she said with a shy smile and looked down as Damali lowered her veil for her. "Thank you for giving me away, Carlos."

"It was time, all way around." Carlos kissed her cheek. "You're a beautiful bride."

Juanita turned to Damali. "Thank you for everything."

"I'm honored that you asked me," Damali said, giving Juanita's hand a squeeze.

"I'm just glad that you would do it," Juanita said and took a shuddering breath. Her eyes searched Damali's for final acceptance. "You are *truly* a matron of *honor*."

The two women stood together in silence for a moment while private understanding bound them as more than teammates, but finally friends. Damali could only nod and sniff, and then she smiled, giving Juanita's hands one last squeeze before turning to march to the music.

Damali tried to keep her eyes on Father Patrick while blinking back tears of joy and wondering about time. . . . How strange a commodity it was . . . so quick to heal, so slow to heal. Tragedy could be triumph and the reverse also true. Sara would always be a blue star in the night, just as Hubert and Sedgewick would be constellations of courage she'd say her evening prayers for. Gabrielle would be her constant wonder. . . . What if things had been different? . . . And God bless Yonnie, where was he? Kamal and his men would always be regal spirit mentors in her dreams . . . the ones who taught her first how to deliver the balm of peace. Today was a gift she wouldn't squander by looking backward.

But never in a million years did she think that time could have healed the wound between her, Jose, Juanita, and Carlos. The look on Jose's face said it all when he glanced past her to spy his bride, letting them all know time was also merciful. The brother almost broke down.

But nothing was more moving than to see Tara come down the aisle on Carlos's arm for Rider. Damali could barely see the white runner for the tears as she held Tara's flowers and walked before her. Rider didn't even try to hide it. After waiting thirty years for this day, he didn't have to and no one expected it. Rider just shook his head and let the tears run while Shabazz and Mike flanked him like kingly sentries.

Tara wore a long, white, beaded Native American–styled gown and a breathtaking headdress of white eagle feathers. A short veil rimmed in silver thread covered her face and her hair hung down naturally to grace her delicate shoulders. She held a bouquet of wild lavender in trembling hands, tears wetting her beautiful face as she walked with the dignity of a true queen. They practically had to help Father Patrick away from the altar—he was bawling so badly—as the tribal shaman from Tara's grandmother's home in Arizona came to the front of the church to unite the pair as one. Mercy of the Mercies had been visited upon the team today.

The private hotel reception that followed was nothing short of decadent, Carlos's orders and definitely his style. Seven cakes for seven brides, all trimmed in the brides' hue of choice. Food enough to have fed the regional teams at *la casa,* and enough champagne to make everybody dance and act stupid. But Carlos made sure he teased every brother real good when they tried to leave early, citing their harassment of him not long ago.

"Yo, dude, where's the fire?" Carlos teased, whisking Tara away to dance to another song. "Y'all ain't leaving yet, are you?"

Rider just laughed. "I still have a firearm nearby, even today."

Carlos danced around, whirling Tara back to Rider. "My bad. Guess I'll just have to get Inez to hang and party with us."

"Aw, man, don't start," Mike said, laughing.

"D, talk to your husband, pleeease," Inez wailed, as Carlos hustled her out on the floor.

"Nope," Damali said, wagging her finger. "Y'all made me stay at my reception for almost four hours." Damali sighed and looked at her watch. "Only been two hours. Fair exchange is no robbery."

"See, I taught her well," Carlos said, teasing Dan as he danced away with Heather. Then he stopped. "Oh, yeah, y'all are *real* new—I'll let *them* go."

The group burst out laughing as Heather blushed and dashed away from Carlos. Carlos cocked his head to the side to see who he could pick on next.

"We're out," Bobby said, glimpsing Jasmine and laughing as Carlos wiggled his eyebrows at him.

"Uh, see ya, Mr. Berkfield—I mean, Dad," J.L. said, body blocking Carlos from taking a dance spin with Krissy.

"Marlene, Marlene, I know you can boogie all night, sis," Carlos said, a new victim in sight.

Shabazz held up his hand with a smile and rubbed his chest. "Newly back from the dead, brother—I get special courtesies. Back off my wife."

Carlos pounded his fist with a broad grin. "Been there—but, uh, y'all ain't give me no special consideration."

Shabazz winked, lacing Marlene's arm over his. "Y'all wasn't *married* when I was considering."

"Oh, oh, so it's like that, now. Okay," Carlos said, laughing. "Cool . . . I'll dance with *my wife* then. How you like that?" Then he stopped and glanced around. "Where's Jose and 'Nita?"

"Gone about a half-hour ago," Rider said, ushering Tara out the door.

"Vamp move if I ever seen one," Carlos said, as Damali laughed and pulled him onto the floor.

"Well you would know," Shabazz said, sneaking out the door.

"Bye y'all—see ya in ten days or so," Marlene called out, laughing.

The room cleared. Marjorie and Berkfield stood with Damali and Carlos.

"Dang, they really left us." Damali put both hands on her hips and then doubled over laughing.

"Sho' did . . . man, and I thought we was bad?" Carlos shook his head and twirled Damali out onto the floor. "I had 'em play oldies, too, for the old-heads."

"What are we gonna do with all this food?' Marjorie said, looking at the nearly untouched silver banquet trays.

"Give it to the church, Marj," Berkfield said, and popped her on the behind to make her squeal. "Let's dance. Send the cake toppers to their rooms, and let's say me and you take a bottle of bubbly back to *our* room?"

"I got the logistics covered," Damali said with a wink. "You guys have fun."

The DJ slowed down the music and put on an old Luther Vandross ballad. Carlos smiled as "Creep" came on, pulling Damali into an embrace.

"Guess it's just me and you and a whole big reception that nobody wanted to hang out at."

"Time," she said, kissing his neck and staining his white shirt collar with lipstick. "Time seems to move *real* slow when there's something you wanna do, but can't . . . and seems to move real fast while you're doing what you really wanna do."

"Now you're talking dirty to me in a public place."

"This isn't a church; it's a nice little hotel reception room."

"Ah . . . but you might get in trouble for the offense." He nipped her earlobe. "Lose the collar, later, okay?"

"Hmmm . . . maybe, maybe not." She kissed the underside of his chin as they slowly dragged around the floor all alone.

"Wanna take a bottle of bubbly up to the room?"

"I have to tell the staff what to do with the food—I promised Marj." She batted her lashes and then chuckled with a sexy wink. "Will only take a minute, but time . . . can move real slow sometimes," she said, drawing out the words as she withdrew from him by increments.

"Keep playing with me and I'll make it stop," he said, his eyes beginning to flicker silver.

"Promises, promises, but you'd better not let the hotel staff see your eyes."

He checked himself with a smile and went over to tell the DJ he could pack up. He kept Damali in his peripheral vision as she spoke with hotel management, giving instructions. She hadn't lied, though, about time moving slowly when there was something else you'd rather do. He watched her body move beneath the pale lavender silk sheath and became riveted to the way her legs flashed out of the slit at the sides each time she took a step. Time made him remember how her cinnamon-brown skin felt when she smoothed on shea butter . . . and it brought her scent to him from across the room, slowing time like a slow drag. Agonizing.

"You know we're officially still on our honeymoon . . . and since it was interrupted, I demand a do-over," he said against her ear when she finally walked down the deserted hall beside him.

"Is that so?" she said, hiking up the bottle of champagne she'd taken from the reception as they leisurely strolled by the open archways, glimpsing the beach.

"Yep," he said, suddenly turning and sweeping her up into his arms. "Besides, with all the drama, we never got to celebrate your birthday right."

She squealed at the sudden change in altitude and held on to the bottle to keep it from falling, and then laughed even harder as he sealed them away in an invisible whirl.

But she stopped laughing the moment he touched down inside their oceanside suite, set her down slowly, and pressed her to the door with his eyes blazing silver.

"I want nine of those ten honeymoon days back, Damali," he murmured into her hair as he took her mouth. "Every delicious second."

Turn the page for a sneak peek at the next Vampire Huntress Legend novel.

THE CURSED

Coming in paperback from St. Martin's Griffin in July 2007.

Their landing, right inside the main entrance, was smooth—not a funnel cloud or a light burst, but rather a mere parting between the fabric of time-space density allowing them never to break stride. The message jettisoned from Carlos's mind to the brothers: *Let me ask for her and Nuit. Then we leave a calling card.*

Silent nods with angry eyes were the response. Carlos glanced at Rider first. The message clear: *No matter what, Yonnie is still my boy. You won. Leave the man his dignity.*

Rider's response was one word as they began walking forward. "Done."

Leather coats dusted ankles, hairs on backs of necks bristled, and heavy weapons caused sweat to slick palms—not from fear, but from fury grips. They stood at the edge of the high crevasse and looked down; their entry had been so smooth that even the Dark side's border guards didn't see them. Then again, it could have had something to do with the heat waves of pure rage rising off each man that blinded them. Right now, the Guardian team fit right in with the population at Hell's gate.

The team stared down at the six-hundred-foot drop to the main floor. As it was designed for a spectacular entry, the only way in was to demon-scamper over the crags, tunnel up from a portal, or touch down vampire style in a funnel cloud.

They'd entered Ground Zero through a small cave slit that opened out to a wider cavern. Glittering gold-laden bars serving blood and human flesh provided an endless demon feast before them. Writhing, naked bodies twisted in every imaginable carnal act littered the floors, as well as the plush, crimson surfaces swathed in Bedouin silks and black drapes.

Persian rugs covered gleaming black marble floors as muscle-bound servers brought fresh golden goblets of blood to sate the en-raptured. Massive gold leaf–covered fountains with depraved images spiraled in orgies spewed human blood for bathers reenacting the last days of Sodom and Gomorrah. Huge gaming tables with world terri-tories and human lives at stake in the gold chips were heavily loaded with gamblers. Carlos motioned with his chin toward the pit bulls walking the perimeter at the top of the cavern with Harpies riding their backs.

Everybody got the layout? Carlos's steely gaze roved the group. *Don't sleep on nothing down here.*

Stone-jawed nods were his answer. With that, he folded the team away and opened them out onto the floor as though coming in for a vamp landing.

Seven battle-ready males wafting adrenaline and more approached the bar, drawing hisses of admiration from nearby female entities.

"Lilith send you boys to join the party?" a long, lithe, snakelike fe-male asked Big Mike as she began to coil around his legs. Her skin was made of glistening, almond-hued scales like that of a yellow boa, and her eyes were an eerie shade of hazel that bordered on green-gray-gold. Each of her long platinum tresses seemed alive, as though they were tiny snakes, as she swayed invitingly before Mike. "And you're dinner, too. . . . She thinks of everything."

The moment she pulled back to strike, Big Mike whipped out a snub-nosed pump shotgun and shoved it into her mouth, fingering the trigger as she lurched forward. "Baby, if you're gonna give me deep throat, do it like a pro—don't bite."

She gagged and eased off the weapon. "I like your style," she mur-mured, uncoiling from his leg and stroking his groin. "What you're packing under the belt ain't too bad, either, lover. My bad, on jump-

ing the gun with a first strike—shoulda known a man like you would
wanna be the aggressor. Let me make it up to you?"

"Later," Mike grumbled, keeping the barrel of his gun trained on
her. "Get off me, bitch."

Carlos cut a glance at the bartender as the Amanthra withdrew
from Mike with sad eyes. A sexy female vampire had blown him a
kiss, and he could tell she'd telepathically told the bartender to give
him whatever he wanted. Although she remained on her barstool, she
shot random erotic images his way, then licked two fingers and
dragged them down her cleavage.

"Keep dreaming, baby," Carlos muttered as she slid her hand up her
shirt and released a soft moan. He glanced at Bobby and Dan to be
sure that the redhead with crystal green eyes and a double-D cleavage
hadn't messed up the younger brothers.

"She has to do way better than that," Bobby said, totally unfazed.

Dan pounded his fist, chuckling when she flipped them both the
bird and strode away. "Goodnight to you, too—skank."

"I guess after being called by Lilith, everything else in here is a minor temptation?" the bartender crooned, his handsome caramel-hued
face flawlessly boyish as he smiled at Carlos. He lowered his lumines-
cent brown eyes, delicate black lashes shadowing them as Carlos gave
him a hard grit. "No response, strong silent type?"

"Your problem, dude?" Rider said in a half snarl, leaning closer to
a second-gen vamp than was normally advisable. "You wanna ease up
off my brother before my trigger finger gets itchy?"

The bartender flinched to attempt a quick snatch at Rider, and six
barrels pointed at him with distinctive clicks. He eased back with a
sheepish grin and held up both hands in front of his chest.

"Like I said," Rider muttered through his teeth, "wanna fix the
man his drink and fuck off?"

"My apologies," the bartender said in a sensuous murmur. "But
the testosterone and adrenaline trail you gentlemen have is captivating
the whole bar . . . with well-fed human blood as the foundation carrier, too. Whew . . . a damned delicacy that only the vixen herself
could provide. Tell me, are you all off-limits and only hers for dinner?

Is that why you're all so touchy, or did she send you as a gift for us? If she gave explicit orders, then no one would dare cross her, but if not . . ."

"Private label, neat." Carlos said in Dananu, ignoring the probing question.

"Yes, *sir*," the bartender said in an awed gasp. "And she trained you in the mother tongue, too? Do you all speak it, or just the hunk that smells incredible?" He drifted away and came back with Carlos's order. "Oh, wait till I tell *the crew.*" His gaze perused the seven stone faces that were ignoring him and staring out on the floor, scanning the scene before them. "After she's done, you have to stay for a while and talk that nasty Dananu to me."

Carlos didn't respond but kept the horny vamp in his peripheral vision until he moved away to serve other revelers. He kept his eyes roving for any signs of Yonnie. In his mind, as much as this was going to end up as a drive-by, he wanted to let his boy know that he was still family and had a haven—if things hadn't changed. But Carlos quickly shook the futile thought. Any emotion considered soft and accidentally picked up on in here would get a man immediately smoked.

The team looked up in unison to see something they'd never seen before. A fine, brunette, female vamp still moving as mist had sidled up to Rider from behind. But before her hands slid across his shoulders, he'd vamp-snatched her and slammed her head against the bar, holding her by the throat.

"Never in the throat without my permission," Rider growled, a 9mm at her temple. "We clear?" He flung her away from him and eyed her with disdain. "Seconds. I hate 'em."

The team tried not to gape. Rider's speed was something they could talk about later—and how he'd seen her behind him at the bar without turning around, as though he had vamp three-sixty sight-line. Regardless, their cover was holding; the old heads had it on lock. Female were-demons were smiling a little too much at Shabazz and Big Mike for Carlos's liking, but he had to let it go. Old tracers, he told himself.

Carlos kept everybody in his peripheral vision. Lilith's lair was heavily fortified, and the bouncers patrolling the upper rims were no joke. Standing seven feet tall with ten-inch fangs and barrel chests to rival WWF wrestlers, those big bastards would have to be shot first, he knew, along with the Hell dogs they held by long chains.

But any minor bar fights, even mortal combat down in the main pit, was nothing more than a floor show—and the spectators would applaud the victor and eat the scraps when it was done. Therefore, for the moment, Carlos took a gamble that they could press for answers without causing a complete riot.

As soon as the bartender leaned over his drink and licked his lips at Carlos, offering him an Ecstasy-laced joint, Carlos snatched the bartender over the bar hard and punched him in the face, breaking off a fang.

"You got something else to say after my boy told you to back the fuck up and stop sweatin' me?" Carlos had placed a 9mm at the bartender's temple so quickly that he couldn't mist out of Carlos's grasp.

The bartender put both hands up in front of his chest, his nervous, red-glowing eyes darting between Carlos and six additional menacing pairs of Guardian eyes. "Hey, hey, hey, you gentlemen never said she'd sent you just for her bed and her dinner. We didn't know."

"So, where is that slimy bitch, anyway?" Carlos said, his lips circling into a snarl as battle-length fangs began to lower.

"She went below to give her husband his due," the bartender said, swallowing hard as his eyes went to half mast. "Damn, I see why she sent for you, though. . . . Are you sure you don't want anything, sir, until she, uh, returns?"

Fury tightened Carlos's grasp on the bartender's throat as he hurled him back against the glasses, several breaking bottles and shelves. "Get that motherfucker out of my face," he muttered and spun toward his team. "She ain't here. Damn!"

"Fallon ain't, either," Jose said, glancing around at the appreciative vampire gazes as phantoms slipped between succubae and incubi, whispering. "So, brother?"

"Let's leave a calling card," Carlos said in a low, lethal voice. "Like right about now."

Weapons came from under coats, double-handed firing in an automatic spray. Hallowed-earth shells whizzed by like tracers, burning the very air as they met targets to incinerate. Guards from the upper levels hurled down to the floor as sulfur rose and screaming demons unprepared for the onslaught took cover, some dying in their mating frenzy only to look up at the last moment. Bat-winged Hell dogs swooped off the ledges, their fangs dripping acid, their twelve glowing eyes roving the floor with rage while their razor-sharp spaded tails lashed wildly in the air.

Mike dropped to one knee and pulled the compact shoulder launcher out of his coat, mounted it on his burly sinew, shoved in a shell from a hidden coat pocket, aimed, and fired. The splatter and cinders from one airborne pit bull ignited another that accidentally flew through its path. Rider had gotten four bouncers in a single shell shot through their heads with his right hand while he fired the Gatling gun with the left.

Dan mowed down anything moving behind the bar and then advanced on the gaming tables. Jose was his tandem street-sweeper with a snub-nosed pumping dead aim, serving chest blasts into high-roller demons and splattering the gaming tables' green felt. J.L. had run up the side of a cavern wall and balanced on a precipice in a ninja move on the edges of his toes to draw a flock of Harpies to him. Blue-arc tactical charge held him in place as he lifted his weapons and took steady aim. As soon as they got within range, J.L. released a hail of bullets from an assault rifle, dropping burning bodies, then pivoted off the cliff edge to land on his feet with Bobby covering him.

Berkfield had run into the teeming throng of an orgy, pulled the pins on two grenades with his teeth, hurled them, and then dove for safety behind a bar. But a were-demon looked up at the same time he did. In two seconds, Berkfield had drawn and blown the back of the demon's skull off. Bobby was over the bar in a blink and reached down to yank his father up. They stood back to back, firing at anything coming their way, blowing demon guts out and spattering gook everywhere.

Carlos flung his spent weapons to Big Mike and Rider, his goal now to run deep into the cavern headed for Lilith's shrine—her bed. The outer area was like her foyer; he had to go in deep to make an impact in her house.

Hand-to-hand combat brought him surreal pleasure. All the shit they'd taken him through . . . Raw battle frenzy rippled through Carlos's system as he heart-snatched stunned male sentries and neutered drone lovers on the way to Lilith's golden, demon-headed sanctuary. To defile that carnal place would definitely send her a message: Her primary lair had been breached after all these centuries, the squad that did it went for broke, and she was vulnerable—thus weak, and her reinforcements weren't shit against the Guardian forces.

But the moment he neared the high monument that sat alone on a steep crag of green malachite almost a half-mile deep into her lair, a giant black cobra—her regular lover and familiar—uncoiled from under her bed in a jealous rage, green eyes glowing, black scales gleaming, fangs dripping as it hissed. Carlos could feel the thing before him hesitate, clearly not sure if Lilith had sent him as a new playmate but furious at the invasion. Carlos stretched out his arm and drew the Blade of Ausar into his grip.

"You tell that bitch that Rivera was here!" Carlos shouted. "And the next time she fucks with *my family* or brings that punk bastard, Fallon Nuit, with her to my door, it's her head and his nuts!"

The serpent swayed its huge, Hyundai-sized head and snapped, its eyes narrowed on Carlos from its position above him. Then from beneath the bed, several more heads emerged, until the thick body came out to reveal that it was a hydra, not a serpent. The tricky question for Carlos now was which head was the main one? Plus, the damned thing moved like greased lightning. He could still hear gunfire report behind him, which meant his team was holding its own. From his peripheral vision, he saw Shabazz and J.L. racing in to assist.

Not even waiting for the command, Shabazz was liquid motion and had stunned the beast with a tactical charge from his locks and right hand. The blue arc rippled right down Black Beauty's gun barrel and discharged the shell to blow away one head. J.L. flipped out of the way of a strike to dig one of Dan's spent AK-47s into the monster's eye, only landing to blow out the other firing from 9mms with both hands.

Sword raised, Carlos took a running leap forward into the air with a Neteru battle cry, his coat billowing out from him, propelled by fury. His silver glare burned the creature like lasers had been trained on it, making it flop and screech to be out of his line of vision, and then he released the blade swing. A huge head crashed to the cavern floor as Carlos dropped onto Lilith's bed. Serpents hidden beneath her red silk sheets wriggled and scampered away at his intrusion, and he pulled a handheld Uzi out of his shoulder holster and began shooting the bed, making it bleed black and green blood.

The hydra went down slowly, the other heads whining and hissing as the mortally wounded creature nuzzled the gushing site of the main beheading. Fury still had a choke hold on Carlos, and he rammed his sword into the center of the bed, wishing Lilith had been there versus her sumptuous mattress, and then he unceremoniously beheaded the golden heads of the four posts.

But he jumped back amazed as they bled red blood and the little gargoyle figures at the top of each post grappled at their cut throats.

Down beside his teammates in seconds, Carlos nodded as they picked up the pace to rejoin the battle on the main floor. Gunshots had slowed so that there were only occasional bursts. Each man's heart slammed into his chest as he ran, hoping for the best, trying to prepare for the worst—only to see the entire team standing in the middle of sulfur plumes rising in hot, yellow smoke from the floor.

A sea of decapitated and mutilated demon bodies stretched out before them on the floors; piles of ash and cinders covered the bars, littering the crevices and crags where they'd dropped. Golden furniture and gaming tables were shot to smithereens. Glass was everywhere from exploded bottles. Guardian eyes briefly studied the carnage knowing that if anything twitched, it could still get up and bite.

"Raze the place," Shabazz muttered.

Carlos lifted his blade, ready to send a blast of white light from it, when a cavern opened behind the far bar, sucking the whole bar and half the shelving behind it down into it. Instantly, Carlos spun. J.L.

was up on the golden surface in two flips, fly-kicking Harpies back, and then balanced on a sliver of remaining shelving to flip off and send two Harpies right into Carlos's blade. Shabazz threw his head back, released a warrior's yell, and suddenly upper and lower canines ripped through his gums. His clothes had been left in a pool of fabric where he'd been standing. Liquid feline motion, Shabazz's body elongated into a huge, sleek jaguar, his claws ridding Harpies of appendages and entrails as he went to J.L.'s aid. The team froze for a moment, stupefied. Berkfield flung a hallowed-earth grenade down into the cavern that had opened, and the team jumped back from the implosion that sealed the hole.

Bobby was blowing away miscellaneous Harpies that had escaped out of the air with Dan standing at his flank and Jose on the other side. A swarm of Harpies came at Big Mike, and the gunners couldn't get a shot off without hitting Mike. He reared back, hauled off, and threw a cinder-block punch into the eye of the small whirl, causing Harpies to fall out of formation and bounce to the ground, stunned. Bobby, Dan, and Jose picked them off like they were shooting pigeons. The moment the team fell back into formation, all in a line near Carlos, he lowered the sword of Ausar, raised the disc of Heru as a shield, and released a cannon jolt of white light from the tip of the blade to flash burn everything demonic in their wake.

"Move out," Carlos said, slowly lowering the shield and watching Lilith's main lair burn with great satisfaction.

Shabazz swept up his clothes and team members shared incredulous glances but remained mute as he hurriedly robed.

Suddenly a deafening clap of thunder knocked them to the ground and scattered them like bowling pins. The sonic boom made boulders begin to fall in on the cavern, pelting the team with dangerous projectiles. He had to get his team out of there—had to get them all into a centralized group so he could burn through the universe's fabric without leaving any of his men behind. Carlos gathered his Guardian brothers with effort, straining to shield them with a stretched Heru discus and helping them up quickly with his energy so they could run toward him.

Dangerous energy fatigue was setting in as he tried to focus. In the midst of the chaos, a massive, blinding-white, winged stallion snorting blue-white flames, eyes glowing silver, its silver hooves razor-deadly, dropped down. The riding warrior owned a familiar face. His dark arm stretched out to the team, the other held a huge crossbow with a silver stake that glinted off his gold Kemetian crown.

"I told you we had your back, brother," Adam said as several more Neteru kings dropped down to collect Guardian soldiers. "We'll seal your home in black-box safety—go to your queens. Rest. This battle is won. Tomorrow, however, is another day."

"Okay, we have already established that they're crazy," Damali said, losing patience with the group's insistent questions, mainly because she couldn't answer them. "I want a prayer line grappling hook on each man in there. White light, pure everything you've got, to bring 'em home. You ladies got that?"

"Yeah," Juanita said, "but what's going on, maybe it's from the Dark side. Like how do we know about them being able to things they hadn't before—"

"It's got to be the marriage merger," Marlene said, her voice quiet and reverent and her gaze distant. "Of one flesh . . . seven joining seven, strengthened by the bond that joins mind, body, and spirit as one under the auspices of white light." She brought her gaze to the team. "They got us in them, and they're in us. I'm calling Father Pat. It's time to get the Covenant involved anyway, if they went after Lilith buck-wild and crazy."

"Whoa," Krissy said, and stumbled backward till her back hit the wall. "The marriage merger can do that?" she asked, totally ignoring the second part of what Marlene had said.

Heather and Jasmine just stared at each other as Marjorie slowly brought her hand to her mouth. Inez began walking in a tight circle, fanning her face.

"This is too crazy," Inez said. "If we're getting juiced up like this, it's gotta be for something scary-big, anybody feeling me? I'm with Marlene; we need all them guys from the clergy up in here, too. Like what if I find out I'm cock-diesel like Mike, and he's fast with a switchblade, like me? Oh, shit, y'all. You hear what I'm saying?"

"Yeah . . . completely," Tara murmured, her gaze distant. "This isn't like times before. They're acting like it's a last stand, and I don't even think they know why."

Damali walked in a circle raking her locks, total frustration claiming her as the puzzle numbed her brain. As much as she hated to admit it, fear for the safety of one half of the team had a headlock on her as well.

"Do you know where the capital city is for ancient Babylon?" Damali finally blurted out, unable to control the volume of her voice as her nerves frayed and snapped. "It's on the Euphrates River, south of Baghdad in modern Iraq!"

Unable to contain herself, Damali paced harder as the group's eyes widened before her. "Pray and pray hard, sisters. They're walking right into part of this whole Middle East madness. There's ground troops from however many nations over there . . . civilians, tanks, tracers, land mines, God only knows what, and our squad could accidentally come out of a whirl right in the middle of a firefight. Who knows? And I haven't even begun to think about what demons are over there right now screwing with everybody, keeping the conflict going, holding humanity in a death struggle against itself. Hell . . . Level Seven might be topside, for all we know!"

"I'll see if I can get maps, something to give us a geographic visual as we pray white light around where they are. It helps." Krissy jumped up and dashed down the hall, returning quickly with her laptop.

Jasmine, Heather, and Marjorie linked hands, making blue-white static zing between them with Tara in the middle to draw her vamp-locator knowledge to the fore.

"The old stones are screaming," Heather said quickly, looking up at Damali. "The region is not just white-hot topside, but underground. The Holy cities . . . with the conflict going on near Beirut, Jordon, and north—Christian and Muslim and Jewish strongholds are in flames."

"But they went to Lilith's bedchamber," Tara said with a shiver.

"To her main lair that has *never* been breached in history. Even warrior angels couldn't find it. . . . It is an insane move, a fool's quest." She covered her face with her hands and breathed into them deeply as though trying to keep from hyperventilating.

"Yeah, but Carlos is the only fool I know who ever sat in the Chairman's throne and lived to tell about it as a living human being," Marlene countered. "Even warrior angels didn't do that. . . . And if he had an old link to Cain that didn't die out all the way, then if anybody could find Lilith," she added, glancing at Damali, "it's him."

Damali briefly closed her eyes, trying to find the silver lining in the mayhem surrounding her. "There's always a reason, there's always a reason. . . . There's always something good that comes out of every bad for the greater good," she murmured like a mantra, trying to remind herself of that and calm her nerves for the sake of the team as another wave of panic threatened to sweep through her.

"Ohmigod," Krissy said, beginning to rock. "From where we are in the South Pacific, they're already into the next day, fourteen to sixteen hours ahead of us, just before midnight there by an hour, perhaps. What if . . . Oh, shit, they're outta their minds!"

"I know, I know," Damali said, pacing. "They're nuts."

"Just like the prophecies," Juanita murmured, holding her hands up in front of Inez as both of their eyes rolled back into their skulls, showing only the whites the moment each seer went under.

"And I saw the Lamb open one of the seals, and I heard, as it were the noise of thunder, one of the four beasts saying, come and see . . . and I saw, and behold a white horse: And he that sat on him had a bow; and a crown was given unto him; and he went forth conquering, and to conquer." Inez's head snapped up with a gasp. Her voice had been a gravelly, chilling tone that was not her own.

"Revelations one and two!" Marlene screamed, running into the bedroom and searching for Damali's stones. "Where's your stones, child? Your divination tool! This is the big one! The first seal is opened! Call Father Pat—this is not a drill!"

1. What do you think about Carlos's acceptance of the possibility that Damali might be carrying Cain's heir?

2. Do you feel that Eve made the right decision when she executed her own child to keep him from his bloody rampage? Discuss the many layers of this scenario. For example, should mothers of killers turn their children over to authorities for justice or hide them as fugitives?

3. What do you think of Damali's growing ability to heal as a Powers Angel?

4. Discuss Rider and Tara's reunion, as well as its implications for Yonnie, plus the loss of Gabrielle.

5. Do you think this is the end for Fallon Nuit?

6. What havoc do you think Lilith can reap in her new position as Chairwoman of the Vampire Council?

7. Discuss the loss of the Brazilian Were-human team and the dynamic among Kamal, Marlene, and Shabazz. Is this who you thought she would wind up with? Why or why not?

8. What do you think the hole that has been ripped in the veil, and the escape of both good and bad hybrids, will mean?

9. What do you think of the role of the Neteru Kings and their assistance of Carlos at this time?

10. Discuss the Neteru Queens and how have they evolved to include Damali as more of a peer rather than a novice in training.

11. How do you feel about Damali's near rape and her handling of the situation once she came home?

12. Discuss the tenderness demonstrated during the bath scene with Damali and Carlos. Do you think this level of forgiveness is possible between lovers/spouses?

A Reading Group Guide

St. Martin's
Griffin